The Witch in the Peepul Tree

Celebrating
30 Years of Publishing
in India

The Witch in the Peepul Tree

Arefa Tehsin

HarperCollins *Publishers* India

First published in India by HarperCollins *Publishers* 2023
4th Floor, Tower A, Building No. 10, DLF Cyber City,
DLF Phase II, Gurugram, Haryana – 122002
www.harpercollins.co.in

2 4 6 8 10 9 7 5 3 1

P-ISBN: 978-93-5699-240-5
E-ISBN: 978-93-5699-200-9

Typeset in 11/14 Adobe Garamond at
Manipal Technologies Limited, Manipal

Printed and bound at
Replika Press Pvt. Ltd.

To Riaz chacha (late Riaz A. Tehsin).

This book would not be what it is without you.
Neither would I.

Contents

MORNING
Makar Sankranti, 1950

LATE AFTERNOON
Makar Sankranti, 1950

DUSK
Makar Sankranti, 1950

12.15 AM
The Night Before
Makar Sankranti, 1950

AFTERNOON

Makar Sankranti, 1950

Ahad, Dada Bhai's Son

Dada Bhai's House

Bohrawadi, Udaipur

THE SKY WAS A BATTLEFIELD. MONKEYS HAD LEFT THE TERRACES, but hateful crows shrieked their disapproval. The kites were a scattering of colourful flower petals thrown on a baraat. They soared, ducked, swirled, tumbled, dragged and bravely hugged each other in a dance of death. The bloodied hands of boys and men pulled and tugged the strings coated in ground glass and flour. War cries boomed as soon as two kites entangled in a fight to the finish. Fists met mortar or punched the air as one of the kites went floating away, a vagrant with no strings attached.

Children everywhere on the streets scuttled looking for spills. But Ahad was past the scavenging stage. He was a grownup—all of nine years and two months. And he would be the king of kites someday. Soon. Right now, he was content being a flag bearer. It was Makar Sankranti, the one-day kite festival that marked the end of the winter solstice. The arid, dry air rushed in whip-smack breaths as he ran from end to end, gaping at the annual arena of patangbaazi—kite fighting and kite flying—from the terrace of his home, the second-highest building in Udaipur after the Maharana's palace. Buildings pressed against each other in the walled city, shoulder to sagging shoulder, cheek to withered cheek, huddled in solidarity below the fortification of the Aravalli hills. The distant top of the City Palace had sprouted kites with the most elaborate tails, but no one else was allowed to cut one of *those*.

The reins were passing hands from the Maharana of Mewar to Hindustan, Ahad thought, just like those of the tethered kites.

Abuses billowed in the breeze. The winter afternoon sported clammy, half-naked bodies. Ahad's forehead oozed with sweat, and his arms felt as if they were carrying a full mashak—a leather water skin—when all he held was the spool. He could see Zain Bhaiya's concentration drawn to a point, while Sa'ad Bhaiya leant low on the edge of the railing.

'Pull, Zain, pull!' His eldest brother, Sa'ad, straightened and sprang back, as if he had a scorpion on his spine.

'This manjha, Sa'ad Bhaiya ... we need a sharper one!' Zain plucked the line with mounting irritation.

'Get the new manjha, Ahad!' Sa'ad came and snatched the spool from Ahad's hands. 'We must launch another kite.'

'Where is it?' Ahad hung his hands with a mix of relief and dismay. He could do with a break. But the spool, the manjha,

that he had especially forged for his brothers over the week was
not good enough.

'In Sanaz Apa's room. Go, go, go!'

Ahad padded towards the stairway as wars raged above his
head. The stone stairs going down the five storeys didn't have
a railing to hold on to. The flights of steps on each floor were
at opposite ends and landed on the sides of large porches—
the common area between rooms—overlooking the open-to-
sky courtyard on the ground. Rays from the pale overhead sun
impaled the house, making darkness lie in peels in the corners.

The cold, coiled in the gut of the house, snaked up Ahad's
backbone. His stomach jiggled as he landed on one precarious
step after the other. He almost lost balance and caught his breath.
He didn't have Zain Bhaiya's physique, Sa'ad Bhaiya's height or
Sanaz Apa's good looks. But he had determination. *Israar* ...
Dada Bhai called it. His father, Tahir, whom everyone called
Dada Bhai, was a stickler for Urdu—the language polished to
a fault. No one talked in the humble Waghari, the dialect of
Bohras spoken in the rest of Bohrawadi, in their household
... Well, all except his own mother, whom Dada Bhai had no
control over. He could control what she was called, though.
Not the graceless Aayi or Hau or Dadi, but Dadi*jaan*. Ahad
loved his father, but his grandmother was no jaan, no beloved;
she was a hellcat!

Hot in the face and cold in the body, he continued the
descent more cautiously this time. The fifth and highest
floor was Dada Bhai's territory, with his living quarters and a
sweeping patio. The bone china tea set kept on his side-table
was the town's envy. A volley of laughter had come rat-a-
tatting out of his drawing room right up to the roof some time

back. He had visitors earlier. Ahad ran to the other side of the veranda and took the next flight of steps to the fourth floor. It was Ammi's dominion. Though today it was silent, his mother had as many, if not more, visitors than Dada Bhai every day—khadi-clad social workers or even a royal lady or two with a small entourage. The princely state of Mewar had been merged into India last year and became independent. But according to Ammi, only half of it. The half that wore pants, kurta-pyjamas and turbans. The fourth floor had a nice little visitor's room with a Persian rug and her bedroom just behind it. On the other side was the kitchen, where a big round thaal on a tarana was fixed every day for the family's meals. He inhaled the smell of til-ke-laddoo, the sweet of honour of Makar Sankranti, wafting out of the open door.

Ahad thumped down. A treepie resting on the eyebrow of a jharokha by the steps flapped away, startled. He saw an untouchable Bhangan standing in the side lane below the house. What was she doing? Her empty basket of nightsoil dangled by her side. These shit-collectors fascinated Ahad no end; he often imagined if the Bhangan wondered whose turds she was carrying on her head, what meal they had last night for some of it to dribble down her face. After all, Dada Bhai's building had the only private toilet in the colony of Bohrawadi, from where she collected the shit basket daily. The rest of the people went to dhoonda—the community toilet.

Ahad reached the third level, gasping for breath. He didn't like this part of the house. It had two rooms—one for his sister, Sanaz, and the other for guests. The second storey was much better, where he and his two brothers shared a room. Though the floor had the only toilet in the house, used by everyone, and his vile Dadijaan lived in the other room on the floor, it was still his sanctuary. The place where he safely stored all his secrets. In his compact trunk. Along with his private fortune—a peacock's crown, two rifle bullets he had sneaked out of Dada Bhai's armoury, a hard-bound copy of *13 Years Among the Wild Beasts of India* and a seashell brought all the way from Mombasa by one of Ammi's uncles, who had two wives.

From the jharokha on the front wall above the main entrance, he could see the peepul tree outside. Every time his aunts visited, they swore that the jeevti dakkan—the living witch—danced under it, long after the lamps were dimmed and the night was dark as a clogged drain. They said she was invisible during the day, hanging upside down in the tree. Perhaps she lay suspended right now, giving him a secret, saw-toothed smile. He shuddered and walked quickly to his elder sister's room and knocked on it. No answer. He lifted the solid brass knocker and brought it down.

'Ahad!' he heard Zain Bhaiya's cry from far away. 'Hurry your fat ass up!'

'Sanaz Apa!' he called his sister, knocking harder. What a day to nap! She should be up on the terrace cheering for her brothers. It was do-or-die out there!

'What's the commotion?' Badi Bi came down the tall steps, double bent, squinting her myopic eyes. A big off-white shawl was thrown over her head. 'Is it you, my prince?'

'Yes, Badi Bi,' Ahad whined. 'Sanaz Apa is not opening the door! Zain Bhaiya is going to spit in my trunk again if I don't go back up with the spool at once!'

Ahad was the favourite of the ancient housekeeper; in front of her, he could still behave like a child and flaunt his baby fat. His brothers would beat him with their back-slaps and hoots if he tried it with them.

'Push a little. She is probably asleep, as usual.' Keys of the entire house jangled at the widow's ample waist.

Ahad pushed. The latch inside gave in a bit, and the door split open a crack.

'There…' said Badi Bi, her voice warm and comforting. 'Wake your sister up.'

Ahad wrestled with the door. The latch rattled and gave way and the door banged open. Badi's Bi's anklets tinkled weakly as she turned to go, now that the matter was resolved.

Sanaz Apa was sitting on a chair in the middle of the room staring right at the door, her bottle-green dupatta thrown carelessly to the side. The latticed frame of the jharokha let in sculpted rays of the winter sun.

'Why couldn't you just get up and open…' Ahad's voice thinned to a tweep.

His sister's face reminded him of the cabbage in the kitchen last week … *wilted*.

Her glassy glare made him take a step back. And then, the same glare drew him towards her, one hushed step at a time, as if sound would disturb her stillness. Sanaz's long, thick braid lay limp on her chest. He reached the chair and squinted at her face. She peered back, her lips parted in surprise. The upper half of her body sat heavy, like a sculpture. He extended a finger and poked her shoulder. The bust turned to gelatine and lolled to a side. A rasping, abrasive cry of a sacrificial goat gurgled out of Ahad's throat and resounded in the building, the walls echoing his terror. For once, he understood what the leaves of the peepul tree outside were whispering in a strange tongue: the living witch had taken his sister.

BEFORE NOON

Makar Sankranti, 1950

1

Rao Sahib, the Zamindar

Dada Bhai's House

Bohrawadi, Udaipur

THE SKY OUTSIDE THE JHAROKHA WAS SHAMELESSLY NAKED. A cold, bitter blue. Rao Sahib favoured cloudy skies that aroused pompous peacocks and far-sighted buzzards. But then, what did you expect of cities but characterless paper kites dancing to the tune of pimps?

'Only two kinds of people have ruled Hindustan, Dada Bhai.' He lifted one of his buttocks and farted with force. He would have liked to claim it was a 12-bore he had fired, but refrained, glancing at Dada Bhai's distinguished face. 'Muslims and Rajputs. You and I. How will a Shudra and Brahmin rule, you tell me? Patel and Nehru? It will be a disaster.'

Dada Bhai smiled at his silver teaspoon, stirred the tea, clinked it on the edge of the cup and replied placing it on the saucer, 'It wasn't me, Rao Sahib, but our Maharana of Mewar, Bhupal Singh ji, who was one of the first from Rajputana to join the Union of India after Independence. Didn't you always say he was a visionary?'

'Dada Bhai, he had visions of a "free" India snatching away all our fortunes, if you ask me.' Rao Sahib fingered his thick up-curving moustache. People misread it as an act of being proud. It was an act of finding relief from his over-charged state. Ah … feeling the tantalizing hair between the fingers and rolling the pointy tips was catharsis … like breaking wind. 'And he chose the path of minimum friction. The state of Jodhpur almost acceded into Pakistan! Even Jaisalmer was in talks with Jinnah. He had given them a blank page to write their terms, they claim. I say, we should have fought harder for our rights! Or remained an independent entity, neither a part of India nor of Pakistan!'

The British had left the subcontinent two-and-a-half years back, dividing it into India and Pakistan with a stroke of imperial genius. Who said the Independence was 'won'? It was doled out. A sugar-dripping gulab-jamun split up between two tussling brats. Fools thought Jinnah and Gandhi were the 'fathers' of Pakistan and India. It was Lord Louis Mountbatten.

Since then, Nehru and Patel, the prime and home ministers, were trying to do just the opposite: get together the warring kingdoms that had shed blood for centuries to come join the Union of India in a great brotherhood. It was like worshipping a god for generations and then discarding him overnight for a new god. Rao Sahib missed the British; Mewar hardly had any independence 'struggle'. The British had a symbiotic relationship with them. They knew it was 'you' and 'I', not 'us', and that made things so much simpler.

Dada Bhai took a small sip from his gold-rimmed cup and placed it down, undoubtedly measuring each word before he uttered it. Rao Sahib's head would inflate if he mulled so much before speaking. He eyed Dada Bhai's breeches and coat with four big, puffed-up pockets. The Maharana referred to him as the best-dressed man in the city. But Rao sahib won't be caught dead wearing such suffocating clothes in his own chambers. He liked his loose dhoti, thank you very much. Where was the place to *expand* in these tight breeches?

'Jodhpur and Jaisalmer are border states, and hence Jinnah was bending backwards to have them in Pakistan. Hindustan and Pakistan have locked their jaws over Kashmir. UN mediation or not, this tug-of-war is not going to end anytime soon. Even the big and powerful states like Gwalior and Indore have joined the Madhya Bharat union, Rao Sahib. Joined the new Al-Hind, Hindustan, India. The Kingdom of Mysore is acceding. The Constitution of India has been drafted and adopted. How could we remain a small independent entity with the Union of India pressing in from all sides?'

The conjured image of 'pressing in' made Rao Sahib look out of Dada Bhai's high-perched room—a hull in the sea of buildings—overlooking the top of many smaller houses. He missed his fiefdom: the wild vastness of his forested estates, the sheer height of the walls of his garh—the fort and the people around him in his control. He always felt 'pressed in' in the city, like the clothes his old maid flattened with a coal iron. Suffocation seeped in for a moment, and he glanced at the large living room with two jharokhas from where sunlight swept in. Frugal yet elegant in its simplicity, reflecting the pretence of the city aristocrats! Solid teakwood furniture. Two snarling leopard heads and a huge sambar antler mounted on one wall. The other covered with the skin of an extraordinarily large leopard. A cheetal skin placed on the back of an armchair resting on a side. Oil lamps crouching in brackets in the walls. Two electric bulbs hanging from the ceiling in eternal punishment.

Dada Bhai continued, crossing his feet on which he still had his horse-riding boots on, 'The world is transforming. East Germany and the People's Republic of China have been officially proclaimed. Everyone is watching Hindustan now. Maharana Bhupal Singh ji has steered Mewar through an era of turbulence. The revolution and the fight for independence from the British Raj has brought in reorder and social and political transformation in the region. I urge you to look at it as an epoch of change.'

'Dada Bhai, you are sounding like Manilal and Ramdas Gandhi pleading to reduce Godse's punishment for Mahatma Gandhi's murder. I need to act like Nehru and Patel and turn it down. Who accounts for our *changes* in fortunes? Your ninety-eight sulphur shops all across Mewar have shut down after Independence. The Government of India wants me to surrender a considerable area of land to the state. It is the land of my ancestors, Dada Bhai, it is not stolen goods I need to surrender. Your business is hard-earned … your monopoly a result of generations of goodwill with the royalty. Everything in a snap … gone? Is this what you call change?' Rao Sahib wiped the froth forming on the corner of his mouth and shooed away a pigeon sitting on the jharokha's ledge, peeping in, and almost knocked off his headgear—the pagadi—that he had removed and kept aside. The damn pigeons, crows, cockroaches and rats of cities! 'What about your children? I have thirteen of them!'

'I would want my children to find their own destiny, their own fortunes. This will only make them better people. Why should I and my family amass such a large share in a world where millions are starving?'

Rao Sahib rubbed his knee, swollen from the long travel on a horse. 'Getting rid of feudal oppression, are we? Taking land and resources from the rich and distributing them to the poor? We'll see twenty years from now how "uplifted" these poor are. Five year plan for development by the Indian government, huh? Did the Maharana ... did *we* ... grow trees keeping five years in mind?'

The coolness of the winter afternoon and the strident cries of kite-fighting entered in waves from the ornate jharokha. Dada Bhai's England-made felt hat, with hawk feathers, hung from a stand, taut and stiff, just like his back. A rare framed photograph (which was supposed to have a glass negative) of his father with a dead tiger of considerable size and all the tribals who had undertaken the hakka for him, hung at the back of the stand.

'No, it didn't matter if trees took many years to grow,' Dada Bhai conceded, running his hand over his thick, greasy hair. He had once told Rao Sahib that guns and hair should always be well-oiled. Rao Sahib scratched his scalp and flakes of dandruff fell on his crisp dhoti. He made a mental note to give a good hiding to the servants if he found the guns in his armoury not as greased as Dada Bhai's head.

'But, Rao Sahib ...' Dada Bhai's coarse voice belied his younger years. 'Aren't we forgetting that Rajputana was anyway under the British since 1818? Once they left, we didn't have much choice, did we?'

'They were good partners...'

'Masters, more aptly.'

'If you may.' Rao Sahib shrugged. 'They made money and let us keep our money too. The Union of India wants us to be a celibate Meera with blind devotion, while Krishna frolics with all the lasses. You tell me, what kind of independence is this?'

Dada Bhai cracked up laughing. Rao Sahib slackened in his cushioned chair and took another slurping sip of tea.

'Tea is a vice I can openly indulge in only at your place, Dada Bhai. It's so grand. One of the good things the British left behind. The way Hindustan is heading, you'll soon have even the untouchables—the Bhangi and Chamar—having tea on the streets. Let it be known, this is my prediction of a day we will all live to see.' Rao Sahib placed his cup on the saucer reverentially. It was not every day he could have a sip of this exquisite drink, delicate in body, stirring in spirit, of the milky golden colour of his third paramour's skin. He then imagined this tea ... the skin of his mistress ... touching the lips of an untouchable ... and shivered inwardly, drawing the cup closer to him.

'Badi Bi has sent this, Dada Bhai.' A stick of a boy stood on the veranda.

'Bring it in, Ismail.'

The servant boy leant low to offer Dada Bhai a plate full of hot onion pakoras.

Rao sahib's mouth watered. The tea and the talk had worked up his appetite, which even Ismail's smirky face couldn't kill.

'Ram-Ram, Namaste, Assalam-alaykum!' Ismail spat out his signature greeting with a toothy grin. Rao Sahib ignored him.

'As you know, Rao Sahib, we do not have separate cooking utensils for our Hindu friends, so I can't ask you to partake of this. But I am rather famished after my horse ride in the morning to Sajjangarh. Please excuse me.' Dada Bhai took the plate of pakoras from Ismail and placed it on a small table by his side.

Rao Sahib stroked the thick hair of his moustache. 'Um … my oldest wife—your bhabhi—is not here to rebuke me. So I guess I can have a quick bite.'

Dada Bhai smiled and asked Ismail to request the housekeeper Badi Bi for another serving.

'See, I am a liberal at heart.' Rao Sahib rubbed his hands in anticipation as the savoury smell of fritters overpowered the noxious odours of the city.

'I believe you are. And a man of honour.' Dada Bhai, who had kept the plate of pakoras on the side table to wait for Rao Sahib's snack to be brought in, said formally.

Rao Sahib nodded in complete agreement. He now sprawled on his chair, spreading the bulk of his legs farther apart.

Ismail walked in with a plate of pakoras and another one stacked with til-ke-laddoo. 'Badi Bi says it is Makar Sankranti, you must have the sweet.' He grinned as if challenging Rao Sahib not to eat the fare prepared by an old Muslim woman. Had he been at Rao Sahib's garh, this bloody houseboy would be skinned! Ismail placed both the plates on the side table near him and left with a lingering smile.

'So are you, Dada Bhai, a man of honour. But you have taken this honour business a bit too far.' It was Rao Sahib's duty to reproach his friend. 'You are excessively lenient. I remember that trip when you hunted two sambar stags in my estate. You almost left when Rashid Ali refused to distribute the shikar meat to the lowly tribals after the hakka.'

'They had risked their lives during the beat to flush the stags out of the thicket. They deserved a part of the hunt … the

Bhils are miserably protein starved. Your man Rashid Ali said he would rather feed the vultures than the tribals!'

It was Rao Sahib's turn to laugh out loud. He was proud of his booming laughter. For a moment, it over-powered all the trumpeting of a city turned into an elephant-in-heat on Makar Sankranti.

'Nothing wrong with his reasoning. You feed them once, they want it always. Since you refused to take any lands from the Maharana, Dada Bhai, you don't understand begaar or its perils.'

'What perils, Rao Sahib? Begaar is free labour. The tribals live on your land, you can call them any time to work for free.' Dada Bhai picked up a silver case lying on his round side table and drew out a cigar.

'Yes, just as the durbar can call me, a Rao ... one of the highest landlords in the order, any time of the year to the wretched city and ask me to provide a month of free service.' He raised a hand before Dada Bhai could protest. 'Yes, yes, begaar has ended with Mewar's merger with Hindustan. I have some work at the durbar and that's why I have come to Udaipur. But before going to the palace, I decided to pay you a visit. Do you know why?' Rao Sahib kept the plate of pakoras on the side and wiped his hands on his thick wool coat, leaving piss-yellow stains.

'Because we are good friends?' Dada Bhai raised an eyebrow, tapping the cigar at the back of the case.

Rao Sahib bent forward, holding another fart coming up, checking the impulse to touch his moustache. 'I have heard a rumour about you. A terrible rumour. And I have come to clarify it. Rectify it, if I can.'

And with this revelation, he let the air pass, held his moustache like an anchor and drew back in his chair, satisfied.

2

Suġra, Dada Bhai's Mother

Dada Bhai's House

Bohrawadi, Udaipur

AN ANGITHI TIRELESSLY BRISTLED IN THE CORNER ROOM OF THE second floor in the winter months. Suġra had made the importance of the charcoal brazier clear to her son, Tahir, whom everyone called Dada Bhai, two years back when she shifted here after her husband's demise caused by a sneeze. He went tumbling down the stairs from the topmost floor and split his head. The four-and-a-half long months of iddat—in which a widow is confined to an isolated cell—had not helped her figure out the purpose of his random life. Or the cosmic plan behind his comic death.

If there was a greater scheme, it was certainly designed against her. First, everyone expected her to break her bangles on his passing away. It worked well for those who wore glass ones; gold was a different story. She remembered sitting by his prostrate body and banging her wrists on the wall, only to bend the gold like her husband's dented head. A crone with henna-dyed hair had come and tried to remove them from her wrists. Her knobbly fingers had refused to part with their proud possession, not letting them pass through her hardened knuckles. It led to deep abrasions and nicks that at least made Suġra cry at her husband's funeral, long after they had taken the corpse to plant him, fruitlessly, in the Khanjipeer graveyard outside the walled city.

Then she was made to shift from the third to the second floor—from where she could access the in-house latrine easily—under the pretext of her own free will. A place where her three grandsons could regale her with their antics, which was supposed to be the only goal in the life of a worthless widow. A room that was cool in summers but in winters grew tentacles that slithered up all her unnameable parts. A room with a divan, a mirror and two mounted four-horned antelope heads staring down at her in elaborate silence. The three insolent imps living in the room opposite to hers would only disturb her peace when they needed betel nuts from the jar. Once she had adequately cursed her grandsons after giving them a handful, she would sit scraping a few more nuts with her pearl-shell scraper. Suġra didn't want to keep an empty jar that would soon be on its way out, like her.

Her six daughters, who used to visit her occasionally, were varying proportions of bitchy and vicious. Her younger son, who lived in the building behind theirs, was just like his father—pointless. But it was her elder son, Tahir, who made her feel threatened by his quiet respect for her.

And then there was her beloved daughter-in-law, Tahir's wife, Mena, whose beautiful face, some said, invoked lore of yore. It was a face Suġra always, every single moment of her life, wanted to see—mounted on the wall of her room with the rest of the game trophies. She fingered the rings hanging in her stretched earlobes and cackled. The gold bangles, which she had reclaimed soon after the months of chaste isolation of early widowhood, felt cool on her skin. But she did not get her nath back. Her husband had never kissed her, as far as her memory went. The only thing that touched her lips was the big gold nath. She would daintily lift it away from her lips as she sipped on milk. It had given her the grandeur of a woman who was kissed. Every day. Her husband had stripped her of that last dignity in his death.

She leant from the well-cushioned sitting area, carved into the thick wall by the jharokha, and glanced at the narrow lane on the side. From the second floor, she had the glorious view of the back wall of a two-storey house and the dirt lane below.

Three kids ran after a kite, winding down the buildings. Makar Sankranti got everyone spiralling on their axes. Suġra could see a blurry form of a woman walking idly by the side of the house. The empty basket of nightsoil gave the untouchable away. She seemed to smell her wrist, and then walked back again to the front of the house. Did this Bhangan, this dirty bitch, think it was her private garden? Suġra was tempted to hurl a few abuses at her, but stopped herself. This, of all days, was not the one on which she wanted to attract attention.

She squinted her eyes to see better. How she missed seeing the peepul tree! From the jharokha of her room on the third floor, which was now her granddaughter Sanaz's, she could always see a part of its nefarious form. She swore she had seen the jeevti dakkan there on a few nights; a dark shadow flitting purposefully between the branches when everyone was drunk on sleep. Suġra wanted to make her acquaintance—a powerful, supernatural ally who was not weighed down by human morality.

'Sasu ji!' The call sent a jolt through her stationary body and running mind.

'*Bhandora!* You want me out of this house and six feet under, don't you? You devil from hell, you!' She shifted on her janamaz, spread on the sitting area by the jharokha, and resumed rolling her tasbi. Sitting on the praying mat all the time gave her the authority to follow Allah's will. Who was she but his instrument?

Ismail stood by the heavy, wooden door, a smirk on his face and a permanent glint in his eyes, which seemed to be caused by opium, not a constant state of happiness. As soon as he stopped his addiction, Suġra suspected, this stick-pile of a boy would scatter.

'Badi Bi has sent you some pakora and til-ke-laddoo. Makar Sankranti … can you see, Sasu ji? Those spots in the sky are not flying bugs, they are faraway kites.' He walked in and offered her the plate of fritters and sesame laddoos in mock reverence.

Suġra was aware of the stale smell of ageing that had become a part of her. The permanent mist in her eyes softened all the edges of the world. Ismail's face came more in focus as he leant forward with the plate. Suġra swung her rosary of polished quartz, one end held in her fingers, deadened as much with years as with the betel nut scraper. It struck Ismail's hairless cheek, lethal and precise, and hung by her hand again in total submission.

The boy's eyes were mirthless as he looked up, his free hand rubbing his dark cheek where an earthworm of a mark was crawling to the surface.

'Thankfully my eyesight is clear enough to see the bugs nearby and squash them, Chora.'

The boy kept the plate by the praying mat and stepped back, his features setting again in amused resentment.

'And, yes.' Sugra's voice always became liquid and reliant, that of a dependent, old woman, when she smiled. 'I am not your mother-in-law. If you call me "Sasu ji" again...' She exposed her gums, with missing front teeth, in a snarl and pushed her tongue in the gap.

Ismail walked out of the room, halted at the door and turned. 'Sorry, I won't ... Sasu ji!' He grinned before he scatted.

'You...' Sugra began in a husky voice and then thought better of it. 'Ya Ali...' She glanced out of the jharokha again, rolling the smooth beads between her rough fingers and looking out at a sky that looked deceptively dreamy with the vague kites. Mena had been offering to take her to a hospital for her cataract. Why wouldn't she? They took all the blood out of your body in those dark buildings smelling of vomit and death. Many villagers and city dwellers chose to die in their homes rather than visit a hospital. Tahir generally remained ambiguous in the disputes between his mother and his wife, but for once he took Mena's side and insisted that Sugra visit a hospital. It was the first time her doubts were confirmed: he secretly wanted her buried.

The wretched Ismail would soon come with her glass of milk. She missed the other two Hindu boy servants, who were on leave the last two days. Gone home for Makar Sankranti. She had vehemently opposed Tahir's decision to keep the needy boys in the house. But she had eventually come to see the benefit of it. These Hindus were napaak—impure—not washing their appendages after peeing, but unlike Ismail, she could bewilder the two cousins. Intimidate them. Tame them.

In Bohrawadi, where the Shia Muslim sect of Bohras lived, married women went to their maternal home every morning before the rest of the household woke up, and returned in the evening. A fair tradition. The mothers had enough to feed the daughters, didn't they? But no, Tahir's precious wife wouldn't go home. Okay, Mena's parents were dead, but the futile brother lived. This bhandori Mena had the longest hair in Bohrawadi, long enough to make a hangman's noose. Her face chiselled by the devil himself to lead men astray. Her form carved out of marble. It best suited the tombstones, if you asked Suġra.

For the last two-and-a-half years, Suġra had been robbed of her daughters' company; five of them were married into the same family that shifted to Pakistan after Partition. The house was so bleak now. Haunted by her daughter-in-law. A slut in a saree, the most obsecene of dresses. Not observing purdah. Tahir's friend in Pakistan, the big business tycoon with emerald and diamond mines and a fleet of merchant ships, had beseeched him to leave Mewar and Hindustan, offering him equal partnership in all his businesses. But the good 'ol Tahir chose to remain stubbornly embedded here. Oh no, he wouldn't leave his *mother*land, even at the cost of his own *mother*.

Suġra caught hold of her walking stick with an ivory head lying prone by her side, and knocked hard on the jharokha, which housed a recent, unsolicited addition. The sparrow, crooning to its chicks in the nest made on the window ledge, let out a startled chirp and flew away. Suġra picked up a pakora— to kill time rather than satisfy a hunger she never seemed to have. It tasted like greased sawdust. Not just her eyes, but her tongue too had gone bad with age. The only thing she could feel was the pain in her bones, the cold on her paper-thin skin.

Old age was butterfly's second cousin, moth, a creature trying to hide its ungainly form in its lacklustre wings. She shifted to the end of her janamaz, wrapping the shawl around her tighter, and waddled towards the door. In addition to the brazier in her room, she had insisted on a tall mirror—a luxury not many could boast of in the city. This was soon after her four-and-a-half mirror-less months of seclusion and her exile from the room she had shared with her husband. But now, she questioned if having a mirror was a great idea. Every time she walked to the door, she could see her farmer's sickle of a form in it, bent and blunt with use and abuse.

She swept a glance around the second floor. There was a railing-less staircase flanking the wall beside her room, going up to the third level. On the other side of the semi-circular porch were her grandsons' room, the toilet and the steps going down to the first floor. If she walked up to the parapet, she could see the open courtyard on the ground floor, where the visitors waited till they were ushered in, but she checked herself. She couldn't be displaying such anxiety. It was supposed to be just another drab day in the life of an old woman who had lived to see two world wars caused by un-contained male ego, the fall of the British empire in Hindustan spearheaded by a 'half-naked fakir', and a husband who didn't have the spine to beat her even once in his lifetime.

Her only daughter, who remained on this side of the imaginary border, was a baanjh—with a dry womb. Eldest of her children and two years older than Tahir, Khadija remained childless even at the ripe old age of thirty-five. She had secretly announced to the whole village of Galiyakot, famous for its mazaar, the tomb of a saint revered by both Muslims and Hindus, that it was not her but her husband who was dry. Suġra wondered if that was true. After all, the husband could have got a second wife on the grounds of being childless, but he didn't. It was telling, if not incriminating.

Khadija was Suġra's confidante. Her foot soldier. Her ears and eyes during the time of her iddat. She could visit only once or twice a month when her husband came to town for work. He was a wholesale dealer of incense, supplying it in bulk to temples to add to the aura of mass piety. He sometimes returned to Galiyakot the same day, even though it was a long journey back, to avoid paying the coachman for an extra day's work. The brief spells were enough for Suġra's purging. She couldn't stand her daughter for more than two straight days, anyway.

But, this time, she wished Khadija had not visited at all.

'Stop acting like a woman!' she scolded herself. 'The jeevti dakkan will not betray those who seek her…' With this assurance, she trudged back to her bed.

3

Parijat, the Nightsoil Worker

Street Market

Udaipur

EVERY MORNING SHE SMELT OF ROSES. THEY COULD CALL HER Bhangan—of broken identity—but how could they take the smell of roses away from her? Even her name meant night jasmine. They could take her life, but not her name. Not the fireflies that pulled the strings of constellations at night as she lay watching them emerge from the holed roof of her hut. Not the Aravalli hills beyond the walled city of Udaipur that stood steadfast, offering her fellowship. There was always a rosy side to life, even if you carried shit on your head.

Maldar ji Street, Ghanta Ghar, Bohrawadi ... the mohallas that she covered every day with her wicker basket were landscapes of hate. She could hold a basketful of faeces and go round and round sprinkling it in all directions and not a single drop would hit a half-decent person. The men with turbans and topi hiding their slithering thoughts spat curses at her if she walked too close to their shops, but she could see the hunger in their eyes. The hunger for her firm breasts half-hidden in her choli, her thick lips a shade lighter than her wheatish skin, her fluted neck, her rounded hips lending her oomph, her wild curls contained by a band of yarn stretched to the breaking point. She could sense hatred sailing towards her from the ghaghra-choli clad upper-caste women going about their duties—the face veils displaying their modesty and hiding their anger and a lifetime of repressed desires.

'You swine! How dare you walk close to me!'

Thunk … A mud pot came crashing to the ground, the water snaking away in a pee line on the dirt path of the Mandi. This was the lane dominated by grain and spice sellers. Only a few shops were open today. Husk spun lazily with the cool breeze. Chilly powder got in the nostrils and caused sneezing fits. Haggling customers clutched their money pouches. Wheat and barley and corn lay in open sacks.

Today, being the festival of Makar Sankranti, most shops had unbreakable iron locks dangling on their eminently breakable wooden doors. The terraces were milling instead of the streets. Children scurried in the lanes. Sugarcane juice vendors pushed their wheeled carts going from mohalla to mohalla, rhythmic in the calls fluttering from their lips. Women looked out from the jharokhas with their veils lifted an inch above their eyes, taking in the noon sky curdled with kites. Profanities flung in the air, hitting all unintended victims caught in the crossfire between warring kite fighters. The city kitchens sent out the aroma of frying sesame seeds.

Parijat was on a mission and wanted to reach Bohrawadi soon. She, as a principle, avoided walking through this lane when she came from their basti, the settlement of untouchables near Delhi Gate. There were five gates to the fortified city of Udaipur surrounded by a moat. One of them, the north-facing Delhi Gate, was never used by a Maharana in his lifetime. Once he was dead, his bier would be taken out of this portal. It was symbolic of the kings of Mewar not surrendering to the Mughals ruling from Delhi; a tradition that continued long after the dynasty of Tamerlane (the lame Timur) was gone and the British befriended.

Parijat preferred to walk through the brass utensils and clothing shops, not those of grains and spices. The upper castes didn't want her ilk close to their uncooked fare. She was polluted by birth. Her proximity could foul their food. Her touch, their frail purity. One of Parijat's recurring dreams was going house to house, putting a finger on the old and the young, corrupting their faith, sending women flying away to purify themselves again. And then she would step inside the imposing Jagdish temple that stood outside the gate of the City Palace. Go right into the sanctum sanctorum and touch the one-that-couldn't-be-touched. She smiled inwardly. It wasn't she who was untouchable. The idol was untouchable for her.

'Give me the money for my broken pot, you!' the woman, with a maroon pallu covering her head and eyes, demanded. 'I not only had to break it, I will have to go home, bring another one and fill it with water again!'

Parijat stood looking at the jingling bangles and sweat marks on the woman's armpits as she threw her hands around. A leper, sporting dirty bandages where his fingers once would have been, walked past Parijat with a theatrical limp, giving her a wide berth, eyeing her empty basket with disgust. A couple of idle shoppers cast a mildly curious glance towards the caterwauling woman and continued with their bargain. This was an everyday scene—a woman or two breaking their pots if an untouchable passed them and demanding money for the loss of their property.

Parijat rubbed her face with her free hand, which came back smudged of the kohl in her eyes, thinking how Gandhi ji had named them Harijan—God's own children. No wonder his people had given him three bits of hard-hitting advice. Right on his naked, skeletal chest.

She lifted her free hand and gestured as if she was shaking a damroo—a small hand-held drum. No money, it said.

'Speak up, cunt!' the woman barked. 'Are you dumb?'

Parijat didn't want to waste any more time. She patted the small pocket on her slime-green ghaghra. It just held a folded paper. She felt all over but didn't find a single coin on her person. Remembering something, she smiled and dipped her hand into her buttoned blouse. It drew out a silver pai from the depths of her cleavage.

'Throw it towards me, *chinaal!*' The woman was vibrating with rage, seeing this immodest display in the bazaar.

Parijat flung the coin on the street. It fell with a sickly tinkle near the broken pot before the woman picked it up. They didn't need to purify money. Money had no caste. It passed effortlessly from the bed of a prostitute to the begging bowl of a leper to the praying (preying) thali of a priest to the bloodstained plank of a butcher.

She scuttled away from the street, aiming to get to Bohrawadi without any further delay. This was normal, this small event. Her community had internalized brutality. And the ever-present stench. Every monsoon, rain would permeate her mother's wicker basket, drenching her head in diluted faeces. First, she started to lose the curls. Parijat's earliest memory was hopelessly trying to straighten each loop as her mother rolled thick rotis by a mud stove, her fingers calloused, her eyes deep moon craters.

The rain achieved what the persistent games of a six-year-old couldn't. The tresses began to fall. Her skin turned scabby and yellow. A charnel miasma began emitting from her pores. That was just before she coughed blood each time they tried to feed her. The day they took her wasted body away, little Parijat did not cry. She coughed and coughed like her shrunken mother had, trying to ease her chest about to burst with panic.

Then it was her uncle. A Bombay returnee zamindar got the idea to make a septic tank at his fort to collect their crap. After a few months of use, it clogged. Her uncle and his partner went inside, carrying their sticks, and emerged dead. Death due to poisonous fumes. No one had come to pull them out as they lay dying for hours until Parijat's father was informed and he rushed with help. A minute too late. Her newlywed uncle breathed his last with Baba wiping someone's diarrhoea from his dying face.

While her mother had shrivelled, her father expanded. No hakim could figure out the cause of Baba's death. His bloated limbs had started smelling like the fetid tanks he cleaned. And soon they were emitting a foul liquid, pooling around his legs every night, saturating her untouchable heart.

Most men in her community died shy of twenty-five. Cholera, typhoid, pinworms, meningitis, upper castes ... they had all the diseases inflicting them. Her cousin Hari's hips had been slashed by the village Thakur's goons. He had failed to get up on time to bow to the zamindar as his carriage passed. He had failed to die on time too. 'Hip-less-Hari' became no short of a legend. He fathered two sons and an intersex child before he passed on to clean the shit-holes of heaven.

But Parijat was sure her brother Valmiki would survive that illusionary age of twenty-five. While the other boys in the village played gilli-danda and mardhari-ka-meetha-laadoo, he would sit behind their hut in the village surrounded by shrub forests, pressing his chapped lips and squinting his eyes hard to read a book, as if the effort would make up for the lack of teaching. He had got a good beating from Baba more than once for sneaking behind the window of the room where a teacher from Udaipur sat tutoring the Thakur's half-witted sons. Baba suspected he sat there to smell the mutton shorba the brats were fed each afternoon. The aroma of this broth—cinnamon, ghee, bay leaves, cloves, chunky pieces of mutton and garlic cooked in ghee—was what heaven would smell like. If the Thakur ever came across Baba's son sitting outside his sons' window, he would not only kill the boy but also feed his entire family to the hyenas. Chopped and properly served.

Valmiki had survived the hyenas. And so had she—sixteen full years of existence. What more, she would earn a big fat coin of one rupee today! It would buy her sixty days of rose-water supply. Thirty drops each in two precious phials. She wouldn't have to skip a month's breakfast to buy it. A whole month of roti with raw onion and salt in the morning coming up! Her mouth watered. It had not tasted anything since last night.

There were no men in the city lanes today pushing handcarts or carrying gunnysacks on their bare backs, their bodies bent with the burden passed on by their forefathers, sticky with a crushing tiredness that didn't leave them till the pyre consumed their bones. '*Hak-klick-klick...*' A tonga driver's whip smacked a horse's backside as he urged the beast forward in the narrow lane. *Tik-tok-tik-tok-tik-tok* ... the tempo of the horse's hooves and the rolling wheels made a noisy jangle.

Her foot almost slipped in the drain-water trickling out of a wall as the tonga rattled past, squeezing her. She felt a creature coiling around her left breast. Before she could smack it, the fat shopkeeper drew back his hand, his smiling mouth dripping red. Parijat staggered away from the wall once the tonga passed, and stared at him.

'What are you looking at, Bhangan? How dare you come close to my shop! Who allowed you to enter this street?' He pressed his obscenely thick lips with his fingers—fingers that were fondling Parijat's breast a moment back—and spat a jet of paan-stained saliva on the wall. 'Scat before I have those brazen eyes gouged,' he snarled. Parijat turned away quickly and ran down the street, reaching the pitted lane that led to Bohrawadi.

Another Bhangi sat on his haunches at the bend of the road, head thrown back admiring the kites that ruled the sky. He wiped his face with a rag and returned to cleaning a pipe hole on a wall with a stick. Slop and slurp. Slop and slurp. Bones jutted out from his spine. He was a breathing cadaver. Parijat had no sympathy for him. He was a fortunate male of their damnable race. The men were paid many times higher than the women, and they had fancy jobs—cleaning drains and sewers and tanks. The women had to clean the dry latrines as they were located inside the house. For being more reliable than men to be allowed in, they were awarded with pittance and some stale roti thrown at them if they gave a good performance of begging. Parijat could not beg. Even when she wanted to. Even when she

starved. She swept her thoughts away from food but they kept
sneaking back. A flagellation of thoughts. Hitting her stomach.

The stunning woman in saree, whom they called Mena
Bai, would throw her a roti now and then, even though Parijat
didn't ask for one. She was Dada Bhai's wife. The suited-booted
messiah of the tribal Bhils. She wished he would cast a glance
at the Bhangis or at least the Hele, the Muslim untouchables.
Wasn't he some sort of an upper-caste Muslim too? A Bohra?
But then, he had cast a glance at her once…

'Don't call yourself Bhangi!' Her brother, Valmiki, had once
glowered at her husband Bhola. 'Our great leader Ambedkar
calls us Dalits—the oppressed. And don't forget, he has written
the Indian Constitution too.'

The ever-biddable Bhola had nodded, his hand with a frozen
elbow twitching to please.

Parijat turned the lane and saw the building that stood
guard to the rest of the houses. Proud and intimidating. The
only building in Bohrawadi that had an in-house latrine. Who
shat where determined the status of a man. But there was no
faeces waiting for her at Dada Bhai's house today. She had
done her rounds in the morning before men and boys filled the
terraces and remained there till the end of the kite-flying day in
a constant state of arousal. The shaded street felt cool beneath
her bare feet. There were hardly any windows opening in this
back lane. It was all walls. Except one jharokha on the second
floor. The path was largely unobserved, away from prying eyes.
She had a spring in her steps. And she soon would have a one-
rupee coin in her bosom. Parijat smiled to herself. Life did have
a rosy side.

4

Hariharan, the Middleman

Dada Bhai's House

Bohrawadi, Udaipur

THE SMILE HUNG ON HARIHARAN'S FACE AS HE CUSSED THE steep steps beneath his stiff feet and the eight gold rings stuck in his swollen fingers and the arthritis that his father had passed on as the only inheritance and Dada Bhai who had built this blasted house. He drew out a pure white kerchief from his pure white kurta and dabbed sweat beads from the flab of his face. He looked up to see the two remaining floors to be scaled but the overhead sun dazzled his eyes, the hovering kites making dark spots in his dizzy vision. The pretentiously simple, white-washed, five-storey residence smelt of conspiracies hidden in its crevices. Hariharan was a firm devotee of conspiracies. Of politics of power. Of power of politics.

A few branches of the spiteful peepul tree visible from the jharokha on the side wall made his back prickle, and not from the cold. Everyone except Dada Bhai knew that the tree was the abode of the jeevti dakkan, the living witch. He cast a quick glance at the two rooms that stood facing each other as he crossed the third-floor porch—one was Dada Bhai's daughter's and another a guest room—both clamped shut, and hurried up the railing-less stairway. He darted a furtive glance towards Mena Bai's room as he crossed the foyer on the fourth floor. The ornate wooden door was closed. Just one look at that goddess of beauty would have made this hideous climb worthwhile.

'What are you looking at?' a gruff voice nudged his disappointment aside.

He could feel the old housekeeper drilling her gaze through her ghoonghat from across the veranda. She was sitting outside the kitchen, frozen in mid-motion, sagging over a grindstone, its wooden handle clutched in her hand.

'Badi Bi!' Hariharan broadened his fixed smile. 'Pranaam. Always a blessing to see your respected self.'

This didn't placate the pugnacious hag. She had the cunning of a politician. She resumed moving her hand in a circular motion, making the heavy, grinding stone go round and round reluctantly, her head all the while turned towards a panting Hariharan. Fine maize flour fell softly around the edges.

'Ah, Hariharan sahib!' The servant boy Ismail—the twig that Hariharan would like to snap someday on his disfigured knee—emerged from the kitchen carrying a steaming bowl of cooked beans. The staple food in Bohras, like most other castes, was roti and dal, or roti and gosht on special occasions. But Dada Bhai had the gall to have vegetable curries cooked in addition to the meals of the lowly masses. Hariharan made a mental note to tell his halwain, his fat squab of a wife, to make him a vegetable curry in the afternoon, although he hated all vegetables except potatoes. His stomach roiled with the smell of the beans.

'Care to have roti and beans, Sahib? The climb doesn't do you much good, I can see,' Ismail chirruped fingering the missing button on his bush shirt.

'Shup up, kambakht!' Badi Bi stopped gnashing the corn. Shut 'Do you want to mar his faith by making him eat at a Mussalman's house? You know how much it'll cost him to purify himself?'

'It will certainly be more than your year's salary, Ismail Bhai,' Hariharan wheezed, wiping the froth forming at the corner of his pasted smile.

'Ah, if you have to undertake something so monumental, might as well...' Ismail dashed inside the kitchen and emerged holding a half-open tin can in his hand. The smell hit Hariharan hard enough to buckle his knees. He reeled. Instinctively, his hand holding the pure white kerchief rose to his nose and covered it. Hariharan breathed the smell of his own sweat to ward off the stench of the long-dead sardines that had travelled all the way from Britain in a silver can. Floating in some unnamed liquid made to keep the dead fresh for the afterlife. Dada Bhai was known for his love for imported sardines, a luxury most would prefer to avoid like the Bengal famine.

'You...' Hariharan managed a stifled threat before Badi Bi pulled out the wooden haft inserted in the grinding stone to rotate it, and threw it at Ismail, who stood holding out the sardine can.

'Oww!' Ismail gritted his teeth as the handle rattled on the stone floor after hitting his arm. 'That hurt, Badi Bi!'

'Kambakht! If Mena Bai had seen you, she would give you a well-deserved thrashing!' Badi Bi lifted her ghoonghat an inch and glared at him with a wrinkled eye.

'Nah, Bhabhijaan would have just joined in the laugh. She is a real connoisseur of a good prank.' Ismail picked up the wooden handle and gave it back to the old bat.

'And be quiet,' Badi Bi went on in a grating voice. 'She is not well today. Resting.'

Hariharan cast a grieved look at Mena's locked room and hauled himself up the last flight of steps.

'Why does he always dress like you, Badi Bi?' He could hear the loud whispers of Ismail and sense the brazen grin in his words.

'Like me?'

'Like a widow, always in white,' Ismail chuckled.

Babi B's laugh was a muffled chug.

Hariharan was never impulsive. He made a note in his mental ledger, which he always kept handy, to deal with this irritant Ismail two years hence. Things would be pretty positive by then. His future was orderly and meticulously laid out like the segregated sweetmeats in his halwai father's shop. The bittersweet confectioner. Always bitter to him and sweet to others.

The malodorous taste still lingered in his mouth and nasal cavity as Hariharan reached the fifth and final floor. He stood there hearing the loud noises of thrill and excitement floating down this highest terrace in town. Feet thumped from one end to the next on the roof above his head. He would rather be on one such terrace today in his cotton vest, gorging on til-ke-laddoo and shouting encouragements to his friend Nana

Sahib, the undisputed kite champion of the Ghanta Ghar mohalla. Uff ... the sacrifices he had to make for his children, he thought, looking at Dada Bhai's heavy wooden door left ajar. An open, inviting ruse. But who was the unsuspecting rat? Hariharan sniggered. Post-Partition Hindustan was the best space for him to prosper. There was so much misery to encash.

He straightened the wrinkles of his chalk-white kurta, rehearsed his most sterling smile, took in a few deep breaths to support his bursting lungs, cleared his conscience of missing the kite-fighting, and walked purposefully towards the door. His sources had told him about Rao Sahib of Singhgarh visiting Dada Bhai. He had to reach the battle lines and make his move before the zamindar made his.

A capacious porch led to Dada Bhai's living room and bedchamber. A heady scent of bokhoor—wood chips soaked in fragrant oils—blended with fried pakoras and cigar smoke wafted from his quarters. Hariharan lifted the brass knocker of an angry tiger's face and brought it down on the oft-slapped cheek of the door as he peeked inside. One day, he too would have all this in his living room—a black telephone on a mahogany table, understated nineteenth-century furniture that cost more to show less, a gold-rimmed tea set made of bones ground in China, a divan with ... no, without a deer skin spread on it, and an ugly, visiting noble sitting on an armchair. But certainly no leopard heads hanging on the walls, frozen in an everlasting snarl.

'Hariharan ji ... come in.' Dada Bhai, seated regally on his chair with Rao Sahib bent forward, squashing his belly on his thighs, gave him a stately nod.

He stood at the door, suitably surprised on seeing Rao Sahib with Dada Bhai. 'Hehe … Dada Bhai ji Sahib, I didn't know you had respected company.'

Rao Sahib jerked his hand, as if a hairy millipede had crawled up his fingers, and drew back on his chair, allowing his belly to decompress.

'Come on in, please,' Dada Bhai said again, placing his tea cup on the table.

'*Khamma Ghani,* Hukam.' He bent his aching back to greet the zamindar.

'Hari—haran…' Rao Sahib's expression was that of a farmer seeing an upsurge of locusts descend on his ripened fields.

'Care for some tea?' Dada Bhai asked, ushering him to sit on the divan.

Hariharan's knees creaked as he slouched on the soft deer skin, silently thanking his personal deity Laddoo Gopal for the respite before the nasty climb down—past that pest Ismail, past that haunted peepul tree. Everyone needed to have one personal deity out of the thirty-three crore Hindu gods. Addressing it to gods in general was an utter waste of a prayer. Hariharan believed in maximum profits out of minimum investments. No investments, preferably.

'You know, Dada Bhai ji Sahib, I have no vices.' He shook his head side to side looking at the tea.

Dada Bhai's living room, separated from his bedchamber with a thick curtain drawn on a low, open doorway was cool after the sweaty climb. But not hushed as it generally was. Hoarse, hysterical shouts of the entire town flowed into this eyrie from the jharokhas, along with the sequinned beams of the winter sun. Rose-ringed parakeets sitting on ledges kissed and made love to while away a day when paper birds and bird-brains ruled the sky.

Dada Bhai's clean-shaven jawline curved up in a smile. 'There is no divine law you'll break by having tea, my good man, nor invite the godly wrath upon you. But why take the chance? Leave this vice to us sinners.'

'Oh no, no. You both are no sinners!' Hariharan grinned sheepishly. 'You are the finest specimens of humanity, reformers of the society, uplifters of the Bhils...'

Rao Sahib groaned. 'And how would you describe your respected self, Hariharan?' His voice was laced with mockery. It was evident he would have loved to squash him beneath his leather mojdi footwear. Hariharan felt energized thinking that the zamindar couldn't. Not in Dada Bhai's domain. Not now. Not ever. Three-and-a-half years from now, he would see who squashed whom. Another note in Hariharan's invisible ledger.

He expanded his smile displaying his pure white teeth. 'I am just a servant, Rao Sahib. Servants don't have descriptions.'

The zamindar farted lifting his bottom, mildly satisfied with the answer.

'I am very, very sorry I just came up without sending you a word first.' Hariharan felt the winter creeping up his skin as the sweat dried. 'Both your servant boys were not around.'

'Yes, Rameshwar and Shiva have gone to their village for a week for Makar Sankranti.'

'You are too liberal, Dada Bhai.' Rao Sahib finished his tea with a content slurp.

'And, ahem, if I may add, a bit, a wee bit incautious too, Sahib.' Hariharan ran his tongue over his dry lips. He continued, looking at Dada Bhai's questioning glance, 'Remember, a year ago, a Muslim servant drowned those two boys … the sons of his Hindu master … in the Ayad river?'

'What about it?' Dada Bhai frowned.

'Ahem, with all due respect, what if the Hindu servants decide to take revenge?'

'Hariharan ji…' Dada Bhai gave him a hard look. 'If all of us start to think like that, whom will we trust? We've seen the worst possible bloodshed during Partition. The Mahatma died trying to make people understand.'

'There is some basis to biases, Dada Bhai. What about Mewar?' Rao Sahib twirled the points of his moustache speaking above the clamour from the roof that rose and fell in waves. 'Hindus and Muslims have lived as brothers here for centuries. The biggest Tazia in Muharram starts from the Maharana's palace. Bhabhi ji lights diyas on Diwali and prepares til-ke-laddoo on Makar Sankranti.' He picked up one and continued with a mouthful. 'We didn't even want the British to leave.'

'What's the point, Rao Sahib?' Dada Bhai's question was a bullet shot.

Rao Sahib drew back, wounded. 'The Sindhis, Dada Bhai. The Sindhis. That's what the Partition has given Mewar.'

Dada Bhai's forehead furrowed. He spoke after a moment. 'And we should open our arms and doors to them.'

Hariharan observed the two friends from his cushiony divan covered with deer skin, happy at the outcome he had initiated.

'Would we have rioted on our own, Dada Bhai? Sindhis brought the riots with them. What about all the Bohra cloth shops they burnt in Bada Bazaar? The Sindhis have started opening their own cloth shops. What will you say to that?'

'I will say they are displaced people; imagine the atrocities they would have faced on the way. Yes, some of them may have engaged in excesses when they came here. But who hasn't? The persecution of the Muhajir in Pakistan—the Muslims who have migrated from India. It's shameful. Pakistani or Hindustani, they are all *our* people. As for the Bohras, they are gravitating towards Loha Bazaar in Chamanpura now. They want to go into a business no one can burn—iron. We'll all find our footings, Rao Sahib. Let's give ourselves time.'

'Didn't the Sindhis come to burn your ammunition shop too?' Rao Sahib clearly wanted to have the last word.

'Yes, and our Hindu landlady deflected them. Told them they'll have to burn her first.'

'Our Dada Bhai ji Sahib here is an impartial gental-man,' Hariharan put in.

'Sure.' Rao Sahib smiled. 'I too am. Impartial. No discrimination. I give a good hiding to the Bhil tribals as well as my wives and kids.' Before Dada Bhai could say something, he added, 'I remember Bhabhi ji and her Ladies Shot Gun when you visited my jagir last year. She was shooting crocodiles from her window. Unlike you, I would never give a shot gun to my wife, Dada Bhai. Guess which crocodile she'd be shooting with it?' Rao Sahib threw back his head, hooting with laughter.

'Rao sahib, call it "shot gun". You will do well to drop "Ladies" when you speak to Mena. I can't guarantee where the gun will be pointed if you do.' Dada Bhai smiled while Rao Sahib continued to laugh, his body shaking.

'You said you wanted to relax for some time?' asked Dada Bhai once the cackles subsided. 'I have told Ismail to prepare the guest room on the third floor.'

Rao Sahib's response was a bit absurd. He suddenly seemed too eager to go, trying to get his bulk out of the chair in sheer desperation. 'Just an hour's rest, Dada Bhai. Then I'll have a word with you and take your leave to visit the durbar. Bonded labour—begaar—calls.' He winked at Dada Bhai as he squirmed out of the chair, crumbs of pakora falling off his kurta.

'I'll call Ismail to take you to the guest room.' Dada Bhai stood up, placing his cigar on the ivory ashtray.

'Oh no, no. I know the way.' By now, Rao Sahib had accomplished the feat of standing on his feet, his once-starched dhoti starched no more. 'Third floor, the room opposite our Beti Sanaz's.'

He rolled out of the room, leaving dandruff flakes and the smell of an Ayurvedic pain-reliever oil in his wake.

Hariharan waited for Dada Bhai to see him off, scratching his two-day-old stubble. The damn barber had caught a cold. The room now smelt of slow-burning tobacco and stale aristocracy. Dada Bhai came and sat on his chair again, picking up his abandoned cigar from the side table.

'There are two Bhils waiting below, Dada Bhai ji Sahib.'

'Yes, one of them has come with Rao Sahib from his estate. The other must be my khoju shikari, my jungle tracker Jaitya, from Jogion ka Guda with the news of a fresh kill. A cattle lifter leopard has terrorized that village, I heard.'

'Is that so … You are the best marksman in Mewar, Sahib. And such a gental-man to go cull the man-eaters and cattle-lifters making life hell for the tribals. They live in grinding poverty. You are—'

'I'm sorry I can't accept your proposal, Hariharan ji,' Dada Bhai cut in.

Hariharan examined him with a glowing smile, a hungry smile. Here sat in front of him the future mayor of Udaipur, the future minister in Nehru's cabinet, the future Prime Minister of Hindustan in twenty years. Who knew?

'That is too bad, Sahib ji.' Hariharan rubbed a hairy mole on his arm fondly. 'Too bad that you are destroying your reputation and a most glorious future.'

5

Nathu, the Bhil

Dada Bhai's House

Bohrawadi, Udaipur

THE EARTH BENEATH HIS FEET ALWAYS SPOKE TO HIM. SHE grumbled when he scraped the colonies of ant eggs with his toes, murmured when his feet sank in grass, moaned when he split her skin with his pickaxe and sometimes, when he spread the dung of his now-dead bull on his tiny tilled field, she sang him a song. She always spoke, except when he walked on the paved paths of Udaipur city. The earth was stone-cold here. Cold like the village moneylender's scrolls gathering interest in their dusty folds. Cold like his mud chulha, the cook fire, which had not been lighted for two days. Click-clack, click-clack, his feet imprisoned in his camel leather mojdi protested in sullen crunches as he walked to and fro, to and fro, on the ground floor of Dada Bhai's house. He had got a big blister around his left ankle. Watery-eyed and layered.

'Stop!' Doonga, the Bhil who had accompanied Rao Sahib, bristled.

'Doon-goonnn-ga ji,' Nathu stammered, halting before his fellow Bhil tribal sitting on his haunches. A big off-white pagadi loomed large over his shrunken head, and his leather footwear was removed and kept on a side. His eyes were bloodshot. The dhoti was streaked with mud and his angarkha—a shirt with cloth buttons and two pockets—was scrunched.

'Just stop!' Doonga rubbed his dark face, smudged with sun; the smooth silver bangle in his hand was a complete contrast to the lines on his forehead. The toes of his bare feet jerked in small shivers.

Doonga drew a long drag of his bidi and looked up listlessly at the kite-strewn sky from the open courtyard of Dada Bhai's home. Nathu followed his gaze and felt as if he was at the bottom of a dried-up well with circling vultures carrying the tiding of his end on their wings. The bulk of the house loomed around him. The ground floor was as big as four village huts put together, a third of it opening to the sky. The white paint was peeling off around the hem of the walls. The slant-eyed jharokhas high up let in languid winter rays. They pooled with the oval patch of sunlight that streamed in from the roof, warming the heart of this slumbering beast. There was a passage leading to the odha that contained a small inner yard and two rooms—a locked one for storage and a servants' quarter. Odha, the masculine of veiled, a place in the house that was always dark and dingy, the feminine being odhani, the stole vital to maintaining a woman's decorum. A flight of stone steps went up the large open courtyard, alternating between left and right on each floor till it reached the roof. Five intimidating storeys rose one above the other, a stack of bricks that could scatter with a storm.

The city dwellers had a way of teasing the gods, trying to nick their heavenly lodgings. These alien gods were known for their spite. Make offerings to their agents—the pot-bellied pandits—or else burn in hell. Do the kariyawar, the last rites, after a family member's death or else the dead would haunt you forever. The gods matched the savageness of their counterparts on earth—the zamindars—making sure the afterlife was as miserable for the slaves they had created in a fit of boredom. Nathu wondered if animals knew about the existence of gods. If they cared. Where had his dead bull Bhoora gone? Would he be punished in the animal hell with vicious resolution? Or would he graze in heavenly meadows humping the cows to eternity? The Bhils had uncomplicated deities like Magra Baba—the hill god and Rana ji—the forest god, and they could be easily pleased. Make an offering to Rana ji of a bottle of strong home-brewed mauda of fermented wild mahua fruits, and you'd be blessed with whatever you wanted—a month without a solid hiding from a zamindar or a young milking cow with heavy udders.

He arranged a smile on his face and tried small talk with Doonga. 'Do-do you know that Vaski ran away with Nanka from the Go-gogunda village? Um ... Sh-sh-she is married to Roda. But since they couldn't catch the eloping couple within the village limits, the elders have decided they can sss-sss-stay together. Nanka will have to give a buffalo to Vaski's ailing husband as com-compensation. If you ask me, I'd much rather keep the buff-buff-buff...' He let the word trail.

Doonga's slow-burning bidi was more responsive than his passive face. A faint odour of burnt wood emitted from the Bhil. His emaciated body sat in a foetal position, half-alive, half-dead.

A butterfly came dipping and upping—a wave in the air. Earthy. As greenish brown as the two Bhils. As lost in the building as they were.

'Have you ever been on a haaa-hakka with Da-dada Bhai?' Nathu tried again to soothe his nerves by making normal conversation. 'My Ba tells me that Da-dada Bhai visits Rao sahib's jagir often for a hunt with a beat. And then makes sure the game is diss-stributed to all the Bhils participating in the hakka equally. That's unheard of. I wish I lived in Rao Sahib's es-estate.'

At this, Doonga looked up at him with hollow eyes, the two silver earrings in his ears flashing defiantly against his sunburnt skin.

'Be-believe me,' Nathu trudged on, 'life in Jogion ka Guda is much tougher than life on Rao Sahib's estate. A cattle lifter leopard has b-brought much grief in the past two months, not just to our village but also to another one. One of those families will die of ss-ss-starvation or the village baniya's interest. That cow was their only ss-source of a half-ss-starved life. I am here to request Dada Bhai to kill the marauder.'

Doonga lowered his gaze to his mud-stained dhoti, ashes from the bidi falling around his fingers. A line of red ants walked past him, haughty and proud. He brought his bidi down on their pompous march, sizzling a few ants alive.

'You know, I loved your performance in Ga-gavari five years back, just at the beginning of the month of Sh-shravan,' said Nathu, taking off his pagadi and scratching the hair. His nails came back full of dandruff wet with sweat. The winter afternoon was fierce and high strung. 'I was viz-viz-visiting with my Ba to give Dada Bhai the news of a leopard kill. Twenty people from your village had come to perform Gavari for Dada Bhai's family right here. You wouldn't remember me, I was just a t-t-t-twelve-year-old ratty boy.' Nathu had always been a fan of the traditional Gavari renditions—a colourful cast of characters and musical depictions of their changing moods, played every year after the monsoons. It was one of the only sources of entertainment in their lives in the forests. 'You were one of the Rai Devi, white in face … twi-twinkling jewellery. I was swinging to the tune of thali and mandal all day. And Buriya, oh, what a wonderfully horrible Buriya you had! One ss-stare from his horse-hair fringed mask and I would ss-ss-swoon!'

Doonga cast him a sharp look, as if he was still the ratty boy.

'I'm seventeen, Doon-doonga ji, married for three years,' Nathu whispered in answer to the glassy stare.

Nathu wondered if Doonga would make a pretty Rai Devi again. He seemed to be touching thirty and had started to wither. He made him think of his father, Jaitya. Nathu shuddered at the thought, snapped the hastada from his shoulder and wiped his face with the absorbent red cloth. There were a couple of wooden benches in the courtyard for people to sit and wait. Not the Bhils though. They couldn't possibly sit on a bench at an aristocrat's house. But the tribals were more fortunate than the Bhangi and Chamar—the untouchables—who couldn't even enter the house. His Ba told him to look at the people below his station in life to find a semblance of happiness. It worked most of the times, until the errant son started to look up.

Dada Bhai was known to be disrespectful to the age-old caste system and allowed Bhils to sit on benches, untouchables to enter his home. But Bhils and Bhangis were wiser than him. Wiser through hundreds of years of oppression, hip cutting, hot-coal branding, soul shattering. Wiser than the proud ants sizzling under Doonga's bidi.

Bawls and bays of the kite fighters on rooftops resounded against the walls of the building. The greenish-brown butterfly beat arcs into the noisy air to find a way out. Nathu tried to direct the insect through the tall open door and stopped looking at the trunk of the peepul tree in the lane. He had not breathed a word to anyone about why he was really in the city today. But surely, the jeevti dakkan that hung right outside the house could see the cobwebs in people's minds more clearly than the gods trapped in clouds. The sullen presence of Rao Sahib's aide Doonga was not helping. Crunch-creak-crunch ... Nathu's mojdi made a fuss as he again started walking from one end of the foyer to the other. He had learnt in the first eight years of his life that you couldn't see them, but witches watched. Ghosts gawked. Spirits sensed. He didn't want anyone to read his thoughts; a witch least of all.

'Nathu ji, Doonga ji ... Ram-Ram, Namaste, Assalam-alaykum!' The playful voice of the house servant, Ismail, came bounding down before he appeared on the steps carrying a plate full of pakoras. 'Badi Bi sends her compliments.'

Nathu smiled. A smile that can only be brought to the surface by primal instincts—food topping them all. His staple diet was raw onion with maize-roti. On good days.

'Sh-she is too kind ... and so are you, Ismail Bhai.' Nathu reached out for the brass plate, hot with the fried pakoras, before Ismail touched the landing.

'Badi Bi says she hasn't seen you for years. Generally, it is your father who brings in the news of game from Jogion ka Guda. What brings you to town today?'

'Um...' Nathu rubbed his left eye, which twitched when he lied. 'Ba couldn't come. He wanted me to inform Da-da-daada Bhai about the leopard kill. Sss-so ...'

It was Ismail's turn to smile. His translucent skin stretched over his jaws to the point of splitting open. The smile from a liar to a liar. From a pro to an amateur. 'You see, Dada Bhai has a couple of esteemed visitors. He'll come and see you at the earliest opportunity.'

'No ha-ha-hurry,' came Nathu's hurried reply.

'I thought so.' Ismail's grinning head went up and down, up and down, in subsequent nods. Nathu had seen such gestures made by puppets. How he waited for all of them—from those who played Gavari and Pad and Kahwad to the puppeteers to the sadhu who got possessed by the resident spirit every moonless night like clockwork.

'Nathu ji ... for a serial stutterer, you talk a lot.' Ismail chuckled as he sprinted up the steps.

Nathu took the plate full of pakoras and sat by Doonga's side. 'My Ba told me Ismail is—' he spied up the stairs to see that the servant was gone—'quite a thief. Keeps s-slipping ss-stuff out of the house. Badi Bi, the old maidservant, wanted him out, and he was removed from ss-service. But Dada Bhai took pity on him and kept him back.'

Doonga didn't touch a single pakora, his hands hugging his legs hugging his chest.

'Ram-Ram, Doonga ji!' A cheerful clatter made Nathu look at the main door. A middle-aged Bhangi clad in a short dirty dhoti and holding a long broom stood outside the door. The left arm was frozen at his elbow, and the left cheek spasmed as he spoke. Nathu wondered if both the deformities were connected in some way.

'How is the forest produce this year?' the untouchable went on without getting a reply to his greeting from Doonga. 'I hope we can get some juicy amla this season.' It seemed his broom was made out of his own spiky hair.

'Ram-Ram.' Nathu felt compelled to answer on behalf of his fellow Bhil. He walked towards the main door, placing the plate of pakoras by Doonga's side. 'Yes, at Jogion ka Guda we have had a good fruiting of belpatra and amla this ss-season. Our men have already ss-started to come and s-sell the wild fruits outside Udaipur's sh-shaharpana.' A tart smell of sweat wafted from the untouchable. Nathu controlled the urge to cover his nose.

'Oh, good, good,' answered the Bhangi, as if he had one full rupee to go outside the shaharpana—the city wall—and buy all the belpatra and amla in the world. 'I am Bhola, but you can call me Loola.' He smiled exposing his yellowed teeth and gesturing at his disused arm. Loola meaning armless.

'I am Na-Nathu from Jogion ka Guda.'

'I ... um ... am here just to clean the street, nothing else. Doonga ji knows me well. You see, my wife, Parijat, works at this house,' Bhola said proudly. 'Dada Bhai's wife, Mena Bai, is quite generous.'

Nathu nodded politely at the wretch with the puffed-up chest of a pigeon.

'Doonga ji is quiet today ... has the jeevti dakkan possessed him?' Bhola tittered at his own joke and stopped abruptly, realizing how close he was to the peepul tree. He cast a glance behind him at the rustling leaves, turned and gave Nathu a nervous smile. 'Ram-Ram, Nathu ji, Doonga ji. I will get back to work. The kite-runners in the lanes are not making the task any easier.' He complained good-humouredly, raised his good hand holding the broom in a salute, and began to tramp away with a limp. A gang of screeching children ran past, slowing down to hurl abuses at him.

'Rat tail!' shouted one.

'Drain flea!' squealed another.

The third held his elbow close to his chest and walked with a limp amid a volley of laughter. Nathu saw Bhola chuckling with them before their attention got diverted, clearly by a falling kite, and they darted after it.

Nathu shook his head in pity and turned towards Doonga. He was an idol—rock-still, silent, the incense of a bidi burning in his fingers and eyes fixed in an angry stare. There was something decidedly odd about Doonga today. But who was Nathu to comment on it? He too was on a decidedly odd mission. One that could cost a life.

6

Rao Sahib, the Zamindar

Dada Bhai's House

Bohrawadi, Udaipur

RAO SAHIB'S DHOTI FLARED UP WITH A GUST OF WIND FROM THE open terrace, as if it was inflatable, when he stepped out of Dada Bhai's room on to the patio. He put the pagadi on his head and let out a long, satiated burp, still tasting the onion and potato pakora. The sunlight was dappled with the flying kites.

'To the right, Zain, a little to the right!'

'This pink one with a tail is the toughest, Sa'ad Bhaiya. I need to take him by surprise.'

'Hold the manjha for a bit, Ahad. There … light-lightly, I said!'

He heard the shouts and thumps of Dada's Bhai's sons floating down the roof with a pinch of envy. If only he could run like that again. Data Hukam, his long-dead father, had often rubbed his knees and looked caustically at him, his eldest son, when as a child he went prancing about their fort. Now he understood why. Rao Sahib felt a short burst of empathy for him.

'Rao Sahib…' Dada Bhai's voice caught him off guard. He turned to see him coming out of the solid teak door in sharp strides—his breeches disciplined and stiff, unlike Rao Sahib's unruly pumped-up dhoti. 'I forgot to mention. Your horses must be tired from the long journey. You can take my buggy to the court.'

'I sent my two aides to the durbar as soon as I entered the city this morning, Dada Bhai. Thank you for the offer. I'd rather go there on my horse's back than in a horse carriage.' He tweaked his moustache. 'They'll escort me to the durbar once they take care of my stay arrangements at the City Palace. The Bhil that came along with me is waiting downstairs.'

They walked to the railing of the patio and looked at the open courtyard four storeys below. Two Bhils squatted next to each other.

'Is it Doonga?' asked Dada Bhai squinting his eyes.

'Yes, if you remember, he had taken some of your old England-made hats and pants a couple of years back to use in the Gavari performances. They make a mean gora sahib with that costume!

Ugam ri dharti ro guriyo aawe re Maharaza
Ugas ro aave ne aatham ro jaave re Maharaza…'

Rao Sahib hummed in Mewari patting his thigh. It was one of the Gavari songs made on a gora English sahib and played by the tribals who had caked their sepia skins in ash.

Dada Bhai gave him an indulgent smile. 'Yes, they performed this one for my kids when we visited your estate last.' He looked at the other Bhil, who had got up and begun to pace in the open courtyard, head down, shoulders slumped. 'That must be Jaitya from Jogion ka Guda. He's an excellent jungle tracker. One of the best khoju shikaris that I have. He will pick up a stone, sniff it and tell me which animal has peed on it, how long back and point me in the direction it went.'

'What's he doing here?' asked Rao Sahib, suppressing a yawn. It was natural for this primitive tribe to know the wild animals. They were akin. Both lived in wilderness. Both understood the language spoken by a leather whip better than words. Both smelt like dogs that hadn't been given a brisk scrubbing in a month.

'Must have brought the news of a kill. A cattle lifter has terrorized their valley. I need to go there today or tomorrow.'

'Come to Singhgarh for a hunt, Dada Bhai. Let's organize a good hakka. Partridges are in abundance at present. So are sambar and cheetal. Bring Bhabhi ji and um … the kids along.' Rao Sahib reached for his moustache and twirled it between his fingers.

'Inshallah, Rao Sahib. Soon.'

'It has been long since I went hunting, Dada Bhai. The last hakka-beat I attended was Maharana sahib's mahurat hunt, the auspicious one on Machla Magra on the festival of Navratri. After that, as you know, ahem…'

'Yes, yes, you got married again! How callous of me, I haven't wished you yet. Please accept my heartiest congratulations!' Dada Bhai extended his hand, and Rao Sahib slipped his sweaty one in his. For some reason, his palms were always clammy, even in winter.

'Dada Bhai…' Rao sahib cast a knowing glance at the open door. '…let me warn you about that leech seated on your diwan.

Such creatures leave their hiding places and come out to suck blood when someone's drowning. They will make the village baniya, who live on interest, look like saints.'

Dada Bhai dipped his head in an understated acknowledgement. Sometimes this overload of tehzeeb ... all this culture ... got annoying for Rao sahib. These civilized ways would please the gora sahibs who anyway considered them uncouth brown *Indians*, but for someone like him, it was plain inconvenience.

'All I'm saying, Dada Bhai, is that you and I are brothers in peril. You are safely living in this city of royals, the capital of Mewar. And I in my forest estate, my jagir. But there are orgies of Mussalman and Hindu killings happening not far away. Muhajir are flooding Pakistan just like the Sindhi and Panjabi Hindus are streaming into our cities.' He inched closer. So close that he could smell the coconut oil in Dada Bhai's hair. 'I may not agree with Maharana Bhupal Singh ji signing the Instrument of Accession to the Dominion of India, but I have a theory. It is that handicaps have a heightened sense of intellect. That goes for our Shree Shree Bhupal Singh ji. He was one of the first to sign it as he didn't want any fixers between him and India later on. Avoid'— the fart that followed was a delicious reminder to the til-ke-laddoo and hot tea—'... fixers.'

If Dada Bhai was affronted by the advice or the flatulence, he didn't show it. Now that was one thing, Rao Sahib had to concede, that was a positive of having tehzeeb.

'I do value your advice, Rao Sahib,' he said after a long moment of examining a jharokha on the opposite wall.

'And don't forget, I am way ahead in years than you are.' Rao Sahib pursed his lips and nodded wisely, trying to press more weight on to his years. 'I'll see you before I leave for the durbar. There is something important that I need to discuss with you.'

'Sure, Rao Sahib. Please call Ismail if you need anything,' Dada Bhai said, before heading back to his room where the hyena Hariharan sat in wait.

Rao Sahib began his descent down the house. He kept one careful foot after the next on the high stone steps, passing the frosted rays streaming in from the jharokhas on the walls. *Chunn* ... the sizzling mustard-garlic aroma of dal being tempered mixed with the smell of an open sardine can stung his nose as soon as he landed on the fourth floor near the kitchen. He held the stone railing of the porch, panting. Finally, there was something to hold on to after the tedious descent. He glanced in the direction of Mena Bai's room, but the teakwood door was shut.

A pigeon landed squarely on the palisade by his side and went around in a circle, confused, tipping his head to check Rao Sahib.

'Shoo!' The swing of Rao Sahib's hand sent it flapping noisily in flight, spurting a long, watery poop on his sleeve.

'*Kode maaro ise!*' he boomed, waving a fist at the slate-grey bird beating its wings, wishing for a whip in his hand to flog it. They were growing in number each time he visited the city, and he feared they would soon outnumber the city dwellers.

'*Kambakht!* Who's shouting outside my kitchen?' Badi Bi came bustling out, her anklets trembling.

'Uff...' Rao Sahib took a step back from the widow, who had appeared on the kitchen doorway. 'What a way to begin my visit to Udaipur!'

'Oh, I'm sorry, Rao sahib.' She pulled her white odhani in front of her eyes, veiling her face, and retreated into the kitchen.

'Rao Sahib ...' Ismail's head popped up the steps leading to the third floor on the other side of the porch. 'You should have simply called me to escort you and avoided days of bad luck by seeing a widow in the morning! Let me take you to your room.' He waited for Rao Sahib to cross the porch and approach the steps.

'Do you need a hand?' Ismail smiled as he extended his hand towards him.

One withering look from Rao Sahib and he took it back.

'You know, Hukam, Dada Bhai intentionally comes in front of Badi Bi on these steep steps, so that she doesn't have any place to run away or hide her face. He says she is like his mother, and to see a mother's face in the morning can never be a bad omen.' Ismail sprinted down and waited on the landing.

Rao Sahib was lost in thought. He ignored the blabber and cast another glance at Mena Bai's room before he climbed down.

'Hukam, Bhabhi ji is not well.' Ismail smirked.

'And who asked you?' Rao Sahib reached the last step, laboriously breathing through his mouth.

It got colder as one went down the house. The midday sun peeping from the rooftop and jharokhas could hardly warm up its insides. There were two rooms on this landing—Dada Bhai's daughter Sanaz's and a guest room—on the opposite ends of the porch. Ismail walked up to the guest room and unbolted the door. The heavy metal latch scraped and clanked.

'You have an excellent view from this storey, Hukam ... of the jeevti dakkan hanging in the peepul tree outside.' Ismail's voice was the static cackle on a phone. He pointed to a jharokha on the wall above the main entrance to the courtyard, through which one could see the many elbows of the peepul tree. 'And, of course, of Sanaz Apa's room.'

Rao Sahib halted right in the middle of the porch and glared at him.

'I've kept your trunk in the room, Rao Sahib. Your wife, Baisa Hukam, had sent it two days back from your estate. It has your change of clothes for your visit to the durbar—your sherwani, Bhupalshahi paag, breeches and yes, the sword in its scabbard.' He walked into the room and pointed to the small iron trunk kept on a mahogany table. The room was sparsely but comfortably furnished. The few small depressions in the wall to hold the oil lamps were stained with accumulated darkness that light leaves behind. An armchair with a sambar skin flung casually on its reclining back. A four-poster bed with a hanging mosquito net. A seating area with cushions by the jharokha. A side table with a bronze jar and a silver glass. A thick green curtain separating the small bathing area. You could pee there if you liked and wash it away with water from the earthen pot kept inside. But for relieving yourself after two plates of potato pakoras, you had to go to the second-floor toilet, which had a hole—the trajectory aimed at the wicker basket placed in a small enclosure on the ground floor, with a separate entrance, to be emptied by a Bhangi the next day.

Ismail passed him, leaving behind the smell of odorous body fluids. 'Call me if you need anything, Hukam.'

Rao Sahib grunted a reply as he sank into the armchair.

'Please accept this humble servant's wishes on your son's wedding ... oh, sorry, I mean *your* wedding, Hukam.' He stepped on the porch, well out of reach of Rao Sahib, with a ghost of a smile on his lips.

Rao Sahib looked up and returned the smile this time. A cold, amusing sneer. 'I wonder what colour blood would look on such dark skin as yours. I guess it will resemble glistening sweat.'

The smile on Ismail's face flickered. Rao Sahib exhaled a loud moan and spun his moustache in satisfaction.

'Um … Data Hukam … I am just trying to apprise you of the baseless village rumours that reach the city and become urban legends. Good-for-nothing villagers, these!'

Rao Sahib removed his pagadi from his head and placed it on the table. 'Next time Dada Bhai visits my estate for a hunting trip, I must insist he bring his cheerful servant along. But, well, accidents happen all the time in the city too. It is fortunate that my two aides carry arms with them.'

Ismail's gaunt face turned grey. 'You have such a sense of humour, Hukam…' He began closing the door. 'I'm-I'm at your service … just call.'

'Leave the door open!' Rao Sahib boomed.

Ismail bowed and left it ajar.

'All rumours are not baseless, Ismail,' Rao Sahib called in glee as the scrawny rat scuttled away.

He spread his legs wide and squinted. The door of Sanaz's room remained still. The peepul tree in the lane swayed. He couldn't see it but heard its rustle. Tales said that the living witch had a scalding touch. And a will that would move hills to rubble, heroes to tragedy. It was known that she slipped into the house through a jharokha at midnight, smelling of a hakim's concoction. If you got up at night, you might find her hanging upside down over your bed, her ghaghra tucked between her thighs and her nebulous eyes fixed on your dreams. He instinctively looked up above the bed and found a gecko staring at him.

Rao Sahib felt a tightening in his chest and straightened in his chair, reaching for the comfort of his moustache. He had not achieved what he had set out to do this morning at Dada Bhai's place.

But the day was not done.

7

Suġra, Dada Bhai's Mother

Dada Bhai's House

Bohrawadi, Udaipur

THE KITES WERE HAZY DOTS ON THE FAR HORIZON, LIKE LONG-ago youth. Suġra craned her neck to see the little patch of sky available to her window and said a small prayer. Ameen ... she finished, kissing the rosary with her cracked lips. The janamaz, her prayer mat, was crumpled below her on the seating by the jharokha lined with bolsters. There she was—the Bhangan, the damn untouchable, loitering in the back lane with the basket dangling by her side. At times, Suġra also called for a Bhangan to stand outside the door with an empty basket when someone was about to travel a long distance. It was considered shagun—a good omen. But no one in her family was going to undertake a journey today. Not that she knew of. What was the bitch up to? Abuses oozed out of her throat and melted on her tongue. But she remained silent. And waited.

'Sasu ji!' Ismail's call made her turn towards the door in anticipation. Even her quickest movements were sluggish at best.

'What is it, Bhandora?' The only fluidity she retained was with expletives. She sat taut, straining to look at the porch through the grain in her sight.

'An elderly woman from the corner khadki is requesting to use our toilet.'

'Uff… Why don't you ask your dear Bhabhi ji about it?' The people living in the community housing khadki had common toilets. Anyone who had diarrhoea felt it was their right to relieve themselves at Dada Bhai's personal latrine. Her loveable daughter-in-law encouraged the behaviour. And why not? The toilet was on her mother-in-law's floor.

'Mena Bai is not well. She's resting.'

'Then shoo the woman away!'

'She is standing right behind me on the staircase,' Ismail shouted back from the other end of the porch. Sugra sensed something off about Ismail. His cockiness was missing.

'Oh, well, I wouldn't want her dumping on my staircase! Tell the woman to empty her swelled bowels and get lost.' She heard a shuffle and saw a flash of purple odhani before she turned away, disgusted.

'Ya Allah…' She brooded chewing on her thoughts. An old photograph of her with her husband hung on a wall. A constant reminder of a wasted life. All her days and years rolled into one. With a glass negative.

There was a damp patch on the wall near her door, which she believed resembled the map of Pakistan. Partition was not a thing that was done and over with. It would never leave her house. She shot curses at the indistinct patch after each namaz, three times a day, diligently, for separating the daughters from an old woman. At least the Bohras had made it simpler; they had clubbed the routine of offering five prayers a day into three. Not that Suġra had any other pressing things to do, but she knew she was approaching her end—one namaz at a time.

Each day was so long and so short. She sat alone listening to life that was passing her by. Her senses dying one by one. More than her skin, her sight and her taste buds, she feared the dying of her brain. To be caged in a body that smells, shits, coughs, swallows, blinks, but can't think.

Their housekeeper, Badi Bi, often told Suġra that she was older than her. That as a child widow with no children or family, she was much lonelier. That even the bhoot bangla—the haunted house—two lanes away in Bohrawadi was chirpier than her late husband's empty house, which she returned to every single night of her life. What did that old coot know? Suġra once had a husband and had given birth again and again. But she had never enjoyed sex. Ever. Badi Bi was a Mussalman, not a Bohra. Her clitoris had not been slashed when she was a child. She could reach climax herself if she pleased. The khatna of women—the mutilation of the clitoris—was a deplorable practice. Suġra had made sure all her daughters underwent it.

'Sasu ji?' Ismail's voice sounded much nearer this time. Suġra blanched as if she was caught in the act. She turned her head to see him standing in the open doorway, the shabby bush shirt hanging loose on his body.

'Someone else here to have a crap?' She rolled one rosary bead after the other, keeping rhythm to calm her nerves.

'No, this someone wants to see you.'

She kept the rosary by her side on the janamaz. 'Who someone?'

'Don't know. He is—she is in a burqa and won't tell her name.'

'Adaab…' The smell of musk was so strong that it twitched Suġra's weakened nose before she heard the greeting and the jingle of anklets. The voice was manly. What stood on the door was a broad-shouldered woman draped from head to toe in a yellow burqa. A purdah fell on her face with a rectangular net screening the eyes. A hand smeared with henna was raised to the forehead in a greeting. Glass bangles huddled with each other on the wrist. Clanking. Twinkling in winter shadows.

Suġra felt skewers of cold impaling her skin. She cleared her dry throat. 'What are you looking at?' she shot at Ismail. 'Run along, Bhandora!'

The woman in the burqa stepped in and moved her head, regarding the room: the bed with the cotton mattress, the lonely mirror, the earthen pot holding water, the oil lamps placed in wall depressions, the two iron trunks with personal belongings, the mounted four-horned antelopes, the hanging photograph, the old woman by the window. Suġra felt like Ismail's bush shirt under the woman's gaze—moth-eaten and threadbare.

She closed the heavy wooden door delicately, without letting one unnecessary creak escape. An affected mannerism that could only be the result of years of gruelling practice.

The woman turned around, walked towards her with a swaying confidence and removed the purdah. There was a sharp intake of breath. Suġra reached for her chest instinctively. She didn't fear lizards or roaches, not even the jeevti dakkan. But she housed a secret, mortal dread of the third gender.

The face came into focus. White, painted skin. Thick, paan-stained lips. Kohl-lined eyes. Grizzled stubble on the cheeks. Hair rolled up in a bun.

'I said, *adaab arz hai*...' The middle-aged person brought her hand to her forehead again, as if she was a courtesan in the Maharana's durbar.

Suġra coughed to clear her throat and said, 'Have you got what we asked for, you greasy scum?'

The person let out a hearty laugh. Suġra looked around nervously. There were others in the house. She glanced down the open window. Sure enough, the Bhangan skulking in the lane was looking up towards her jharokha, the only window of the house that opened in the back lane.

'Oh, stop it, you! You've got your payment. Just hand over the damn thing and scat!' Suġra adjusted the odhani on her head and covered her shrunken toes sticking out from under her ghaghra, as if the cloth was her armour of steel.

The person flippantly tossed her burqa to a side, revealing a strapping body half-covered, half-exposed in a sky-blue ghaghra-choli lined with golden lace. Jewelled earrings hung from her ears and a lurid pendant lay contently on her tight choli that clasped her twin melons.

'You don't disappoint me, Suġra Bai.' She smiled like someone who doesn't care about their kismet. Blood-lipped and assured of authority. Striking and fierce. A Durga idol come to life.

The person, oozing of oomph, sat down beside her. 'I am not surprised that a spiteful crone, who has everything in life, wants to invoke evil. You fit the bill. But just be warned...' She leant towards Suġra and looked at her in amusement with her kohl-lined eyes. Suġra reached for the wall on the side for support.

The stone felt cold beneath her palm. Her leftover teeth began to clatter. A blanket was rolled up and propped against the wall, but she didn't have the courage to reach out. The things a mother had to undergo for her children! Motherhood was a curse. A lifelong one.

The triumphant cries of someone winning a kite fight floated in from the window, followed by whistling and thumping and abuse. All this while, the person kept checking out Sugra as if she were a second-hand garment on display in the cloth Mandi.

'Be warned, Sugra Bai—an evil invoked can merge with any darkness it chooses. Within or without. It is not in your control once it is ... *unleashed*.' As the person drew back, the limp pendant on her chest caught a shaft of light and came to life.

Sugra was in dire need of a glass of water. She tried to control her limbs shivering with cold, her tongue trembling with insults, her bowels churning to be emptied.

The person put a hand inside her choli and started to fondle her breasts. Sugra watched in fascination. After a long moment, she fished out a small yellow velvet pouch. She slowly moved her fingers to caress it, all the while staring at Sugra. Then, with a sudden movement of handing out alms, she extended it towards her.

'Place it down,' Sugra heard herself saying through a parched throat.

The person tossed her head back in a mad, manly laugh.

'Keep it low!' Sugra hissed.

'So the blue blood Sugra Bai won't touch a hijra.' The person pretended to scowl. 'But will take a handout from the same eunuch on her bed. *Tuch-tuch-tuch* ... how the mighty have fallen.' She pouted her stained lips, placed the velvet pouch near Sugra with mock reverence and drew back. 'Go on, open it. I don't want any complaints about our services later on. We have a reputation too, you see.'

Suġra ogled at the bulges of the eunuch's stomach between the choli and the ghaghra. Her skin exuded the sheen of polished mahogany. Suġra reached for the pouch as if it was a living creature with a sting. Loosening the string, she let what was inside drop on the seating. A small phial rolled over to her feet. It was full of a dark green liquid.

'One drop will make you shit buckets. Two drops will make you bleed from you-know-where. Three drops ... well, you do not want to go to three drops, do you?' The person's lambent face twitched in a smile.

Suġra dipped her head in a slight nod. That was as much courtesy she would extend to a eunuch.

'What if there are...' Suġra's voice quavered, giddy with anticipation, 'there is...'

'No trace. Guaranteed. It will be gone like ripples in water.' The person arched her eyebrows and struck her palms with force. Suġra cringed, feeling the vibration of the thunderclap in her chest.

'Old goat, you are meeting a hijra up close for the first time in your long, tedious life. The experience wouldn't be complete without our signature clap, don't you think?' She let out another rattling laugh.

Like ripples in water ... Suġra thought, looking at the laugh lines disappear from the hijra's face.

She picked up her burqa with a flourish and put it on before she reached for the face veil sewn in a flat topi to be worn over the head. She posed near the door with one hand on the handle and turned, her every movement liquid. 'Since I am the sick conscience of your society, let me give the secret advice once more. One extra drop is *one—too—many!*

With this, she raised her henna-painted hand to her forehead in a salaam, opened the door and stepped out with an elegance that Sugra would never again witness in her life.

8

Parijat, the Nightsoil Worker

Dada Bhai's House

Bohrawadi, Udaipur

AN EMPTY STOMACH DID NOT MAKE PARIJAT FEEL LIGHTER. IT made her feel bulkier. Her fingers clumsy on the wicker basket. Her actions driven by impulses. Hunger was a greater intoxicant than liquor. Noon was approaching and there was no sign so far. She'd heard a manly laughter floating down Dada Bhai's second-floor jharokha, the only window that opened on this alleyway. Didn't his widowed mother live in that room? Who was there with her? Her son didn't possess that grating laughter, Parijat was certain. The peepul tree in front of the house, with its branches reaching out to the side lane, rustled a soft reply. She brought her wrist to her nose and inhaled deeply. The sweet fragrance of long-dead roses never failed to calm her.

The smell of til-ke-laddoo was overpowering in the back alleys on Makar Sankranti. It got caught there, pinned by shafts of winter sun and weighed down by the cold. Parijat wished for the wind to blow it away, just as it had gusted the thick fumes rolling from her mother's and father's pyres. The aroma of food on an empty, grinding stomach ... the misty breath of death over a loved one. Some things were unbearable, even for an untouchable.

A gang of street kids ran past her, shouting and chasing a kite swinging away in the breeze. Wild and free at last. She glanced at her basket and sighed. The work should have got done by now. What was taking so long? This had never happened before. She sensed something was wrong. Taking a few cautious steps, she approached the end of the alley and peeked into the lane that led to the main entrance of Dada Bhai's building. A bhishti lugging a black leather mashak lumbered by, calling out to the women of the houses for replenishing their water supplies. A shrunken, rheumy-eyed man sapped under the weight of life-giving water.

Parijat inched towards the two steps that led to the building's main door, which stood ajar. The thick trunk of the peepul tree right opposite the house came into full view. Brooding under an awning of pea-green leaves. If this tree was in her locality, people would have tied threads around its thick, veined trunk, making it a votive space. Bees and dragonflies worried over its strong branches that reminded Parijat of the arms of the man she loved (oh, so hopelessly). There was an intact kite caught on a bough, well within reach. No one had dared to pluck it from the armpit of the peepul and invoke the rage of the resident witch.

The two steps to the house set in stone. That a Bhangan could never cross. That she would give anything to cross. Even a year of rose-water supply. She slowly walked up the steps and peeped in. What she saw caught her unawares. A gasp escaped her mouth. There in the open courtyard sat a Bhil on his haunches drenched in sunlight. Doonga! A younger tribal was walking the length of the hall that opened to the sky, thick silver anklets in his feet shining like shackles.

She drew back on the steps and leant on the tall stone wall of the house, her chest heaving, her hands clutching the basket in a death grip. A couple of twigs snapped under her fingers. She closed her eyes and started to drag her feet back towards the alleyway. Bulbuls, warblers, starlings and barbets trilled from the peepul tree, doing a roll call for the witch lurking somewhere in the obscure shadows.

'Parijat!' A friendly voice sent a shock through her tense limbs. She turned around, breathless and sweating. 'I thought you would have left by now.' The familiar smell of a wet dog made a cloud around her. It was unsettling yet assuring to be in that cloud.

Her husband, Bhola, came limping towards her, a buckled hand pressed against his puffed-up chest. The broom in his good hand trailed in a bushy tail behind him.

'Why are you still here?' he asked, his eyes shiny, his lips brittle.

Parijat gestured for him to keep his voice low.

'Oh, sorry.' He grinned, exposing a set of rotting teeth. 'Work's not done, I guess.'

She nodded imperceptibly, her thoughts four years away in a murky past.

'Here,' he crooned, 'I'd saved it for the evening, but you can have it now.' He dropped the broom on the paved path and dug his intact hand into the pocket of his shabby kurta. When he drew it out, his dirt-filled fingernails held two grizzled lapwing eggs. Til-ke-laddoo! Parijat's lacerated thoughts smoothened around the edges. She snatched the sweets from her poor husband's hands.

He smiled.

Her heart surged with gratitude … and pity.

'I'll see you later, my pari,' he said and winked at her, limped back on to the lane and turned the corner, humming a happy tune.

The coarse confection dug into Parijat's flesh as she balled it in her fist. She stepped into the shade of the alleyway, away from the glare of the afternoon sun. A chorus of shouts rang around the terraces, the peepul tree breathed quietly and she found herself being sucked in a time warp. Her thoughts swept her back to the past with a bristly broom.

A twelve-year-old orphan girl sitting by a window. The sun resting on the keekar canopies. The pinkish-white flesh of keekar fruits splitting out of their green skins. The old zamindar's bald pate. One of his feeble hands fondling her half-formed breasts, all the while moaning and whimpering. The cry of 'Hey bhagwan!' and a jet of white, sticky cactus milk covering her face and hands. The old man, dressed in a cotton vest, crumpling on his bed.

They said the elder Rao Sahib was on his deathbed. He needed a beautiful apsara to take him to swarga. They said he couldn't do the act, but his hardened stick would help him walk to heaven. They said his heir, the future Rao Sahib, wanted to speed up his nirvana. He had sent many paramours to him. They would do mujra swirling their abundant ghaghra-skirts. Thump their anklets to the rhythm of the tabla. Make their eyebrows jump and bangles crash. But he would just turn in his urine-soaked bed and sleep. Until one day he saw *her* walking with her wicker basket at the back of his toilet. He gurgled a demand to his servant, wiping his drool. Parijat was promptly brought to him the same night.

At first, the zamindar's men would slip in the untouchable girl in the dark. But then his son became impatient. She would be brought to sit by the old man in the day, in the night, in the evening, whenever he demanded. She sat fully clothed on the edge of the bed that smelt acrid, tasting bile, looking at the world that constantly changed outside the open window. The fumes of burning wood rising from a distant field on the slope of a hill. Wind combing through the branches of the two shady mango trees, tussling the leaves with their deft fingers. Wisps of clouds unable to hide the naked sky or her naked shame. The only thing that remained constant day after day was the sticky cactus milk.

Valmiki, her brother, had run away from the old Rao Sahib's estate after their parents died. He had joined Gandhi ji in the independence struggle. 'He's an insect, he'll be crushed like one!' she had heard some women talk near the well. The untouchables had a separate basti—a settlement—on the edge of the semi-arid, bushy forest, away from even the Bhil adivasi villages in the estate. They had their own well from where they could draw their water. No Rajput or even a tribal would step inside their basti. If someone was ill and dying, a Vaidhraj or Hakim would prescribe medicines based on their symptoms, without having to touch them, of course.

But there was always a rosy side to life. One summer, three years back, someone had shaken her gently from her slumber in the dead of the night. She was sleeping on the cot in the yard outside her aunt's hut. In the moonlight, she

saw Valmiki sitting on the cot, with a finger on his lips. She
hugged him with the force of flood waters. He fell back on the
cot, suppressing a yelp. They slipped into the forest and sat on
the rocks by a half-dry stream shining in the moon rays. The
brown summer landscape was grey-haired at night. Parijat cast
a glance around for the leopard whose fresh pug marks she
had seen in the morning going towards the goat pen of the
upper-caste village.

'The women say you're an insect and will be crushed,' the
nine-year-old Parijat had confided.

'They also say your engagement has been called off, and one
day you'll fall off the tree a ripe old maiden!' Valmiki's laughter
had disturbed the fruit bats. But not the sleeping monkeys.

'Be quiet!' Parijat didn't like his joke about her dying a
spinster. She had been betrothed before she was born. 'If it's a
daughter…' The ten-year-old boy's father had come to a pact
with Baba. Her Baba had breached the pact by dying and not
leaving any dowry.

'This year, I will pass my metric exam and study to become
a lawyer,' Valmiki had said under the stars—the dimly lit
lamps of their ancestors' catacombs. 'I have people in the party
supporting me. And then I'll take you with me, forever away
from this hell.'

Parijat loved her brother wantonly. More than her doll with
a broken leg. She swelled with pride every time she saw him. She
remembered how he used to open his books and escape into a
world of black symbols on yellowing pages. He was condemned
because he wanted to escape condemnation. In all her wisdom
of nine years, Parijat knew the doll can't grow her wooden leg
again. But she loved him, this broken doll of hers, for being
hopelessly sure, for fighting a war that would not free them.

For the next three years, there was no sign of him. Only stories and rumours brought in by an odd villager who visited the city or guests who came to Rao Sahib's estate. Valmiki seen marching with the freedom fighters in Delhi. Valmiki making a speech in the medical college of Udaipur, crisply dressed in khadi. Valmiki with a beard. Valmiki with a shaved head. That night, when the Bhil Doonga, sent by the son of the dying Rao Sahib, came knocking on her aunt's hut for the first time, she was so sure it was her brother that she ran to open the door. Her aunt insisted she accompany the Bhil and pushed her out of the hut. Doonga led her to the old zamindar's Haveli apologetically. She was confused. What was this about? The tribal shook his head sadly as he stopped in the corridor of the Haveli, guiding her into the chamber before he closed the door, leaving her surrounded by the odour of age and decay.

As the weeks passed she was not confused any more. It was not a glamorous garh—the fort she always wanted to see the interiors of. It was a ruined landscape with rot in its bowels.

One afternoon, when clouds were weaning the day off light, Doonga came to escort her from their hut in the basti of untouchables. She stared at her fingernails crusted with dung, the cakes of which she was pasting on their mud wall. Her widowed aunt, who was stacking the firewood in the yard, turned her face away from Parijat in disgust.

A cow bayed at a distance. A snail crunched beneath her bare foot as she took a step back from Doonga on the mud porch. A cry bubbled out of her throat. A yap that became a roar. A mangy stray stopped to see the commotion. A group of mute spectators from adjoining huts came shuffling on their untouchable feet. An oriole flapped its wings and flew away, terrified. A sticky-white cactus-milk bitterness filled her mouth.

A warm breath of bad advice hit her—the aunt shouting at her to be quiet. Doonga stepped back and left.

She was sitting on the porch dry-eyed and silent, with her ghaghra spread around her like the broken wings of a butterfly, when the men came for her in the evening. Three of the zamindar's men, without Doonga. They dragged her to the banyan tree in the middle of the settlement for everyone to see. The dung cake was still cupped in one of her hands as they pinned her against the tree, forced open her mouth and slashed her tongue with a knife. Her vision darkened and her gullet gurgled with blood.

The sheer impact of the recollection nailed Parijat to the wall of Dada Bhai's house, her hands splayed on the sides, her fingers clasping her wounded basket in the alleyway. She took shallow rasping breaths, tasting the memory of her own blood. Five days after her tongue was slashed, the Bhil Doonga had again come to her aunt's door, intense sadness gathered around his stubbled cheeks. He had not asked her to come along when he started walking away from the hut. But this time, Parijat had followed. In her indestructible silence.

And then, her inflamed, puffed-up face and blistered lips had started to tremble, sending jabs of pain down her neck. She would never forget Doonga's face as he had turned to look at her, his hand placed on his stomach, where he tied his dhoti, eyes wide with the creeping suspicion that she had gone insane. Parijat laughed silently through her stinging stiffness, her flooding tears, her shrunken horizon. She had lost her voice, so what? The three robust upper-caste men not only had to touch an untouchable, but also her sweat, her saliva, her blood! Life had a rosy side, after all.

9

Hariharan, the Middleman

Dada Bhai's House

Bohrawadi, Udaipur

CURSES FLUNG IN FROM THE WIDE-OPEN JHAROKHA, HURLED from the terraces of Bohrawadi. What a pleasant day. Nippy breeze, laddoos, cuss words, kites, coercion—all served in precise pinches. Just the recipe Hariharan liked. Dada Bhai's cigar lay forgotten on the exquisite ivory ashtray on the side table, burning slowly in the oblong shadow of the latticed side window. One day, Hariharan's son would sit in one such room, not minding a forgotten cigar, with a pot of sinful tea sitting by his side. In his eldest son's soft hands, he could see the making of a fat man. That's exactly what he wanted to leave for his sons and family. Decadence.

'Your green B-Model Ford car is nothing short of a legend, Sahib.' Hariharan's fixed smile was not forced now. 'There are stories told and retold about you bringing leopards lying stretched on its bonnet. I've seen street brats run behind your car just hoping to lay a finger on it. Tooting that rubber horn would be their dream come true. Even mine, for that matter.'

The dapper aristocrat in breeches, with a gold watch chain hanging out of a puffed pocket, looked out of the window, sullen but cocksure of himself.

'Oh, sorry, I forgot,' Hariharan continued in a drone, 'the Maharana ji Sahib had you remove that horn so that people don't confuse your car with one of those from the palace. I've seen the rayyat, the citizens, lie on their stomachs in the street to pay you respect, assuming it is royalty passing by...' He chuckled.

Hariharan had a whole new world to create, his own little universe in a brand-new Hindustan. He was eternally grateful to Mahatma Gandhi ji, who made it all possible. This kind of opportunity presented itself once in many generations. But creation couldn't all be calculation. It had to be part impulse and part play too. He straightened his starched, pure white kurta in admiration of his calculative and creative skills.

'And your horses, Sahib, your Marwaris ... uff.' Hariharan, sitting on the grandiose divan, was beginning to enjoy this immensely. 'Who owns the likes of them in this walled city of Udaipur but Maharana Shri Shri Bhupal Singh ji Maharaj himself? I just passed your two beauties tied on the Five Foot Road leading to your house. I heard you're going to give away that part of your land to the municipality to broaden the road. Are you going to shift your stable to Hathipol then? You are such a gental-man, Dada Bhai ji Sahib. Noble, magnanimous.

What a shame it would be to lose your benevolence. Mahatma Gandhi ji says there is greater pleasure in giving away than in amassing wealth. But for that you should have something to give away, na? Your humble servant can be ever so wrong, though.'

Dada Bhai's breath rattled. He remembered his cigar and picked it up. Hariharan looked at the effect he was creating with relish.

'You think the world is an honest place, full of gental-man like you? Think again, Dada Bhai ji Sahib. It is full of parasites.'

'Like you?' Dada Bhai snapped in an uncharacteristic flash of anger.

'Alas.' Hariharan pulled his lips down, looking deeply hurt. 'I am just a lowly well-wisher, Sahib. And a Gandhian, like you. That is why I follow the great Mahatma Gandhi ji's advice and speak the truth, even if it may torment me.' Hariharan imagined his pure white kurta covered in the contents of the sardine can and didn't have to pretend to look most tormented. He straightened on the divan and continued grimly, the serrations in his voice near visible, 'As soon as the truth comes out, the collector, the top city officials, your zamindar friends and the lower landlords, who come to pay you respects, will all be gone, just as your days of shikar with the angrez, the gora sahibs, have gone. And like the white men, those days will not be coming back.'

A sudden gust of wind made the curtain separating the bed chamber from the living room flap. Hariharan caught a glimpse of a typewriter on a table with a high-backed chair. Not having a typewriter was barely tolerable for him, even though he didn't know how to type.

Dada Bhai got up from his armchair and walked to the open jharokha, the main window of the living room that was not covered with latticework. He folded one of his hands at his back, brought the other near his lips, holding the cigar and stood looking out at the distant Aravalli peaks, as if he was staring at those bygone days, which would never return.

Hariharan got up, his knees creaking, and ambled to stand by his side. The house stood guard over the city, overwhelming in its size. Men and boys bounced below them on the terraces. Colourful kites tried to escape their tied fates and fated ties, just as Dada Bhai did. Hariharan had a healthy liking for growth, which he believed was a relative concept. One's growth could mean another's downfall. It was all about balancing it out. He spread his mental ledger and was happy with what he saw. For that moment, he even forgot the unsettling proximity with the jeevti dakkan somewhere below them in the peepul tree. He felt content. A god looking down at his helpless creation.

Someone knocked on the door. Both the men turned around to see Ismail's face. He looked pale, as if he had seen the witch crouched in a dark corner, bits falling off her ghastly neck. Breathing steadily. Feigning dead.

Hariharan was happy to see the change in Ismail's demeanour and made a note in his mental ledger to find the cause of his distress, which could be used next time.

'Badi Bi says lunch is ready, Dada Bhai.'

Without getting a reply, he turned and walked away.

'Have you heard how Bohras kill a child every time they have to cook a pulao and use his blood to prepare it?' asked Dada Bhai, pulling a long drag on his cigar. The smell of burning tobacco smoked Hariharan's nostrils.

'I … ahem … why yes.' Hariharan was caught off-guard by this question. He answered without losing his smile, 'That's what gives the pulao its flavour, I hear.'

Dada Bhai tossed his head back in laughter. The veil lifted from his face, and the furrows became laugh lines. The sound regal, abundant, a rumbling boom. And then he stopped as abruptly, eyeing Hariharan sideways with disdain.

'So what are you proposing, Hariharan ji? What is your idea to stop my imminent downfall?'

Hariharan looked mortified, a difficult feat to achieve with a fixed smile. 'It is not imminent, Dada Bhai! We'll steer you clear of ... this disgrace.' He tried to turn a gold ring studded with a yellow sapphire in his swollen pinkie, caressed and cajoled it, and then gave up the effort. Had the darned Rao Sahib made his move before he came? He wished he could decipher the zamindar's cryptic farts.

The afternoon sun streaming in from the jharokha washed over his hands, cleaning it of shadows. It was not a time to fumble, but to show authority. 'We have two options in front of us, Sahib. Two tangible, solid and sure-shot options. Kamruddin Hathiwala and Lal Chand Mahajan.'

Dada Bhai turned his gaze at him, amused. The laugh lines still lingered on his clean-shaven cheeks. 'An aspiring Humphrey Bogart and an established Shylock.'

'Ahem ... no, no, Kamruddin Hathiwala and Lal Chand Mahajan.' Hariharan suspected this was the effect of tea this man had just had. No wonder it was considered taboo. He would any day go for the good old opiated bhang.

Dada Bhai smiled and nodded at the strapping Aravallis robed in their nut-brown winter skins. 'You had fleetingly mentioned but not elaborated on your proposals last time, Hariharan ji.'

Hariharan beamed inwardly, that special smile he reserved only for himself. He was not going to remind this man how he had cut him short when Hariharan wanted to explain his proposals.

No, Sahib.

Hariharan was not the one to give someone a piece of his mind; it was too precious to give away.

'Now since your respected self is asking me, Dada Bhai ji Sahib, I must give you the options. I am your true servant, with only your best interest at heart. You must believe me.' He shifted on his stout legs under Dada Bhai's stern gaze. The man was a good foot and a half taller than him. 'The less savoury option first. Being your true...'

'Yes, yes, I know.' Dada Bhai flicked the cigar with his nail, dropping ashes on the window sill. 'What is your proposal?'

'To be honest...'

Oye! Cut it, cut it! A savage war cry and thumping of feet right above their heads made them look at the ceiling. Outside the jharokha, clouds blew in with a gush of air. It made the colourful kites rock and dazzle in the greying sky. Hariharan shivered as a cold wind invaded the room and rolled up and died under the snarling leopard head.

Hariharan cleared his throat and began again, 'The easiest way out of your ... ahem ... situation is borrowing money from Lal Chand Mahajan. He is the only one in the state of Mewar with that kind of money to lend. The sums that you will require are rather ... huge. Not *cosmic* ... but big, yes. But ... *but.* I am your well-wisher, Bhai ji Sahib. I owe you big time. You helped my father out of the dumps and never asked for your money back. My family would have been on the street. Not just me, you have helped so many in this city, this state. Your large-heartedness...'

'Hariharan ji...' Dada Bhai turned his gaze from the kite-fighting to look at him. 'What is your objection to my borrowing money from Lal Chand?'

'I'm not even talking about the monstrous interest you'll have to pay ... unless the Union of India grants you the tender of the catechu forests you've applied for, the chances of which are slim, if you don't mind me saying so ... you will never, *never* be able to repay those kind of interest rates. Ah ... how I wish your sulphur and ammunition monopoly had not been taken away. This unholy union of India is based on the firm foundation of discrimination, Sahib.' He let his suffering pour out in a sigh.

Dada Bhai's lips curled a little, scoffing Hariharan's genuine distress over him losing his generations' old businesses.

'The interest rates apart, my bigger concern is that he's most *indiscreet*, Sahib. Most.' He shook his head violently, the triple chin wobbling from side to side. 'The whole of Mewar will know of your situation if you take money from him. Mark my words. The pandits would no longer be tolling their bells for you, nor the mullahs turning their rosaries once they know of your financial distress. You need someone who is tactful, judicious, tight-lipped.'

'And that is...'

'No one,' Hariharan asserted. He was looking out of the window all this while, but turned to look at Dada Bhai whose face was hard set. Immobile. Puffing away his cigar. Looking at the shrieking masses running on their boxy terraces. Hariharan was no fool. He had not expected Dada Bhai to be pliant. On some level, Hariharan truly pitied this man, who held his belief in the goodness of people and disbelieved the existence of the living witch in the peepul tree.

'So you suggest…'

'Kamruddin Hathiwala. I am completely out of line to say so…'

'You are.'

'He really loves your daughter, our Sanaz Beti…'

'Has he even seen her, to fall in love with her?'

'…he's ready to give the entire sum you need, interest-free.'

'An old fox with his legs dangling in the grave.'

'…much respected.'

'With two wives and children of his own, some even older than my daughter Sanaz.'

'…contribute a part of the sum as an investment to your new business.'

'Struts about as a cock.'

'…consider.'

'No.'

'…and he's a Bohra!'

Something slapped Hariharan's face. Dada Bhai's hand had not moved. The engraved wooden frame of the jharokha had banged with the wind, sending a gust of cold smack. The hatch flew out again. Hariharan looked out, stunned. The mood of the sky had darkened. The winter sun had disappeared behind the gathering clouds. Hariharan wished for a warmer layer on his kurta. This unexpected weather on Makar Sankranti was not a good omen.

He touched the blue sapphire on his middle finger. These stones had the power to flip fortunes. He always left home armed with astrology gems, one on each finger. He was sure the bad omen was for Dada Bhai and would turn the tide in his favour. This was god's doing. He sent a silent prayer to the sky and dipped his head.

'Your respected self should give it a thought…'

'Enough.' Dada Bhai didn't shout, but his voice was the low growl of thunder. He kept looking out of the jharokha, at the sky bloating up and turning bruise purple. The stubbled cheeks of Aravalli hills grew dimmer. The kite fliers continued their battles, hoping that the imminent storm would surrender to boyish hands on spools and strings. There were no women on the terraces, but you could hear their disembodied voices, shouting encouragement and curses at their men. 'You should leave, Hariharan ji. There is a storm coming.'

'If…'

'Please leave.' Dada Bhai's head swirled towards him. He glared at Hariharan with the red-veined eyes of an insomniac. His sleepless nights were as much a legend as his B-Model Ford.

Hariharan crept away from the man who was looking out of the window at his impending ruin. The faraway hills sent in the drowsy-sweet aroma of wet mud. He crossed the room, went to the door and stopped, his hand on the handle, his eyes on the aristocratic arse in breeches.

'Bhai ji Sahib, zamindars are friends to no one. Taking money from your zamindar friends will only lead you to be a pawn in their hands. They will force you to represent their interests in the Union of India. So much for your high principles.'

Dada Bhai turned around at the other end of the chamber, his forehead grooved. 'What are you talking about?'

'I am just talking about the natural order of things, Dada Bhai ji Sahib. And the balance.'

He brought his hands together in a namaste, bowed and left the outlandishly understated chamber.

10

Nathu, the Bhil

Dada Bhai's House

Bohrawadi, Udaipur

WHY DO OLD MIRRORS GET BLACK SPOTS LIKE AGEING SKIN ...
Nathu had wondered early that morning, staring at the small, rectangular mirror in which his face barely fit. He had thought of many inane things so that his courage didn't leave him before he left for the city.

Now he looked at Doonga as he sat bundled, his eyes feverish, a dull smell of wood emitting from him, and remembered how during the Gavari performance, all those years back, Doonga-the-Rai-Devi smelling of flowers had given him a piece of sugarcane. There was something sinister about his silence, about the breathing memory of the man who was no more.

The empty brass plate where the pakoras were a few minutes back shone with a film of oil. Nathu belched. He had earlier eaten the thick, grainy makki-ki-roti with a crushed onion and salt that was packed for his journey in the morning. It was not often that he got to eat so much before half the day was done. *Thak-thak-thak* ... faint sounds of chopping drifted down from the high-up kitchen followed by a whiff of frying onions. Sounds were strangely amplified in this monster of a house. He could see all the semi-circular porches on the floors, except that of the highest one, where there was a larger veranda.

'Haa-have you seen Dada Bhai's armoury on the f-f-first floor?' he squatted by Doonga's side and asked. 'I was lucky to go inside it with my Ba, five years back. You should sssssee the guns and ammunition there—double-barrel rifles, muzzleloaders, 12-bores, sh-shot guns...'

The taste of fritters lingered in his mouth like the taste of his thirteen-year-old too-plump-for-a-Bhil wife. She still hadn't lost her baby fat ... he didn't want her to. Her breasts were not fully formed yet. Just an indent between two sloping Aravalli meadows.

What was he thinking about! It was debauchery, at a time like this! She had an important task in hand today, just as he had. Only guilt could make his insides warm up on a cold day. Bhairon ji—the godly rock foiled with silver and studded with two white eyes—just might forgive the sinner. But there was no escaping his agent, the Bhopa—the priest in a tight-fitting dhoti. An illiterate goat herder in a village could instantly sense a missing goat from his herd of more than two hundred. So could the Bhopa sense what you hid: the missing goat.

Nathu didn't often visit the devra, a small worshipping place under a tree or by a stream where the Bhils prayed to Bhairon ji or Rana ji. Not that he didn't want to pay his respects to the gods, but he was afraid. Afraid since the day he had seen a child possessed by a spirit beaten up by the Bhopa whose safa—the big headgear—had come undone in rage. The afflicted boy grinning through bloody teeth, telling the ganja-smoking Bhopa that the spirit will not leave his body till he stopped beating him. The smell of incense, mud, fury, marijuana, tears and tantrums crowding the village air. The boy lying unconscious in mud and the Bhopa with crazed eyes not allowing anyone to touch him for hours.

Nathu worried that if he went too close to an afflicted person, the spirit would slip into him. It was like catching choti mata—chicken pox—through contact. All those possessed, young and old, went to the devra to get cured. If they got rid of the spirit, it would certainly be hanging somewhere in the vicinity, waiting for another unsuspecting idiot.

A blast of wind blew in grey clouds over the city. The leaves of the peepul tree sent in forbidden susurrations and pricked pins on Nathu's skin. He was too close to the jeevti dakkan. Why was the weather becoming gloomy on Makar Sankranti? Surely, it had to be the doing of the witch.

He looked up for any sign of Dada Bhai. He had seen people go up and down the house—a tall, clinking woman in a burqa with a fearsome gait visiting the second level where Dada Bhai's widowed mother lived; Rao Sahib of Singhgarh trudging down from the fifth to the third floor; an ungainly man in a white kurta pumping his fat legs up the building and coming down later, red in the face, thundering out of the main door into the rambling streets of Bohrawadi; the pathetic Bhangi Loola stopping for an idle conversation; a beautiful untouchable woman peeking in from the main door—her eyes widening as if she had seen the living witch crouching next to Doonga. Ismail had appeared a couple of times, but his demeanour had turned combative, snarling when Nathu tried to give him the empty plate. But there was no sign of Dada Bhai.

Jets of wind continued to blow, sending the kites helter-skelter amid a clamour of confusion. The Bhil children in his village today would have caught a dooski—a robin—and would be going door to door to collect anything they would be handed down before they released the bird in the evening. He slipped his hands into the pockets of his angarkha to escape the inescapable wind. The air smelt of approaching rain, the sweetest scent in a semi-arid zone. But today, it brought a sense of foreboding. He twirled the end of his dhoti into a knot.

'Doon-doon…' He let the name trail. '…ji. I think it is going to rrr…rrrr…rrrrrr….' He blinked rapidly getting not even a twitch in reply from the other Bhil. Doonga was colder towards him than their village Baniya Pannalal, the moneylender with gout. Marriage and death—at both junctures, Bhils had to pay their respects to Bhairon ji the god and Pannalal the gouty moneylender and sit at their stony and smelly feet in turn.

There was a Bohra, a distant relative of Dada Bhai, who lived a few furlongs away from his village Jogion ka Guda. He also gave money on interest and entered into partnerships with Bhils by giving them seeds to plant and mortgaging their land. He cracked his knuckles before accepting money and put on his milk-white turban with a golden border only when dignitaries like Dada Bhai visited. He would oil his grizzled, tapering beard, stare at the small dust twisters in his yard and crack his knuckles in anticipation. Dada Bhai always cleared part of a loan of one of his jungle trackers when he visited. He had helped Nathu's father, Jaitya, and his family much through the years. Jaitya and other Bhils sang songs in his praise ... *Topa wala Bapu aaya* (The man with the hat has come) ... and awaited his visit as much as they awaited the first clouds after planting season.

Nathu glanced up at the sky, which had turned pale and smudged. Not the robust grey of the first monsoon showers. Dark clouds reared up from the east and a thunder stifled a groan beneath the churning billows. The wind popped goosebumps on his arms. He looked up the floors of the house, hoping to catch a glimpse of Mena Bai, Dada Bhai's kind wife, who had once given him an angelic smile and an orange candy, pulling on a dull-blue pallu covering her head. But there was no comfort for Nathu as all he saw was an irate Ismail flitting about. The kite flyers had begun to draw back the strings. Crows screeched. The thunder sounded closer this time—bare and boundless like the boom of Dada Bhai's rifle, the crack of a zamindar's whip, the cackle of the living witch.

Nathu had a sudden urge to empty his bladder. He got up from Doonga's side to go to the odha, the dingy ground floor quarters.

'I'll pee and k-k-k-come.'

No response from the man. He had grown quieter and more distant, receding into himself.

Nathu walked through the passage into a small and rather dark yard with two rooms and a bathroom, where the servants could urinate or take a bath. A hammer with a solid wooden handle hung by a nail in the passage. A stack of fresh sugarcane lay on the floor, a gift from a grateful villager. Nathu had seen heartfelt offerings made to only two entities—Bhairon ji in the devra and Dada Bhai in Udaipur. The room used for storage was cautiously bolted and locked. The door of the other—an almost empty servants' room—was carelessly left open. A musty cavern. Shafts of sunlight seeped in through the rectangular slanting windows high up near the ceiling. They hardly made a dent in the darkness gathered wall to wall in the servants' quarters.

Pat-pat-pat … fat droplets dribbled down the open courtyard into the covered passage. *Whoo … whish … whoo …* the peepul tree outside complained. Ribbons of rain splattered on the ground. The roof of Nathu's mouth felt droughty. What kind of an omen was this … rain on Makar Sankranti? He felt exhausted as he stepped in and relieved himself in the bathroom smelling of the urine lodged in its cracks, and splashed water on the curling, yellow line of pee. The walls seemed to be closing in on him, willing to crush his bones. Yet he couldn't move. His hand, roughened and toughened with earth, lingered on the latch of the wooden door, which was rotting from the bottom. Nathu didn't want to go out and confront the winter thunder. He longed to feel the earth between his toes. All he felt was the jeevti dakkan's rage.

The door screeched open and he stepped out with the effort of a man pulling himself out of a swamp. He walked down the passage, emerged in the courtyard open to the ether and instantly felt absences around him.

The first was of missing raindrops and the impending storm that was no more. The wind had blown away the clouds … or was it the living witch's angry puffs? The silent, white-washed walls of the building gleamed with winter sweat. He stared up at the house's very own piece of sky wrinkled with thinning clouds and thickening wizardry. A myna called in clipped notes as the people again launched their kites in the wind. The butterfly he was trying to chase out of the house lay dead at his feet, its wings folded.

Nathu glanced at the passageway that led to the odha. The second absence made its presence felt. The hammer hanging on the wall was gone. Nathu's gaze swept the entire hall in slow motion. The other Bhil had vanished. And that's when the third and final absence struck: the living witch had taken Doonga!

MORNING

Makar Sankranti, 1950

11

Rao Sahib, the Zamindar

On the Way to Udaipur

Aravalli Hills

WITH THE END OF EACH WINTER CLIMAXING IN MAKAR Sankranti, Rao sahib's bones settled in his flesh like spokes of an old fence—brittle and bent at an angle. He could almost hear them grind as he swayed from side to side on the horse's back. The brown-green landscape rose and fell in wave after wave of hills full of bushes, shrubs and winter shadows. It was a semi-arid forest of dhok, bui, seeno, desert capers and grasses spread over the low hills. The sun lingered on the sleepy horizon before it was hauled up by the brisk new day. Two Rajput aides, straight-backed and hairy, followed him on horsebacks and a wasted Bhil half-trotted, half-ran by his side. The gold rings in Rao Sahib's earlobes flashed gaudy smiles.

'Dada Bhai's wife Mena is a wilful person. My friend doesn't know how to keep his woman leashed.' Rao Sahib looked at a peahen standing right in the middle of the *kutcha* path, regarding him disapprovingly.

'Hukam,' grunted one of the aides with an up-curving moustache and a pendulous stomach resting on his horse's saddle.

A babbler darted out of a bush, babbled to itself and hopped on to a shrub. The horse shat, one plonk after the other, filling the air with fresh-dung smell.

'I had to give a good hiding to my youngest Thakrain after I saw her touching the saree seller's hand. Oh, yes, the story is true. I saw it with my own eyes. My young wife's hand reached out on the other side of the purdah, separating her and the merchant, and held not the silk but the man's hand! And she says it was by mistake. Ha! A tight slap goes a long way with mistake correction.'

'Hukam,' the younger aide, whose knotted muscles and solid calves made his dhoti-kurta ripple, replied this time.

'Do I need to say what happened to the insolent imp of a trader who touched my wife's hand?' The horse neighed through drool as Rao Sahib's grip tightened on the reins.

'No, Maharaj Sahib.'

'I share the bloodline with the Maharana of Mewar. My libido is good enough for dozens of wives and I just have four. Only four, mind you. And a few concubines, all of whose children carry my second name. I have done a lot of good.'

'Hukam.'

He turned around to see if either of the aides objected to what he said, knowing fully well that all the illegitimate children of zamindars carried the name of the father but were not given any share in the property or equal social standing. Seeing no dissent, he faced the mud path again. The young, muscular aide riding behind him had spawned from his groin.

'And they tell me to travel in a buggy to Udaipur, as if I am a rickety old man ... or a woman to be taken in a palanquin! I'll travel in a horse cart when my spearhead can't dig into a woman anymore. And that day is unlikely to come.'

An assertive 'hukam' followed. Dew drops shone everywhere, trapping the forest in bubbles.

'Ah, the treachery of women ... a T-Model Fort with silk purdahs is what I bought for this youngest wife of mine. I dressed up for the wedding in a gold achkan, an Amarshahi paag, breeches-style pyjamas and a hanging sword—a costume I only wear in the durbar. It makes me feel as if I am a character in Gavari. But I dressed up for her. Didn't I?'

'You did, Hukam.'

'She fell ill five months back and didn't trust my Vaidhraj to treat her. Wanted a city doctor. Have you ever got treated by a city doctor, Banna?' He again turned back and looked at his illicit son.

'No, Hukam.'

'Neither have I. Nor did my mother—my Baisa Hukam or my father—my Annadata. If my parents didn't need it, why should I? And our Vaidhraj is no less than the Hakim in the Lucknow court combined with their Khansama, the highest-ranking chef in their kitchen. Generations of our Vaidhraj have been in our family. They have been advising us on our diets—we have wild boars and sambar in winters but no poultry; hares in summers but no partridges or quails. He says they have warm *taseer* ... warm efficacy. But mind you, I don't follow traditions blindly. I allowed meat to be cooked during Sawan for my young Thakrain, though I don't consume meat myself during monsoons. I just consummated the marriage. Haha ... see what I mean?'

'Hukam.'

'Not just in the month of Sawan...' Rao Sahib stopped to listen to the loud trumpeting call of a winter visitor. 'Ah, the demoiselle beauties!' He craned his neck to see the cranes. 'They must be in one of the water bodies below the hill. And if I remember correctly, there is a lair of a wolf in that grassy valley as well. Wolves often litter in that rocky cave.'

'Hukam,' came the non-committal grunt of the older, pudgy aide. An outbreak of thick curly hair had escaped his nostrils and covered his upper lip, cheeks and chin in an untidy beard.

'You know, Amar Singh ji, I love the Aravallis and their arresting beauty. I will not let anyone wound them, dig them for mining or slash their timber. I can't fail the forest gods ... pollute the pious rivers, which will carry my ashes someday or have their waters imprisoned in a dam.' A sunbird confirmed his claim with a shy chirp. 'Who dares to contain the moody Banas River and evoke its wrath ... who dares cut down a peepul tree and be haunted by the spirits that dwell in it? Only short-sighted fools. I didn't let East India Company rape my forests. But do you think I will be able to stop the Union of India once they strip me of my ancestral lands?' Sunlight spilt on the dusty road. A discarded snakeskin lay by the side near a bush. 'Get me that.' Rao sahib commanded the Bhil Doonga, who went and picked it up, dusted it carefully and handed it to the pudgy aide Amar Singh.

'Snakeskin kept in your coffers is meant to bring you wealth. Do you think it'll help me any bit? My Annadata has left me an inheritance of *freedom*.' Rao sahib gazed dolefully at the far-away clearing, which hosted a tribal village and their rectangular agricultural lands. The field of vision was clear on the curvaceous path, taking him down his realm of prickly hills. He breathed in a stream of nippy air, flowing right into his lungs, and opened a couple of buttons of his woollen coat. He admired the unobtrusive company of the squirrels stamping the branches in abiding haste; the seven sisters raising a ruckus on a babul tree, its tiny yellow flowers dozing in the protection of thorns; the tart scent of ripened berries of ber. He sent a sigh skywards, knowing the wings of his prayers had been clipped.

With a press of Rao Sahib's leather heels, the horse clomped onwards. 'Lankeshwar here understands me better than my wives.' He rubbed the horse's neck fondly. 'So I was saying, forget about Sawan, I even let the youngest Thakrain have meat during the period of Shradh.'

This revelation was taken kindly only by the horse Lankeshwar. Even Doonga, looking pitiably lost and jogging by his side, cast a sideways glance at Rao Sahib.

While the younger aide maintained a stoic, affected silence, Amar Singh cleared his throat aloud. 'Ahem, Maharaj sahib, forgive my saying ... but having meat in the Pitra Paksh ... the fortnight of the ancestors! Observing Shradh during this period by a son is compulsory, and you are the eldest one. Our three previous generations are stuck between heaven and earth in Pitraloka. How will they be heralded to heaven if we pollute ourselves during that pious time?'

'He ... he ... he...' Rao sahib rumbled. 'Yeah, the fortnight of gods and ghosts. I imagine Yama's buffalo farting while lugging my fat ancestors' souls from Pitralok to heaven. I am sure my Annadata will fart louder than the buff! He will insist on having his karmic account settled then and there.'

'Don't make fun, Maharaj Sahib. Since I am your father's third cousin, I will take the liberty to speak my mind.' Amar Singh's stomach was jostled by the horse's back. 'Our holy scripture the Garuda Purana says that there is no salvation for a man without a son. A son must not take the nirvana of his forefathers so lightly.'

Rao sahib's laughter sent two startled treepies flying away from the keekar tree. 'How many times have you been in love, Amar Singh ji?'

Amar Singh just squinted his eyes, puffed up from sleepless nights of alcohol and mujra.

'See, Doonga here is more hungry than in love, Sujan Singh here is more angry than in love, and you … well, let me not be indiscreet considering your age and stature. But I can tell you that I am always in love, sometimes even with two women at once. Love makes you risk the fate of your ancestors in the ether. Love makes you a drop of wax trying to hang on to the candle flame. Uff … what a shayar I am! A poet wasted on my Rajput brethren.'

Just as they reached the bend and turned around, Rao sahib drew the reins of the horse, who neighed in protest through his bridle, exposing a perfect set of teeth and gums. An oxcart loaded with dried stacks of barley stood right in the middle of the narrow path, which had the hill on one side and a steep drop on the other. An ox and a farmer, whose head was wrapped in a huge white turban, looked at the little entourage of Rao Sahib, bewildered.

'*Ghani khamma*, Maharaj Sahib…' The farmer bent forward and bowed to the zamindar, touching his head on the butt of the ox. Rao Sahib glared at him.

'I'll—I'll be out of your way in a moment…' The farmer fumbled with the rope and tried to take the ox on the edge of the hill. The animal stood rigid, refusing to go to the steep side. *Hak-klick-klick-klick* ... the farmer urged him, pulled his ropes, tried to cajole him by slapping his backside, beat him with a stick, but the ox stood rooted in fortitude and fear.

The forest hummed with the small talk of thorny bushes, blowing the smell of wildflowers and the farmer right on to Rao Sahib's face. A capricious smile left and found his lips again and again. He looked at the slouched farmer with mounting interest. What do you do when a doll stuffed with hay crunches beneath your foot? You kick it to the side. His mojdi-clad foot jerked in reflex hitting Doonga out of his trance.

'*Kode maaro ise!*' he commanded his aides, his fingers itching for a whip to flog the farmer with.

Doonga ran up to the flummoxed farmer, held the rope tied on the nose ring of the ox and led it, uttering soothing sounds, to the side of the hill. The cart squeaked, the wooden wheels emitted a sharp *chunn* sound, the farmer oozed beads of sweat, a few twigs of barley spun in the air and Doonga crooned a Mewari song, softly.

'See?' Rao Sahib asked his aides as the three horses trotted past the cart dangerously balanced at the edge of the hill. 'Don't ask me again why I take Doonga to the city with me every time.'

'Hukam.' The younger aide Sujan Singh's voice carried more conviction this time.

Doonga ran back to Rao Sahib's side, barefooted, his copper hands gilded with sweat.

Rao sahib lifted his pagadi from one side and scratched the back of his ear as they went down the hill on the dirt track. He picked up the casual chit-chat from where he had left it. 'Now, you'll be thinking that I am critical of Dada Bhai's handling of his wife and so lenient with mine. That is because his wife Mena Bai is not just misbehaving herself, she is unleashing a whole army of women who'll misbehave. She is running a school to educate *girls*. What do you get when you educate a bunch of giggling girls … or a gaggle of geese?' Rao Sahib let the question hang. Getting no response, he answered it himself. 'Quack-quack-quack. You don't get Hakim or Vaidhraj but quacks, get it?' The forest air trembled with his laughter.

He looked back to make sure both his aides were smiling. Satisfied, he turned his bulk to the front. On the side of the hill was a jamun tree bending low on the precarious slope. A troupe of Hanuman langurs sat feeding on the juicy purple fruits, picking lice off their relatives and crunching them between their teeth. A few babies with deep perception on their puckered faces, timidly peeped from behind their mother's backs. Rao Sahib was nodding appreciatively at his favourite primate when a langur bared his canines and coughed aloud. The monkeys stopped their tomfoolery in an instant. The large male coughed again. And again. The piercing call of a sambar made Rao Sahib double back on his horse and the equine halt with a jerk. Suddenly, the forest burst with alarm calls and a frenzy of activity.

'There seems to be a leopard in the vicinity, Hukam.' The younger aide Sujan Singh had reached for the 12-bore strapped around his back. He clicked open the lever of the barrels with one hand, took out two LG cartridges from a leather pouch on his waist with the other, slipped them in the twin barrels, cracked shut the bore and unlocked the gun with a deft flip of his thumb, keeping it aimed at the ground all the time.

The troupe began moving on the tree, peeing and excreting and twitching their tails nervously. A mother quail bustled away with her little ones in the bushes. Lankeshwar beat his hoofs.

The reins slipped from Rao Sahib's hands, and he gasped with a visceral fear. The air grew weighty carrying the forest's warnings.

'Easy, easy...' Doonga stroked the neck of the horse, holding its rein. His eyes darted around the narrow valley they had nearly descended into, where the morning mist hung low. 'I can sense the leopard passing that gorge,' the Bhil said in a hushed voice to no one in particular. 'I don't think it will pass our way.'

Rao sahib pulled the mane of the horse as if he was going to de-weed the hair from its neck. After a few long-drawn moments, the jungle began to sober down. The horse was back to being pliant. Rao sahib wiped his face of any traces of fear and snatched the rein away from Doonga's hand, urging the horse forward.

'Nowadays, every other time I visit Dada Bhai in the city...' Rao Sahib paused to look back at his aides challenging them to mention his scared state moments back. '...I come across this city dog Hariharan, sifting through the refuse of the rich. He is feeding on the flesh of a wounded nation split in two at birth. Well, I have a very important task to do in Udaipur this time.'

'Hukam,' replied the aides in unison, as if their conversation was never broken.

'And by the way...' Rao sahib gazed at the drowsy, early morning sky, still sunken in its nightly dreams. 'I am not carrying my beloved England-made rifle. Needless to say, if I had it, I would have loved a leopard hunt.'

Silence lingered in the fast-approaching mist of the valley. Rao sahib turned and threw a fierce glance at his aides.

The 'Hukam' that followed was the loud alarm call of a langur on the advance of a hungry leopard.

12

Suġra, Dada Bhai's Mother

Dada Bhai's House

Bohrawadi

'ASK YOUR PRECIOUS HUSBAND TO COME AND PAY HIS RESPECTS to his old mother-in-law someday.' Suġra squinted at her eldest daughter Khadija sitting next to her by the jharokha, cradling a steaming glass of milk. 'Tell him, regards are not taxes. They won't empty his coffers.'

Early morning rays were even more miserly than Suġra's son-in-law. They fell in tepidly through her jharokha, wrapping her room in gloom.

Khadija slurped on her milk, her attention focussed on the squeaks. Ismail had informed when he escorted Khadija to Suġra's room at dawn, just as Suġra was heading to the latrine with a lota, that a jackal had littered in a drain two streets away.

Municipality workers would have come to catch the family and take them to no man's land, if any such land existed.

'They are killing them,' Khadija said sweetly, picking up the silver bowl filled with peele chawal, the sweet yellow rice. Her corkscrew ringlets below her odhani made her head a covered cauliflower. 'Life is so unfair. A mother killed trying to defend her newborns.' She drew a long, sad sigh, which was anything but. Rolling the sticky rice in her fingers and putting it in her mouth, she smiled at Suġra. 'Aye, Aai, why fret over my old Qurban Ali? You should be happy that your son-in-law takes good care of your daughter.' Khadija licked her fingers with relish before she pressed another ball of peele chawal between her nails. Leisurely. Sensually. Like pressing ... Tauba-tauba ... god forgive!

Suġra closely observed her daughter, a sugar-coated repository of hate. She sat at the most focussed point of her vision, only the odhani covering her head hazing out at the periphery. No doubt the apparently seedless son-in-law was taking good care of her ... to keep her mouth shut about him. She was weighed down with gold. Bands around her wrists and fingers and neck. Suġra eyed her enviously each time she lifted her nath, the nose ring, to sip on the hot milk. Milk ... these children of hers had suckled her. Bitten her teats when they couldn't get any more. All these years later, they were still sucking her dry.

The voices of the electrified crowd receded from the streets. The jackal and her kids were gone—either captured or killed—after giving the people a healthy morning dose of carnage.

'Can't say I feel too sorry about these wild animals in our cities. You remember, Aai, the year I got married, Badi Bi had left a pitcher full of sugarcane juice in the courtyard to prepare vinegar? The golden girl forgot to close the door. The jackals had a good party with it that night. All of us sisters would have died of fear thinking it was the jeevti dakkan in the peepul tree! Only when Tahir banged on our door did we realize it was jackals who had finished the drink, broken the pitcher and started howling. Hehehe…'

Oh yes, how could Suġra forget! The girls were wailing louder than the wild beasts.

'You have all the entertainment you want in your big city, Aai.'

Of course, Suġra was knocked silly with entertainment. The happening sparrow nest on her ledge. Her grandchildren's oh-so-innocent capers. Ismail's rib ticklers, thigh slappers.

'We have enough share in our little town of Galiyakot too.' Khadija adjusted her ghaghra. Why did her skirt look flared like a Rajput's? Bohra women were supposed to wear *dhai-ghaz* skirts with much less flare. It seemed her daughter's husband was not just seedless, but spineless too, giving her all this leeway.

Khadija wiped her mouth with the corner of her odhani and slurped on the milk. 'Last week, there was a commotion in my neighbour's house. Their kitchen is built on the roof and is covered with mud tiles. Two civets entered it by removing the tiles and had a good meal of jaggery. Can you imagine how frightened my neighbours were? You know, civets carry away young children!'

Suġra was getting intrigued now by her daughter's anecdotes and beating around the thorny bushes.

'They didn't carry away any of mine, so I can't say for certain.' Suġra smiled her best two-front-teeth-missing smile.

'Aai! You can be the naughtiest!' Khadija hit Suġra's hand with the end of her gold-rimmed odhani, her eyes crinkled in fake amusement.

Ah ... daughters. The loveliest of things made by Allah. Paraya dhan ... someone else's wealth, since the day they are born. Shedding a million tears in the farewell when they go to live and die by their husbands' sides. Taking along half of the wealth of their parents. Only to come back again and ask for more. *Tweep-tweep-tweep* ... The sparrow family on the ledge had started their day with the mum cleaning the nest and flying away to find grub for her chicks. After a few days, they would fly away and the mum would have nothing to do with them ever again. The lucky sparrow Aai!

'Oh, before I forget, Qurban Ali, whom you are so angry with, has sent you a gift.' She took out a small, wooden box from her embroidered cloth purse. Suġra took it in her wrinkle-carved fingers and opened it.

Her thoughtful son-in-law had sent bokhoor, the perfumed lumps of room freshener, which she couldn't smell. Or was it her ever-scheming daughter who had picked it up from Galiyakot? Hah ... so this aromatic clump was the harbinger of a favour-to-be-demanded.

Suġra tried to remember the taste of the sticky-sweet peele chawal and the smell of bokhoor. She closed the ridiculous box politely, waiting for the daughter to go on. Dawn had reeled into morning, sending the sun rays reflected from the opposite building into Suġra's room. Which was near the latrine. Which was arguably the most important part of Suġra's life.

'Does Tahir still see Badi Bi in the morning? The sight of a widow brings bad luck. Not just to him, but to the entire family. The day his position in society stands ruined, I will tell him I told you so. It'll break my heart, but I will be compelled to tell him that.' Khadija shook her head in anticipation of her deep remorse.

Suġra wrapped the woollen shawl around her tightly and looked down the jharokha. Every morning, as the birds began their day with a bang, sleepy men dragged past her house, carrying bucketsful of clothes to be washed at Lake Pichola or Lake Fatehsagar. That's where the scum of the society went to wash their scum. Most Bohras lived in a khadki—buildings with a lane in between and a common loo—in Bohrawadi. Suġra was proud to have married her daughters well; each one had a private roof above their heads and a hole below their bottoms. Today, there were no men passing with dirty laundry. It was Makar Sankranti, after all. The men would not be fondling small clothes but paper kites.

'Tahir calls me a prudish woman, *me* … his own eldest Apa. And Mena, his wife …oh, the dear, dear woman. She is headed straight to hell. Even in the town of Galiyakot we hear her stories, Aai. How this "modern" woman in Udaipur is educating other women. I thought she'll just go as far as sending her Sanaz to a co-ed school. But tutoring both Hindu and Muslim females … running a centre to empower widows by honing their sewing and embroidery? *Empower* … what does it even mean? Such pompous terms. Widows are supposed to remain chaste, pious … pray for the family and count their days to be united with Allah. What kind of devilry is *empowerment*? Next she'll be asking the widows to wear coloured clothes!'

Suġra nibbled silently on her daughter's sermon about widowhood, remembering the days when every other year her belly would bloat like a festering wound. At thirteen she had her first child. Stillborn. Covered in slime. A bad crop. Many such years, with brief spells of relief in between leaving her with eight living children, seven dead. *Ya Ali* … she sighed inwardly. If only she had become a widow sooner.

'With some people, I have to pretend I don't know a Mena Bai from Udaipur. With others, I can't escape the confession. 'She's my bhabhi…' I whisper, shamefacedly. Qurban Ali is so understanding. He tells me often that I shouldn't burn my blood for the sins of my relatives. Speaking of which, I had called Ameena in Pakistan.'

Sugra's interest was instantly drawn to a point. She sat a little straighter and stopped rolling her rosary. Khadija smiled and drew back. 'Why is the hurricane still on?' She jerked up an eyebrow looking at the kerosene lamp. It was burning on low flame in an indentation in the wall. Gathering her flared skirt, she got up and walked up to it, her gold bangles jangling. She rolled the knob to extinguish the flame and walked back to the jharokha. 'This Ismail is totally useless. When has my darling brother Tahir called the two Hindu servants back from their holiday? He is such a softie, this Tahir of ours.'

Sugra got off the seating by the jharoka, held the ivory head of her walking stick and limped to the small bathroom, its privacy hanging by a curtain. She would not give her cauliflower-headed daughter the satisfaction of asking her about the well-being of her sisters in Pakistan. If there was one thing Sugra had learnt as a woman, it was not to show her weakness. Especially to other women.

'You know, Aai, every time I come here, I get a feeling that this giant of a house wants to throw me out. Or swallow me whole,' Khadija went on as Sugra peed, splashed water on her private parts and came out of the bathroom, wiping her hand on the curtain that separated her bed chamber from it.

'It threatens me. I feel I'm a fly caught in a spider's web.'

'It's not the house … it is the presence of the jeevti dakkan,' Sugra said sagely, hunkering on her bed now and not on the seating by the window.

'Oh, don't say that, Aai!' Khadija shuddered, her eyes widening. 'Anyway, I have to get going in an hour. Qurban Ali will be done with his work and we've to leave for Galiyakot soon after. I don't have time to meet Tahir and Mena. And the kids, well, they don't care much about their aunt, do they? Abbas and his family are in Galiyakot, but he preferred to stay in the Musafir Khana rather than with me, his elder sister.'

'He has gone on a pilgrimage to the mazaar. He has to stay at the community guest house to visit the holy tomb easily.' Suġra had no love lost for her younger son Abbas, a useless souvenir of a trip once taken. But he was *her* souvenir.

When Suġra still did not show any inclination to ask the news of her five daughters, Khadija walked towards the divan and plonked herself on it. 'You know the phone lines to Pakistan are so second rate! I wonder if they catch a cold in the winter to get that nasal sound,' she cackled. 'Ameena was telling me that the Bohras of Pakistan make exactly the same sweets—zarda, nukti ke laddoo, kalakand, suji-ka-halwa, double-ka-halwa … though they call double-ka-halwa "Shahi Tukda", like the Miyan-bhai call it here.'

'How are the little ones?' Suġra couldn't help asking.

'Oh, the baby ducks were quacking at the back.' Though her smile didn't waver, her sweet voice turned sour.

Suġra knew that Khadija earnestly hated her youngest sister Ameena, who was the most happily married with a large brood.

'And your other sisters?'

A spotted dove sitting on the jharokha eyed the leftover sweet yellow rice in the bowl. Khadija got up and shooed it away. Truly her mother's daughter.

'I couldn't ask about the other sisters. All I could hear after that was the squawking phone line.' She went to the earthen pot of drinking water. The four-horned antelope heads regarded her with bleary eyes. 'I'm sure Ameena would have told me if any of the others were not well before she went blabbering about the Bohra desserts.' Khadija took long gulps of water from the copper glass. Ah ... to be young and hot-blooded. Suġra's intake of water reduced drastically in winters, just as her intake of food reduced in summers. What more, an abiding rainy season ruled her cloudy eyes.

'But then,' Khadija continued, ignorant of the seasons of old age, 'I can't be sure, actually. Ameena, poor soul ... she is too caught up with herself.' She came back and settled on the divan again.

Suġra chewed on the morsel of information about her family in Pakistan doled out by her embittered daughter.

'You stop worrying about them, Aai. At least they don't have sounders of wild boars romping on the lanes at night and breaking open the doors with their tushes to get to wheat flour!'

Suġra had waited patiently enough for the small talk to end and the favour to come; the gift box of bokhoor lay on a side, biding time.

'You start talking good of your husband and bad of animals when you have something sinister in mind. Come on, out with it now.'

'Sinister...' Khadija looked aghast. 'You do me great injustice, Aai. You always take Tahir and everyone else's side, when I am the one who brings in news ... does all the worldly work for you.'

A yawn bloomed from Suġra's mouth and ended in a long yowl.

'So, tell me, why are you here?' Suġra smiled broadly, exposing the dark tunnel between her teeth.

Khadija got up from the divan and walked up to her mother. 'I have finally found out what I must do. I ... *we* have to invoke the jeevti dakkan.'

Sugra continued to smile in confusion, as the full import of the words first ballooned and then exploded in her head.

'Say again...' Her throat was instantly dry.

Khadija bent forward, her eyes screwed up and feral. 'The jeevti dakkan ... you have to help me invoke the living witch.'

13

Parijat, the Nightsoil Worker

Kachchi Basti

Delhi Gate, Udaipur

SQUICK ... SQUICK ... SQUICK... CRIES OF A PIG'S DISTRESS
pierced Parijat's dreamless sleep. She got up with a gasp as
the screams stabbed the dark, frigid hours of the morning. Her
husband Bhola lay snoring on the sagging cot, tangled in a torn
blanket. A parcel with no takers. Even his own mother preferred
to stay with his younger brother, not with Loola the handicap,
the sad-smiled, charcoal-skinned son, bent at the wrong angle.

Parijat was full of gratitude towards him, even after three
years of marriage. Once the old Rao sahib had attained nirvana
and the reins had passed on to a brand-new Rao Sahib—the
oldest son of the deceased—Doonga had stopped coming to

take her to the Haveli every day. She was a discarded toy, whose eyes are gouged or a hand come loose or tongue slashed. When the death of the zamindar was announced in their village, she had run away into the forest to her favourite stream. And there she had cried. And laughed. And cried. Soundlessly. Tears had seeped out of the cracks in her thirteen-year-old heart.

Her fierce relief didn't last long. Parijat's aunt had always been cold towards her. Now she looked at Parijat as if she was a turd she couldn't sweep out of the house. The villagers would scold their daughters if they played with her. The old hags would spit when she passed their crumbling bodies and sturdy huts. She could go to the stream in the forest and scrub herself raw. But she couldn't wash away that sticky-white liquid that had erupted out of the old zamindar in spurts and coated her existence. She had become an untouchable among untouchables.

Parijat had waited and waited for her brother Valmiki to come and take her away. Only the stories of his role in the Indian independence movement trickled into their remote village in the Aravalli hill range. A tribal returnee from the city had claimed that Valmiki had even met the great Mahatma Gandhi once. He had heard it from someone who had heard it from someone. She was the spoils of a dead zamindar. He was the stuff fables are made of.

And then one day, while returning from her refuge of a stream in the forest, she had seen this person stop in his tracks as a few quails scuttled away in the bushes. A short man scrunched up from a side, with a bundle pressed below his intact arm, on the way to the village. He had gaped at her dripping form and wet hair weaving her face. The following day, his mother had visited her aunt and asked for her hand, stiffly. In tart sentences. No dowry needed. Her aunt almost fell to her saviour's feet.

Her relief was so great that she didn't mind pawning her only gold bangle to organize the small wedding before the groom returned to his work in the capital of Mewar—Udaipur. Rumours said no one wanted to marry their daughter to a Loola ... a handicap with only one functional arm. The relief for his mother had also been great, if not greater than Parijat's aunt. It was a good bargain for everyone—even for Parijat, whose hopes had now rearranged themselves around meeting her brother one day in the city.

The walled city was everything she had imagined it not to be. It boiled and roiled. It was flush with crowds. The ravishing palaces and lakes of the city were a mirage to the poor deluded men and women. Even the sky was caged. There were no courteous spotted deer turning their dainty heads towards her. No green pigeons looking at her kindly with their ruby eyes. No forest stream drawing her mutilated body in its rippling arms. There was only a sewer at the back of her house, slicing the dirt path in a festering sore.

Ggul ggul ... groin groin ... the pathetic squeaks of the pig continued that morning, as she left her night-long warmth packed in the bedding on the floor, tightened the strings of her choli her fumbling husband had loosened the night before, wrapped the shaggy blanket around tightly and groped her way to a canister of water. Picking it up, she walked out of the tiny dark hut, willing the sleep to lift its bulk from her eyes.

A big, open drain where the city belched, its waste flowed through their kachchi basti—the shantytown—in a thick soup, its smell indescribable. A smell that was part of their routines—eating, sleeping, hugging, cooking, kissing, in sorrow and in health, till death did them part. The fragrance of her gulab jal overpowered it in fleeting, intense moments of solace.

There was an old mango tree right outside her hut. It always had a beehive or two hanging from its chin. There were beetles, squirrels, palm civets. Caterpillars that morphed into butterflies. Ants who got wings after the first shower of rain. And died soon after being liberated. It was a secret world right in front of everyone's unseeing eyes, one that only Parijat could take in. There was always a rosy side to life.

The rusted canister winked at her in the paling darkness as she took some cold water in her cupped hand and splashed it on her face. She chewed on a twig of neem and gargled away the stale morning breath. A few huts away, near the wall of Delhi Gate, stood two Bhangi men holding a hog down, its legs tied. One had pinned it to the ground with a knee and the other was plucking the bristly hair from its shivering back. Bhangi and Chamar raised pigs and let them loose in the runnels to feed and fend for themselves. A Jain merchant bought these animals regularly and transported them to a paramilitary facility to be used for consumption. Before each dispatch, the owners plucked the hair out of the pigs. The coarse hair, which was used to make brushes, fetched good money. *Squick ... squick ... groin ...* the frantic cries and appeals of the swine fell into an abyss of apathy.

Maulvi Syed Ali, walking towards the mosque in the adjoining slum of the Hele—the lower-caste Muslims—cast an appraising look at her. A priest had to be from the upper caste. Syed Ali, who was Dada Bhai's accountant, spared some time daily to show his untouchable brethren the pious way of life. Their god liked to be addressed in Arabic, as hers liked to be addressed in Sanskrit, which only the pandits could read. She stepped back on her porch, with the impact of his blustering look, and cast her eyes down. He left in his wake a trail of

Kewra attar and the pride of a predator who has graciously left its prey for now.

Today, she had to start early, before the break of dawn, if she had to complete her work routine and then the special task handed to her. A centipede crawled inside her stomach and climbed on its many feet up to her chest. She stood in the bitter-cold air, waiting for the feeling to pass. The hundred-footer didn't stop tingling her insides. She looked at the mango tree for help. It sensed her plight and rustled in the quiet, inert hour. A murmur sent from one dumb creature to another.

Parijat slipped into the hut that hummed with Bhola's snoring. She lighted the oil lamp and turned the knob to increase its flame. They didn't have enough oil to keep it lit for the whole night. It made a small globe of light around her, too feeble to penetrate the night that crouched in the corners. She went to her thin mattress, rolled it and propped it up on a wall. There was a tear on the side with cotton balls bulging out of it. Parijat dug her hand into the tear, pulled out something in her fist and buried it in her blouse. Then she walked to the soot-blackened mud stove, where she had stacked the thick maize rotis prepared last night for breakfast, and wrapped a roti and an onion in a piece of torn cloth, leaving two for Bhola. Tiptoeing to the cot, she tenderly tucked in a sad foot sticking out of the blanket. He mumbled something in his sleep and half-turned on the bed. She felt a surge of pity for this man who had freed her from the village and bound her in wedlock.

Parijat cradled the bundle of roti and onion in her armpit, stepped out of her hut, picked up the basket from the porch and strode out into the maze of lanes.

She could see the silhouettes of a few peacocks and peahens resting on the contours of the shaharpana. The fixtures on the city wall that would get wings and fly away at dawn. A fox trotted to the side of the dirt path and stopped to look pointedly at this intrusion into his morning stroll. Parijat crossed the adjoining colony of Hele Muslims and reached another kachchi basti with a generous view of the big gutter. Some of the huts had skins of cows, goats, dogs and donkeys hanging to dry on their mud walls. The stench of rotting flesh here overpowered the smell of the drain. This was the colony of Chamar—the caste of tanners. No self-respecting Bhangi would touch a Chamar, and it was true the other way around as well.

The Chamar collected dead animals and supplied the skins to the leather industry. The upper-caste Hindus would not touch a cow once she was dead. They worshipped Gau Mata only while she lived—consumed her urine to cure ills and milk to satiate appetite. Until a Chamar came to claim a holy cow, she would lie untouched in death in a debris of devoutness.

Parijat walked up to a tiny door. Dried, hairy strips of goat skin lay scattered in curls around the hovel. She rapped on it. Once. Twice. Waited and rapped again. With a shuffle from inside, the little shanty-house came to life. She stepped back and brought her wrist close to her nose. No aroma of rose water there today. Only ant bites.

Metal scraped on wood and the door opened, one shy bit at a time.

'Parijat Didi...' said a voice as tired as the hovel. A form appeared at the door. A limping quilt with a human somewhere in its core. Parijat reached out for the forehead above the two puffed-up eyes and drew back her hand. It was hot as the metal base of the oil lamp she had lighted at home. The gaunt boy of fourteen or fifteen years, just a couple of years her junior, dropped the quilt draping his head in a hood. 'You have come very early today.' His face crumpled in pain as he shifted on his legs.

Parijat extended the bundle holding a roti and an onion towards him. He took it gratefully and muttered a small thanks.

Three years back, when a freshly married thirteen-year-old Parijat came to the city, she saw this brat every day. Gokul would go screeching in all the slums, rolling his tire with a wire or playing football with a band of soiled kids. He seemed to be their undisputed leader. There was something tall in his smallness. Something powerful in his frailty. He reminded her of Valmiki, the brother she longed for. She would look at the kids with an unfeigned yearning to play. To kick a ball. To climb a tree. To cover herself in delightful mud.

As if Gokul sensed her urge, he stopped rolling his tyre one day in front of her hut and held out the wire in his extended hand. Parijat walked up to him, looked vacantly at it for one long moment, snatched the wire from his hand and ran away, rolling the tyre on the dirt tracks, her ghaghra ballooning in the wind.

After a long sermon from a neighbourhood shrew about the decorum of a married woman, Parijat did not play with Gokul or the tyre again. But she never forgot his small act of kindness.

The last of Gokul's family was his grandmother, who was indeed grand. Her laughter was the only boundless thing in this walled city Parijat had come across. Once her husband Bhola left for work, she would slip into the Chamar basti and pay grandma a silent visit. She was always greeted with a generous cackle, a glass of buttermilk and returned with her hair tied in a tight braid. Gokul had started to spend most of his time working with the other men of the basti, helping them collect and skin dead animals.

Parijat had slowly got used to the smacking and squelching sounds of skinning, the putrefying odour and the thickened, darkened blood.

It was an open secret that Parijat visited the Chamar basti. Bhola played along and let his young bride do what she pleased despite the displeasure of others in their community. Soon he landed her some work collecting faeces from a few private toilets of the rich. It was an easy job and they could certainly do with an additional income. Even after she started working and the intimidating maze of the upper-caste quarters turned familiar, Parijat continued to visit grandma. Till the day she died. Laughing over a handful of rice she had overcooked.

That was a long month back. A Chamar boy didn't have the luxury to mourn for more than a day. Gokul had to get back to work to fill his ever-demanding stomach. Maybe it was his deep sense of loss that made him lose his balance and break an ankle. He couldn't go to work and earn a daily living. The neighbours tried to send him some food once a day, but they had their own families to feed. Parijat skipped one meal daily and decided to give him her share till he got better. He was getting worse.

She patted his shoulders, swaddled in the quilt, and gave him a sullen smile before walking away briskly through the flaccid skins and sleeping slum. The world was starting to stir, and pink rashes had begun to surface on the sky. It was a momentous day. Finish the work quickly. Go earn her extra four-annas that would get her a month of rose water supply. And … above all … do a personal favour to someone she loved the most in the world.

14

Hariharan, the Middleman

Ghanta Ghar Mohalla

Udaipur

THE MAKAR SANKRANTI THIS YEAR WAS A DAY OF GREAT IMPORT … if Hariharan struck a deal today, his fortunes would balloon, by god's grace. His wife had stained his forehead with a flaming red tilak, dividing it in two. The thin tendrils of smoke rising from the sickly-sweet incense sticks had mixed with the miasma of his wife's stale breath as she did the aarti, tinkling the tiny bell to wake the god. Hariharan prostrated before their personal deity Laddoo Gopal—the baby Krishna—promising him a whole month of fresh curd if his deal brokered today. No, no, why would Laddoo Gopal bother to get him thousands of rupees for a measly supply of curd for a month? He closed the offering at four months with a reverential touch of his forehead on Gopal's cold cradle.

His feet trawled on the silent mud paths of the city as he practised his smile walking towards Ghanta Ghar, the old clock tower, in the supple morning hours. He clutched his shawl and rehearsed his spectrum of smiles—the one with marginal sanity, the one with controlled madness, a sad smile, a surprised smile … A single wrong twitch of the lips could cost him a fortune. His ludicrously rounded belly, he liked to believe, was an occupational hazard. Why would anyone trust him if he looked like a half-starved labourer who would run away with their hard-earned money? His gouty knees, which froze during winter nights and thawed only by noon, moaned beneath his crisp white pyjama.

The deep blue sky was wrinkled with a few pink lines. The city had started to twitch in its slumber. The puddle of vomit at the side of the lane—the smelly remnant of someone's revelry—had not yet been cleared by the Bhangis. He caught a movement at the corner of his eye and didn't turn around; kept walking. Hariharan knew it was a jackal sneaking in the lane. But this was the hour of dreamwork and the occult. What if it was a living witch … you never took the chance of turning around. If you did, you would find a woman, with a long trailing ghaghra, crawling with her fingernails just behind you. One jerk at a time. You must keep walking as if you know nothing of her presence: that was the only way to save yourself.

He would generally not step out of the house in these murky hours, but he wanted to finish the first task of his well-planned day before sunrise. He felt the cold jabbing at his head, which was full of ledgers and protected by a white topi, as he climbed the two stone steps to a wooden door and lifted the brass knocker. Rap-rap, rap-rap ... he kept pounding with persistence. The world inside the house in the back lane of Ghanta Ghar refused to yield.

Finally, something stirred. A shuffle of guarded steps approached the wooden door.

'Whozz it?' The house asked in a grouchy grumble.

'I am here to see Lal Chand Mahajan ji.' He came closer and whispered the secret to the blind door, 'This is Hariharan.'

'In the middle of the night? Who has died?'

'Oh no, no, god forbid. No one has died. But it is urgent. Really urgent. Otherwise, I wouldn't have dreamt of disturbing the venerable Mahajan ji out of his slumber.' Hariharan added as an afterthought, 'It is almost morning,' and immediately regretted it.

The house seemed to have gone back to sleep. No one answered. The door stood its ground stoically. Hariharan cursed his big, fat tongue. Saliva gathered in his mouth and instead of spitting it out, he gulped. Rigid with anticipation, he let out a long breath, which formed a mist around his nose. Just then, the iron latch scraped harshly against the door and clanked it open.

In the dim light of the pre-dawn hours, Hariharan saw a hunched figure bundled up in blankets, only a pear-shaped nose peeping curiously out of his face.

'Ram-Ram, Mahajan ji.' He pulled out his hands, warm with the body heat gathered inside his shawl, and folded them in greeting.

'This better be worth my sleep.' The man took a step back to let him in. As he shut the door, darkness closed in from all sides, suspending the weight of reality. Had it not been for the biting cold, Hariharan would have imagined himself to be floating in a dream.

'Follow me,' Mahajan said in a nasal voice, heavy with sleep.

Hariharan couldn't see where he was headed in the cavernous house, but he could hear Mahajan staggering ahead. He followed the sound, knowing in which direction Mahajan's den lay. As his eyes acclimatized to the dark, the passage and doors took vague shapes. In one of the rooms, this honey badger of a moneylender kept the collateral—all the shiny items stolen from the barrows of the living. Hariharan often imagined the room as a chamber of buried treasure. One day, he would set his eyes on it. Or better, have one such chamber for his own respected self.

'*Aji* ... who has come at this hour?' A pointed voice fell from the first floor in a dripping icicle.

'Go back to sleep...' was all the old man commanded.

Keys jangled as Mahajan searched for the right one in the big iron ring. With a delicate click, the daunting lock lolled to a side helplessly. He unlatched the door and stepped in.

Mahajan struck a match and lit the kerosene lamp placed in the taak—a bracket in the wall—turning the knob to lengthen the flame. The cramped room got drenched in a feeble yellow light. Thick parchment rolls and bonds, swollen with the mounting interest and misery of countless borrowers, lay in dog-eared piles along the walls and on a greying wooden table. A stout granite statue of Laxmi, the goddess of wealth, squatted on a counter littered with dry parijat flowers—one of her favourites. Two incense sticks made a V-pitchfork on her side.

Mahajan slumped on a flattened mattress by a wall, with a bolster to support his arched back. A low, sloping wooden table, with a pot of ink and pen was placed by its side. As he sat down, his elephant foot popped out of his dirty pyjama in full view. Bloated like a dead lizard in water. The purple-veined foot had always repulsed and fascinated Hariharan in equal measure.

'What is it that you want to feed me before I have cleared my bowels today?' Mahajan said, pushing his elephant foot forward for a better view. Hariharan gave him an embarrassed smile.

'Let me catch my breath, Lal Chand ji.'

There was another mattress lying limp on a side. Hariharan unrolled it sending clouds of dust into the musty air. He coughed bending his stiff knees as he sat down on it cross-legged.

'Which is the gang of dacoits you want to fund with my money?' Mahajan asked again, suppressing a yawn. His skin, with an unhealthy pallor, stretched on his emaciated cheeks. Wisps of grey hair stuck greedily to his balding head.

Mahajan wore a facade of poverty because he had wealth. Hariharan wore a facade of wealth because he didn't have any. The two men understood each other perfectly. There was a bond between them—that of brazen lust for money. That's the reason, Hariharan believed, they wholeheartedly mistrusted each other.

Lying on the side of the mattress, spread on a threadbare silk cloth on careless display, were coins. Small pieces of one paisa coins, three paisa coins with or without a hole in the middle, one annas which equalled six paisas and one rupee that amounted to sixteen annas. Bait for the dispossessed. Lures for the starved. It could be all yours just for an impression of your thumb on one of Mahajan's ledgers with prodigious memory. The debts would outlive the borrowers. And hopefully their children too.

Two rupees was the monthly earning of many of Hariharan's acquaintances. He found his mouth salivating.

'Mahajan ji,' he gulped. 'I want to know if you could give a serious thought to my proposal.'

'You woke me before the sun is up to ask me this?' The old man bent forward, his small eyes constricting with annoyance.

'Today is the day.' Hariharan shifted on his buttocks. 'By today evening, I intend to close the deal.' He blew air in his hands and rubbed them for warmth.

Mahajan eyed him distastefully. 'My answer is no.'

Hariharan's insides churned but he shook his head nonchalantly, as if he was expecting this reply. 'You are a clever man, Lal Chand ji.' He scratched his stubble tearing his gaze away from the thick-veined elephant foot again. 'This is an assured interest payment over the fattest capital you could ever think of lending. The man is a stickler for decorum and you're sure to get the interest on time year after year.'

'I have no objection to lending Dada Bhai money. What I have an objection to, is you.' Mahajan reclined on his bolster.

Hariharan took the blow valiantly, rubbing his double chin with unfeigned hurt. He looked at Mahajan, sitting still like a snake playing dead before a strike.

'Lal Chand ji, I don't question your wisdom…'

'…or my ability to lend such a big amount of money.' Mahajan's lips curled up in a half-smile exposing a gold tooth sitting proudly amid its yellow brethren. 'No other moneylender in the city has it, na? Why should I pay *you* a fat chunk of *my* profits when Dada Bhai would come to me anyway?'

Hariharan leaned forward and whispered, as if there were spies eavesdropping from behind the ledgers, 'That old debauch Kamruddin Hathiwala. He wants to give the entire amount to him *without interest*, if Dada Bhai weds his daughter Sanaz to him.'

'Is he now? I don't understand how Dada Bhai's reformer of a wife Mena would let that happen.' Sleep had abandoned Mahajan's hazy eyes, and they were narrowing into slits, his groggy voice turning incisive. 'From what I hear, she has his unbending support. She is stirring shit here in our Ghanta Ghar mohalla too, trying to fill women's heads with the idea of educating themselves. Learning the letters ... hah! My son gave his wife his clear opinion, printed in five fingers on her face.'

'Did you hear about Dada Bhai's employees walking down from seven of his bases in Chandesara, Gogunda and other villages and towns to give a dharna ... a peaceful sit-in protest at his house in Bohrawadi two weeks back? He hasn't paid them in two months, is what I hear. Of course, it was all cordial and they went back with a promise and no money. Everyone loves Dada Bhai. But how long can love survive on an empty stomach?' Hariharan's legs were cramping with the cold and sitting on the ground. He agonized to move his finger rings that refused to budge, like Mahajan. He was the safer bet compared to Kamruddin Hathiwala. Hariharan needed to convince him, without seeming desperate.

'So?' Mahajan put a long nail between his teeth trying to dislodge the remains of last night's meal. The gold tooth was the only luxury Hariharan had seen him succumb to. All his wealth—his cave of treasure, his display of coins, his ledgers gathering interest—he was saving from himself. Just as his forefathers had saved their wealth from themselves.

Hariharan inhaled the mildewy air in a deep breath. 'Kamruddin has already lent him money in the past. *Invested* ... he said. What if he summons a kurki to Dada Bhai's house to liquidate his properties? That will be a humiliation to match no other—the government officials coming with a drum-beater to announce to the whole colony about his going bankrupt. His wife Mena Bai will do anything to salvage her dear husband's reputation. Even if that means marrying her daughter to an old fart.'

The room, which was all shades of wretchedness and plunder, seemed to be swaying on its unsteady feet with the flame of the lamp. A drunken crook. A moment passed as the old moneylender chewed on this information. He may be a blood-sucker, but he was known for his word. You only needed to convince him to give it. Hariharan wanted to get up and stamp his feet to ward off the creeping cold, but he kept sitting with a bogus smile. His stealthy moves were juvenile compared to the deviousness of this veteran master.

'Hmm ... and how are you so sure about what Mena Bai thinks, you great psychic?' Mahajan allowed himself the opulence of a small, grating laugh. 'Till the time he has that beautiful daughter of his, these possibilities remain. If not that old lech Kamruddin, it'll be a wealthy young Bohra man. Mena Bai would not object to marrying her daughter to a deserving youth with respectable money.'

If nothing else, Hariharan had the instinct to know when he was beaten. But he didn't believe in closing doors. Or fire escapes.

'Mahajan ji Sahib, you are my elder and I revere you like my father.' He got up with a groan and rubbed his knees, summoning a smile back to his face in a haze of pain. 'I promise you, you'll see the advantage of doing business with me. With all due respect, it'll be sooner than you anticipate.'

With folded hands and a bow, Hariharan made his first exit of the day.

15

Nathu, the Bhil

Jogion ka Guda

Aravalli Hills

'*JUNGLE HAATH MUNDA JAI RAYO HAI, NATHU?*' A FEEBLE VOICE, rising from the condensed darkness of the hut, asked if Nathu was going to the bushes to relieve himself. His father, Jaitya, had been drifting in and out of consciousness, saliva coagulating by the side of his pillow.

'Ha-haan, Baa,' he answered as he stepped out in the early winter morning, dense as moss. The cold pressed against his shins and stomach and ears, sizing him up.

He inhaled the frosty air, hoping to push out the smell of blood, pus and urine ensconced in his lungs. The Bhil village of Jogion ka Guda lay scattered in twelve huts on three hillocks. Constellations blinked at him as he walked into the wilderness and squatted behind a bush, dewy grass tickling his bare bottom. The forest was in a deep lull, birds and beasts resting at this darkest hour before the sky was splattered with the natal blood of a newborn day.

He stood up, hitched and tied his langot, the loincloth, around his waist, picked up a bit of mud and rubbed his hands, pouring the water he had got along in a leaf cup. There was no need for him to clean, nothing in his bowels to empty. His mud stove had not been lit for three days and he had not seen the cinders rise with the smoke like fireflies. A few village women had managed to get them a little food, but he and his wife had fed it to his delirious father, who burbled it out. Their bull was dead and the goat demanded all the attention of a surviving child. Though they hadn't eaten much, gone to their field to work or collected firewood, his wife Thawari had not failed to get the goat her fodder.

Three nights back, Nathu had heard a long moan of '*Aye Bai...*' and ran out of his hut to see a group of tribals carrying his father home, a dislodged hand hanging by his side, glistening with blood. Deep claw marks ran on his bare chest like four dug-out rows of a sowing field, his flesh gathered on their sides. A female leopard with two cubs had terrorized their area. As her cubs grew, her range increased. Of late, the leopard had been frequenting their sugarcane fields and had killed a bull and a goat so far. Jaitya was supposed to go to Udaipur and request Dada Bhai to come and shoot the cattle lifter. It was as if the cat had read his dark intentions and slapped him for his naughty thoughts.

The other Bhils informed that Jaitya had wandered too close to the cubs at dusk after winding up the day's work in his tiny field—a small farming terrace levelled on a sloping hill. Nathu had rushed to get the Hakim—the doctor of Unani medicines—from the adjoining village of Kotra, but he was travelling. Not expected to return before a week. He was the only Hakim in the fifteen villages of the region. There used to be a Vaidhraj, an Ayurveda physician, in one of the bigger villages. He had died last year, choking on an overdose of his own herbs, which villagers suspected were potent aphrodisiacs.

The village elders of Kotra had sent a midwife to attend to Jaitya's wounds after Nathu had stuttered his spit-deploying pleas for help. The old woman almost fainted seeing the mangled man who had started to emit the smell of half-fermented mauda liquor. His broken ribs pierced the chest with each breath that heaved with the burden of his remaining days. Thawari had to steady the midwife's wildly shaking hands as she sat squashing neem leaves and turmeric bulbs to be applied to his wounds.

They had managed to tie his hand that was torn from his shoulder and remained connected to his torso with a web of raw flesh. It was kept on the side of his sagging cot, as if a broken branch would reattach itself owing to proximity to the trunk. A sticky doll lying by the side of a sick kid that he just wouldn't part with. The hut, plastered with mud and thatched with bamboos and straw, housed a little horror story. The hand with a hundred hues. Changing colour with each passing hour. Emitting foul-tasting fumes. Attracting wide-eyed flies, rubbing their legs in glee.

The hut, on the flat belly of the hillock, had a mahua tree to which parakeets, koels, squirrels, barbets and ants paid daily homage when it fruited in the honeyed summer sunshine. A small inviting porch with a goat tethered under a mud-tiled shed. An inner chamber divided in two with a woman's faded odhani separating the living space of a father-in-law from a young amorous couple. Shelves holding a few copper plates. A pot of water. A dark fireplace for cooking. A cot. A dying man.

'Ba, we can take you to the hosss-spital in the city,' Nathu had whispered to his father during a spell of his alertness. Jaitya's eyes shone. The chest with a few grey puffs of hair and four lateral wounds lifted and fell erratically. His hair was sticking up on one side. The odhani that cut the hut in two had been thrown carelessly over the string. Nothing in this household went to waste. The worn-out odhani were converted into curtains, the torn curtains to scrubbing cloths, the threadbare scrubbing cloths stuffed in blankets, the blankets used as pall for the dead.

Jaitya, ever the clown, gave him a crafty grin, which came out as a grimace. 'And what ... are you now an agent for the village Baniya?'

Nathu knew he had asked a moot question. It was well-known that city doctors removed all the blood of a patient admitted to a hospital. But ... but! He had heard of a man being brought back from the verge of death. Surprisingly, in a hospital! His father was right, though. They would have to borrow a big sum of money from the village Baniya moneylender and take the help of four healthy men to carry his cot through the hilly forests on a tedious trek to the city. If Jaitya survived as a cripple, for him to be dependent on his son lifelong would be a fate worse than death.

It didn't matter to Nathu if he now lived in a free India. His jungle tribe would always be lesser people. Secondary. Tertiary. Or whatever came after that. They had been exploited, abused and preyed upon for centuries. They would be, for time to come. Theirs was the story history would repeat but never change; always leave it without a happy ending. Over centuries, their hearts had turned porous, not able to hold the flood of suffering. These people of the forest had learnt to handle death and loss as the city people had termed: practically.

But Nathu loved his father with the love of a frog for his little puddle of sludge. A father who welcomed joy with a handshake and grief with a hug. Who kept holding his wife's hand till they put her on the pyre. He had his own theory about life: Life is a net. Only if you let your sorrow, pleasure, greed or anger expand, will you get caught in it. Else, you can caper away, carrying your delicate little bundles of hope and happiness to eternity.

Jaitya had toiled for his little brood—one son and two daughters, who survived the age of ten, and sang them the Bhil songs in his trembling bass voice welcoming each dawn with a melody. He never remarried, though. The Bhils were guided through life simply—following their instincts and needs. Their societies didn't have monstrous morals or sins that would toast them forever in hell. Nata pratha was prevalent; the wife could run away with another man and she would be spared the ignominy. The husband was compensated by the lover in the terms decided by the Panchayat of village elders. Justice, love, need … all prevailed; one did not come at the cost of the other. Jaitya was too busy chasing the little things in life, such as the fluttering smiles of his children, to go after the big things that mattered such as getting another wife.

Jaitya's love for all things little had given him a jungle sense rivalled by the best khoju shikaris of the region. He didn't miss a small displaced bush, a hint of a smell, a twisted twig, a faraway warning call, the dryness of animal droppings, the wetness of trampled dew, the thin layer of dust settled on a pug mark. No wonder the celebrated, disciplined hunter Dada Bhai called Jaitya the heartbeat of the forest and counted him among the best of his khoju shikaris. A tracker who drifted through the wilderness like forest breeze. Deft. Unseen. Unremembered. Nothing escaping his shifting touch.

And Jaitya was attacked by a leopard. The irony was not lost on Nathu. He felt his arm sag under the crushing heaviness of the hasthada—the featherlight handy cloth—flung over his shoulder. The weight a male must carry. He didn't want to be the man of the house; he wanted his father to carry this bulky title for him. Nathu was not tough. He wanted his seventeen years to be a secret the world didn't know of. He would rather splash in the muddy ponds after rains, climb mahua and mango trees to pluck the fruits before squirrels, monkeys or parakeets got to them, and marvel at what lay beneath the girls' spiralling skirts.

Jaitya knew Nathu was a soft boy and never asked him to toughen up. Not even when his mother died. He married off both his daughters, borrowing money from the village Baniya, with whom he had a running account, and kept paying the mounting interests every month, knowing fully well he would never be able to pay back the capital.

Nathu rambled in the dark semi-arid wilderness in the early morning hours, spreading his anxiety on the grasses like the wildflowers he used to scatter in the wind. Why hadn't his father slapped and told him that plucking flowers is what girls did, not boys! He squinted his eyes at the morning star and demanded that his father not leave him. He had not prepared him for it!

It was deja vu. Nathu had felt such intense despair many years back on a duck shoot. Two city doctors, Dada Bhai and a Thakur Sahib had come to Purohit ji ka Talaab, the lake where migratory birds descended in clouds every winter and remained moored to the waters. The retrievers, posted at various spots

around the lake, were firing their muzzle-loader guns to make
them fly; it was not considered sporting to shoot sitting birds.
Shots reverberated, ducks took to wings, gunpowder spiked
up the air, the gentlemen aimed and fired their 12-bores and
excitement made little Nathu whizz on the shore of the lake,
one end to the other.

Jaitya swam and retrieved a couple of bar-headed geese,
bhatiya as they called them, from this side of the reservoir
when, on an impulse, he decided to venture into the waters
thick with weed to get his hands on two more fallen ducks.
That was when he got entangled. *Bachao ... Bachao ...* the cries
for help boomed louder than the gunshots as Jaitya began to
sink. The Thakur Sahib and the doctors joined in the cries for
help, but they couldn't possibly wet their shiny leather shoes.
The seven-year-old Nathu began to sob and whimper. Dada
Bhai bolted to his car, flung open the boot, got a long bamboo
with a rope tied to it and rushed into the lake. Only the hairy
top of Jaitya's head was above the water now. From the point
Dada Bhai couldn't wade any further in the weeds, he threw the
bamboo at the sinking Jaitya, holding the rope. There was no
response. By then, the other tribal retrievers had come crashing
to the scene, shouting in Mewari, '*Haatho haath bandho*', a cry
to make a human chain, clenching hands. Dada Bhai, with a
human chain holding him from the back, threw the bamboo
with force for the third time. It hit the chest of a half-alive man,
and he caught it. Jaitya was hauled to the shore, one pull at a
time, and lay on the mud, unconscious. His dhoti was bunched
up his thighs, one hand clutching the neck of two dead ducks.

As the other Bhils started a small fire, stacked Jaitya with
warm clothes and the doctor pumped out the water from his
lungs, Nathu stood a little away, weeping like Dada Bhai's

drenched breeches. It was after a few long-drawn moments of his father's chest being pounded, and Nathu's terror reaching a full-frenzied boil, when Jaitya opened a set of beady eyes that whirred in focus.

'You must change your clothes, Dada Bhai.' Words wheezed out of his frozen jaw. 'Otherwise you'll catch a cold.'

A cheer rose. Nathu, standing forgotten a little away, had smiled through a running nose and swollen eyes.

A scuffle of a disturbed partridge resting in the bushes made Nathu blink out of his reverie and look at the tangled shadows of the early winter morning. Blunted peaks of hills after hills melted in the dark sky. He had wandered, lost in thought, and arrived on the fringe of the thicket—the sacred grove where Rana ji resided. Their gods Rana ji and Bhairon ji didn't live in elaborate temples, but in the littlest devra in the wild. Just like Bhils did. People didn't cut the wood of gods and over the ages, these became ancient forests. He folded his hands and sent a long-distance prayer to the devra, not risking to stepping inside the grove thick with solitude.

Nathu prayed for courage. He knew Jaitya would not succumb to despair in his penultimate days. But he had one last wish. A small, doable wish. Which would release him from the net called life.

'Be strong, Nathu. Be strong,' he said to himself without a stammer and turned to walk back to his hut, the end of the night squeezing her cold, dying lips on his. He understood what Jaitya had asked him to do. He prayed for courage not to do it.

16

Rao Sahib, the Zamindar

Surajpol Gate

Udaipur

RAO SAHIB FELT NAUSEOUS. HE ALWAYS DID, IN THIS CRADLE OF claustrophobia. Solid rocks, gouged out from the aged Aravallis, encaged Udaipur in a shaharpana. The high wall was surrounded by a moat filled with water from the lakes of the fortified city. On the turrets stood soldiers, shelled in their armours. Waiting eagerly for trouble. Watching the movement of humans trapped in the walled city. The streets had the fishy stench of a woman's vulva. The pigeons, the insolence of naked babies. The vendors, the shrillness of bats. Baniya to Kshatriya to Muslims to Bhangi-Chamar ... one and all incubating, shagging, eating, scheming, screaming, masturbating, menstruating, dying, huffing, coughing in the same enclosed space.

Rao sahib's fingers twitched for his whip again. A stream of humans had moved too close for his comfort, in an ant line. He was outside the Surajpole Gate from where he had to enter the city with his two aides and his Bhil Doonga. The winter morning had turned clammy, a far cry from the loam fresh with forest dew. If the forest had a thousand eyes, the city had a thousand mouths. With pouting, adulterous lips. A Marwadi seth wearing a gold-rimmed orange pagadi had got down from his tonga and was trailed by servants. A seth of Shekhawati, Marwar, was a proud creature. To get the title of 'seth' he was supposed to have a minimum number of people working for him, sponsor a temple, run a dharmsala, and a gaushala. What was the point of a title, Rao sahib wondered, that was not through bloodline? Vulgar vainglory.

The seth had made a beeline past a couple of bullock carts rolling in the direction of the Surajpol Gate, towards the Bhils. They were sitting outside the moat of the shaharpana, under shady trees, waving off flies from their baskets full of kotbadi, belpatra, amla and other forest produce. He was greeted with a loud *khamma ghani, Seth ji* as his servants got busy buying from the depredation of tribals.

An enigmatic smile played on the merchant's lips as he rubbed his ego, going up to the Kalbeliya gipsy selling the oil 'sande-ka-tel' believed to have mystic properties. The nomadic tribe of Kalbeliya, known for its snake handling, folk dances and herbal remedies, could be trusted to give you the most kosher treatments. A large monitor lizard lay curled up in a deep plate full of oil. Inert. Framed in death. Releasing its healing powers in the oil. A rugged brown cloth on the side groaned under the weight of semi-precious stones. The seller, dressed in a red pagadi, white dhoti-kurta and silver jewellery produced phials with a sweep of his hand from below a sack and dipped them in the oil with a flourish. He pushed the dead lizard tenderly while doing so, trying not to disturb its eternal slumber—a stirring performance. The seth bought no less than eleven bottles of the healing oil, undoubtedly for his disease-ridden family, sending the seller in raptures.

Rao Sahib had entered the city with a sour mouth. The seth had sensed his displeasure, just as Doonga could sense the presence of a leopard in a thicket. The impudent merchant had smirked at him. Given him a smile that was teasing. Hostile. Challenging. The notional nation of India would not take anything away from these remarkable men who didn't live on their ancestral lands but on the blood of the society. Businessmen. Moneylenders. Cheats.

With his sour mouth turning acidic, Rao Sahib sent his aides Sujan Singh and Amar Singh to make preparations for his stay at the Maharana's City Palace. Or so he told them. He wanted to be alone for what he had set out to do today. There was this one place he had to go to before visiting Dada Bhai and then the Maharana's durbar. He could only trust Doonga to be with him, for what was he but a shadow?

'The Union of India is giving voting powers to each and every man. And *woman*.' Rao sahib's horse *tok-tok-toked* on the maze of kutcha lanes. 'It would make thugs in-charge of running a country that is a hundred times bigger than the state of Mewar. Not just that, it is giving the right to anyone ... *anyone* to fight an election and become a leader. Even a hijra. Tell me Doonga, how would you like serving a eunuch?'

Doonga walked by the side of the horse, holding the rein of the class through the milling masses. Rao Sahib didn't expect a reply from him. It would be like expecting a response from his horse Lankeshwar. And yet, there seemed to be an invisible ghost that capered about Doonga that day, just as the jeevti dakkan flitted in the peepul tree outside Dada Bhai's house. In frightening quietness.

'And do you think India would become as great as Britain? Mark my words, Doonga ... it never can. You have to loot other nations to become great. These thugs, our 'leaders', will be looting their own people.'

Two men in tight loincloths with gunnysacks on their slender backs, went in tow of a hollow-cheeked man pulling a loaded handcart. They left a pungent smell of turmeric in their wake. Their hair was bleached brown in the sun. The activity was much less today near the Dhan Mandi, the grain market, as almost everyone was preparing for a day in the company of kites.

Most of the shops were closed. A small corner boutique, with a smattering of colourful kites, had attracted a pack of little rascals pooling their coins to buy one.

Rao sahib passed a dharmashala near a Jain Mandir. Doonga's knowledge of the city lanes was thorough. Just a twitch of Rao sahib's lips and he knew where to take him.

'You know which are my pet places in this city? The lakes, Doonga, the lakes. Chocked with crocodiles, skimming with migratory birds, churning with fish. That is the last wild bastion left in Udaipur. How long will these beasts survive our 'independence'? There are already rumours of the authorities wanting to give contracts for crocodile hide ... they plan to mass murder these ferocious reptiles to make shoes and purses—'

Before he could finish his remorse, Rao Sahib's horse, led by Doonga, turned on a wide road shaded with trees. There was a boundary wall on one side to stop a forest from spilling into the city. Gulab Bagh. The exquisite zoological and botanical garden of Udaipur.

'How can I forget that *this* is my favourite place in the city?' Rao Sahib closed his eyes and inhaled, taking in the sudden burst of green. The temperature dropped a few degrees as the breath of the geriatric trees washed over him. Villagers made it a point to visit the zoo and the park when they came to the city. It was quiet today. Makar Sankranti. For the first time after entering the city, Rao Sahib heard Doonga's panting. The horse's snorts. The convivial morning chatter of birds.

On the side of the road stood a banyan tree. A ponderous head of a canopy resting on sturdy, brown shoulders. A nude man—an Aghori—was half propped up against the trunk. His legs were spread in all defiance of decency, with scattered thickets between his groin and on his chest. Half of his hair was coiled on the top of his head in a sloppy bun. Coarse dreadlocks hung around his dirt-caked neck. His mustard teeth were bared in a leer. His face and body smeared with cremation ash. A sullied blanket was spread on the ground below him. An open box of barfi lay on the side covered with flies. A half-broken human skull was tossed carelessly near the sweets.

Rao Sahib's first impulse on seeing the man lying naked in the biting air was to close the two buttons of his woollen coat.

A middle-aged man, another seth, stood with folded hands a little distance away, his bright blue kurta, white pyjama and orange padagi making him an assortment of cheap candies. A servant stood behind him, one hand raised to protect his nose from the tart stench of the nude man. In the other, he held a small bundle.

'Oghad Baba, give me a few digits please.' There was a trace of strain on the seth's feminine voice. It seemed he had been standing there for long.

'Cunt, how many wives do you have?' the Aghori asked petulantly.

'One, Baba, only one.'

'Scat, you! Even Draupadi had better sense to have five husbands!' He spat on the side, a thick blob of cough.

'One … Five … Many, many thanks, Baba!' The seth buckled up in reverence to do his Pranam.

On cue, the servant put the bundle of ghee-smeared rotis on the side of the blanket and hastened after his smiling seth.

'*Khamma ghani*, Thakur Sahib,' the seth sang as he walked past Rao Sahib's horse. 'I got my numbers for satta.'

Rao Sahib looked at him with distaste. He was not here to get lucky numbers for *gambling*. His purpose was much more complex. Only an ascetic who consumed cadavers, worshipped Shiva the destroyer and Kali the goddess of death, and sought moksha from this cycle of rebirth, could guide him.

Doonga held the reins as Rao Sahib fumbled down the back of Lankeshwar and stretched his own back. It took his disused legs some time to adjust to the weight of his torso. He walked up to the banyan tree, his body tipsy, his mind alert, his dhoti crumpled.

Rao Sahib bowed to the Aghori, who flung a string of abuses at him.

'Curse as you may, Oghad Baba, but your child needs your help today.'

The Aghori kept swearing, asking him to leave him alone.

'I've fucked four-thousand-five-hundred-and-fifty-five times in my life,' the Aghori snapped, picked up a barfi and chewed it with an open mouth and exaggerated chopping sounds.

'I do not want numbers, revered Baba,' Rao Sahib pleaded. 'I just want your blessings. Before I left my estate today morning, I went to the mazaar—the tomb of the Peer Baba in my fort. I also visited the shrine of Hanuman ji, my personal deity.'

The Aghori toyed with the Rudraksha beads around his neck and rubbed his hairy nipple. Birds made a racket on the branches of the banyan tree.

'I only want your *ashirwad,*' Rao Sahib begged again for his blessings. He straightened up, looked around to check no one was within hearing range except Doonga and Lankeshwar. The audacious seth he had encountered at Surajpol Gate turned the bend and began walking towards the banyan tree with purpose. Two servants tailed him. Another greedy man coming to the Aghori to seek fortune. Rao Sahib had to hurry up.

'It is about Sanaz, Dada Bhai's daughter,' he whispered urgently.

The Aghori straightened, stood up on his blanket and grazed his back on the trunk of the banyan, all this while his lips trembling. He cocked his head from side to side, scratching his balls and looking intently at Rao Sahib. His face warped in a smile ...he laughed. And laughed. And laughed.

17

Suġra, Dada Bhai's Mother

Dada Bhai's House

Bohrawadi

SUĠRA HEARD THE DOOR GROAN AND WHEELED AROUND. THE other widow stood there. The widow who ran their house and understood Suġra's grandchildren better than she did. Who was nondescript in her bearings and prodigious in the respect she commanded. The widow with whom she had a combustible relationship. Badi Bi. The magic creature of the house. Bent double under the invisible weight of family secrets.

What her daughter had just told her was whizzing in Suġra's head as the widow in a white salwar kurta, one of the three dresses she owned, greeted Khadija with a cheerful Aadaab. An off-white woollen shawl looped around her arms and head loosely covering her grey hair. The shawl was poised on the forehead, just a pull away to veil her face in a ghoonghat if a man came by. She lugged her heavy, bent frame into the room with sluggish grace, her silver anklets tinkling thinly.

'Did you have your milk, Suġra Bai?' Badi Bi asked Suġra to get her out of the conversation's way.

She sat on the divan by Khadija's side and patted her cheek.

'My Badi bi …' Khadija held the old housekeeper's hand and brought it to her fleshy lips. 'The peele chawal were sublime! No one can make this sweet like you do. I long to have it in Galiyakot.'

'Stay back for a couple of days and we can make all your favourite dishes.'

'Na…' She kept Badi Bi's hand back where it belonged. 'I am leaving in an hour. Qurban Ali will be done with his work. We want to avoid the afternoon throngs on Makar Sankranti.'

'Leaving already? Travelling so much in a day is not good for your back and hips,' Badi Bi croaked rubbing her knees.

'What good are women's hips if they can't give birth?' Khadija drew her legs to her chest and held them like a child she'd never have. She looked piteous, dejected. Another trick she had learnt from her mother. 'Every month, after Mena Bai married Tahir, I used to tease that her belly was not swelling up. Now look at her cache of kids.'

'I don't have children, Beta, but I have all of you, and you have your brothers' and sisters' kids…'

'You are a child widow, Badi Bi. Your husband died when you were just seven years old! Everyone calls me baanjh. Mothers don't want their newly wed daughters to meet me, convinced that my shadow will shrink their wombs too.' A sob escaped Khadija's lips, which Suġra knew was for her benefit.

'Such dark talk at the start of the day! Listen, I've made preparations for mutton and roti. Ask Qurban bhai to drop in and have lunch before you leave for Galiyakot.'

Sugra rolled her rosary piously, learning a lesson from the old sod on how to change a disagreeable topic ever so agreeably.

'He won't, Badi Bi...' Khadija looked at the widow with doleful eyes. The same widow she was insisting Tahir should not lay his eyes on every morning. Sugra smiled inwardly.

'I heard your younger brother is visiting you.'

'Not me, Badi Bi. Abbas has come to pay homage at the holy mazaar. I just met him and his wife once in Galiyakot this time. What fun is it to visit a sister whose house is not bursting with nephews and nieces?'

'*Aye Chori* ... you think most unnecessary things! He hardly visits his own mother. Ask Sugra Bai.'

Sugra's grunt was non-committal.

'*Ya Allah*...' Badi Bi got up from the divan, putting the whole weight of flab on her stiff knees—her dearest woe. 'I think Sugra Bai will have to settle for dal-chawal-palita instead of mutton-roti.'

'I am just an old, lonely woman who has lost all interest in life, Badi Bi. I am no Mena Bai you need to please.' Sugra willed for Badi Bi to stay back a while longer. She didn't want to resume the dreaded conversation with her daughter in this cold-hearted winter morning.

Badi Bi didn't take the bait. 'So dal-chawal-palita for lunch, then.' She trudged towards the wide-open door and stopped. 'My salaam to Qurban Bhai. Stay for longer next time!'

With the last command, she waddled towards the steep staircase on the other side of the veranda.

Khadija waited for her to climb a few steps and disappear from sight. She turned towards her mother, quick as a cat.

'Aai, did you hear what I said?'

'I guess I heard it wrong. It can't be about invoking the jeevti dakkan. Excuse my fading senses, Beta...'

Khadija got up from the divan and sashayed towards her, placing her bottom on Suġra's bed firmly. 'Do you want to see me happy, Aai, or what? Finally, when I have found a way out of my misery, you are turning a deaf ear towards your daughter's pleas.'

'I am deaf from both ears...'

'What you are is partial,' Khadija's voice reduced to a threatening whisper. 'You try to shelter Mena, who has rained disgrace on the family by crossing all limits—educating other women, wearing a saree, having visitors the whole day. Next thing she'll do is wear pants, like Tahir does. Mark my words, she will!' She waggled her finger furiously. 'If it were any of your other children, who had asked for a *small* favour, even your precious daughters who have abandoned you and gone to Pakistan, you'd have pulled the living witch out of the peepul tree by her petticoat!'

'Pull the living witch out of the tree by her petticoat! Ah-ha-ha-ha...' Ismail's laugh shattered the disquiet. He had stepped in holding a tray with two glasses. 'Khadija Apa, you're my hero!'

The daughter and mother sat stunned on the bed, gaping at the servant boy.

'Badi Bi's compliments.' The bamboo of a man pushed through the room against their combined will. 'Hot and sweetened saffron milk.' With an elaborate, practised sweep of a hand, he placed the silver tray on the bed.

'Run away, Bhandora!' Suġra collected her wits and swung them at the servant. 'This pig will give me a heart attack someday.'

Ismail took two steps back and pouted his paper-thin lips. 'Khadija Apa ... tell Aai not to be so hard on me. It is not only you she is unfair to, see?'

Khadija froze. Suġra wondered how much of their conversation he had overheard.

'I am not your Aai,' she said instead, silently cursing the idiot of a daughter.

Ismail smirked and pointed at the jharokha. Khadija spun her head towards the seating by the window before Suġra could move hers. The gift box of bokhoor lay asleep on it, face down.

'Can I take the empty bowl?' Ismail held his chin with two fingers, as if he was meditating on a philosophical question.

'Shut your trap and get lost!' Suġra remembered the bowl of sticky yellow rice lying near the bokhoor box.

'I guess that's a yes.' Ismail walked to the jharokha smugly, whisked the empty bowl and walked towards the door. 'See you later ... *Aai!* With another laugh, he was gone.

Khadija got up, went to the door and closed it. Suġra was a trapped mouse. Trapped with a cat. Her throat ached with the cold water she had guzzled down a while back. The holler of a kite flyer made her jerk. The early war cry of Makar Sankranti had managed to stir even Suġra's feeble ears. The other call that reached her thrice a day without fail was the azaan from the Bohra mosque. War and religion had what it took to get themselves heard.

'You know, my dear daughter ... a piece of my own heart, you'll go away to your caring Qurban Ali. Even though you may believe I don't have many days left, I have to live those days in this very house. In this pleasant room near the toilet, in the excellent company of the two stag heads.' Sugra had placed her rosary on a side and moved to the edge of the bed.

'This dog Ismail should be thrown back on the street! Tahir is too lenient to keep him despite knowing that he is a thief. Look at him creeping in on us!' Kadija rolled the corner of her odhani around her middle finger in an angry knot.

'The walls may not have ears, Khadija ... but *we* sure have a brain in our heads. Have you heard about being *discreet*?' Sugra's own voice sounded to her more crusty than usual owing to a trace of pleading, which she was not used to. 'Just leave me out of this.'

'But Aai, I'm not asking much of you. I know someone who'll come and give you the potion today. This is *one* thing you can do in your lifetime to make me, your eldest daughter, happy.' Khadija got up from the bed, agitated. The odhani covering her head fell on her shoulders, her curls springing up in freedom.

Sugra clutched the ivory head of her walking stick and shuffled to get up. Fear ballooned in her chest, making it difficult to breathe. She wanted to go. Go anywhere away from this devious bed. She got to her feet and looked up at her daughter. There was a time when she was as tall as Khadija. The growing years had made her shrink to Khadija's shoulders.

'Do what you must, but keep me out of this.' She tottered to the door and flung it open.

'Aai...' Khadija's voice turned balmy. 'You are not Adam Nabi who has tasted the fruit of the forbidden tree. This will not be your original sin.'

Sugra remained fixed on the spot. Needles of cold jabbed from underneath her skin as she contemplated her lifelong confidante. The schemer of her little schemes. The executioner of her little commands. The blackmailing bitch. Suǧra learnt that there are many lessons to be learnt, even in your dry old age (why did they call it 'ripe old age' when there was no juice left in you?). The lesson: there are no such things as confidantes. A secret should be best kept a secret.

18

Parijat, the Nightsoil Worker

Kachchi Basti

Delhi Gate

IN THE EARLY MORNING CHILL, PARIJAT STRODE FROM THEIR settlement near Delhi Gate to the main town with purpose. She wanted to put her morning rounds behind her, scrub herself clean and be free for the afternoon. A dull gold light flushed the stubbled cheeks of the Aravalli hills, reminding her of Gokul's feverish face.

The part of the city where she worked was divided into neat little chunks. Karwadi for Muslims. Khateekwada for halal butchers. Bohrawadi for Bohras. Mochiwada for mochis—the cobblers. Choti Bohrawadi lined with grocery shops. Maldar ji Street and Ghanta Ghar dominated by Hindu Baniya shops.

Bada Bazaar for Bohra merchants selling clothes and utensils. Life was straight lines in the city. Unlike her forest back home, where it was crooked and amorphous and misbehaved. Trees leaning over each other, green with immodesty. Squirrels sniffing and biting what they fancied. Breeze caressing or whacking at will, accountable to no one. It was a world not run by the rules of religions. The conceit of clerics. The lechery of landlords.

The city had its own advantages, though. So far, it had been caning-free. It had given her a solid career in manual scavenging and a few interesting chance encounters. Like the one with Dada Bhai's wife. It was a crisp summer afternoon when Parijat had halted in a by-lane in Hatipol hearing Mena Bai's name. A few Hindu and Muslim ladies in various stages of purdah were stepping out of a building, filling the path with soft jingles and titters. Some had completely covered faces, others half-covered eyes. Most of them said their Aadaab and Pranaam to Mena Bai and left, walking past Parijat, maintaining an arm's length from the untouchable. This building was called Mahila Sabha—the assembly of women. Parijat had stopped to hear the talk, pretending to sweep the other side of the path. Only two women remained.

'…but we must go to Garima's house tomorrow and get her. Even if her in-laws protest.' Mena Bai was in a green cotton saree, with the pallu thrown carelessly over her head. Her face was exquisite. Chiselled by a god in love with his own creation.

'She is a child widow, Mena Bai,' the Hindu woman said disapprovingly from behind her red veil, which she had pulled in front of her face as soon as she left the confines of the building.

'Precisely why we should convince the mother-in-law to let her learn how to read and write,' countered Mena Bai, whose long, thick braid reached her knees. 'She is nine, Sunanya Bai, just *nine*. The union of India is giving equal rights to both men and women. Society as we know it is going to change drastically in the next ten years. We need to prepare these little girls for a new world order.'

'I understand what you say about female literacy. You've succeeded in convincing more than half of your Bohra community and some of the Agarwal and Rajput families about it, even at the cost of men pelting stones at your place. But child widows are a different story.' Sunanya shook her head, her pose uppity. 'This time they wouldn't pelt stones, they will set your house on fire.'

'You have achieved what no one else could in this city. Don't throw it all away.' The older Bohra woman clad in a plain ghaghra-odhani, her head covered and face bare, rubbed her puffed-up eyes. 'Dada Bhai is very supportive of what you do, Mena Bai, and we know his status in society has helped us with the literacy drive. But the road to rebellion has to be tread with gentle steps. Sunanya Bai is right. To disturb the equation of child widows in society ... It is not a beehive, it is a snake's nest.'

'I am attached to that girl. It is not about this big cause of child widows. It is about Garima. *Her* life.' Mena Bai's thin gold bangles scintillated in the sunlight falling in the by-lane.

'Have you heard that age-old adage of "greater good"?' the Bohra woman said sagely, her nath trembling as she spoke. 'We'll fight this battle when we are prepared for it. Right now, even our allies will turn against us if we do. It is all overwhelming— the exodus of the British, the end of monarchy, the emergence of a new political order ... democracy they call it. We have to allow society to churn internally.'

'My mind understands what you mean. But I have a heart, which just wouldn't agree.' Mena Bai's thick, curving eyelashes fluttered, two free-spirited sunbirds.

Parijat could sense Mena Bai's form under the cotton garment. The delicate curve of her neck. The gentle bulge of her breasts. Her midriff flat and smooth. Her complexion creamy and delicate; she was a *gori mem,* a white madam, with glistening black hair.

The oldish woman answered in a voice used by priests before a funeral, 'The heart doesn't listen, Mena Bai, it beats its unreasonable whims into you.'

'Choose your crusades smartly, Mena Bai. Say…' Sunanya turned her head and pierced her gaze through her veil at Parijat working on the side. '…who will send their daughters to study here if you get *her…*' She jerked her head in Parijat's direction. '…a Bhangi or a Chamar, to study at Mahila Sadan? The families might still accept a tribal … a Bhil girl sitting on a side and learning. But an untouchable? Never! Even I wouldn't.'

Mena Bai sighed sadly looking at Parijat for a long moment. Something changed under the veneer of Mena Bai's soft gaze; it acquired the dogged look Parijat had sensed in the posters of leaders. The look that chose the battles they would fight. And those they would abandon.

'So be it then.' Mena Bai turned to the two older women. 'We will not go to Garima's in-laws' place. But … *only* till the time we are prepared to fight the harder battle.'

The women managed a half-triumphant, half-grudging nod as Mena Bai walked back into the building.

Parijat heard the tautness in Sunanya's words as the two women passed her, their clothes swishing, anklets clinking. 'Mena Bai is un-contained. The British shared some of those values. Our society doesn't. Some may admire her, but others hate her guts.'

'I agree, Sunanya Bai,' the Bohra woman replied anxiously. 'It is not men but women who despise her. Many of them are just waiting for her to make one wrong move. All our efforts of the last seven years ... burning the night oil ... everything that we have done together ... even fighting the resistance from our families, will come to nought.'

Parijat had squeezed herself against the wall to give ample space to the passing women. They kept on talking as if they would never run out of conversations, like she had. For them, Parijat was no more than a lizard stuck to the wall.

She had often thought about that encounter recalling each detail. How graciously Mena Bai turned her head on her delicate neck. The magnificence of her long-drawn sigh. She was a mythical being come to life. An extraordinary woman, both in her grit and her form. The real-life Rai Devi of a Gavari performance. And each time she thought of that bright afternoon with Mena Bai, her mind was pulled to that grey afternoon, three years back, in her village.

Her thirteen-year-old bare feet had slurped and squelched on the dirt path as she kept rhythm with Doonga's gait, walking to the Haveli where the old Rao Sahib was waiting to die. Mud puddles dimpled the trail, nourishing the parched skin of the Aravalli hills. Her hair had sprung up in little curls with the dampness. Winged insects sprung in the still air, making the most of the short lull in the rains. The tanned landscape had donned a velvety odhani of green. Grass had sprouted on the slopes and the thorny shrubs had lost their menacing look to the tenderness of new-born leaves. The air carried the delicious smell of wet earth.

Doonga made her wait in the middle of the Haveli in the open courtyard, which had corridors running on three sides, as he went to get water to wash her feet. It was then that this man with brisk steps walked towards her from the main entrance. He wore a smart hat with two hawk feathers and was clothed in the suit-boot of the British gora sahibs.

'Little girl…' He stopped before climbing the steps to the corridor. 'Are you from here?'

Parijat swung her head from side to side, holding a pleat of her ghaghra for support.

'I am looking for Rao Sahib's quarters.' His voice carried the sound of rushes by a rivulet. 'I sent the boy, who had got me here, back to the stable. Forgot my walking stick there.'

Parijat stood looking at him as if he was the most perfect thing she had seen in her life. Long fingers ending in half-moons of nails, clean-shaven jaw, liquid eyes holding her forest stream in them.

'Is it here, or there?' The man tried again, pointing at the corridor on the other side.

'*Khamma ghani,* Hukam!' Doonga chirped his greeting with a broad smile, holding a jug full of water in his hand. Parijat had never seen him so happy.

'Doonga!' said the man turning on his shiny leather boots. 'Just the man I wanted to see. How are you, my friend?'

'What a surprise, Dada Bhai ji Sahib!' Doonga bent low, his hands folded over the jug.

'Well, I'm here on a short hunting trip. My friend Jaswant Singh ji has invited me for a hakka. I'm staying at the fort with him. Just came to the Haveli to pay his father, the old Rao Sahib, my respects.

Doonga remembered the water in his hand. He couldn't hand over the mug to an untouchable so he poured it on to Parijat's feet. She rubbed one foot above the other as Doonga continued to talk to the visitor from the city with genuine respect.

'I was just asking this little girl where his quarters are.' Dada Bhai came and stood near them.

'This one can't speak, Hukam.' Doonga kept the mug on a side.

'I'm so sorry! Is she one of your daughters?'

Doonga cast his eyes down. 'Um … no, Hukam. A relative.'

Dada Bhai patted a couple of his puffed-up coat pockets and dug his hand into one. He drew out a fist. 'Here, child, take this.'

Parijat was the trunk of a banyan tree that couldn't move even if it willed.

Doonga said in a comforting voice, 'Take it, Parijat.'

She extended a hand, shyly. The elegant man dropped a few hard toffees in her hand. Night blue, moss green, dusk red. He patted her a couple of times on her head.

Doonga nodded appreciatively and glanced back at the man in raw devotion. A strong gust of wind herded dark clouds in the sky, wrapping the three of them in monsoon shadows.

'You'll show me where Rao Sahib is?' Dada Bhai asked Doonga, half-turning towards the steps.

'Right away, Hukam!' Doonga turned towards Parijat. 'Wait on the side. We'll do our work later.'

He hurried away, leading Dada Bhai towards Rao Sahib's room, leaving Parijat in a pool of bewilderment. Except her brother Valmiki, whom she had seen years back, no one had been kind to her. No one. Men gaped at her body, which was changing form, with lewd interest. Women looked at her as if piss ran in her veins. She looked at her extended hand holding clumps of coloured sugar. Words congealed on her amputated tongue. Tiny needles stabbed her skin, making small eruptions of goosebumps. She could feel her heartbeat in her fingertips. Her eyes stung. A tear spilt from the wild waterfall she had contained within her.

Plop ... A thick raindrop fell on her face. Wind blew, lifting away the sadness that blocked her pores. A bolt of lightning came crashing out of the clouds, and left the world with a roar. It resonated in her chest, warming up her body. For the first time in her life, Parijat felt *she* was the lightning. There was fire in her mouth and she wanted to roar like a thunderclap. He had given her toffees. She had given him her heart. Parijat would never forget the moment she fell in love with Dada Bhai.

19

Hariharan, the Middleman

Bohrawadi

Udaipur

H ARIHARAN'S FINGERS WERE CURLED AROUND A GLASS FULL TO the brim with Rooh Afza. He didn't sip it. He sat there, trying to match its red hue to the carpet and curtains on the small windows of the ground floor room. He loved the voluptuous body of anticipation ... the thrill of feeling the small of her back, the unexpected bulge, the sudden sensual sweat, an abrupt crease. Today, there was too much at stake to enjoy the foreplay. Today, anticipation made him nervous. Didn't give him a hard-on but an uncontrolled bowel.

'*Naush farmaiye*,' the man with a henna-dyed beard and paan-stained mouth urged him to drink in forced Urdu. He had a feeble, womanly voice. A silver spittoon was placed at an arm's length on the carpet.

Hariharan, seated on a mat spread on the lush rug to protect it, widened his smile. 'I didn't know you had such nice living quarters, Bohra ji Kamruddin Sahib. Last time I met you in your shop.'

Kamruddin smiled condescendingly, exposing a set of betel-stained teeth that Hariharan immediately matched with the colour of Rooh Afza. He rubbed his forehead and flakes of dried-up tilak fell down his face; red again. *Omens can't be ignored*, he thought and held the glass tighter. He would never have a drink in a Mohammedan household. Dada Bhai understood this and did not even offer him. But, here, he couldn't refuse, couldn't let a sweet red liquid come in the way of his future prosperity. His polluted dharma could be set straight with a pandit's purification puja. But a deal once broken ... no pandit could set it right.

'It's not that your shop is not nice ... it is. *Very*. Rolls and rolls of the finest silk from Benaras, Kanjeevaram, Mysore, Assam. You may be the biggest silk supplier in Mewar, but what makes you stand out is taste. That is something not many people have, if your humble servant may say so.'

There had been clashes between the Sindhi refugees from Pakistan on their arrival after the Partition and the Muslims of Udaipur. The Bohra shops that dealt in cloth were burnt in the riots. The Sindhis established their own cloth businesses soon after. Kamruddin was one of the few who had sensed the shadows approaching and diversified into iron. Something which fires of hate couldn't consume. He was able to deal with the losses better than most other Bohra businesses in town and had even managed to restart his silk trading.

'Yes, you may say so. Mashallah, my taste is legendary.' Kamruddin's smile turned self-indulgent. He knew a few Urdu words and stressed on them in his speech, which was a weedy garden of the Waghari dialect. He sat bare-headed at home. Hariharan saw his ginger hair with middle parting for the first time, finding it to be more vulgar than anything else on his person—the silk kurta pyjama, the lopsided smile, the wrinkles covered in a film of oil, the strong smell of sandalwood attar, the tapering face ending in a broom of a beard. The head with ginger hair looked as if it had rusted but didn't have the decency to crumble.

The Bohra merchant's chambers were decorated according to his garish taste. A thin stream of music trickled in from the adjoining room, the one that belonged to his second wife; a juicy pear if accounts were to be believed. The record of a black-and-white Hindi film played on the gramophone; the only other in town was owned by Dada Bhai.

Hariharan understood the importance of preliminary small talk. It blunted sharp-edged truths to rounded lies. There were protocols to perjury. And Hariharan was intent on following them.

He spun small webs of talk, rubbing his knees and Kamruddin's ego. Men had begun to gather on the rooftops, clutching their kites. A bunch of little rogues ran past the window, shouting and rolling a tyre with a long stick.

'I am happy to see your respected self, first thing in the morning on this pious day of Makar Sankranti.' Hariharan folded his hands and bowed his head.

Kamruddin nodded in acknowledgement of this obvious fact.

Happiness is the most overrated thing in the world, Lal Chand Mahajan had told Hariharan when he had tried the same line on him, some days back. *Ever heard of a really happy koel or a jubilant tiger?* he'd asked. *The well-being of a koel hangs on her cunning, on the devoted crow couple she will deceive by planting her eggs in their nest. That of a tiger on his ferocity, on the throat he will rip apart. Koel and tigers are celebrated in cultures and literature, and not because they are happy. The only happy beings are dogs,* he'd said, *who should be used for their loyalty.* Parting with another rare morsel of wisdom, Mahajan had added, *the real successful people are those who can sell this ridiculous commodity—happiness—to others with the sincerity of a dying man.* Hariharan had not noted it down in his mental ledger. He had let this hard-earned advice become a part of his functioning.

'So what brings you here?' Kamruddin asked with feigned interest.

Hariharan cleared his throat of phlegm, the by-product of an early winter morning foray.

An elderly man stepped into the room, a scruffy white topi placed on his head. 'Maimoona Bai says we have run out of mutton. I need to go to Khateekwada, Sahib.'

'Today is Makar Sankranti, you fool! No butcher would be open, tell this to the old hag.'

Hariharan had passed this servant sitting on the porch making soap with harandi oil and caustic soda. Most people in Bohrawadi made their own soap. Hariharan wanted to pick up a soap and scrub his hands raw. He was a pious vegetarian man, and yet he was holding a glass which had been in the same kitchen where they cooked meat dripping with blood ... probably prepared by the 'old hag' Kamruddin referred to— his first wife. Hariharan steadied his shiver and rearranged the smile on his face. His family should damn well remember the sacrifices he makes for them.

'You were saying…' Kamruddin picked up the spittoon and spat a jet of red saliva in it.

'You had shown some interest in marrying Sanaz, Dada Bhai's daughter,' began Hariharan.

'Only after you gave me the idea.' Kamruddin's smile was of a hyena in the middle of its meal, salivating and blood-splattered.

Sell happiness … Mahajan's advice purred in Hariharan's head. 'She is the loveliest of creatures … imagine the ethereal beauty of Mena Bai combined with Dada Bhai's handsome features.' Hariharan recited the rehearsed words.

'So you say. I haven't seen her.' The words came out wimpy.

'Will your honourable self lend Dada Bhai the money without interest? If so, I can drop a gentle reminder to him that you'd like his daughter's hand in marriage. And, of course, to offer you a partnership in his business.'

'I haven't seen the girl,' Kamruddin repeated. Caution had crept in his eager, moist eyes.

'But you've heard the rumours of her beauty. And seen her apsara of a mother?'

Kamruddin wiped the corner of his mouth with a pensive thumb. The Bohras had nicknamed him Vichuda Kamar—Kamar the scorpion. Bohras of Udaipur had this irrepressible habit of giving nicknames to one and all—Bastar (the bed) Burhaan, Dadu (granddad) Damani, Gorkha (Nepali) Hatim. No one had dared given a nickname to Tahir, aka Dada Bhai. Dada plus Bhai was just a way to address him with double the measure of respect.

'You know I am a big disciple of Mahatma Gandhi ji Sahib. I work tirelessly for the greater good of society. I believe in getting two parties together who will benefit the most from each other.'

'Does that mean you don't want your cut in the deal?' Kamruddin asked, fussing with his overgrown toenails.

'Hehe ... you have a great sense of humour, Bohra ji, that is why I like doing business with you. A most refined sense. It is so disarming.' The day was turning warmer and Hariharan fidgeted with his shawl. 'What all I had to do to convince that leech of a moneylender Lal Chand Mahajan to not lend money to Dada Bhai. How shrewd that old man is! I had to warn him that he might never get his interest back. Or the capital. Dada Bhai might not land the tender for catechu that he has applied for.'

'You think so?'

'No, no, I don't!' Hariharan's double chin wobbled as he shook his head. 'But I had to convince Lal Chand about it. The Indian government is struggling to find its footing. They would certainly want to lease the catechu forests to a man of Dada Bhai's stature and experience in running a business of that scale. With his erstwhile ninety-eight sulphur shops in Mewar, his appeal to both Hindus and Muslims and not to forget the trust that Maharana Bhupal Singh ji Maharaj has in him ... well, he stands a better chance than anyone else to land the contract.'

'Ba ji ... Are you coming?'

Hariharan turned towards the door to see a light-skinned young man standing with a kite. The long kite-tail trailed on the floor. He was a good specimen of youth—cheeks darkened with careless stubble, hair slick with oil, half-bored, half in a hurry to get on with life, confident posture, sufficiently rude.

'I will soon join you on the terrace, my boy.' Kamruddin nodded at the young man, who Hariharan noted was older than Dada Bhai's daughter Sanaz.

'My oldest son,' he said grandly, once the boy left leaving a scent of springtime behind.

'Masallah…' Hariharan too had learnt a few Urdu words to impress his prospective clients, though the 'sha' always came out as 'sa'.

'So if you have already convinced Lal Chand to not lend any money to Dada Bhai, what is the hurry? Why do you want an answer from me right away?'

'Thing is…' Hariharan agonized over his whispering from a distance and bent forward. 'I have inside information. Rao Sahib of Singhgarh is visiting him today. He wants to make an offer to his dear friend, Dada Bhai.'

'What kind of offer?' Kamruddin's question gurgled with the paan spit gathered in his mouth.

'There is some speculation, but what seems probable is that he has come to offer him fat chunks of land from his estate. Landholdings will be annexed from the royalty and landlords all across Hindustan by our new masters. For a more equal distribution of wealth. Hah! As if that can ever happen. Anyway, Rao Sahib will have to surrender it in due course. Might as well gift it to his trusted friend.'

'Isn't your Dada Bhai a man of high principles? I don't think he'll take it.'

Hariharan knew the lofty image of Dada Bhai was a sore spot for Kamruddin. A few years back, there was a meeting of the top merchants of the region. The uptight gora—the British Resident Col. Beetham—had actually got up to shake the young brown man's hand when he had walked in, offending Kamruddin profoundly.

'Your wisdom is unquestionable,' Hariharan put in, a bit too eagerly. 'Yes, he might reject his offer. But what if he accepts? If he knows he has another option … *you* … he just might not.'

Kamruddin ejected red saliva in his spittoon again, wiping the side of his mouth with his silk handkerchief. 'The man thinks my prudence and pragmatism is beneath his nobleness.' He glanced out of the window, drawn to the high-pitched voices of the kite fighters.

'Bohra ji, Dada Bhai is ministerial material, prime ministerial, even.' Hariharan veiled his desperation to get the merchant's attention under a forced sneeze. 'Imagine the social ladder to be climbed if you're tied in marriage with his family.'

The song on the gramophone finished, and the record whirred in suspenseful silence.

'As you know, I have an Agarwal partner,' Kamruddin said, eventually. 'I want five Bohra cooks for the Muslim guests and two pandit cooks for the Hindu guests at the wedding dinner.'

'Ah,' Hariharan drew back and exhaled, his guts wanting to empty in relief. 'That's very doable.'

'I can give you only five per cent for your services. That is the final offer.' Kamruddin got up, spilling the smell of sandalwood attar in the room, a merchant done with the bargaining for the day and ready to swing down his shutter.

Hariharan's smile, plastered to his face, threatened to chip off. But he nodded in complete understanding of his partial failure and gulped down his drink of Rooh Afzah.

20

Nathu, the Bhil

Jogion ka Guda

Aravalli Hills

THE FIRST THING NATHU WAS TO LOSE TO ADULTHOOD WAS
the love of everything tangy. His tongue had always been a
slave for the citrusy and lemony. The wild amla, lime, tamarind,
karonda ... he used to compete with birds and squirrels to raid
the fruiting trees and shrubs. That tingling on his tongue. That
swell of saliva in his mouth. Since last night, his father Jaitya
had begun to reek of a zesty fruit. Nathu controlled his urge to
retch as he stood, in the early morning hours, away from the
porch, staring at the hut he dared not enter. The hut with a
solitary flavour.

The first stirrings of dawn were all around him. Nathu
would never again be able to chew on amla. Ever. Each time his

171

father Jaitya visited Dada Bhai, he carried a handful of dried and salted amla for him. A small gift, of a small forest produce, from a small forest person. Dada Bhai's gratitude was always large. A bit out of proportion. Like the reaction of the workers on that hot summer day. Jaitya was to meet Dada Bhai in the village of Chandesra, where one of his many sulphur shops was located. He had taken little Nathu along with him on the journey. That day, Dada Bhai had unwittingly stepped into the hut where his workers kept their matki, the clay pots for holding potable water. Soon after he left Chandesra, the workers had taken out the pots one by one and smashed them on the rocks, spilling the cool, drinking water. The cracked earth had slurped it away hungrily. He may be their boss, but he was a Mussalman. They couldn't let his presence stain their dharma. Nathu thought it was absurd. The workers had bought the pots from that very Mussalman's money—one anna for each matki.

Nathu stood near the porch and rubbed his eyes. A snake, which had probably gulped down a frog, lay curled on the side of the mahua tree with enduring patience. Nathu was wary of gods, witches and spirits, but strangely, not of snakes. He felt kinship with them. These reptiles protected their wealth—the food grains and agricultural fields—by eating rats. In turn, they were persecuted by humans for their service. A lazy note of a grey hornbill made him look up a fig tree. The bird sat half-awake on a branch, killing time. Like Nathu.

'*Hangaar karwa chalo!*' Jaitya's cry sent a sharp jolt through Nathu's spine, making him shiver. His father had been raving on and off in delirium, repeating the call of the tribals to gather for a hakka. They would go cheerfully with Dada Bhai for a beat as they were sure to get a share of the hunt. With the zamindars, the only thing the tribals got was a hiding if an animal escaped from their side of the circle or if they failed to flush out the beasts from the thicket.

Nathu pictured his wife Thawari bending over Jaitya in the hut, wiping the sweat off his forehead and cooing him back to his unconscious state. Yet he kept standing outside feeling short of breath, with pinpricks on his nape and barbs on his lips. He craved the calming smell of his now-dead bull Bhoora. The soothing rhythm of his jaws moving as he regurgitated … *kat-kat-kat-kat*. His dung cakes were plastered on the walls of their bamboo hut in dense circles. His cool nonchalance to the ways of the world. On Bhoora's death a week back, Nathu had seen his father lament loudly for the first time; Jaitya had lost the company of the only male in the world who shared his burden.

Thawari appeared at the dark door of the hut and stepped out with an aluminium jug full of Jaitya's vomit. Seeing Nathu, she halted for a moment. Placing the jug on the mud porch, she wrapped herself tighter in her own arms and walked towards him.

'Why are you standing here?' Much shorter than Nathu, she always had to throw her head back to look at him.

A faint smell of vomit and gossamer-covered moneylender's ledgers smothered him. He opened his mouth, gasping for breath.

Thawari slipped her plump fingers into his hand, which hung by his side. A moment passed. Then two. She came closer and gently rubbed her thumb on his knuckles. His slamming heart slackened its pace.

'Calm down…'

'Ak-ak-ak…' The plough of his tongue was lodged in rocks.

'Shh…' Thawari quietened him and drew him in an embrace.

Nathu held her tight and glanced up in a silent prayer. The sky was a shimmering black garment of silk he would never own. He looked down at the bundle in his arms and realized he didn't need the sky. As his rigid body started to loosen, Thawari pulled away. Her lac bangles clicked thickly.

'Listen, Nathu.' She had not let go of his hand. It was way too early in the morning and no one was out to see this public display of affection. 'We have to do this. I have taken out your pagadi and dhoti-angarkha. Get dressed. I've also packed two maize rotis and an onion that Chatra Ba had got yesterday for your journey, and kept a char-anna coin in your angarkha's pocket. And yes, a small packet of salted amla for Dada Bhai.'

Nathu shook his head.

'It will not be such an arduous journey. By dawn, you'll meet other Bhils on the way. Before you know, it you'll be at Dada Bhai's place.'

Yes, towards dawn he would find Bhils from the nearby villages marching to the city in dusty strides, intent on selling their forest produce outside the shaharpana. Some of them would be carrying grains of millet or bajra to the grain Mandi. There would be women carrying on their heads what they called mooli—six- to seven-foot-long bundles of firewood—to be sold to the city households.

But he was not going to the city to sell a sack of wild berries. No, no … he moved his head again from side to side. Fear drummed his chest in a dozen different beats.

'You know it's not that, Th-th-thaa-thaa…' Blue veins bulged on his neck. He couldn't move the rock placed in his mouth.

'Look at the hut, Nathu. Your beloved father is lying inside with one last wish.' Thawari kept her gaze fixed on him, her round face a calm full moon floating in a river.

The hut stood where it was. It was the resident in it who was hurtling towards his end. Nathu could hear the muffled steps of Jaitya's departure. The man with a set of unequal eyes taking away with him a hundred melodies. Every Bhil was born with the failures of his forefathers. A few could cradle them like a baby and sing them a lullaby.

Jaitya had spoken to him coherently last evening. This was after hours of writhing and sweating in pain and waking up every time with a '*Hangaar karwa chaloo!*' cry. His father had called him to sit by the side of his cot and patted Nathu's hand to console him. Thawari, the only one in her senses in the household, had sent out the word to Nathu's sisters in two distant villages, but he knew the news would not reach them in time. Nathu had sat in the light of the sticky lantern, squeezing back his father's good hand and tasting snot and tears in his mouth.

Puk puk puk ... the coppersmith's notes echoed in the hills, imitating the noise of a grain grinder. Jaitya's dirty langot was clumped around his thighs. Nathu could see the roof of his mouth where a white layer had deposited, a pall covering him from the inside out. Red veins had appeared in his eyes, cracking them up.

Jaitya had gone on talking, his ravaged chest heaving with effort, 'Too many holes on my little boat. It is sinking now ... This is the last thing I ask of you, Son.'

And maybe the first, Nathu had thought. But he sat exasperated. He had let go of his father's trembling hand and his fist lay on the cot in an angry lump. Nathu clenched his teeth in rage, biting his tongue. Tasting blood.

Jaitya's red-veined eyes had been imploring ... asking for a favour, asking for a final act of solace, asking for forgiveness ...

since he had revealed his terrible secret. Silence had curdled in the hut. There on the cot lay Nathu's angel of woe. Flavoured with the rot of decaying days.

And now, Nathu stood in the hours that were passing hands from night to morning, staring at Thawari with a hunted look. The wilderness stretched and scratched in its sleep. A rustle here. A swish there.

'You must get ready to go, Nathu,' Thawari said in a temperate voice, much too wise for her young years.

He didn't move.

She placed her hands on his shoulders, hauled herself up on her toes and whispered in his ear. And then, she gently put herself back on her bare feet.

Nathu looked at his wife swathed in a shawl, her breath still moist on his ear. She moved her hand to her belly and rubbed the slight bulge.

He swayed on his feet. Suddenly, the world had become immense. A mountain without a peak. He was overcome by vertigo. He tried to concentrate on the small hut. With a small secret. Someone in it passing effortlessly through the net called life.

Nathu turned his head to Thawari and nodded before he shut his eyes and gave himself to a free fall.

LATE AFTERNOON

Makar Sankranti, 1950

21

Thanedar Tapan Singh, the Inspector

Dada Bhai's House

Bohrawadi

HE WANTED TO BE CALLED 'INSPECTOR'. THEY CALLED HIM Thanedar Sahib. Everyone except Dada Bhai, who had been Tapan Singh's paragon. The man he aspired to become, who everyone would look up to. Tapan liked telling anyone who would lend an ear about George Orwell—his other hero. Orwell had served in the Indian Imperial Police in Burma under his real name Eric Blair for seven years from the year 1920. Tapan would often recount Orwell's lament in his essay 'Shooting an Elephant': 'In Moulmein in Lower Burma, I was hated by large numbers of people—the only time in my life that I have been important enough for this to happen to me.' Tapan wanted to reach that woeful state when people hated him for what he did.

Tapan's path of progression was laid clearly before him. First, he had to reach the top. Then he would get disillusioned with the ways of the edgy, blundering, post-imperialist Hindustan. And today, Dada Bhai's daughter Sanaz's mysterious murder presented him an opportunity to rise in the ranks in this new epoch, which was the offspring of the forced marriage of the princely states into a nation.

This part of the house—the cold, dark odha on the ground floor—had two rooms. The locked one was for storage and the other, which Tapan had decided to use, was servants' quarters. The sun rays fell in two shafts from the square, slanting ventilators high up in the thick walls. The room smelt of mouldy bedding. Of cold sweat breaking in warm nights. Of a lingering memory of marijuana going up in smoke. Tapan pulled out his black leather pocket diary from his coat. Similar to the ones the gora sahibs used. The room had been converted into a makeshift office for Tapan and his team. Three chairs and a spare table from Dada Bhai's quarters were hauled down the steep steps of the building and dragged inside. Four lamps had been set ablaze and placed in the corners. Tapan wanted to catch each nervous twitch of a suspect who stepped in his net. Every move of his ambushed prey.

He had come there with two accomplices. The bushy sub-inspector Madho Singh and the corpulent constable Haider Khan. A year after independence from the British, in 1948, the Indian Imperial Police was renamed the Indian Police Service. Except that, nothing had changed. His colleagues still sat in the courtrooms with their hands at the back of their chairs—to accept bribes and change their stance at the last minute. Under oath. Tapan often pondered over the uselessness of oaths—either taken by placing your hand on Gita in the court of law or taken in the presence of fire when you got married. All for optics. The thought of the drooping udders and hairy thighs of his wife made him wipe the ink of his pen on a torn rag. He preferred both his wife at home and Gita in the courts wrapped in swathes of cloth.

An hour and a half back, he had received a call from the Inspector General of Police, who in turn had got a call from the Maharana's durbar. The very best in the police force were to be sent to Dada Bhai's house; didn't matter if their thana—the police station—had Bohrawadi in its jurisdiction. Tapan Singh had been summoned not from the Hatipol thana, but from the annals of the police headquarters behind Ghanta Ghar. This was a case of the highest profile. Juicy with prospects. Saddled with high expectations. Tapan couldn't separate his anxiousness from excitement and felt hot and cold alternately. He rubbed his left eye, much smaller than the right one, always wet and grainy like moisture-laden salt. The sub-standard police force considered Tapan a reasoned-seasoned detective. No one else but he knew that most of the cases he had solved were by accident, not design. But a reputation once built had the strength of a bull. All it needed to keep going were some angry grunts and horns pointed at someone's ass.

He threw his khaki coat on the back of the chair and sat down to calm his nerves and collect his thoughts. Madho Singh filled the ink pot fixed on the table with blue ink and placed a pen holder on the side. Tapan fit his pen in it. The nib, meant to write in the Devnagari script, glistened with memories of half-forgotten crimes. Noises of lament poured down from the lofty building. '*Aye, Bai…*' A woman was crying in a constant tempo, the pitch heaving and falling in tireless waves of grief. A girl would soon be wrapped in a white sheet and swallowed by earth.

'We have cleared all the nearby terraces of kite flyers,' Madho Singh informed Tapan Singh's khaki shirt. He had a habit of speaking to people's elbows, to tree trunks, to chair handles, to anything without eyes. His furry hands were folded in submission over his crotch. Madho carried a pen with a nib to write in the Nastaliq script. Tapan Singh was practising his Urdu writing and one day soon hoped to solve its mystery as well.

'I believe no one has been allowed to leave the premise. I saw a Bhil on the porch.' Tapan Singh placed his small diary with a leather cover on the table.

'No, Sahib, no one goes past this,' said Haider Khan patting his morbidly fat hips.

'Find out each person who has visited this house last night or today, or even peeped inside. Get what I mean?'

'Sahib!' Haider Khan's moustach shivered as he saluted. He went to the door, stopped and turned. 'Even the living witch who lives in the peepul tree outside?'

'Even her.' Tapan Singh's gaze was steady. 'And cut a little on the melodrama.'

Haider Khan had the puppy eyes of a trusting person. They crinkled in a smile as he padded out of the door. He completely lacked the bitterness of the creatures who are themselves distrustful.

Tapan Singh glanced at this little tenacious room. He had to keep moving to ward off the cold in this cavernous place, but he had to keep still to harvest his thoughts. To understand the story of a dead girl. Forever sixteen. A bloodless murder. Poison ... strangling ... motive ... weapon ... black magic? He too had a fourteen-year-old son, his only child. People thought his thin frame was somehow responsible for him not being a virile man. Arrogant simpletons. He was not dry and shrivelled up. He had conducted his marital duties for at least a few years in the mousey morning hours when he was half-torn between sleep and desire. Not anymore. Not anyhow. Not when his morning sleep had left him. Everyone was not Dada Bhai tied in wedlock to a nymph plucked from heaven's gardens.

The man was a myth. The stuff folk songs are made of. An aristocrat, Dada Bhai's father had left him much wealth. But he had not puffed on a hookah and grown fat on it. After obtaining the monopoly for sulphur from the Maharana, who was truly fond of him, he threw a bag, a cook and a stove in the backseat of his car to travel the length and breadth of Mewar, entering into partnerships, giving the franchise of 'Tahir and Sons' to ninety-eight agents—both Baniya and Bohra merchants. He fought with his feudal friends for the rights of the oppressed, especially the tribals, and was a darling of the royalty and politicians. His wife, Mena Bai, to the utter dismay of many a respectable family, had started a women's education movement in Southern Rajputana with his backing. Even the British had sought the company of this straight-backed, disciplined big-game hunter, who was the second-best shooter in the kingdom. His celebrated B-Model Ford attracted hordes of rascals running after it in the streets whenever it carried a proud, dead leopard on its hood. He was famous for his aim, his stubbornness, his acumen, his England-made hat (with hawk feathers), his Urdu, his etiquette, his attire, his fairness, and his partiality towards a well-cooked tongue of a goat. The beautiful dead daughter would not make his myth fall like a shooting star. It would deepen it. Impregnate it with mystery. For what is more lip-smacking-ly alluring than naked grief?

'Everyone has lost interest in kites…' Haider Khan came blundering in, his khaki shorts taut over his pillared thighs. '… and developed it for Dada Bhai's house. We've herded them into their homes, but rumours are in full blast. Sahib, men are lying in wait to get a sneak peek. This is the biggest thriller of the year.'

'Hmm … Has more force arrived from Hatipol police station?' Tapan Singh drummed his long fingers on the table.

'Yes, I've posted the constables around the house and cleared the lanes. Imagine, men were trying to make their women sit on their porches to catch some gossip. I sent them in with a shrill warning.' He fingered the whistle hanging on his liberal belly, which had room for another belt. The buckle bit into the last hole on the belt's tip.

'So everything's in control?'

'Yes. But whose control, we are yet to figure out.' Haider Khan made his earlobes jump.

'We'll need to start questioning those in the house.' Tapan Singh ignored his constable and rubbed his clean-shaven cheeks that collapsed below the cheekbones. The smell of kerosene in the burning lamps had chased away much of the mouldy air. The yellow light cast an illusion of a warm, cosy quarter.

'The Bohras believe in burial on the same day of demise,' Madho Singh's surly voice escaped somewhere from the curls of his black beard. He was almost the same age as Tapan Singh, in his early thirties. But the bushy landscape of his body made him look as primaeval as the Aravalli hills.

'That means we just have two to three hours to examine the crime scene as it is and speak to those who were present, in their most emotionally raw state.' *And preferably solve the case.* Tapan Singh said to himself as he removed his stiff black-and-brown police hat.

'Dada Bhai's brother and his family are visiting the town of Galiyakot, where their holy mazaar is. The sister lives there too. The brother has been sent a telegram and might arrive only by late night. His sister Khadija was visiting Udaipur today morning with her husband, but they left a while back. A constable has been sent on horseback to catch them mid-way and convey the news,' Madho spoke to Tapan Singh's hat. He was of medium height and built but the weight of all the hair pulled him down and made him appear stocky. 'Dada Bhai might want to hold off on the funeral till tomorrow, early morning.'

'He may ... or he may not,' said Tapan. 'If he insists on a funeral today, we have just a couple of hours.'

Madho nodded broodingly. 'Five of his sisters are anyway in Pakistan now. The family has some relatives in Bombay too. Of course, none of them would be able to make it to the funeral.'

Tapan Singh had once visited Bombay. He had seen the sea there and thought it to be as vast as night.

'Sahib, our men are inquiring about those who called on the house since last night. I'll go get an update from my foot soldiers.' Haider Khan rolled out of the room, leaving behind the smell of armpits. Tapan Singh had solved a few cases but he could never solve the mystery of fat men sweating in winters.

'Who all are in the house?' asked Tapan. 'I heard Rao Sahib of Singhgarh is visiting Dada Bhai. Speaking of high profile...'

'We should talk to him first and let him go,' Madho Singh suggested. 'It would create a big fuss if he is held back for long.' The topi on his head was secured in unruly hair. The bulges of his knees were visible between his nut-brown shorts and socks.

He didn't have his winter coat on. Tapan assumed his hairy hide was enough protection against the cold.

'Who else?' inquired Tapan.

Madho brought out his very own pocket notebook and wet a finger with saliva to grease and turn the page. 'From Dada Bhai's family—his three sons, his mother Sugra Bai and his wife Mena Bai.'

'Everyone has heard what a looker and a go-getter Mena Bai is. Didn't you say that the resident witch was his mother Sugra Bai, and not the one in the peepul tree?'

'Hukam, those were not my words. Haider Khan would have described her to you.' Madho's eyes were deadpan.

Tapan Singh chuckled, 'Okay, who else?'

'Badi Bi, their old housekeeper. She is a child widow. A servant Ismail, who's a credible crook. Their two boy servants are on leave. Dada Bhai gave them a week's off on Makar Sankranti.'

'A week! I wish our masters were that generous. Get what I mean?'

'Haider should confirm it, but according to the initial inquiry in the last hour or so, I have drawn a list of those who visited the house today. Two Bhils. One came with Rao Sahib and another one from the Jogion ka Guda village, probably bringing news of a leopard kill. The infamous fixer Hariharan came in at noon. Not sure yet, but a Bhangi or a Bhangan would have cleared the basket of faeces from the outhouse below the privy that has a separate entrance; you can't get inside the house from the outhouse. They have a private toilet, Sahib.' Madho imparted this important piece of information, his head still bent towards the notebook.

'I know. And it seems they have a private hell too.'

'Being Makar Sankranti, the usual vendors are not out on the street. No bhishti came to give them potable water today, but a Bhangi was seen loitering in the street.' The overgrown moustache and beard covering Madho's lips and cheeks gave his face a menacing quality of stillness even when he spoke. He licked his finger again as he turned a page and drew a blank. 'That's about it for now. Apparently, the room where the body was discovered was closed from the inside. I've examined it. The jharokhas are latticed. There is no way someone could have entered the room either through the main door or windows.' He closed the notebook, inserting a down feather as a bookmark.

'A closed-room murder.' Tapan Singh felt his stomach groan as anticipation built up. He stood up, scraping the chair on the ground. It emitted a sharp sound of a pebble in a chalk scratching against a blackboard. A leather holster was strapped across his chest with a revolver on a side, the only metal ornament he allowed himself. He straightened his khaki shorts and pulled up his brown socks to his knees. He preferred not to wear full-length pants even in winters. They made his legs look like two candlesticks. Wrapped in brown paper.

Tapan walked to the door, which was right opposite the passage that led from the darkling odha to the open-to-the-sky ground-floor veranda. On his right was a storeroom, with a big rusty lock holding the door in a clasped jaw. On the left was the servant's bathroom. Winter sunlight snuck into the mouth of the passage, failing to creep in any further into this dusky side of the house.

'Tell me all about Rao Sahib before we call him.' Tapan Singh removed watery mucus from his small eye, held his hands at the back with professional curiosity and pondered on the cause, the culprit, the crime (and the curse?).

22

Thanedar Tapan Singh with Rao Sahib

Dada Bhai's House

Bohrawadi

THE ZAMINDAR WAS A TRAIN THAT HAD RUN OFF THE TRACKS. A few grizzled hairs curled around the Bhupalshahi paag on his head, making untidy halos around his gold earrings. It seemed a whole bottle of Kannauj attar had been sprinkled on his sherwani and achkan—the velvety green coat—and the off-white breeches-style pyjama. But it didn't mask the smell of fresh vomit. His face was puckered like a baby's. Frazzled. Demanding its toy back.

'Forgive me, Hukam, for troubling you on such a day. But for your friend Dada Bhai's sake, we need to ask you questions before you leave for Maharana Sahib's durbar,' Tapan Singh spoke reverentially.

Rao Sahib flicked a bulky hand, as if shooing away a pestilent fly. Rings studded with precious stones sent angry flashes in the light of the four lamps blazing in the room.

'Your two aides...' Tapan looked at sub-inspector Madho Singh standing by the side of the table for help.

'Amar Singh and Sujan Singh,' Madho told the ink pot.

'You left them near the city gate of Hatipol around 10 a.m. and asked them to go to the Maharana's durbar. You reached Dada Bhai's place before noon with the Bhil Doonga. Could you please tell us, Hukam, where you were and if you visited someone during that interval?'

Rao Sahib shifted uncomfortably in the teakwood chair. It was an inch too small to accommodate his royal buttocks. 'It is none of your business.'

'Ahem ... With all due respect, Hukam, we need this information.' As an afterthought, he added, 'It is a *standard procedure*,' in English.

He could see Rao Sahib slack a little under the weight of the heavy English term.

'I went to visit Oghad Baba ... the one who sits near Gulab Bagh. To pay my respects to him.'

'You came straight from there to Dada Bhai's?' asked Tapan.

'Excuse me, Hukam,' Madho Singh cut in, staring at Rao Sahib's green achkan, his own expression concealed by the dense growth on his face. 'Is this the naked Aghori who tells numbers for gambling?'

Rao Sahib threw a distasteful look at Madho and turned to Tapan Singh condescendingly, the sub-inspector too low in his ranks to be addressed directly.

'Yes,' was the curt reply. 'That's the answer for both the questions.'

Tapan Singh dipped his pen in the ink pot and continued to jot away tiny words the small diary could accommodate.

'Hukam...' Tapan Singh looked up. 'Hariharan, the exact nature of whose work remains a bit murky, visited Dada Bhai when you were with him in the drawing room on the fifth floor. Is that correct?'

'He's up to no good.' Rao Sahib placed a hand on the table and leant forward giving Tapan a clear view of his horse teeth. 'I have a feeling he is trying to lure Dada Bhai into a disastrous deal.'

'What kind of deal?' Tapan Singh leant forward as well. The zamindar's breath, smelling of stale retch, came to him in puffs. It seemed he hadn't been able to stomach the murder.

'These pure vegetarians, they are the biggest bloodsuckers. I suspect Hariharan is trying to get Dada Bhai a loan on murderous interest rates.'

'Loan? For what?' Tapan Singh's eyebrows creased.

Rao Sahib reclined, the chair sighing with his bulk. 'Dada Bhai is facing ... I am not sure I should be telling you this. Have you heard of honour among friends?' He twirled the end of his up-curving moustache.

'Rest assured, Hukam, if there is anyone you should be telling this to, it is me. Get what I mean?' Tapan kicked himself internally for his verbal tic. Outwardly, he followed it with a most winning smile. It was not winning enough.

Rao Sahib stared at him with surly suspicion; Tapan looked back submissively. A long silence ensued.

Tapan Singh felt the room growing a bit chillier around him. He cleared his already cleared throat. 'Hukam, what I mean is, this information can be vital in solving the case. I request you to help us.'

'So now the *Gole-Thole* will patronize me, is it?' Rao Sahib's lips formed a gruesome smile.

The derogatory term hit Tapan Singh in his stomach. It was used for the bastard sons of Thakurs who didn't have any share in their father's property and landed jobs like the one he had. Of a Thanedar or Daroga. Or a security guard in the Maharana's durbar. They were even exchanged in dowries. He suppressed the yelp of a kicked pie-dog and shook his head meekly, not venturing to clarify that though he was a lower-caste Rajput, he was not a Gola.

Rao Sahib seemed to be enjoying the familiar ambience of terror and nervousness around him. He relaxed spreading his thighs as wide as he could in the narrow chair. 'My friend is in trouble. What is the extent of the trouble, I do not know. He is the most idealistic man I've known, or even heard about in fables. Even the devi-devta are not so ... the gods are all flawed. Such an overdose of idealism is ... how do I say ... unnatural. It goes against the ancient instinct of survival. The Maharana had offered him a hundred villages. Dada Bhai refused. We all will have to surrender large chunks of our properties to the socialist thugs of the Indian government. We might as well give it to our friends and relatives.'

'So you had come to offer him a part of your estate that you might have to surrender to the government?'

'Three hundred and fifty acres of it. Sign it over to him over a one-rupee stamp paper.'

'With all due respect, Hukam, why do you think Dada Bhai would take land from you when he refused the kind offering of the Maharana?'

'Because I am his friend, you eediot!' His fist came crashing on the table. The fixed ink pot sent a few blue drops flying to

Tapan Singh's ironed shirt. He picked up the piece of rag lying on the side and wiped the ink from the table.

'I don't mean to upset you, Hukam,' Tapan Singh apologized, as if he was the one who had spilt the ink. 'Could you make your offer to Dada Bhai?'

'I would have! Had that ma-fucker Hariharan not barged in on us! *Kode maaro use!* Rao Sahib tried to reach for an invisible whip and spat a globule of spit on the side.

Tapan Singh let a long moment pass for Rao Sahib to stop grinding his teeth.

'I'm sorry to hear that, Hukam.' He referred to his pocket diary. 'Sometime past noon, you went to the guest room on the third floor, where Sanaz's room is. Were you inside for an hour or so until her nine-year-old brother Ahad pushed open the door of her room and discovered her body?'

Rao Sahib rubbed his rough cheek in an attempt to control his convulsing face. 'Yes … the body.' It seemed he would throw up again.

'Did you come out of the room in the meantime? See anyone there?' Tapan's pen was pinched between his pencil-thin fingers, as if he was throttling it to come out with the truth.

'No, I didn't.' Rao Sahib's lips kept moving, even during pauses. 'I saw the face of that widow Badi Bi near the kitchen, when I was climbing down from Dada Bhai's quarters. I am damned! What do you expect of a day on which you see a widow's face? And my friend Dada Bhai will still claim it is *superstition*! Would you believe that? It is a bad omen, and it will not change if you don't believe in it. Omens are our friends, sent to warn and prepare us. Our ancestors were not fools to believe in them. Were they? Am I?' Rao Sahib eyeballed Tapan Singh, the paag on his head a little askew.

'Of course not, Rao Sahib.' Tapan Singh was quick to react this time, waving the question away as if it was the most ridiculous thing he had heard this Makar Sankranti. He quickly dipped and upped his pen in the pot and scribbled a few words in his diary with glistening ink. 'Didn't see anyone else, Hukam?'

Rao Sahib shook his head sullenly. 'I was resting and then getting ready for durbar.'

A cry spilt on the ground floor. It seemed someone from the household had just laid their eyes on the girl's dead body. The crescendo rose, reducing the world to a sharp point of lament. A barrage of sobs followed, which only an unburied child can invoke.

Rao Sahib looked around baffled, and Madho Singh bent down to whisper something in Tapan's ears.

'Oh yes, yes! I forgot to tell you.' Rao Sahib seemed to have caught the collar of his fleeing memory. He crunched the ends of his moustache with his fingertips. 'I met that thief of a servant Ismail too when I was climbing down the floors. He was loitering between the kitchen on the fourth floor and Sanaz's room on the third. He is a sneaky character, that.'

Rao Sahib tried to raise one of his buttocks to give way to flatulence, but the chair shifted with the movement, its arms stuck in his bulging bottom. The wind that passed had the sound of a flute and the smell of rotten pakoras.

Haider Khan, who had stopped at the door seeing Rao Sahib seated inside the small room, shook soundlessly. His belly wobbled with suppressed laughter.

Tapan Singh strained with the effort of not raising his hand to his nose.

Rao Sahib, unaware of the brief misery he had caused (rather drawing in a few long breaths), went on, 'I'm sure that knotted twig Ismail is bringing in to take of threads and bones and charms in the house, burying them under the beds. I can put my estate's seal on it that you'll find enough black magic in the house if you start looking.'

'Technically it's not a crime, but why would he do that?' Tapan Singh brought his hand to his nose and rubbed it, as if he was collecting deep thoughts set adrift by this significant piece of information.

'Hah! You city dwellers who have turned your pious rivers into drains, you will not understand simple logic. To get some money, what else? He is a scoundrel. A thief! Even Dada Bhai knows that. But he is too large-hearted to kick him out. When a man has a stature like Dada Bhai, there are enough who are jealous of the success. Of his extraordinarily beautiful wife and children. Of his tremendous future. And he is a happy man too.' Rao Sahib squeezed the tips of his moustache again. 'Was ... was a happy man. For all you know, the imp Ismail is colluding with the jeevti dakkan! I would never allow such a man walking freely around my daughters!' He ended with a string of swear words.

Tapan Singh glanced at his sleeve, where the ink drops had grown petals and waited for Rao Sahib to complete. He was not done yet.

'And, of course, Bhabhi ji should have had better sense to stop her nefarious activities.' Rao Sahib scowled and stopped.

'You mean Mena Bai's women's education drive?' Tapan put in.

'She has ruffled many feathers for an inappropriate cause. And at what cost? I don't need to tell you how many distinguished, time-honoured families are left disgruntled. They are enduring the shameless exercise of sending their daughters out *to study*.' Rao Sahib's nostrils flared. His eyelids flitted in fury. 'I should have advised Dada Bhai long back that a good hiding is generally the best cure for a wild horse and a wild wife. I am sure a police *inspector* would agree with me on the virtue of swollen asses?'

'Rao Sahib, you give too much importance to the opinion of a lowlife like me.' Tapan Singh smiled ingratiatingly, turned the page of his diary and asked in the most nonchalant tone, 'Do you know, Hukam, that your man Doonga is missing?'

'What do you mean he is missing?' His whisper was menacing.

'He is not here, Hukam. Disappeared. Gone without a trace.'

'And where do you think he's *gone*?'

'We have no clue. We thought you'd be able to shed some light. Have you sent him on an errand?'

'How can I, Thanedar, when I have been resting and getting ready in my room?' Rao Sahib began scratching the wooden table with his overgrown nails.

Madho Singh standing on the side flinched at the sound and touched the two-starred insignia on his shoulder.

'It seems a hammer, which was hung on the wall of the passage that leads to this part of the house—to the odha—is missing.'

'If you're telling me that Doonga had a hand in Sanaz's murder ...' Rao Sahib's puffed-up face split into a smile. 'Thanedar, use your brains, if you have any. Will a cat go in pursuit of a diamond? If it goes in search of fish, I would believe you. Get what I mean?' The sly old-timer repeated Tapan Singh's catchphrase. 'Who ratted on him? The other Bhil outside?'

'Yes. He was just concerned that he hasn't seen Doonga for some time now.'

Rao Sahib squashed a cockroach who had the audacity to approach his mojdi-clad feet. 'Doonga will be back before I leave, you'll see. Take my advice, give a hard belting to the servant Ismail and you'll know the truth. Isn't that the purpose for which the government provides you with these black and brown belts?' Rao Sahib tried to extricate himself from the chair holding him down firmly. 'Our daughter Sanaz…' All the glee of a moment back fled the zamindar's face. 'This can't be happening…' He stood up looking at his plump fingers splayed on the table.

'Before you leave, Rao Sahib,' Madho Singh spoke up, his stare fixed on a scab on Tapan's knuckles, 'one last question. Rumour says that you recently married the girl whose proposal had come for your son. Is that true?'

The last word swilled out of the room as Tapan Singh gulped. He stood up slowly.

When Rao Sahib looked up, his face was raw as a skinned goat. 'Police force … bloody dacoits in uniforms.' His gaze shifted to Tapan Singh, his fat lips turning up in contrived humour as he asked, 'Aren't you that policeman 'with a future'? Do you want to shit in your pants and paint your future yellow?'

'I-um … Hukam … Madho is just asking a routine … um … *standard question*.' This time, Tapan's English term had little impact.

'You scumbags at least dreaded Maharana's justice in the pre-independence time. If you do not solve this murder, Tapan Singh ji … I'll make sure your career bites your balls. Dirty degenerates!'

The landlord gave Tapan a severe look from below his royal Bhupalshahi paag and thumped out of the dingy room. Haider Khan jumped on a side, sending a tremor on the floor as Rao Sahib stormed past him. He left in his wake a bubble of spit, a fading clang of hip joints, the smell of vomit mixed with attar, and the arms of cold collapsing around Tapan's hairless chest.

23

Thanedar Tapan Singh with Ismail

Dada Bhai's House

Bohrawadi

Tapan Singh had felt the corroded ego of the building since the time he set foot in it. He could feel a presence. Frigid and numbing. Staring disapprovingly at the intruders. Rao Sahib's warning had left Tapan picking his lips only for a moment or two. But he couldn't shrug off the feeling of being watched from behind every minute.

'So it is true then, Hukam.' Madho Singh sat on his heels near one of the lamps, turning its knob to increase the flame as Haider Khan rummaged through Ismail's meagre belongings kept in a trunk in a corner. 'Rao Sahib of Singhgarh married the girl who was meant to be his daughter-in-law. Some say that his eldest son has decided to remain celibate, lifelong.'

Haider Khan chuckled. The iron trunk squeaked. 'Thanedar Sahib, men like Rao Sahib scare me.' Just as Tapan Singh began to nod in understanding, Haider added, 'Men with boobs. I don't like competition.' He strained to stand back on his feet and pointed an accusing finger at the trunk. 'Nothing here except foul underwear and smelly clothes. Sahib, we'll be able to gather more information from the dhoonda where women squat in a line, gossiping and exchanging stories. Sanaz's murder would make the daily defecating ritual in the community toilet much longer tomorrow.'

Madho thumped down the three frayed mattresses stacked against a wall. A rancid smell filled the room as the beddings unrolled. The odour of men who had spent long, hushed nights alone. The cotton had flattened, the colours blanched.

Tapan Singh got up and donned his coat. Neither of his subordinates seemed to feel the chill and went rampaging as if it were a warm summer evening with women hovering on terraces to check on their pickle jars.

Tapan juddered out his plea, 'Madho, be a little diplomatic dealing with the aristocrats. They have many more means at hand than our everyday criminals to screw us or the investigation.'

Madho negotiated through the mattresses, poking his finger in every hole and tear. The sub-inspector ignored Tapan's appeal and said instead, 'Dada Bhai would have never accepted Rao Sahib's lands.'

Tapan didn't pursue the matter with him. He considered the three of them as the three parts of an insect—Madho the head, Haider the sting, and Tapan the thorax that contained the chief processing organs. He vaguely recalled there was one more part to an insect that contained the rectum, but that was a part he could do without.

Madho Singh finally pulled out a small packet from a corner of the mattress, where the seam had come undone. A neatly pleated and tucked newspaper.

'Ah, *The Statesman*.' Haider Khan stomped on his great thighs towards Madho, belly first, and took the folded paper from his hand, ignoring the stink of dried semen emitted by the bedding. 'Sahib…' He turned to both his seniors, one at a time, in the order of seniority. 'Dada Bhai gets this English newspaper all the way from Calcutta. It is delivered to him the next day. The servants are putting it to good use, it seems.'

Tapan took the packet from Haider and opened it carefully to find a light brown powder inside. He rubbed it between his fingers. It felt like butterfly wings. 'Opium.'

Tapan Singh preferred his opium in the good ol' bhang. He avoided liquor; it was astonishing what a bit of alcohol could do to men of honour. Bhang, on the other hand, just made him laugh hysterically. Deliriously. A cheerful, dark-skinned asura before he tore a fair-skinned Aryan from leg to leg.

He placed the packet on the table in full view, right beside the ink pot. He couldn't understand why many in the ranks sighed about the banality of police work. It was anything but.

A scraggy boy in a loose pyjama and a faded blue bush shirt with two missing buttons came to the odha. He gazed at the servant's billet, his very own sanctuary, turned upsidedown. The packet of opium lying exposed on the table had done its trick. The shock on his face disintegrated into a weak smile.

'You called for me, Sahib.' His voice was smudged with fear.

'Come in.' Tapan breathed in the air, rank with the smell of unwashed clothes, as Ismail walked in with his oversized pyjama flapping like fins around his gangly legs.

'Sit down.'

Ismail sat on his haunches on the floor and looked pitifully at the upturned mattresses, the spilt contents from his trunk and the three khaki-clad men in his room.

'Tell us all you know about today's murder.' Tapan Singh pulled his chair away from the table and sat on it again, placing his feet close to Ismail.

The word 'murder' made the boy's limbs tremble.

'I-I don't know anything, Sahib.' He sat just near the spot where Rao Sahib had spat. The phlegm lay by his side in a translucent blob.

'Let's start with telling us when you saw Sanaz last. Alive. Get what I mean?' Tapan Singh crossed his legs first and then his hands on his chest in an attempt to hide his frailty from another frail man.

Ismail pinched his forehead, holding the fold of skin between his thumb and index finger in concentration. 'Sahib, the three boys, Sanaz Apa, Dada Bhai and Mena Bai had their dinner last night on the fourth floor, as usual. Mutton gravy with paper-thin pore roti. They had it sitting around the thaal placed on a tarana in the kitchen. I took the dinner to Sugra Bai's room ... you know, Dada Bhai's mother. She can't climb up to have her meals every day. Sanaz Apa went to her room once the housekeeper Badi Bi cleaned the kitchen and left at around eight. I went and locked the main door and retired to the odha. Today morning ... Sanaz Apa didn't come for breakfast. But we didn't find anything amiss. Since she has passed out from school, she gets up very late.'

'Did you go to her floor today?'

'I did, Sahib. I crossed her room a few times, it seemed locked from the inside.' He fidgeted nervously with the end of his bush shirt gathered on his lap. 'I go up and down the whole house many times a day.'

'So you didn't go up to her room last night?' Tapan uncrossed his hands and tapped his nails on his knees.

Ismail opened his mouth like a carp caught in a hook. 'Why would I do that, Sahib? I'm-I'm too afraid to get out of my room at night. There is a jeevti dakkan in the peepul tree outside. Believe it, Sahib! Dada Bhai says there is no living witch ... that it is all hogwash ... but I have heard her whisper in my ear when I step out to go to the bathroom in the dead of the night ... I've once felt a spectral hand graze my shoulder. I didn't turn ... if you turn she'll dig her long nails into you and drag you down the thick shadows. I'm waiting for the two boys Shiva and Shankar to return from their village. It is difficult to sleep in the dark odha all alone at night, Sahib. I-I don't know anything about the murder, Sahib. I didn't see anything. I treat Sanaz Apa like my own sister. Who would want her dead?' He began to sob in his hands, wiping the snot on his discoloured shirt.

Tapan Singh drew back, repulsed. 'Who all have visited the household today since morning?'

'Badi Bi came very early, as always, but I was not awake then. The three boys went to the terrace in the morning, with their flying gear. I took freshly made til-ke-laddoo and water for them a couple of times. Dada Bhai has a lot of visitors daily. Badi Bi complains of having to keep the tea vessel on boil the whole day. But due to Makar Sankranti, there weren't many guests today,' Ismail babbled away. 'Dada Bhai's sister Khadija Bai visited her mother early in the morning, before anyone had woken up in the household. Of course, Badi Bi was there. Khadija Bai left for Galiyakot without meeting her brother or sister-in-law. Rao Sahib came with his Bhil Doonga before noon. Hariharan Sahib came a little after. And yes, Nathu … Nathu also came from Jogion ka Guda to inform of a leopard kill. His father Jaitya is the one who comes generally.' Ismail rubbed his sunken eyes eaten up by shadows.

'Did you see anything unusual during the day?'

'No, Sahib, it was a normal Makar Sankranti. Kids busy with kite flying. Mena Bai resting in her room. Badi Bi cooking in the kitchen. A few visitors. That's all.'

'Nothing stands out?'

'No, Sahib.'

'And no one else visited?'

'No, Sahib.'

'No one?'

'Ah yes, a woman had come to meet Sugra Bai.'

'A woman?'

'A burqa-clad woman. I didn't see her face, Sahib. Occasionally, some relatives come to pay their respects to Sugra Bai.'

A fist came flying his way. Ismail clattered against the ground. His shirt turned up, exposing a flat stomach with white patches on it, as if fungus had sprouted on his skin. Haider Khan stood over him, towering, with a happy glint in his puppy eyes.

'So you were saying…' Tapan Singh uncrossed his legs and sat rubbing his knees with both his hands.

'I-I don't know anything, Sahib,' Ismail whined crawling backwards on the floor, making his shirt wrinkle further up his sternum. The stomach was sunk beneath his ribs, making a smooth valley. The legacy of the underfed. Or the addicted.

'Your tits are not turning me on, Sugar. Cover yourself up!' Haider ordered.

Ismail fumbled to roll his bush shirt down, lying on the floor. He couldn't.

Tapan could feel Madho Singh flinch by his side as Haider pinned Ismail's wrist with his boot and crunched it delightfully. Saliva dribbled from the sides of the servant's mouth as his lips pulled back in pain.

'Can you deny that you are a thieving wretch?' Tapan picked up the open packet of opium from the table and brought it close to his nose. He stretched his legs and threw the ankles one above the other, watching Ismail impaled on the ground through the V-shaped window of his feet. Tapan too was skinny, alright, but this boy could be picked up by his nape and hung on a hook to dry. 'How much would such a packet of the best quality cost, Haider?'

Haider adjusted the stiff topi on his head and pulled out the lathi slung on his belt. 'One rupee, give or take a few pai, sahib.'

'And what is your monthly salary, sub-inspector Madho?'

Madho tried to look at the mould on the wall and the cobwebs on the ceiling. Anywhere except the boy lying prostrate on the floor. 'Three rupees, Hukam,' he managed to say in a voice as scratchy as his hair.

'You should rather work for Dada Bhai, na? How handsomely he pays his servant boys!' Tapan got up and stifled a yawn.

Haider kicked Ismail on his shin. And his stomach. And his hands. And his shoulders. The boy writhed. Finally, Haider bent his toes with his boot.

A cry rasped out of Ismail's chest. Dry and taut. 'For god's sake, Sahib, stop please.'

'Which god's sake? Tell me, who is the god of derelicts?' asked Tapan, raising his hand for Haider to halt. 'He is a derelict god,' Tapan graciously answered for Ismail. 'So where do you get the money from?'

'Sahib … I steal,' Ismail hiccupped.

'From the house?'

'Yes, Sahib … Dada Bhai … he-he knows,' the servant snivelled. 'He wants me to get rid of my addiction … so he hasn't fired me. I'm trying, sahib, I'm trying…'

'Trying to what? Hide-things-from-me?' Tapan made his words sink in, cocking his head to a side. He felt warmth spreading within, devouring the idle cold.

'No, Sahib, no-no-no…' The drool from the boy's mouth was slick on the ground.

A myna hopped in from the passage, hungry but free. It stopped at the door and looked in with its bandit eyes for worms. Finding all the grub in the room too big for its beak, it flew away with a shrill rebuke.

'Who was the 'woman' who visited Dada Bhai's mother?' Tapan Singh walked to Ismail's face, the tip of his polished black shoe touching the boy's jutting cheekbone. Haider stood on the other side, clutching his lathi, waiting for half a chance to practice the swing of his *gilli-danda* arm. Tapan knew Haider was a kid at heart—he had never grown out of his childhood games.

'I-I…' Ismail whimpered, 'I didn't see her face, Sahib. I swear I didn't!'

Tapan's boot jerked towards the cheeky servant's cheek. His head hit the ground on the other side, splitting open his lower lip. A muted cry escaped with droplets of blood. His forehead shone with fresh beads of perspiration.

'Did you need to see her face to know who she was … *what* she was?' Tapan went and sat on his chair. 'Get me some water, Madho Singh.'

Madho galloped out of the room, quicker than his darting gaze, happy to be briefly away from the blood and spit and bleating and all those unavoidable parts of their job. Tapan knew crimes could not be solved with smiles and roses. He was confused with Madho's irrational aversion to violence. But he was grateful for his clever inputs. His sharp observations. His comprehensive calculations.

Early on in his career, Tapan was smart enough to learn that he was average at his job. Be it deduction skills or strength of muscles. But he was exceptional at management. He could pinpoint who could do the job, and get it done. And then, as much as he loved his jester-cum-henchman Haider, he was a Mussalman. Tapan needed his caste-brother Madho Singh to fetch him water and food.

'Rao Sahib claims you have sold your soul to the witch. Now I see how. Get what I mean?' Tapan awaited a denial from the little shit.

Ismail turned a truant kid, aloof and silent, at the mention of Rao Sahib.

'Sahib is asking you a question!' Haider aimed his lathi at his groin. The hard blow snatched away his last vestige of dignity as a pool of urine spread shyly around his hips.

Another man peeked out from Ismail's sunken eyes. The anger in them was much older than the boy. It was late afternoon and the room became populated with smells: red and yellow in colour.

'Wash it!' Tapan commanded.

Haider stepped back as the houseboy got to his feet slowly and walked to the door, his pyjama and bush shirt blotched at the back. The sound of grief continued to come to the odha in waves from the torso of the building.

Madho returned with a glass of water for Tapan as Ismail hauled in a bucket from the bathroom and splashed it on the floor. His face had started to swell up. Tapan's throat burnt with the cold water. He tasted rotten fish in it, spat it on a side, and asked Ismail to wash that too. When Ismail hunkered near his chair, Tapan grabbed the rough hair and pulled his head back, the thin neck stretched to a snapping point, his mouth wide open. 'Who was the woman who visited Suġra Bai today?' Tapan hissed in the boy's ears.

Ismail smelt of piss and insubordination.

'Give me your belt.' Tapan let go of Ismail's head and extended a hand towards Madho without looking at him. He could sense his sub-inspector fumbling as he undid the clasp and removed his belt.

Tapan stood up, wrapped a part of the belt around his blue-veined hand, and smiled at the revolting undergrowth of hair that peeped from Ismail's armpits, giving him enough reason to beat the daylight out of this trash.

'Shy as a bride, are we?' Haider's fat cheeks were pushed back by his smiling lips. 'Don't be suspicious of the big worm in my pants. It is averse to virgins.'

Ismail remained silent and immobile. Tapan was raked by the boy's bold denial of his lowly station in life. He raised his hand to smack him with leather, but halted hearing a rustle on the door.

'Who knew the thief in the house will be the one with morals?' A heavy woman, dressed in faded white salwar-kurta and a coarse off-white shawl stood at the small door, a thin white odhani veiling her face.

Tapan's smile collapsed.

'Get up and get out, Ismail!' the woman commanded, her authority unmistakable, unchallenged, undoubted by the group of men.

The servant boy dusted his bush shirt as he got up, his legs shaking, lips inflamed.

Tapan had a violent urge to shove this boy with urine-soaked pyjamas down the toilet hole. Instead, he watched him stumble towards the door.

As if on an impulse against self-preservation, the piss-logged boy stopped and turned placidly to face Tapan's small eye. 'If you need anything, you know where to find your servant, Sahib.' He bowed dramatically to the three men, one by one, and straightened his back. 'Ram-Ram, Namaste, Assalam-alaykum!'

Ismail grinned and left. Red-toothed and victorious.

The unused belt hung from Tapan's hand—a teasing, twitching tail that a fleeing gecko has left behind.

24

Thanedar Tapan Singh with Badi Bi

Dada Bhai's House

Bohrawadi

THERE WAS A FURIOUS SPLENDOUR AROUND THE WIDOW rusting with rheumatoid arthritis. In the soggy, lamp-lit odha, she moved like a white cloud and settled on the chair meant for the witnesses. A barely detectable tinkle of anklets clung to her movements. Even with her curved back, she seemed taller than the stocky Madho and grittier than the flabby Haider. The arms enshrined in her kurta exuded strength coming from a life spent in grinding the millstone and carrying the weight of desires wrapped in the white clothes of a child widow. A faint smell of garlic and burnt wood filled the room along with a sense of overwhelming bereavement.

'The person who came to see Dada Bhai's mother Suġra Bai today was a eunuch.' The woman's voice was steady as the hand with which she adjusted her odhani on her head. A bare hand. Without bangles. Calligraphed with deep wrinkles. 'But I assume you know it already.'

Tapan found his bearing as Haider stepped back from the table reverentially, the lathi suddenly a vulgar addition to his ungainly body.

'Badi Bi ... am I right?' Tapan handed the belt back to Madho. He sat down after Badi Bi. 'I am Inspector Tapan Singh.'

'You would have heard stories of Suġra Bai being spitfire. That she had started telling Mena Bai just a few months into the consummation of her marriage that the street dogs in the lanes were breeding but not her. Don't all the mothers-in-law say those things, Thanedar Sahib? Did your mother not tell your wife?'

Tapan Singh entwined his fingers in mute understanding.

'Mena Bai had two miscarriages. And then ... two stillborns. Sanaz was the first one to survive.' The widow looked at her hands as if there was a baby curled up in a bundle there. 'Ah ... to have that first child at home. To tell her stories. Listen to the tinker of her laughter ... who'd have thought I'd be preparing my princess for her funeral and not her marriage ...' Her words trembled. 'For whom will I make the sweet nukti ... and face masks of turmeric and curd ... who'll come and give me a hug as I sit rolling rotis...' The old woman's voice was shaky with spent rage, the inflections brought in by gusts of regret. 'She often sprinkled extra salt around her food in the thaal. I used to warn her that she'll have to lift that wasted salt with her eyelashes in heaven. Allah forgive me ... had I ever imagined ... *kambakht zindagi!* The hand wiping her face under her veil came away wet with tears. 'I am the one who should be carried to the graveyard. Not her. Not my Sanaz.'

Tapan couldn't believe his luck. Even if that meant speaking to a luckless widow. Before he arrived at the house, Dada Bhai's wishes, aka orders, had been explicitly conveyed to him. He could not interrogate his mother Sugra Bai (but, of course) or his sister Khadija Bai whenever she arrived or their respected housekeeper Badi Bi. They were off limits.

But this repository of family secrets had walked into his domain out of her own free will and sat pouring information into his pricked-up ears.

He waited for the torrent of grief to subside before he said, 'I'm truly sorry, Badi Bi.'

'You look truly happy to have me here, Thanedar Sahib,' she said with blistering acumen. As a true Muslim woman, she believed in hiding her face and form, but not her rancour.

Tapan felt a warm stone at the pit of his stomach. He would have to tread more carefully with this one.

'I am happy about you offering your help to solve this case. It is extraordinarily courageous of you to come and speak to the authorities in the face of such a calamity. I thank you for that.' And he was. Thankful. 'You must really love Dada Bhai and his family.' He could sense she loved them. Unbearably. And enough to save their honour, even if that meant safeguarding a murderer lifelong.

The odha went still for a long moment. But the house was alive. Breathing, bleeding, tendrils of pain moving under its skin. It seemed thoughts were gathering around the old woman like birds coming to roost at dusk to a time-honoured tree.

And then Badi Bi spoke, her voice focussed and clear, 'Dada Bhai might disapprove of me speaking to you. But he will not tell me he disapproves. That is the kind of man he is. A man who believes in letting people choose. Even if that person is a greying servant.' She looked pointedly at the three men in the room, one by one. 'If you expect me to divulge any family secret, I should have your word of honour that it will not leave this room.'

Tapan chewed his lips as he scanned Madho Singh, who was staring at the ink pen, and then Haider, who had put the lathi against the wall. He stood with his hands hooked behind him, on his fat ass, and his eyes cast down, submitting to the glory of Allah, the merciful.

'We give you our word, Badi Bi.' Tapan Singh's response matched the firmness of the woman's demand.

'Your intelligence is correct. A hijra visited the house today. Came to meet Suġra Bai. But your crass assumption is not correct.' Badi Bi shifted her mass on the chair.

'It is known that some of these eunuchs are expert concocters of lethal poison.' Tapan regarded how appropriate the chair was to seat his witnesses, not letting them get too comfortable.

'And potent herbal potions. Especially for baanjh women.'

'Who is the childless woman in this household?'

'Suġra Bai's daughter Khadija Bai.'

Tapan stared at this child widow, who was known not to spend a single night at her employer's place; no one could ever accuse that she didn't sleep under her husband's roof. It was said she returned home every night, even for a couple of hours, to guard the virtue of her dead husband's memory. A husband she had never met. How fiercely would she guard her master, who treated her as a mother? Tapan knew an adversary when he saw one.

'You know the rest of Sugra Bai's daughters have moved to Pakistan. Khadija Bai is the only one around for the last three years. She is ageing … running out of time to become a mother. But what do men know about childbearing and birth? Except having a few more pegs of mauda with other men as the wives are lost in screams and agony and fluids pouring out of their wombs.' Badi Bi's hand thunked tiredly on the table, a hand Tapan now understood was not hardened by years of grinding stone, but by clutching on to pride.

'So the eunuch had come to give a potion of fertility?' asked Tapan.

Badi Bi didn't care to assert it. 'You would have asked me about Shiva and Shankar, the two Hindu boys working in a Bohra Muslim household. The usual suspects, right? *Allah ka shukr hai*, they are in their village now. So who's next?'

Tapan referred to his small notebook. Flipped its tiny brown pages.

'If I may,' Madho Singh spoke up.

Badi Bi turned her veiled face towards the sub-inspector.

'Mena Bai's work with women has antagonized a lot of people in and outside the community,' Madho stated the well-known fact. His rasping voice coupled with his brambly physique had the remarkable quality of putting a person at unease. But not this person. He plodded on regardless. 'Men and women are angry. Do you think anyone is angry enough to have killed Mena Bai's daughter?'

The white widow shimmered in the harsh light of the lamps. 'There are enough and more who hate Mena Bai's guts. Maybe you do too, Thanedar Sahib. Would you find it agreeable if your daughter goes to a school or to work?' She unknowingly brushed Tapan's yearning for a daughter. 'Mena Bai has all the qualities that men and women despise. She is a mean shot with her 28-bore. A prankster too. She had once dressed up as a ghost and scared an old man out of the house. The fellow had started to turn up almost every evening to lure Dada Bhai to fish at Udai Sagar lake. Dada Bhai loves his fishing and tends to his rods like children.' There was a fondness in her words now. And then they turned laden with sorrow. 'How will he ever deal with this loss ... his own first born...'

The deep anguish was the only vulnerable spot in this buttress of a person fastened to the family. A person who had jumped from childhood to widowhood, and missed everything in between.

In a blink, she hid her blind spot. 'I'll tell you the story of Mena and Tahir, Thanedar Sahib. Their engagement was sealed over sugar lumps of misri and a coconut by four men from our family who had gone to her home. The wedding was a simple meal in the Jamaat—the community hall. The women of the mohalla came and helped us prepare stacks and stacks of pore roti for the repast. Mena was a petite girl of nine and Tahir a sturdy lad of eleven when they wed. Even before the girl came of age and their marriage was consummated, they both had become the objects of envy and admiration. After finishing all the work given by her mother-in-law Suġra Bai, Mena would not sit on a porch outside a neighbour's house and play looji-boot with other girls...' Badi Bi stopped, dreadfully perspective. 'I can see you don't know what looji-boot is.'

'Yes, I don't know, Badi Bi.'

'The thing is, Sahib...' Badi Bi picked on a corner of her face veil and pulled it slightly. 'One should not pity an old child-widow in a ghoonghat. I can clearly see your expressions, but you can't observe mine. It must be rather taxing to maintain a face that is neither disbelieving nor judgemental while you are trying to study others. With them being privy to every twitch of your mouth, the suspicion gathered in folds around your eyes, the doubtful wiggle of your nose. *Tush-tush...*' She moved her head from side to side. 'Must feel like being ... naked. That is what I tell Mena Bai—my veil is not oppressing; it is liberating.'

Badi Bi seemed to get comfortable in her chair. She held her hands in her lap and said loftily, 'I pity you, Beta, to be frank. A harmless old widow can do your job much more effectively. Without the cost of the extras.' Her head turned towards Madho and then Haider.

Tapan admired her. While most women would sit weeping and howling in the midst of such a numbing tragedy, this one sat in the dingy room with three uniformed policemen, her mind sharp as a meat cleaver.

'You couldn't be more right, Badi Bi. But you have to do your job, and I have to do mine.'

'And that is why I am sitting here with you now, to do my duty, against Dada Bhai's wishes.'

'You were talking about looji-boot...'

'It is a game our girls play. Every afternoon, the women in Bohrawadi finish their daily chores and lounge on their porches facing the lanes. The men are at work and there is no need for purdah. They sit and gossip while the girls play this game with buttons, often broken ones. Even though Mena always had the supply of the best of buttons from Bombay, she would never join them. Instead, she and little Tahir would sit on the terrace, where he taught her the alphabet. They were out there, roosting on the top of the world, for everyone to behold their verdant love.' Her sigh encompassed her unloved youth. 'You know, we get Pola now and then. If someone has returned from a place like Bombay, they send their neighbours a little gift. Apples and bananas are the rarest, and sometimes we get half or a quarter of the fruit. I used to save it for Tahir. He would kiss my hand gratefully and take it to his little bride. Ah, the audacity of young love ... his younger brother has tied the knot too. But it didn't work out quite like Tahir's. He and his wife are visiting the mazaar in Galiyakot at the moment.'

'Isn't that the holy tomb where they take those who are possessed?' Madho Singh asked the opposite wall. He had inched closer to the table.

Badi Bi examined him through her veil and nodded in quiet approval. 'Yes, Fakhruddin Sharif Maula buried there has the power to yank out the spirits possessing the victim.'

'Are you suggesting that Dada Bhai's sister-in-law is possessed?' Tapan asked, making his pen spiral between his thumb and fingers.

Badi Bi's approval turned to ash. 'I am told the police force lacks imagination. There are some things that can't be spelt out, Thanedar Sahib. Since you ask, well, some say she has an unstable mind.' She reached out for the packet of opium lying unguarded on the table, picked it up, sniffed it. 'Do you have to see things to believe them?'

A sharp rap on the door saved Tapan Singh from answering this indestructible woman. Another police constable stood there, not in khaki shorts but full winter pants. 'Sahib, we got the two people you wanted to speak to. They're waiting outside the house.'

Tapan Singh signalled Haider, and he skittered out of the room, lugging his weight without grace.

'Let me spell out Dada Bhai's status and standing,' Badi Bi rasped. 'He wanted to build five storeys in his house. The durbar forbade him to do it. Why? Because there can't be a building nearing the height of the royal palace. The celebrated kite-flyer Babuji of Karwadi wants to come to our terrace, the highest of all, and fly his kite on Makar Sankranti. Mena Bai's work with women is as revolutionary as the fight for independence. Together, Tahir and Mena will make history.' She tipped her head back and looked at the high ceiling. 'You are sitting under four storeys of history in making, Thanedar Sahib. You too carry some of its burden.'

Tapan Singh shifted in his chair. His was the one that had turned uncomfortable now. He wanted Madho Singh to come up with a question, but he didn't.

'Do you realize there will be thousands of mouths discussing this house today? A god-sent case for your career, na?'

The cold had again begun to inch stealthily around Tapan. He felt a meaty aftertaste on his tongue. As if he had bitten a dead rat.

'There is a five-foot road on the side of the house where his horse stable is. Dada Bhai wants to gift that part of the road, his stables, to the municipality so that they can broaden the path. The idle women who sit and gossip on the porches outside their houses feel the widened access to Bohrawadi will expose their haya—their modesty—to the world. There is much anger among them with Dada Bhai's decision. But no one dares tell him that. His reputation ... which you may think would give you vertigo ... is in reality punitive. I don't want it to be the end of him.' Badi Bi's buzzing voice was an angry wasp. 'His stature. His house. His intellect. His beautiful wife. His wife's works. Thanedar Sahib, women and men have hated others for much less.'

'Have there been any … threats?' Madho Singh finally came to Tapan's rescue. He had dislodged his gaze from the wet floor and hooked it on Tapan's hand placed on the table now.

'If you consider the traces in the house of tona-totka … those black threads and packets of vermillion mixed with Allah-knows-what tucked away in hidden corners … then yes. Enough and more.' She waved a hand, which sent a whiff of garlic and burnt wood.

'You mean you have found traces of devilry and witchcraft in the house?' Tapan's voice was hushed. This old woman, who stood perfectly poised between a garlicky life on one side and an incredible murder on the other, was an indication in itself that there was something paranormal with this house.

'Do you believe in spirits? Those shades that are neither living nor dead?' Her stare blazed across her veil and he felt a prick in his spine.

'I believe in the spiritual.'

Koo-Ooo … koo-Ooo … koo-Ooo ….

The sudden whistle of a koel gave Tapan a start. He rubbed his clean-shaven cheek scowling at the lamps burning themselves away.

Haider had moved his bulk into the room again, but kept a little distance from the old woman. Madho stood quietly by her side.

'We use coal in our kitchen. Sometimes firewood too. There is a heap of coconut husks lying on a side to light the fire. I've found bloodied rags beneath it. With a lemon. I've seen unholy things under the children's bedding when they sleep on the terrace in summers. There are many who have tried to invoke the jeevti dakkan to harm this family. I do not know who slips these demonic charms into the house … we have enough and more visitors. But I do know that with big names come big curses.'

Tapan heard footsteps thumping up the house followed by a tearing cry and the flutter of a dozen startled pigeons taking to wings. He looked at Madho and saw a shadow flit across his face.

'That must be Khadija Bai, Dada Bhai's sister.' Badi Bi's voice hollowed out.

She was right. Tapan couldn't see her face or read her expressions. He had gathered though that she was no one's confidante in the family, but she knew it all anyway. Her rough knuckles kneading her thighs betrayed her anxiety.

'I think I have told you enough. I must take your leave. A housekeeper is needed the most in a house of death.' Badi Bi got up slowly to her feet, her back warped further under the staccato of sobs cascading down the house. Instead of Tapan Singh, she turned to Madho. 'There are things you know, Son, and things you don't know. Sometimes it is best to let the unknown be.'

Tapan Singh scrambled to his feet as she got up. He folded his hands in respect.

The bow-legged widow shambling on her feeble limbs, donned in the dull-white fabric made soft by a hundred washes, and followed by three pairs of eyes stopped near Haider on her way out. She inspected him like a child looking at an upturned beetle waving its six barbed legs in the air.

'You sounded a bit unbalanced, dear, talking about the worm in your pants to Ismail.' The ice in her voice was as palpable as the silence on Makar Sankranti. She opened her fist and let the white opium powder from Ismail's packet dissipate in the air. Haider gasped.

'Don't agonize over it. A bit of meditation will help. And yes, reserve the worm in your pants for making worthless sons.'

Imparting the last nugget of wisdom, this one-woman squadron disappeared, one shuffle at a time, into the corridor of the cursed house of death.

25

Thanedar Tapan Singh with Parijat and Bhola

Dada Bhai's House

Bohrawadi

THE BLEAK, WINTRY ODHA HAD BEGUN TO SMELL LIKE A FLOWER bed. Tapan gazed at the garden of roses that had walked right into his domain. A young untouchable Bhangan he so wanted to touch. Caress. Console. And fill her wounds with gold.

A patchy jackal pretending to be a human squirmed in after her. Emitting fumes of ferment and felony. Making the odha a strange hybrid of a forest and a drain.

Madho bent down to whisper something in his ear and the subordinate's unruly beard tickled his smooth cheek. Haider followed the Bhangi and Bhangan in the room, swinging his lathi.

'What is your name?' Tapan asked the pathetic man with a deformed arm, his dhoti-kurta pickled with sweat, his hair mired with sludge and crawling with lice. This scum looked decidedly out of place in the grand house.

'Bhola, Hukam.' He bent double to pay respect with his head almost touching his crooked knees. 'But you can call me Loola.'

'And what is your name?' Tapan tried to maintain a very objective, unaffected voice addressing the girl.

'Her name is Parijat. She is my wife, Sahib.' Bhola's smile made his sunken face more hideous.

Haider's lathi hit his knee and the man doubled down on the floor. 'I thought sahib had asked your wife a question.'

Parijat, looking at Haider with the eye of a storm, extended a hand to get her husband to his feet.

'Apologies, Sahib.' Bhola's mouth dribbled. 'I answered because she can't speak. She is goongi ... dumb.'

'A loola and a goongi ... what a pair! *Ram banaye jodi!*' Haider laughed. 'I told you Sahib, marriages are made in heaven.'

Tapan begged to differ, remembering his own marriage. 'They are made in hell, Haider.'

Haider chuckled. Madho Singh pushed his chin higher, obviously disagreeing.

'We have enough witnesses who have informed that both of you have been loitering around the house today, without any work in particular. Why is that?' asked Tapan.

'Sahib, I was only sweeping the lanes. I begin from that last mud-roofed house at the end of the lane and work my way to Dada Bhai's place by noon. Parijat collects the basket of faeces every day from this house in the morning. There is a small outhouse with a separate entrance where it gets collected. On festival days, Mena Bai gives her a bit of baksheesh. Being Makar Sankranti, she came again and was waiting for Mena Bai to come out.' Words tumbled out of Bhola's twitching mouth. Rehearsed. Stage managed.

'And you got to enter this house today, imagine! If it was not for Dada Bhai's unconventional ways, I would be meeting you in the thana. A filthy untouchable can't dream of stepping inside such a stately home in their god-forsaken lives. Forget about stately, not even in a dilapidating hut of a poor upper-caste man.'

A smothered sound escaped Parijat's throat. The inspector found her smiling.

'Funny, isn't it?' said Tapan. 'The way you started your day today.'

The statement claimed the smile from her face. Tapan regretted it. The ladybird stood dressed in her red-and-black ghaghra-choli, kohl-smeared eyes, curly hair held captive by a red thread, reticent, proud, every inch a princess. He imagined her on her nuptial bed with this sorry millipede arched over her, and tasted bile. But then, gods needed to create freak stories for their entertainment. Immortality was a very long time, after all.

'She starts her day by coming to Dada Bhai's house, Sahib,' Bhola offered.

'But today morning she got up very early and went to the Chamar settlement.' Tapan was fond of fishing and always collected his own bait of worms. Ah, digging in the wet mud and pulling their soft bodies out with the earthy scent of anticipation. He rubbed his palm on the smooth wood of the table, focussing on Parijat. She tilted her head to one side—a worm trying to escape his fingers.

'Um … did she, Sahib? Chamar basti … did you?' Words bubbled out of Bhola's mouth as he looked from Tapan to Parijat. She looked at him sheepishly and nodded.

'Maulvi Sahib going to the Hele Muslim masjid for conducting namaz just before dawn saw Parijat outside her home. And another woman with an upset stomach, who was going to answer nature's call, saw Parijat entering a hut in the Chamar basti.'

'Entering a hut…?' Bhola's words came out limping. 'Oh yes, Sahib. She has a rakhi brother there. A Meghwal boy. Though we don't touch these Chamars, you know, they skin dead animals … but he is a good boy, lost his grandmother recently. He's not well too … Parijat goes to hand over food sometimes.'

'Rakhi brother, huh?' Tapan smirked.

Bhola pulled on his torn kurta.

Tak … tak … Haider gently hit the lathi on the floor to fill the silence.

'How much time did you spend with your young brother?' asked Tapan. 'Too bad you have to visit him in the dark hours when the world sleeps.'

Parijat's eyes were a fierce jungle fire. Her feral beauty untamed.

Haider clapped hard on his bulging calf, killing a mosquito. A startled Bhola backed off and clung to Parijat's arm, vibrating with the echo.

Tapan Singh got up from his chair, stretched his legs and yawned aloud. He kept a hand on Madho Singh's shoulder. It was padded with hair.

'What else were you telling me, Madho?'

Khat … klak.

A muffled click and snap made everyone look up at the ceiling … it resembled the sound of someone loading a gun. A treacherous note.

'Old houses have a tongue of their own,' Madho Singh told Haider's belly. 'I was saying, Sahib, that Parijat is originally from the village Phootia in Rao Sahib's jagir, Singhgarh.'

'Interesting. Phootia, the village with the broken dam.' Tapan moved a step towards her. Breathed her in. Began to drown in roses.

Parijat stiffened.

Tapan surveyed the peak of her breasts, the reservoirs of her eyes, the gorge between her parted lips. She was the spitting image of a god's curvy concubine. Of a jeevti dakkan at her tempting best.

'So you were aware that Rao Sahib is visiting Dada Bhai today?'

Parijat answered Tapan with a confrontational silence, not born out of handicap but defiance.

Tapan flicked his hand and Haider's lathi landed squarely on Bhola's stomach. There was a muted squelch, like a ladle circling in a soupy pot, and a breath sucked in as he fell. The man scratched the floor with dirty fingernails trying to get up. His soles were stained yellow; perhaps the shit he collected had permeated his skin over the years.

Parijat tried to help him up but Haider's swinging baton sent her a warning to keep away.

'So you were telling me you knew about Rao Sahib's visit,' Tapan tried again, returning to his chair.

When Parijat didn't move, Haider's lathi found Bhola's ribs. There was a small, sharp crunch.

Madho recoiled. Bhola simpered. Haider hummed, wanting to burst into a song.

Parijat shook her head violently from side to side, loosening a few sensual locks of hair. It reminded Tapan of his secret, prized treasure—a calendar of Raja Ravi Verma's paintings he hid in his trunk, his only source of porn. Not Raja Sahib's paintings of the goddesses, of course (god forbid!), but those surreal busty women draped in translucent saris with pricked up, hardened tits. He felt a familiar pull in his pelvic region and shuffled in his chair, willing it away.

'It is too much of a coincidence, get what I mean? You hanging around the house unusually on a day when Rao Sahib is visiting, a day when Dada Bhai's daughter is murdered.'

Bhola drew pained breaths, huffing.

'I like stories. Tell me a few stories from Phootia, Madho.' Tapan fondled his pen.

'Two of the men from the police force will be reaching the village today, Sahib. They are on the way right now. We'll have all the information in a couple of days.'

'You see,' said Tapan, rubbing his cheek, 'this one here, sub-inspector Madho Singh, is our very own Narad Muni. He will return to me with all the news and gossip from the universe. And then our in-house god of death, my beloved Yamraj Haider Khan, will get to work. And yeah, he has faster means than riding a buffalo to catch the fleeing men.'

Parijat looked at Tapan with a steadiness that made his small eye twitch, until a faraway wail filled the room, landing pinpricks on their skin. A long, sad cry. Death was an urchin running unbidden around the house. Toppling things. Poking needles. Throwing tantrums. Spilling pots. Ripping curtains. Raising hell.

The women of the family would have bathed and wrapped the girl's body in a white sheet for her last journey. Fresh and ready for her new abode. On the police's request, Dada Bhai had conceded to not utilize the excellent funeral service provided by the Bohra community till the initial interrogations were done. The two solid spots of sunlight from the ventilators had been lugged up the opposite wall, reminding Tapan of the time left to him to sort out his glorious career. Precious little. That's how the important people and days were. Always in a hurry.

The animal stench of the Bhangi mingled with the smell of kerosene, making the air oily and heavy. Tapan would soon have to open up the house to the mourners outside the family. As there wasn't enough time to break Parijat, this magnificent haughty creature, he turned to the more fragile and diseased in the room.

'Do you have anything to tell me, Loola ... anything at all? See, Haider is a man of great restraint. He will not beat you to a pulp and mess Dada Bhai's flooring. But the police station? You can't imagine how filthy it already is.'

'I don't know anything, Hukam,' Bhola rasped.

Glass bangles clinked as Parijat moved again to pick up her uprooted husband slumped on the ground. This time, Haider didn't stop her.

Bhola coughed blood as he stood up, swaying on his feet as if he was being pulled down in a vortex. Parijat was quick to rub the blood off his unlovable face. She wiped her angry hands on her ghaghra.

'Technically, Sahib,' Haider said with a pout, examining his lathi, 'Do I have to purify myself or purify this after it has touched a Bhangi?' He pointed at his baton.

'I appreciate your philosophical question, Haider. We'll try to find the answer before we see our esteemed guests again. Which I believe will be soon.' Tapan let the quiet menace dripping from the pores of this building seep into his voice. He wondered if some of his lust had slipped into it as well. 'Scat!' He pointed at the door. 'And don't leave Udaipur without our permission.'

The tousled, brutalized Bhola, with lice crawling in his hair, bowed his head. His wife held his buckled elbow and led him out in a cloud of swishing ghaghra, jutting hips and tinkle of cheap glass bangles. She gave Tapan an off-shoulder glance. Shearing. Thorny.

The rosebud of a girl vanished in the darkening passage that led to the open-roofed veranda. The flowers were taken away from the odha, leaving Tapan in the fumes of lamp oil, unfulfilled desires and bad intent.

26

Thanedar Tapan Singh with Nathu

Dada Bhai's House

Bohrawadi

'MADHO, WHAT IS THIS LEADING TO?' TAPAN PACED UP AND down, up and down, stepping outside the wooden door, stepping back in. A goat tethered to a long rope. The walls watched. The cold nibbled. The afternoon sat cross-legged, ready to lie down and stretch any moment.

'Hukam, information is trickling in. The force is tracking down the Bhil Doonga's movements. I'll soon be able to tell you where he is.' Madho had brought in another sub-inspector a while back, discussed a few things with him and sent him on the field.

'The girl's burial will be tomorrow morning, I believe. It is too late for them to take the body to Khanjipeer graveyard outside the city now. But they will want us to get the hell out of here soon and let the mourners visit them.' Tapan rubbed his small eye with the back of his palm. 'You need to tell me where the missing Doonga is before I speak to Dada Bhai.'

'I have a feeling this rambling mansion has swallowed him whole, Sahib,' Haider, seated on the beddings they had stacked again, said dizzily. 'I have been hearing strange sounds ever since we stepped into this house. Don't laugh at me, Sahib ... I just used the servant's bathroom and felt the ceiling bending low to observe me closely.'

'The bathroom has a low ceiling, Haider,' Madho said, lifting his topi and trying to flatten the pubic curls on his head.

'You are right, Madho Sahib, but listen to this. I was standing under the peepul tree outside and giving your search instructions to other constables. A sharp whistle made us all start. Each one of us. There sat right above our heads an eagle, glowering at us, a crow chick pierced in its talons. Tell me, Madho Sahib, have you ever seen an eagle so low down in the city? It was clearly a warning from the jeevti dakkan.'

Tapan dug a thumb into the clasp of his belt and chewed the inside of his cheek. The jeevti dakkan was not an outlandish creation of a storyteller. The world was not free of spirits. Or free of gods. He had gone to inspect the room of the deceased. There had been a slight shift in the air as soon as he had stepped in. A stench of burning flesh had wafted in from the jharokha and pinched his nose. A faint crunch had made him turn to find the echo of his boots following him. He had felt a presence in this house. Was his mind pulling cheap tricks of a roadside magician? Or did the magician's biin actually make the rope sway in a snake-dance?

'The biggest thorn lodged in our throats is that the room was locked from inside,' Madho conceded this much and no more.

'*Khamma gh-gh-gh-ghani, Hukam...*' A young Bhil stood with his fingers entwined in a greeting. He was sheathed in the aroma of semi-dried meadows and faraway lands. Tight muscles ridged his calves and arms, not a single ounce of flesh lost to flab.

Tapan called him in with a whisk of his hand. The boy was no more than seventeen years of age. He was dressed in the proper city attire of Bhils—feet held in camel skin mojdi, torso and thighs in kurta and dhoti, earlobes, wrists, ankles and neck in rings of silver, head in a big white pagadi. But his toned, firm body could not hide a tenderness around him. The tenderness that comes from years of leading a protected life, even if one lived in the merciless wilds.

'Did you inform the police about the missing hammer from the passage on the ground floor?' Tapan rested his bum on the side of the table and folded his arms on his chest.

'Hu-hu-hukam'

'You were sitting with Doonga since the time he came to the house with Rao Sahib. But you didn't see him leave?'

'I haa-had come to the sss-servant's toilet in the odha, Hu-hukam, when h-he went away. Just when it s-started to rain. The brief sh-sh-shower.'

'How old is your friendship with Doonga?'

'Friendship? No, Hu-hukam, I just-I just saw him perform Gavari once, all those years back. When my Ba had brought me along to the c-city. There was a leopard kill near our village and Ba ha-had come to inform Dada Bhai about it. Ss-some twenty odd villagers from another village in Ss-singhgarh had come to perform Gavari here ... at Da-dada Bhai's place. For his family.' Faint tremors wobbled his lips. 'Doon-doonga ji had played Rai Devi in the play. I was just a boy then.'

'Hmm...' Tapan looked at the boy he still was. A lily-livered, spluttering one at that. 'What did you chat with him all the while he was with you today?'

'Nothing, Hu-hukam. He hardly ss-spoke a word. Didn't even touch the hot pakoras Ismail Bhai h-had got for us. There was ss-something off about him. He ss-seemed...' Nathu halted, his hands held in servility, as if deciding whether to spell it out or not. And then he did: '...possessed.'

Tapan's small eye felt gummy all of a sudden. He contained his urge to clean it or to steal a glance at Madho or Haider.

'And what do you think we are, your village temple's Bhopa to believe in your nonsensical tales?'

Nathu's despair was visible on his face as he shook it from side to side.

'If I come to know that you are withholding any information from me—' There was no need for Tapan to complete the threat.

'Hu-hu-hu-hukam ... I am not.' Glistening beads of sweat had started to appear on Nathu's burnished skin.

'Doonga-said—' Tapan scribbled in his pocket diary, holding it in his left hand and dipping the pen in the ink holder with his right, '-nothing-to-Nathu.' He ended it with two question marks and placed the pen delicately in the ink pot. 'Do you know anyone from Doonga's clan? His village?'

'I've never been to Doon-doon-doon—Doon-doon-doon....'

Tapan knocked on the table impatiently, waiting for him to finish.

'—ji's village. It is far away. I've never been to Ssinghgarh.'
The Bhil began to nibble on the skin peeling around his
thumbnail. 'I sss-smelt mauda on h-his breath.'

'Uh-huh…' Tapan flashed a look at Madho. 'So he was
drunk in the morning hours. Interesting.' Jotting this in his
diary, he turned to the Bhil. 'You told constable Haider that
you were sitting on the ground floor the whole time and saw
everyone who visited the house since late morning—Rao Sahib
of Singhgarh who arrived with Doonga, Hariharan who came
soon after, the servant Ismail going up and down, a woman
dressed in a burqa, a Bhangi with a bad arm sweeping the street,
who stopped for a chat, and a young Bhangan who peeped in
inquisitively. Anyone else?'

He shook his head.

'You only visited the bathroom once?'

Nathu nodded nervously.

'Do you know what is on the third floor?'

'I ha-ha-ha-have only seen Da-dada Bhai's armoury on the
first floor.' His eyes rolled as he tried to pull out the hitched
words. 'I'd come with Ba a few years back, the same year I met
Doon-Doonga ji and saw the Gavari performed here. Daa-bhai
h-had taken Ba to the armoury to show him his new rrr-rrr-
rifle.' It came out as 'rai-phal', as if it was a winter fruit. Like
sitaphal.

'Ahh …was that the custom-made Rigby and Sons' take
down model?' A sudden wave of curiosity hit Tapan. The rifle
had made more than a few zamindars turn green. The British
Resident of Udaipur, Col. Beetham, had visited to check the
gun, the sight of which was sent thrice to England to be fixed.
Dada Bhai wanted his aim to be perfect. This half-incubated

egg here had seen the rifle, held it even. And for all this boy cared, it could have been the backside of a buffalo.

'Hu-hu-hu-hukam…' He confirmed.

Tapan was beginning to lose his patience with this Bhil and his tethered tongue. Slower than a woman in labour.

'Tell me the *real* reason why you are here today, Nathu.'

The boy looked at him for a moment with his mouth open, shaking feebly.

Dust motes floated in the slabs of early evening light that punctured the room through the high ventilators. Haider stood up from his smelly roost as if on cue, his quaking mass sending tremors down Nathu's legs. The Bhil's eyes were wide with the fright of an animal caught in a beat.

'Why couldn't your father come?' Tapan rapped the table with his nails. 'It is not even the harvesting season … what is Jaitya possibly busy with?'

The boy stood in the middle of the cheerless room.

'Hu-hu-hukam…I d-d-d-d-didn't d-d-d-do…' Letters tripped out of his trembling jaw like drunks.

'That's not what I asked, did I, Madho?'

'No, Thanedar Sahib. That's not what you asked.' Madho eyed the puffs of hair on his fingers.

'Did I ask that, Haider?'

The constable shook his head as he walked slowly towards the boy, his smile widening, his hand caressing the lathi with a lover's gentle strokes.

'I didn't d-d-d-do anything, Hu-hu-hukam. I just made a promise to my father … I sss-sss-swear upon Rana ji…' Spit bubbles burst at the corners of his mouth.

'Oh-kay, a promise. A true Bhil would break his back rather than break his promise, right?'

'No!' Nathu shrieked before Haider could hit him. No faltering words. No rolling eyes. Tapan believed what the British called the sixth sense was actually jungle sense. Your survival depended upon knowing when the predator meant business. And when she didn't. This forest man, raised in the wilds, had his natural instincts in place.

'Interesting. Explain, Nathu, my boy.'

Tears began to pool in his eyes and remained there in two bucketsful. 'A couple of d-days back my Ba ha-had gone to check on our fields at d-d-dusk. I was in the h-hut, h-helping my wife with the firewood when I h-h-heard this commotion outside. The villagers were k-k-k-k-carrying my Ba, torn and bleeding.' He heaved a breath.

Tapan stopped drumming the table. He had not expected this outlandish story. Nothing that couldn't be verified though.

'A female leopard with two k-k-cubs is living near our village Jogiyon ka Guda, Hu-hukam. Sh-sh-she has been hunting the livestock. My Bhoora...' A tear from his eye decided to take the plunge.

'Your...?'

'Our bull, Hu-hu-hukam.' His mouth funnelled, as if he was blowing into a cook fire.

'Hmm ... and the leopard attacked your father Jaitya too?' asked Madho Singh, rubbing his bushy eyebrows drawn in concentration.

Nathu's face convulsed.

Goon ... goon ... goon... A few pigeons gurgled outside, calling it a day already.

'H-h-he is h-hurt very badly. H-he chanced upon the leopard in our barley field, while h-he was checking the k-k-crop at dusk. The stalks are big and if the wind is not blowing in the r-right direction, the leopard can't sss-sense a man ... not until they come face to face. These cats generally don't attack humans, Hu-hukam, but she is with cubs. Ba's bad luck, he ventured too close...' An invisible weight pulled him to the ground. His legs bent and he sat on his heels holding his pagadi-clad head in his hand. 'My Ba ... h-h-h-he is dying, Hu-hukam.'

Tapan frowned at Madho, who stood biting the side of his lip along with some of the beard hair in the process. Haider had lost the happy smile on his face. He looked sullenly at his escaped prey, who sat defending the killer of his father.

'And why,' Tapan turned towards the Bhil and asked, 'have you been sitting here like a first-rate idiot since morning?'

Nathu began to rock, back and forth, back and forth. His knee-length dhoti yanked up, winding tight around his exposed thighs. He removed his pagadi and placed it on a side, digging his fingers into his hair. His eyes had grey winter clouds in them. His movements sent sharp scents of baked cow dung.

The hoarse words came out in spurts, 'I d-didn't want to come. I d-d-d-didn't! I wanted to be with Ba. But the old man just wouldn't let me! For h-him, Da-dada Bhai is his d-devta on earth. He wants to see him before he passes on into the forest of Rrr-rana ji. He insisted I k-come to Udaipur and bring Da-dada Bhai to the village with me ... to see his loyal jungle tracker one last time before h-he d-d-d-dies.' He stopped and drew in a ragged breath. 'I d-didn't lie, Hu-hukam, I have come to inform Dada bhai of a leopard. My Ba is the kill this time.'

The voice lingered in the room, buffing the halos around the kerosene lamps.

'Why didn't you inform him then?' Madho Singh asked. 'He would have come immediately with you if he knew his trusted khoju shikari Jaitya is … um … injured. Why were you putting up this charade?'

Nathu sputtered out a lot of Os before he said, 'Oath … the damn o-oath!' His upper body had tightened with the effort. Thin veins crisscrossed around his eyes. There was anger in them, anger and defeated hope. Stretching from the eastern to western sky of the forest that he had brought along.

The three men in the room waited for him to go on.

'H-he made me ss-swear that I will not tell Da-dada Bhai that he is injured. And dy-dying.' He stopped as if his horizon had come to an abrupt end.

'Why?' Tapan asked incredulously. 'That's absurd. He wants him to come but doesn't want him to know he is injured? Why not convey the urgency?'

'Dada Bhai is known to respond promptly to requests from villagers,' Madho told Tapan. 'He is famed for risking his own life to cull cattle lifters that are frequenting the poor, far-flung villages. Maharana Sahib's durbar used to request him to cull the leopards, and now the Collector sends him the requests, Hukam, when villagers visit him with grievances.'

'Don't try to make a fool of us, Nathu,' said Tapan. 'I'll ask once again. Why?'

Nathu raised his wet face to Tapan Singh looming over him. 'To not k-k-k-cause Da-dada Bhai pain.'

The logic was illogical. Timorous. Tortured. The boy crouched on the floor carrying the dead weight of an oath before he carried his dead father on his shoulders.

'Ba wanted to spare h-him the pain for as long as he k-can. H-he has always wanted that for Daa-dada Bhai. His love for him is incurable, Hu-hukam, and that's why he just wants to see h-him once … before…' Both his hands had found their way to his head.

'And now you've broken that oath. That's shameful. Who breaks an oath to a dying father?' Tapan asked Madho, who refused to answer.

'Has to be a real lowlife, Sahib,' Haider put his honest opinion forth. Before his lathi had made welts on their back, how could someone spit out the truth? These jungle men or their lesser gods had no honour.

'Get out and go to your sinking father whose trust you broke, Nathu.' Tapan touched the boy's arm with the rounded toe cap of his boot. He had no use for this guy if the sap story was true. He was sure Madho would send his men to Jogion ka Guda to corroborate it. They would confirm it by tomorrow. Tapan turned to Madho to call in the next person, turning the pages of his little black secret-keeper urgently.

Nathu got up on wobbly feet. He pressed his pagadi against his chest. 'Hu-hukam…'

Tapan looked up.

'I beg of you … Please tell Da-dada Bhai about my father Jaitya. It is horrible what happened here today with his d-d-daughter. I am truly ss-ss-sorry….' He tapped his feet; the plea strangled. 'But please tell h-him. That my Ba die-die-died waiting for him in v-vain.'

He walked to the door, slightly bent forward, as if he was walking against a raging gale. The off-white cloth of the undone pagadi trailed behind him. He stopped there and turned. His free hand went to his waist, the fingers tugged inside the fold of his dhoti and fished out a small packet.

'Hu-hukam … a small gift for Da-dada Bhai…' His voice was gutted.

Haider stepped forward and took the neatly folded package from his hand.

Nathu nodded to the floor in mute acceptance of his fate, and receded in the passage, never to be seen again.

27

Thanedar Tapan Singh with Hariharan

Dada Bhai's House

Bohrawadi

'CARE TO HAVE SALTED AMLA?' TAPAN SINGH ASKED THE FAT man dressed in the perversely white kurta-pyjama and topi of a politician. He sat wiping his forehead with a white kerchief, flaking off the tall, red tilak. Tapan had opened the cloth packet containing amla as soon as the distraught Bhil had left, thanking gods for providing some nourishment on this gruelling day. A burst of tangy saliva had filled his mouth as soon as he kept a piece of the dried fruit on his tongue. While Haider had taken a fistful, Madho stoically refused to eat the gift left for Dada Bhai, the stricken man of the house.

'It is fresh from the forest, Hariharan ji.'

'It is very kind of your respected self to offer it to me, Thanedar Sahib. But I am devastated. No food would pass my constricting mouth...' The man, who looked like an obese force-fed chicken, glanced at the salted amla in the little packet hungrily, wetting his thick lips with his tongue. The chair protested under his heaving stomach. 'I think the funeral is tomorrow. How very terribly unfortunate.'

Tapan gulped down the water brought by Madho Singh. It left a sweet aftertaste on his lips. He licked the salt from his fingers, folded the cloth around the remaining amla and slipped it into his shirt pocket.

'I had seen Sanaz a few days before Eid. Badi Bi and a couple of women from Karwadi were rolling noodles of sewaiyyan on a wooden board outside the kitchen. Sanaz and her younger brother Ahad sat organizing the thin wires to dry on the thorny white kanthi bushes. She was so deft with her fingers. How she had grown into a graceful young lady...' The eight gold rings that squeezed into the flesh of his fingers clinked softly as he fiddled with his hands. Patted his palms. Touched fingertips with fingertips. His clothes reeked of incense.

Visitors had still not been allowed in the house and the moaning had reduced to a dull but continuous, tired warble.

Hariharan went on without being asked any questions, offering all that he could. And a wee bit more. 'She would have been one of the first girls to attend a college, Thanedar Sahib, Daroga Sahib ... and that too outside Udaipur. I was told she had got admission in Aligarh Muslim University.' He turned to Madho, not wanting to miss stroking the sub-inspector's ego. 'But of course, your very efficient intelligence network would have informed you of that.' A slight inflection in his voice.

'Your humble servant assumes you don't really need a network to find this out. It is a known fact.'

'What is?' Tapan kneaded the skin between his thumb and finger.

'Um ... it is not right for me to say, Thanedar Sahib.'

'Then do the wrong thing and tell me ... lest you forget, you are a suspect too.'

Hariharan let out the sigh of a faithful husband being accused of infidelity.

'This is not my opinion, of course. Um ... Dada Bhai is a great man, but people ... there is no cure for people. Both Hindus and Muslims say he doesn't care for propriety much. Neither does his wife Mena Bai.'

'I thought he is widely loved. Get what I mean?' Grains of dark, oily grime formed on Tapan's skin as he continued to rub his hand.

'He is, he is! I worship him, Sahib.' Hariharan's gaze scuttled from Tapan's normal eye to the small one, trying to decide where he should look. 'But you know how people are. They are angry. They say it is wrong of him to let his wife fight for educating an entire generation of women. Women with letters are like childbearing men, Sahib. Some of these "educated" women have not only started to shed their purdah, I hear, but to even keep their heads uncovered. The world is slowly changing, I know. But, in my humble opinion, it is not ready for an overnight makeover.'

This grave thief was cleverer than he let on. Tapan needed to dirty his nails with a bit more digging. 'I agree with you, Hariharan ji.' He levelled him with an unassuming smile. 'I appreciate your insights into the case.'

Hariharan's smile reminded Tapan of Shakuni Mama, one of the sneakiest characters of Mahabharata, before he rolled his dice.

'Anything else that you can help us with? I will put in a good word in our police ranks about you.' He leant forward on the table, toting the pen in his fingers. 'You and I are going to be around for a long time. Get what I mean?'

A calculation flicked behind the eyes of the middleman. He gave Tapan a crafty smile and said, 'One sly character in this house is the servant Ismail, Sahib.'

'Hmm…' Tapan fingered the pages of his little pocket diary. It made a gentle flapping sound.

'Ismail is a thieving wretch.' Hariharan's eyes gleamed. 'Dada Bhai is too naive. He will even step into quicksand if someone begged him for help. He shouldn't have kept the swindler after he was caught red-handed.'

'Did you catch him doing anything unusual when you visited the house earlier today?'

'He is always up to something, Sahib. But he would not be sly if I caught him doing it, right?'

'What about Rao Sahib? You met him today.'

'He is a sleazy feudal lord, if I may say so, but he can't commit murder, Thanedar Sahib. For that, you need cool calculation.'

Yes, that's what you have, Tapan thought. 'Why was he here, you think? A friendly visit?'

'Ah, no, no, Sahib, don't let this social-visit business fool you. I mean-I mean…' he floundered, 'of course, nothing can fool your clever, discerning self…'

Tapan nodded impatiently for him to go on.

'…Rao Sahib was here to dole away the crusting of his estate that he will have to anyway surrender to the government of

India. The zamindars of the region, well … they want Dada
Bhai to be on their side. You must know, he has a brilliant
career ahead in the great churning that is happening in the
subcontinent. A Muslim with a big following of Hindu royals
as well as laymen, not to forget tribals and untouchables. What
could be sweeter than that kind of vote bank in politics?'

'Hmm…' Tapan hummed the hum of a lazy fly. He needed
this fat whore to disclose more tricks. 'Tell me something I don't
know.'

'Dada Bhai is in a financial mess.'

Tapan stretched back in his chair disinterestedly, spreading
his legs with lethargy. 'He will recover from it.'

'With all due respect, esteemed Dada Bhai has the business
sense of the leopards he hangs on his walls.' The bulge of
Hariharan's stomach pushed against his white kurta. 'These
aristocrats and landlords … all these Thakurs, Zamindars,
Jagirdars and Rao Sahibs … what do they know about business?
About maximizing profit and minimizing loss? Some of them
spend mindlessly on mistresses. Others on patronizing art and
culture. Where is the profit in that? They have had wealth passed
down on a platter for generations. Yes … Dada Bhai opened
his *Tahir and Sons* shops all over Mewar, ninety-eight of them.
Tell me, Thanedar Sahib, your servant might be wrong, but can
anyone without the patronage of the Maharana ji Sahib do it? Is
Dada Bhai's success based purely on merit?' He wiped the froth
from the corner of his thick lips with the white kerchief rolled
up in his fist. 'These aristocrats and royals, they are incestuous.
That is how wealth *breeds* wealth.'

Tapan awarded this opportunist, who wanted to replace
the incestuous royals, half a smile. An opportunist like the
missionaries who had covered the scandalously exposed bosoms

of the native women with pious blouses. Nehru-collared and button-fronted. The missionaries who had influenced the making of the Indian Penal Code by including Biblical prohibitions such as adultery and sodomy as punishable offences. Tapan the student had asked a question to his gaunt, thin-lipped professor about polygamy equalling adultery. It had earned him a sarcastic smile and the advice, 'Try punishing the royals for their many wives, Chora…'

Tapan looked with distaste at this sample of a new breed of profiteers, half-British and half a corpse-mutilating Thug. A new kind of liquor being brewed out of the fruit of independence. With a horse-piss aftertaste.

'What are you arriving at, Hariharan ji?'

'Um … if you'll allow me to say, Sahib, people salute the rising sun. *And* everyone likes to see a giant fall.'

A swell of perspiration rose around the table as Haider raised his hand to pick on his nose. He stood there rolling the snot in little grey balls pressed between his fingers and flicking them to a side. Deferentially away from Tapan. Scornfully towards the servants' beddings.

In the silence, Tapan could hear the heavy breaths of the meatloaf positioned on his witness chair. 'I still don't understand.'

'Dada Bhai is smart enough to realize his fall is near. That is why…' Hariharan frowned. 'This has to be confidential between you and me, Thanedar Sahib … if Dada Bhai hears of it, my … I mean *his* prospects of recovery are lost.'

Tapan nodded tersely.

'He had agreed to marry off his daughter Sanaz to Kamruddin Hathiwala.' He spread his chunky thighs and placed one hand on each, as if he was ready to get up.

'You mean the old Bohra merchant of silk who has what, two … three wives?' Madho Singh drew his woolly eyebrows together, intrigued, as if he had not caught the words correctly.

Hariharan dislodged a gold ring from his little finger and pushed it down again.

'What is the catch for Kamruddin Hathiwala?' asked Madho. 'It can't just be marrying a young, beautiful girl.'

'Well, for many old men that *is* the motive, Daroga Sahib. But you are right, it is not just that. Dada Bhai has contacts. A lot many of them outside Mewar. From Bombay to Karachi. Imagine the business he could generate from them.'

'And why would Dada Bhai agree to such a sordid proposal?' Tapan inquired.

'Because Kamruddin Hathiwala will bail him out … give him a loan for the entire amount he needs, interest-free.'

'Dada Bhai could just take the gift of land from his friend Rao Sahib or from the Maharana Sahib, who has offered him a hundred villages. What's stopping him?'

The beefy man tipped his head to a side, making ripples on his bull-neck. 'His ego, Thanedar Sahib. Dada Bhai will not be accepting someone's handout. It would be a deal. Give and take.'

Tapan said tautly, 'So you were striking this deal for him, huh? This murder would be a great personal loss for you too.'

Hariharan's smile was sterling, as if it was not a personal loss but a personal gain. 'I will find other ways to help his honourable self, Thanedar Sahib. I can't betray him in his hour of dire need.'

'Since you have such a deep knowledge of Dada Bhai's affairs, I would like your most valuable opinion.' Tapan could play the same game. 'Who do you think could have gained from Sanaz's murder?'

'Dada Bhai himself.' The answer came without missing a beat.

Tapan looked up from his squiggly handwriting to Madho's eyes, which had finally settled on Tapan's. Haider held the bump of his stomach with the caution of a pregnant woman. *Burr ... Ommm ...* His burp filled the room with rotten eggs. Haider smiled apologetically at his seniors, waved the reek away, and ended up dispersing it towards them.

'That is quite some insinuation.'

'Hypothetically, Thanedar Sahib, hypothetically.' Hariharan smiled an obnoxious smile. 'Don't look so appalled.' The man who had walked in taut as a wasp's sting had now slackened comfortably in his chair.

'Will you elaborate?'

'Sanaz has a small fortune to her name, passed on to her by her late maternal grandmother. It was to be given to her at the time of her wedding. Now someone in financial distress can use it.'

Madho Singh grimaced. 'Is the inheritance enough to settle Dada Bhai's losses?'

'Far from it. But it will give him a breather. More than that, Daroga Sahib, the death of his beautiful, young daughter earns him sympathy. If he fights an election in the newly minted Hindustan...' Hariharan's smile was pasted to his corpulent jaws. 'What do we love more than seeing a giant fall? Our very own noble charity in making him stand again.'

A sad, lacerated lament from somewhere above thinned into hitched sobs. The wail of a child. The house of death had stirred again.

Hariharan's face blanched; all his cheekiness vanished in a moment. 'I-I have never been to this part of the house before. There is something not quite right about … you know, Thanedar Sahib, the peepul tree outside. That … that *being* on that tree would need some refuge during the stark daylight. Maybe she hides in the unlit parts of this house until everything is consumed by darkness, and then crawls out…' The way his voice plunged to a low gurgle betrayed the fear. 'She is supposed to feed on death and loss.' He looked at the two ventilators near the high ceiling.

The winter afternoon had sniffed the distress in the house and tiptoed away with elongated arms towards the waiting night.

'Any other information you'd like to share?' Tapan asked his odious ally.

'I've told you everything I know to galvanize your investigation, Honourable Sahib, even if that means putting my own neck on the line. There is an evil influence in this house, something which is not human.' A shiver made his body wobble. 'I will need to drink some gau mutra to purify myself today … cow urine is the cure for all evil. I recommend you have a palmful of it too.' He reverentially closed his eyes and parroted a prayer, unable to contain his terror of the darkening room.

Tapan saw he had outlived his utility. 'I appreciate your help, Hariharan ji. We will get in touch with you again.' Tapan put both his hands on the table and shoved his hips to pull back the chair.

The layers of flab on Hariharan's face were wallowing in winter sweat. He stood up clumsily and seemed in a hurry to scat. *Shrrr* …. A rustle, probably of a pigeon who'd come to roost on the high ventilator, made the man flinch.

'Respected Thanedar Sahib, Daroga Sahib…' He joined his hands in a parting namaskar and cast a regardful smile towards Haider too as he straightened his kurta. 'Your humble servant will be at your beck and call.'

Madho nodded to his broad nose, Haider took him out and Tapan watched as his shapeless form walked into the dense shade of the passage and became a white smudge. The house had warded off this evil eye.

28

Thanedar Tapan Singh with Dada Bhai

Dada Bhai's House

Bohrawadi

HE SAT ON THE CHAIR. AS LONELY AS A THORN. BREECHES AND a coat with four puffed-up pockets. Well-oiled dark brown hair, unnaturally ablaze in the lamplight. A thin watch-chain, more coppery than gold, hanging limp from a pocket. Gaze steady, like his legendary aim. Eyes dry. He was in control. The whole of him, except his treacherous fingers that held a cigar. They trembled. A young man with an old man's hands. Silence cocooned him. Harsh. Bloodless. Graveyard-bound.

Tapan Singh sat with—as Badi Bi had pointed—history in making. He looked with awe at the dapper aristocrat. The man possessed what most lacked. *Presence*. The arrow of a Parker Pen pointed towards his heart. It was equal to carrying a Rolls-

Royce in a pocket. Tapan shifted his humble pen to the side of
the table, away from his own sight.

'Dada Bhai, this is Madho Singh from Chetak thana and
Haider Khan from Bohrawadi chowki. The Superintendent
Sahib asked me to gather the best in the force for this task.'

Dada Bhai nodded at the sub-inspector and the constable.
Smoke rose in a thread from the cigar and infused the air with
the sharp smell of burning tobacco.

'I can update you on our findings, if you'll permit.'

Another terse nod.

'Your Vakeel Sahib Manohar Lal ji had contacted us. But we
told him you would not need a lawyer.'

A wicked itch on Tapan's balls made him shift, but he didn't
venture to scratch his sacks in such illustrious company.

'Many people have grudges against your family, Sir,' Tapan
said in the most reverential tone. He did not bestow a 'sir' even
upon his seniors. Dada Bhai was the closest thing to a knight
he would ever know. 'We were told Bohra women are not
happy with you giving away your stable to the municipality
... to widen the Five-Foot Road, that is. The narrow entrance
is a purdah to their mohalla, they believe. But once the road is
widened, they would not be able to sit freely on the porches.'
Get what I mean? he quietly said to himself.

A rumble, a quiver of Dada Bhai's lips.

'Sorry, Sir, what did you say?'

'Any other grudges ... people have?' He sat unbuckled.
Resigned.

'You must not take it personally, Sir. I am sorry to tell you
all this on a very difficult day.' Tapan dislodged a grain from
his small eye and wiped the little finger on his shorts. 'The
activities of your wife Shrimati Mena Bai are not looked upon

kindly either. But then, all revolutionaries have to face this.' He brought the butt end of his shoes together and recited what he had learnt by rote to impress his hero, 'Churchill had said in 1931 that it was alarming and nauseating to see Mr Gandhi, a seditious Middle Temple lawyer, now posing as a fakir … striding half-naked up the steps of the Vice-regal Palace. But sir, Gandhi ji trampled on the British Empire, half-naked.'

His little speech didn't gain him a single appreciative look. He put it to the aristocrat's post-traumatic shock and moved on, 'Hariharan ji said he is trying to help you ease um … some financial stress. Kamruddin Hathiwala ji has agreed to…'

Tapan flinched as Dada Bhai gently knocked the cigar on the table. 'You think I pledged my daughter Sanaz to Kamruddin?' The question was not loud. Not accusing. Just a question.

Tapan cursed himself for not verifying the slurs and lies of the middleman before regurgitating them in front of Dada Bhai. 'I regret the crass assumption, Sir.' He referred to his little black companion, anxious to put this slip behind him. 'I will try to finish this as quickly as possible. There are two Bhils who visited your house today. Nathu and Doonga. Nathu had just come to report a kill.'

Madho Singh shuffled noisily, prodding his boss to tell Dada Bhai about the attack on Nathu's father Jaitya, the family's trusted khoju shikari. Tapan ignored him and strode on like a half-naked Gandhi up the steps of the Vice-regal Palace.

'Doonga, on the other hand,' Tapan said, 'was missing from noon with a hammer from your ground-floor passage.'

Dada Bhai's response was sharp as the tobacco smoke. '*Was* missing?'

'He has been found.'

Madho, who had got the news through his super-efficient network of busybodies, twiddled his beard.

'Dead,' Tapan declared. 'He committed suicide in Fatehsagar Lake. He jumped in the waters after tying the heavy hammer around his waist. Two people on the embankment saw him take the leap. The body has been fished out.'

A thin, screeching sound made Tapan grind his teeth instinctively. Dada Bhai had dragged his chair back and his eyes had turned expressive.

'*Why…*'

'As you know, he lived in one of the villages in Rao Sahib's estate. Six days back, his little sister and his son were beaten to death by the villagers.'

Dada Bhai's face contorted, as if he was breathing noxious fumes. The next 'why' was stitched on his face. He didn't need to spell it out.

'They had defecated in the open near the agricultural fields of the upper castes. It seems they had upset stomachs and couldn't hold it till they reached the wastelands.'

'Oh, Doonga…' Dada Bhai moaned running a hand over his face.

'It is tragic, what happened,' Tapan consoled.

'Rao Sahib?'

'He knew, of course. But he had to get Doonga along with him to Udaipur as the Bhil knew the city quite well. We conveyed the news of his suicide to Rao Sahib. He is quite shaken, naturally. He has excused himself from the durbar and is returning to his estate today itself. Isn't he, Madho?'

The sub-inspector confirmed it with an incline of his beard-heavy chin.

'Those are pious, pure vegetarian Baniya and Brahmins in that village, Sir. They must have been outraged to see their dharma being polluted.'

Dada Bhai's lips twitched in a snarl. 'Yes, Inspector, who can question the devout and god-fearing upper castes?' He ran a paw over his face again; a tiger licking its wounds. 'Rao Sahib should have told me about Doonga's family.'

Haider swatted a big mosquito on his neck and flicked it with his nails. Winter had caved in around the odha. Mosquitoes had risen. Insects with transparent wings droned around the sacrificial fire of the four lamps. Shadows were clotting on the ground, on the walls, in the corners. *Coop-coop-coop-coop* … the deep, cascading call of a greater coucal from the peepul tree echoed Tapan's worries, gathering around the dimming daylight. He had to salvage some bits of the day before the jeevti dakkan claimed it from him.

Tapan had learnt early on in his career that *insaaf*—justice—was the most unnatural thing. The system should not topple. All he hoped to achieve was balance.

'They say a living witch haunts the peepul tree in your lane. The jeevti dakkan. And many believe it to be a fact that she haunts this building too.'

Dada Bhai looked at him with the incredulity of a non-believer, too polished to call the inspector ignorant. 'There is no witch in the peepul tree. *That* is a fact.'

'With all due respect, Sir, it looks probable that there is black magic behind this death.' Tapan trod on with the certainty of a believer. 'You know, Sir, your daughter's room was locked from the inside. No phial of poison. No wound. No strangulation. How do we explain this, even if we establish a motive?'

'I understand that is the job of the police force. To explain the how.'

Tapan tried hard not to make his tone rattle. 'Talking of how, Sir, we have intelligence as well as witnesses that the infamous hijra Roopali Bai visited your mother today.'

A fleeting look of horror passed the sharp, angled contours of Dada Bhai's face. He remained silent.

'This eunuch's herbal poisons and concoctions are known to sell for a little fortune.'

'Are you insinuating my mother for my daughter's murder?'

'Oh no, Sir, I would not dare to! I am just stating the *facts*. The hijra probably has links with your servant Ismail. He scurries in the underworld, you know.'

'Neither my mother,' said Daba Bhai evenly, 'nor my helper Ismail has anything to do with Roopali Bai. It is I who called her here.'

Tapan cast a look at Madho, who seemed calm behind his mane, as if he was expecting Dada Bhai to take the blame even for his thieving servant. He remembered Madho's prophetic words spoken a few minutes back in private: *Dada Bhai is a die-hard socialist like Charlie Chaplin, Hukam. We will not know if we have to laugh or cry at the end of the act.*

'For what purpose did you call her, if I may ask?'

'I choose not to answer, unless I am a suspect.'

Tapan found himself unfairly at the receiving end of his hero's wrath. It should have been directed at his mother Sugra Bai or the jeevti dakkan or that ill-bred Ismail.

'You are not, Sir, but I can charge others with plotting. The Bhangi Loola and his wife Parijat, for instance.'

Curiosity made Dada Bhai blink. 'What could the cleaners possibly have to do with this?'

'I had dearly wanted to spare you this ignominious detail … but I am left with no choice.' Tapan jerked his chin towards Haider and he went and stood guard at the door, making sure that the walls were deaf.

'Your daughter Sanaz,' said Tapan, 'and the Bhangan Parijat's brother, the ex-student union leader Valmiki, have been seeing each other for more than a year.'

The ash from Dada Bhai's cigar fell softly on his breeches, digging a hole in the Egyptian cotton. He bunched his fingers in a ball, as if he was holding a fistful of dust to be thrown on his daughter's grave.

'It seems the Bhangan Parijat has been helping them exchange letters. Since you had permitted me to examine the victim's room, I went through the possessions in her trunk and found this …' Tapan squinted at Madho who conjured a handful of letters from his shirt and placed them on the table.

'I will not be filing this as evidence, of course.' Tapan gave a discreet push to the pages. His long finger directed them towards Dada Bhai with the assurance: 'They will be destroyed.'

The aristocrat stared at the letters—pages torn from notebooks. Frayed. Nibbled on the sides by insatiable Time. He picked up a letter and held it parallel to his eyes. Tapan could read a couple of lines visible between his fingers, written in a tilting handwriting at the back of the page.

> *…you are the Kali that devours all of me. The good and the evil and the untouchable making her a goddessly whole.*

Words on the myriad letters lay strewn on the table …

> *… in your arms I am weightless.*
> *… the small of your waist. The world is a small place.*

And the letter on top. It was a poem:

Happiness, unravelled.

How wonderful it would be
— To be a giant tortoise
On the Galapagos islands
— To be a lake
Untraceable on the map
— Or to find Livingston
And become a catchphrase

How marvellous
— To be a toy clock
Holding time with its hands
— To be a dzong
At the sangam of two rivers
— Or to be a heartbeat
Waltzing at a lover's touch

How incredible to feel
In someone's presence
Aflutter (like a heartbeat)
Embraced (in a confluence)
Timeless (as in a toy clock)
Found (just as Livingston was)
Happy (like a fish in an untraceable lake)

And believing
In someone. Simply.
Like an ancient giant tortoise
Who has looked forever at the

Galaxies and the ocean
Convinced that the Milky Way
Is the jellyfish of eternity.

The words were pooled on the table, which had an ink pot and a cheap pen pushed to one side.

A silent storm billowed in Dada Bhai's eyes as he kept the letter back with the others.

Tapan smiled sadly at him with the intimacy of someone who has seen you naked, who knows of all your hairy moles. Even the secret of your daughter copulating with a shit-cleaner. For that moment, Tapan felt superior to this man, who had acquired the proportions of a legend. A man whose sky had just fallen and was being washed into a drain.

'I am not pursuing this matter with the Bhangi or his wife, Sir. If the news of this love affair comes out, there will be no sympathy for you or your deceased daughter Sanaz, or for that matter your wife, Mena Bai. Many wise men have been saying that educating women will lead to disastrous consequences. It would reinforce their belief.' Just as it had reinforced his own.

A thick grey block of ash hung on to the cigar with its last stretch of will. A fractured sigh escaped Dada Bhai's lips.

Tapan decided to break the silence in a lowered voice. 'If we conduct a full-fledged inquiry behind the murder, the dirty business will be out in the open.'

Two of the lamps had got extinguished. The other two blinked, competing with each other to survive the onslaught of cold. The ululation in the house was now a long hum of a pandit chanting indecipherable words.

Tapan needed to close the case before day end. The future promotion and accolades lay suspended above his thin shoulders. *It was teamwork, Sahib,* he would bow just a little and say graciously. *I couldn't have solved the case in a day without my team, or your kind support and faith in me.*

'I have complete trust in my team, Sir. The story will not leave this odha.' Tapan turned towards his sub-inspector. 'Do I have your word, Madho?'

'Hukam.' Madho scowled at the door.

'Haider?' Tapan turned towards his jester.

'It is haram for me to disobey a senior's orders, Sahib. I would rather eat a pig.' He gave both his seniors a cherubic smile.

Tapan could always count on the believers of warring faiths to stand united against the godless. The gods had given them collective wisdom to know the greater enemy.

Dada Bhai took out his gold watch from his pocket, opened it with a *click*, saw the time and placed it back near his distinguished heart. All the while his hands trembled wildly. Trying to dig their way out of a deep, deep grave.

'It was a room locked from the inside. No one, except the jeevti dakkan, could have crawled her way in through the black of the night to inflict a curse. Get what I mean?' Tapan beheld the walls on which the lamps' shadows twirled in a Kalbeliya dance. 'Sir, that is the most plausible explanation everyone would believe.' Including Tapan himself. 'And would spare your wife, your late daughter and the family lifelong disgrace and stigma.'

The block of ash from the cigar lost all hope and hurled itself to the ground. Dada Bhai stood up slowly, defeat making him rise. A faint smell of cologne lingered for a moment.

He stood straight. Gallant. Claiming every inch of the legend that he was.

Tapan scrambled to his feet after him.

'Inform Doonga's family ...' The aristocrat's voice was so brittle it split. 'Inform his family that I will pay for his funeral and the kariyawar.' His eyes peered at the floor, plucking a distant memory from its cracks. 'I understand he is survived by a wife and three daughters. Please convey ... that I will bear the expenses of their weddings. They must not despair. Tell them that.'

He turned and walked to the door, his shoes click-clomping, to where Haider stood. The constable straightened his mass in attention.

Dada Bhai stopped in the mildewed doorway, the breeches hugging his hips and ballooning around the thighs in a calculated flair. The cigar in his right hand had burnt itself away. The fingers trembled against the will of this iron man, who had not fallen for the overtures of the Muslim League to seduce him to Pakistan, the Congress to take him in their fold, the landlords to give him the sweeping expanses of hills and valleys, or the mullahs who promised to secure him a certain heaven.

He would walk out of the door and get accustomed to a new reality. Or he might mourn for a century. But Tapan would always find him, in the years to come, with trembling hands.

An old man in a young man's body.

A prisoner of his ideals.

A river that had been dammed.

A man in breeches long after the fashions changed.

A relic of the British India time, which once had the promise of a path-blazing future.

'There was nothing wrong in it,' Dada Bhai said, his head bent towards the cold, unyielding floor.

'Sir?' asked Tapan, who had followed him out, just as he had ushered him in personally.

'A boy and a girl loved each other. There was nothing wrong in what Sanaz did. Love. That is what is halal for me.' Dada Bhai patted Haider on his shoulder without rancour. He took a drag of the now extinguished cigar with his lips pressed in agony, not shame, and wafted towards the passage; a ghost with the past of a future. A ghost whose fingers shook against his will. A ghost who would haunt the building along with the jeevti dakkan for as long as he lived.

Haider let out a confounded burp. And filled the odha with the juices of a tender halal goat.

DUSK

Makar Sankranti, 1950

29

Rao Sahib

On the way back to his estate

Aravalli Hills

CLIP … CLOP … CLIP … CLOP … CLIP … CLOP … THREE horses swaggered along in a tired dusk nicked by Rao Sahib's sobs. A grey hare zigged and zagged in the bushes in long leaps trying to get away from the strange vision of two-legged beasts slung over four-legged ones. Maybe the very picture of a jeevti dakkan for him, an apparition. *Beliefs are not baseless*, Dada Bhai always said.

Piyooo-piyooo-piyooo… A peacock with a heavy tail took a short flight from a keekar tree, carrying the burden of beauty on his buttocks.

The low, brown-skinned hills of Aravallis stretched up to the horizon, smouldering in the last rays of the sun.

Brahma had expectorated his betel-spit in the sky, streaking it with red and orange spittle.

Pity-to-do-it … pity-to-do-it … pity-to-do-it. The did-he-do-it bird notified Rao Sahib, reminding him of what a macabre day it had been.

A woollen coat held him in its arms, a muffler covered his neck and a light blanket was flung over his thighs. When he had insisted on returning the same day to Singhgarh, his aides had packed him up like a crate of mangoes for safe transport. He could only feel the chill around his nose, lips, chin and mojdi-clad feet seized in stirrups.

Aaack-thoo! The snot gathered in Rao Sahib's mouth made a disgraceful landing on his mojdi as he spat. He jerked his foot to get rid of it, kicking the stomach of the horse in turn. The beast shook the shiny mane and neighed his disapproval.

'The horses are tired, Rao Sahib. And so are you.' The fat aide Amar Singh's words came out in a motherly drone.

Rao Sahib swung back and forth on the saddle; a pendulum trying to wind back time.

'Annadata, I had sent a messenger on horseback to inform the owner of the sarai by the Jain mandir. We will stop at the temple inn for the night. We can't reach your fort by nightfall.' Sujan Singh, with the 12-bore slung on his shoulders, had taken charge. The illicit son had invoked his authority.

'Sujan Singh has also asked the inn to arrange for some mauda and saathiya for you,' Amar Singh comforted him. 'He is carrying a bottle of liquor bought from the Parsi baba's distillery in Udaipur as well. You will need strong spirits to put you to sleep today, Hukam.'

Rao Sahib continued to oscillate, eyes swollen, breaths industrious.

The air was rank with the reek of decaying flesh. A wake of vultures sat surrounded by their own guttural calls and thresh of wings.

'Doonga…' Rao Sahib muttered as they began their ascend into the hills. A small, winding path through shrubs. Alive with a burst of life at the precise time which was neither day nor night. A false-hearted time. The unconquerable demon Hiranyakashipu was promised a boon by Brahma. He couldn't be killed in either day or night, by neither man nor beast, not from inside or outside, not by any weapon. The ferocious man-lion avatar of Lord Vishnu had stepped out of a royal pillar, torn open Hiranyakashipu's belly and worn his demonic entrails around his godly neck. A garland of gore. Gods could always find loopholes, even in a boon. Perhaps it was not the betel-spit of Brahma but the blood of Hiranyakashipu that blotched the sky with a deep red every dusk.

'Doonga's body is in police custody now,' Amar Singh informed. 'Why did the fool have to kill himself!'

Rao Sahib rocked on his horseback.

'It was sad what happened with his son and sister. But then the rage of the people is understandable. Their fields were defiled. Their religious sentiments greatly hurt.' Amar Singh looked personally affronted. 'The fool Doonga didn't have to kill himself! He still has family left behind him. Who is going to feed their ever-hungry mouths? They will come begging to Rao Sahib for help.'

'I understand Dada Bhai has offered to take care of Doonga's last rites and also bear the expenditure of marrying his daughters,' said Sujan Singh. 'Our source at the police station told me.'

'Hmmm…' Amar Singh's sigh was that of relief. The jagir, the estate of Rao Sahib would not have to look into the unwanted mess. 'Total bloody waste of a good tracker, don't you think, Maharaj Sahib?' He tried to loop the landlord in their languid evening conversation. 'And a hell of a butcher too. He had almost skinned the sacrificed goat last Diwali before I could wash my sword after severing the head. What a waste.' He grieved amid the hills drumming with the animated clatter of birds. 'Remember the last Diwali, Maharaj Sahib? It was quite eventful.'

Rao Sahib remained sullen and silent. The visions came back of the goat's head in the puja thali with a fire burning on top, ready for the Durga aarti. Of his adolescent deflowered wife, who was meant to be his daughter-in-law and warm his son's four-poster bed. Of the splendid trophy of a snarling wild boar fixed by the posh taxidermists Van Ingen and Van Ingen and sent in a wooden casket from Chennai. Of the chance encounter after the festival with Vyas ji, the famous announcer of All India Radio, who was visiting Dada Bhai's house. But none of it could make him see the beauty in the world.

'Doonga's lad was a sprightly boy of eight. His father was training him to become a tracker, not just a farmer-gatherer, so that he too could serve Maharaj Sahib.' Sujan Singh's voice was loaded. 'The young boy could talk to the jungle. Track animals for hours. Dig a small hole in a bed of sand and find water. The last time I met him, he funnelled his hands around his mouth and imitated the call of a bar-headed goose. If you had your gun, Hukam, you would have fired in his direction believing him to be a duck.' He was silent for a moment gripping the reins of the horse. Smartly dressed in an achkan, breeches-styled pyjama and a golden-rimmed paag for the durbar, but called in haste to undertake the return journey to Rao Sahib's jagir, Sujan Singh had no woollens on. His young flesh was protection enough against the old clutch of the winter evening. 'What happened to Doonga and his family is reprehensible.'

'Yes, yes, who denies that, Banna?' Amar Singh snapped. 'You are a young man with hot blood and all the wrong ideas. Next you'd be defending that Chamar, the Meghwal kid.'

'He didn't deserve to be killed and thrown into the pile of dead animals that he collected. Only because he failed to get up and greet that spineless turd Chitranjan Singh.'

'*Tuck-tuck-tuck...*' All the wisdom of Amar Singh's years had compressed in his frown. 'This kind of talk is fruitless, Banna. The traditions that our forefathers have passed on are sacred. Our Vedas, Puranas. Learn to respect them. You carry the royal blood of Rao Sahib himself in your veins.' He stressed on the last part, making it public knowledge for the trees, hills and nightly denizens of the Aravallis.

Sujan retreated into his muscular shell. The man who treasured and measured his words had not spoken this much in a long time. Rao Sahib sensed a barbed fence rising around his son, riding in an armour of silence.

Amar Singh went on, undeterred. He was never the one for subtleties; always believed in drilling home the point or drilling a hole in the chest. Only those who lacked the pride or weapons of a true-blue Rajput would shamelessly tread on the 'middle path'. If you asked Amar Singh, all those in the middle were hijras, the cursed eunuchs.

'Our integrity and valour are the stuff that stories are made of. We are Suryavanshi Sisodias, the Descendants of the Sun. Rana Kumbha, Bappa Rawal, Lord Ram ... we all share the same lineage, Banna, same lineage,' Amar Singh's voice boomed, silencing a mob of sparrows till they figured the ineptness of the intruder and resumed their dialogue. 'And how inclusive and large-hearted are we! Our Maharana's durbar has a seventeenth Umrao—Sindhi Sarkar—a Mussalman! Maharana Sahib could have placed him in the second-ranked thirty-two Chote Umrao, but he didn't, did he? He gave him the highest honour. Rana Pratap proved we will not bend for a Mughal. We are Mewaris, Banna, we can break but we can't bend! And yet, our Rao Sahib here will even eat with Dada Bhai off the same plate ... eat his jhoota ... he loves him as his blood brother. What's more, Rao Sahib's chief cannoneer is Sajjad Saifi, isn't he? Our noble Rao Sahib is a man who trusts his cannon to a Mussalman. Let no one, *no one* say we are bigots! Including you, young man.'

Emboldened by the cursory 'hukam' from Sujan, Amar Singh turned more garrulous. 'You tell me, if we don't have our honour, our age-old traditions, what are we left with? Tell me, Banna!'

Rao Sahib couldn't see the honour of age-old traditions for now. And he wanted others to see that he didn't see it. He coughed aloud.

'The duvet is slipping from Maharaj Sahib's legs.' Amar Singh's patriarchal rage was replaced by his maternal instincts towards his lord, who was his ward right now. 'Set it right, Sujan Singh.'

Rao Sahib let himself be tucked in by his son on the horseback.

'I want to form a trust,' Rao Sahib said in a thick voice, 'And put all the hundreds of acres that I have to surrender as forest land under it.' He perhaps could not save his friend Dada Bhai, but he must save his forests from the myopic leaders of the Indian Union, their new sarkaar. Yes, the royals and elite hunted, but no one else could hunt in their protected hunting reserves. They had strict laws on shikar. This had curbed poaching in Mewar. The villagers used to sit the whole night in their fields lighting bonfires to ward off the raiding animals, but did not dare to kill them. The new sarkaar was already giving contracts for felling jungles and butchering crocodiles for their skin. They had plans to auction all the confiscated old guns from the royal army and sell them at throwaway prices. The whole populace would be armed, not with flintlocks, traps and nooses, but good -quality weapons. Game animals like deer, antelopes and wild boars would be massacred. That had started to happen in other erstwhile states, which had merged into India.

'Maharaj Sahib,' said Amar Singh, recovering from the initial shock. The extra land was supposed to go to deserving relatives like him. 'You are not thinking straight. It has been a gruesome day.'

'This independence is going to cost our wild animals dearly, Amar Singh ji,' Rao Sahib's tone was tormented. 'The destruction of the wild causes most pain to the ones who have been closely associated with it. The big game hunters will be the biggest conservationists of the future, mark my words! What do those milling crowds in the city care? They will clear forests and exterminate wildlife mercilessly to build their towns and roads and farmlands there. All they will end up saving is the dogs of their city lanes.'

'I think it is a noble and commendable idea, Hukam. One that generations will remember you by.' There was a glint of respect in Sujan Singh's eyes. 'They speak highly about that gora hunter Jim Corbett and what he has done to conserve wildlife.'

Amar Singh gave him a look that he especially reserved for traitors. 'Banna, you don't understand the import of what you're saying!' His pudgy stomach rolled left and right and left and right as he turned back to Rao Sahib. 'Hukam, let the new leaders be worried about the wild animals. We should be thinking about our families, our bloodline.'

'What do this new breed of politicians, babus and those milling crowds in the city care for the jungles? The forests will be raped, the wildlife will crash.' Rao Sahib snarled. 'The forests are our real gods. I will not let them destroy our true heritage ... *that* is our age-old tradition! If there is an ounce of Rajput blood in you, you will not let them touch it! Not in our part of Mewar!'

No one could challenge Amar Singh's stock in vain. 'Hukam,' he growled and said no more.

Neither did Rao Sahib. He became quiet again. Shadows began to soften the sharp outlines, merging the land of the living with the netherworld. Bushes linked arms and jostled with each other for space. Night was a python swallowing the earth whole. They were already treading on Singhgarh's soil, but Rao Sahib's garh, the fort, was still quite some distance away. Their layover at the inn was in a Thakur's thikana—one of the sub-lets of Rao Sahib's own estate—from where he collected taxes. A fleeting thought of his patwari, the tax collector, coming empty-handed from this thikana passed Rao Sahib's mind, when he heard Amar Singh whispering to Sujan Singh.

'Mind your tongue, Banna. Don't try to exploit Rao Sahib's disturbed state of mind.'

Rao Sahib turned and gave Amar Singh a vicious look.

'You remember Parijat, Hukam?' Amar Singh brought his horse parallel to Rao Sahib's on the widened path as a way of reconciliation. They had climbed the hill and reached a flat road that cut the wilderness in a straight line. 'That Bhangan girl

who helped your father, the late Rao Sahib attain, um, nirvana?'
he explained tactfully but received no reply. 'She was loitering
around Dada Bhai's house today with her husband. Can that be
a coincidence?'

Rao Sahib raised his stinging eyes to look at him. '*Kode
maaro use!*' he shouted spraying spit, reaching for an invisible
whip, pressing his thighs and bouncing his rein, which sent the
horse in a canter.

Amar Singh brought his mount forward. 'I didn't want to
agitate you, Hukam. It just seems to be a weird coincidence.
She can't possibly have anything to do with the murder of Dada
Bhai's daughter.'

Murder. Just like that. Without warning. Someone's time
was done. A half-empty bottle of kohl, a few petals of gulmohar
near a mirror. Left behind. Just like that.

'Dada Bhai's house is under the influence of two witches,'
Amar Singh pronounced, 'one that hangs on the tree outside
and the other that hangs around the women of Mewar. His
wife! Teaching letters to women! After some time, the only ones
obeying our commands will be our horses, Hukam, not our
wives and daughters. You are Dada Bhai's friend. Try to talk
some sense into him about our Sanskriti ... our *culture* ... that
has stood the test of time.'

His appeal was met by Rao Sahib's silence.

A small sanctuary of light shimmered on the darkening,
bleary-eyed horizon. The old Jain temple, made by the wise
merchants keeping the Hindu sensibilities in mind—every Jain
temple had the head of Shiva's devotee, the demon Kirtimukha,
carved on the entrance step—was perched on the feral landscape.

Amar Singh found his escape from the one-sided dialogue
with Rao Sahib and made his stallion gallop towards the

mandir. Sujan Singh had found his escape from both the elders in the rear. Rao Sahib had nowhere to escape to. He was left alone to deal with a world where Sanaz didn't breathe, didn't smile, didn't come to him running on the ramparts of his fort, pleading, 'Chacha, won't you let me fire your 22-bore?'

Sanaz, whose smile was monsoon to the aged Aravallis. Who was the only one who touched the pointy tip of his moustache, said 'oww' and kissed her finger to ease the pinch. Whose open arms, when they greeted her Rao Sahib uncle, were the yawn of spring. Whose laughter was the toss of a dust storm. Whose odhani never stayed on her head. Who was delicate as aniseed liquor. Strong-headed as a hungry wild boar.

Rao Sahib had seen her grow from a toddler to a lively young maiden through his various visits to the city and Dada Bhai's hunting trips to Singhgarh with his family. He could never catch the exact moment when he fell in love with her. Was it bit by bit? Was it all at once? There was no love stronger than the love denied. He married his youngest wife, whose proposal had come for his son, because she mirrored Sanaz's youth. But she was not her. Oh, what could an old fool in love, bound by the diktats of society, do? Gods forgive him for taking his son's prospect away. Gods forgive him for loving his friend's daughter secretly. No, no, no … Rao Sahib shook his head. The vengeful gods did not forgive. They believed in ripping the intestines of the rakshas and quenching their thirst with their demon blood. Had they punished her for his desires? The Aghori, the naked sadhu whom he had visited in Udaipur, had sensed their revenge. That is why he had laughed and laughed and laughed.

Rao Sahib had not offered his excess lands to his sundry relatives—the Thakurs scattered over Mewar—but to Dada Bhai, so that it could help him. Help *her*. All he wanted the

Aghori to do was make her fall in love with him for his large-hearted gesture. But she was *dead*. He would not let the same happen to his beloved forests!

'Why, Lankeshwar? Why?' he demanded of his horse. The duvet slipped from his thighs to the jungle floor. His torso bent till his head rested on his horse's neck and his arms wrapped round it. His headgear, the gold-rimmed paag, toppled gracelessly to the ground and rolled away till a bush caught it in its thorns.

Rao Sahib shook from the remnants of the shock of dashing out of Dada Bhai's guest room that afternoon on hearing his youngest son Ahad's cry. Seeing Sanaz in her room finally, a sight that he had been pining for. And how! With two flies trooping in and out of her dead mouth!

'Who killed my Sanaz?' His howl echoed in the valleys, suffocating the sounds of dusk.

The cooing of Amar Singh *Now, now, Maharaj Sahib … we know she was like a daughter to you* … the strong hold of Sujan on his horse's reins … the day closing its tired, drooping eyelids around him … the stars floating up in the proud Mewar sky … the tears mixing with suds of saliva.

The day left.

The sniffs and sobs remained like true friends.

Rao Sahib cried. And cried. And cried.

'Sanaz…' His wet whispers got lost in the silky hair of Lankeshwar. 'You can fire the 22-bore, Sanaz.'

A soft neigh from the horse.

There was nothing more to say.

30

Suġra

Dada Bhai's House

Bohrawadi

SUĠRA WAS A BROKEN WINDOW HANGING BY A HINGE. EACH small swing closer to a certain shattering by fall. She had sought the jeevti dakkan at the bidding of her eldest daughter. And the witch had found her. In her darkest hour. The tainted hour, whose stain would blot her remaining days. The bundle wrapped in white was her granddaughter, not the day's laundry that would be returned home—washed and ironed. Though her vision was fogged, the bundle had a morbid familiarity to a dead husband.

The house pulsated with the shrieks, shrills, sobs and snivels of women. Some theatrical. Others unaffected. The cadence rose and fell with each new entrant. Even someone old as her with absconding senses could feel the vibrating air. It was like Tahir's modern house—electrified. The no-good police team had left, leaving the floodgates open for Bohras as well as per-castes to pour in.

Her grandson Ahad's piercing cry at noon, from the third floor, had held the house by its throat and throttled it. Suġra had hobbled out, her stick clattering to a side, and dangled from the railing on the porch to look up. Cry after cry followed. Shredding the winter afternoon to pieces.

Her heart had sagged as she had croaked again and again, 'Aye bhandora, bhandori … will someone tell me what's going on?'

A burp born out of stress had brought along the greasy pakoras she had eaten earlier to her mouth. Grainy and half-processed. A chill slithered up her bent spine as a shivering Ismail focussed on her vision, descending the railing-less steps. Coming and standing by her side. An Ismail without his cocky smile was a world without war. Inconceivable. What he said had filtered through fumes of a fantasy. Sanaz had been found dead in her locked room!

When Ismail held her by her shoulders, she didn't flinch. She collapsed in his wiry arms, unable to feel her knees anymore. The deserters! Just when she needed them! She saw the dead body of her granddaughter long after the brawny twelve-year-old Zain had run up to the terrace to tackle his grief and anger in solitude. The sagacious and sharp-witted Sa'ad had taken their mother Mena, who had fainted on sight, up to her room with the help of his father Tahir. The fat Ahad had cowered in a corner, simpering, too afraid to go back to his room alone. The loud Khadija, Suġra's daughter, had made her entry with her slimy, moss-covered husband, and raised the bars of moaning a notch higher.

Badi Bi had taken control in the chaos, bathing the body and dressing Sanaz up for her last journey with Khadija's help, laying out mattresses covered with white sheets for visitors to sit on, fixing a herbal concoction for Mena and dousing the kitchen fire for good. Sugra had not imagined she would miss Ismail's greeting 'Ram-Ram, Namaste, Assalam-alaykum!' to visitors one day.

Tahir had put his head on Sugra's lap and cried like a new-born babe. Cried unforgiving tears. Her heart had broken over and over again. Her fingers had dug into her son's well-oiled hair and remained lodged there.

As Sugra was made to lay on her bed that afternoon, by Ismail and Tahir, she sensed two wings clipped and fallen by her sides. Of the fledgling Sanaz, who had not yet taken off in flight. It was on that long winter day, the Makar Sankranti of 1950, that her senses began to return to her, one by one.

Sugra felt. Goosebumps on her arms. She had got the chills as a child and was taken to the gora British doctor when all the traditional doctors—the Hakim and Vaidhraj—had given up. She was the first in the mohalla to be touched by a white man. She felt them again. The goosebumps, and the touch of those hands, which were as white as the walls of the hospital room.

Sugra heard. Her childhood nickname Roohani, the soulful. She had earned it on the day her family was returning from a pilgrimage to Galiyakot. They had got delayed on the way back. The gates of the fort city of Udaipur closed at 10 p.m. You needed special permission from the Maharana to enter the city from the main gates after that. For those who didn't have it, the sentry asked, 'Who's it?' If the answer was 'rayyat'—subjects—he would open the small pedestrian door on the side to let you in. After asking the reason for being out so late, of course.

That was a night of nights. The moon was a thin, unholy crescent of teej, the third day of the month. The sky was star-scorched. The wind held its breath. The horses of their tonga shifted nervously. Sugra's family had stepped out of the carriage and stood knocking on the gate. The two sentries on the other side kept asking 'Who's it?' each time they knocked. They could not hear their cries of 'rayyat!' As a gruelling hour passed and the family tired and began to settle around the gate, Baby Sugra, in the arms of her uncle, cried her first word: rayaaaa ... aa ... aa ... and the gate flung open. The baby's voice had cut through the influence of occult, or a bottle of strong-brewed country mauda, they would never know. The sentries had heard her. Her first word was a consummate success.

Sugra smelt. Cooked quails on the breaths of the beggars sleeping in a wide city drain. The eight-year-old Sugra had gone on a leisurely ride in a covered buggy with her mother. The horses cantered on the dusty summer roads of the city, past the clock tower Ghantaghar. Just before the imposing Jagdish Mandir outside the city palace, a convoy of startled quails crushed under the wheels. Two beggars, an oldish man and a youngish woman near the temple, had rushed to claim the dead birds. Animated on finding quails in the city, they had linked their promiscuous hands and blessed the girl peeping from behind the curtain of the buggy: 'May your flight be luckier than the quails.' Her mother had later whispered to herself, 'Tauba-tauba, these vagabonds have no morals. I am sure they sleep together at night, hiding in the drains.' But she had not failed to claim that it was their blessing that saved Sugra from a near fatal fall from a mango tree, on the very day she turned a woman from a girl.

Suġra saw. Herself clearly in the mirror as a twelve-year-old applying kohl from the night lamp around her doe eyes. She had become a strange thing as a grown-up girl. But then, girls are complicated beings. They metamorphose. They start to have cycles like the moon. They are expected to become mahouts and train their bodies on how to act (gracefully), laugh (softly), obey (without question), pray (for the family), sit (with their legs together), eat (in delicate morsels), fart (as if it's a secret). Spread their legs for their husbands to push their way in and for the babies to push their way out. Suġra was ready to do it all for Khuzaima, that lanky boy in his patent striped bush shirts with a devilish smile. The assured swing of his hand as his *danda* hit the *gilli* each time he played the game in the Bohrawadi lanes, sending up dust devils. The firm grip on his little sister's wrist when the lanes transformed into rivulets in monsoons. His paper boats that were bound for the sea ended up anchoring on Suġra's porch. Now that's what she believed was providence. But there was one more thing required of girls. To not, under *any* circumstances, fall for Satan's favourite invention—love.

She was betrothed the day she was born. 'I ask for your daughter's hand in marriage for my Saifuddin.' The sweet misri on the tongues and a smear of attar on the back of the hands. Two beards scratching two friendly necks in a hug. The cries of mubarak-ho, congratulations, in the carpeted rooms. And Suġra's life was sealed before she had opened her eyes covered in her mother's juices. Her Khuzaima, who gave her secret smiles and sent her paper boats, passed her lane one day sitting on a horse, head hanging under the weight of a groom's ornate safa, decked up like a glittering Tazia in a Muharram procession; another martyr to the ways of the world.

Sugra tasted. Lying prostrate on her bed. The citric bile of sadness pooled in her mouth. The years had come and left, breaking all their promises one by one. And now, life was spurring up her senses, cruelly, when what she wanted the most was to forget.

Ismail came to check on her again, his dirty bush shirt torn from one side. The purple of a bruise surfacing around his left jaw and chin. So stark was the contrast that even Sugra could see written on his face the pivotal tenet of the police. Brute force. He had brought in a glass of warm water and gently placed her walking stick by her bed. She could not get up. Ismail bent down, put his hand behind her curved back and propped her up.

'Some milk for you?' he asked, taking the empty glass from her deliriously shaking hand.

'Tahir...?'

'He is making ... the arrangements.'

Sugra thrust herself to the end of the bed, her ghaghra clumping at her knees, her odhani discarded.

Ismail gave her a hand as she reached for her walking stick.

She waved him away. 'Go help Badi Bi.'

He gave her a reluctant nod and hustled out of the room.

The head of the walking stick, made of ivory that had once adorned an august African elephant, sat robust beneath Sugra's feeble hand. She balled her fingers around it and stared at the four-horned antelope, molten pity dancing in its glass eyes. Guilt leaked from her pores and swam around her feet.

Her daughter Khadija had avoided her unambiguously since she had stepped into the house of death, called back from her way to Galiyakot. The husband Qurban Ali had come to Suġra as she sat on a chair near the body, and had held her rough hands in his soft ones.

Once the words of shock and condolence were spoken, and the dry, tearless convulsing of her body subsided, he had bent near her ears conspiratorially and whispered, 'Hope you liked the fragrance of the box of bokhoor I sent along with Khadija.' He had drawn back and given her an ugly half-smile. His voice carried the crackling of Radio Ceylon and she felt it in her teeth even after he left her side.

A perfunctory hug is all that her daughter had bestowed upon her worn and frayed mother. Khadija had been busy in a flurry of activity: consoling the kids, rubbing her brother Tahir's back, checking on her sister-in-law one too many times, helping Badi Bi bathe and dress the body. Suġra had never seen her so industrious. Even when her father had left the world for good.

The majestic eunuch's words, spoken as she had left her room, sang a funeral song in Suġra's ears—*One drop will make you shit buckets. Two drops will make you bleed from you-know-where. Three drops ... well, you do not want to go to three drops, do you? One extra drop is one-too-many!*

Suġra shuddered. Her chest ached. Remorse coursed down her thin veins. She reached for her tasbi, the rosary, and began rolling it. *Ya Ali ... Ya Ali ...* her lips moved wordlessly keeping to the rhythm of her fingers. She stopped with a start, kept the tasbi down on the bed and covered it with her hand, as if putting it to sleep. No prayers could help her now. She was no fool. *Nijaat ...* deliverance ... cannot come to those who invoke evil. The mother sparrow on the jharokha watched this act of submission in silence.

Her daughters in Pakistan would have got the news by phone. Her youngest son Abbas would be on his way back from Galiyakot.

Throes of childbirth were not the worst agony in life. Throes of guilt beat them without breaking a sweat. Suġra lifted the side of her mattress and pulled out a yellow velvet pouch. She hauled herself up, leaning heavily on her stick, and began a slow march towards her bathroom. A march past the baby Suġra, who had said her first word 'rayyaa...', making the sentries fling open the gates for them, the young Suġra who had marvelled at the spunk of the beggars and swore to herself to possess it one day, the girl Suġra who had loved Khuzaima whose paper boats were destined to sink in drains. All those Suġras were dead. Like her flowering granddaughter Sanaz. They had never got a proper funeral though. No one had mourned their passing.

The velvet in her palm reminded her of her son-in-law Qurban Ali's touch.

Oh, the notions today's girls like Khadija were fed with ... a child for a child. Kill one, get one of your own. *It will not work!* Suġra wanted to shake her daughter. Make her see reason. You could invoke the witch by giving her the sacrifice of blood. That was not enough. The boon came at a greater cost. The witch was a moneylender. She would suck the interest out of you with her pointed teeth. But no, Khadija wanted her sister-in-law to lose a child to get one of her own womb.

Mena was again three months pregnant with Tahir's child. The couple had not yet announced it, but not much missed Suġra's rusted eyes. Ya Allah ... why ... *why* did she have to confide this to her embittered daughter! The news had festered inside Khadija, rising up in a boil of a scheme. She had gone to the woman in Galiyakot, whose curses were known to work better than Qurban Ali's member. The offering that she needed was of an unborn child. The witch would be pleased, grant Khadija her wish, the woman had professed. *The price was not high to claim from someone who already had four breathing and growing children*, Khadija had argued with her mother. All Suġra had to do to cause the miscarriage was a flick of her wrist. A drop of poison in Mena's evening glass of milk. Ismail always got two glasses of steaming milk on a tray; gave it first to Suġra and took the other down to Mena. Every evening, her daughter-in-law would be on the ground floor, meeting women who came to ask for her help.

The bathroom was bitterly cold. Suġra drew the curtain, let her stick fall to the floor and strung open the velvet pouch. A transparent glass bottle tumbled out on to her palm, full to the brim with a dark green liquid. The stuff that nightmares are made of. The wall supported her crooked back, bent under the dead weight of sunken paper boats and beggars' blessings. She uncorked the bottle with unsteady hands, poured the liquid on the floor and splashed it away into the drain with a mug of water. The liquid, diluted to a light green now, went down the slope sluggishly before the hole belched it up.

She had not used a single drop of poison from the bottle.

She knew that the jeevti dakkan had sensed her mutiny and snatched away the sacrifice that was her due, regardless.

A child of Tahir's.

The faces of all the dead she had loved most dearly a long time ago, reflected on the splash of water on the slick floor … her mother, Khuzaima, her feisty cousin Bilkis who had died in childbirth, the snake charmer who brought a cobra and tales in a basket. The journey had been so long, full of things that she never did. The lives she never lived. Was it possible to go on living when most of you was gone? Losing your yearnings was no joy. But losing the memory would be what the kafirs, the infidels, called nirvana. Soon, one day soon. She would forget all about her ally the jeevti dakkan, her husband who never kissed her on her lips, the betel-nut scraper that was her last loyal companion and the striped-bush-shirt-clad Khuzaima of paper boats and secret smiles.

Poor Suğra, she thought, *you deserved better.*

31

Parijat

Kachchi Basti

Delhi Gate

PARIJAT AND THE EVENING TALKED. EACH TELLING THE OTHER her travails. Wordlessly. Parijat wanted to flee from the basti of Bhangis, just as the day had fled. But there was no playful dusk, no gentle night to fill in her space. The red and grey streaks in the sky were alive with everything she loved—roses and forest streams and Dada Bhai's smile that dipped down a little before it rose in a wave.

The fading beams of the sun rested on the rooftop. The mango tree outside her hut took in all the free boarders returning to its branches with forbearance. Parakeets. Bulbuls. Babblers. Sunbirds. A lone koel. Pouring his heart to anyone who would listen. The birds beat their wings, shrieked and claimed the best

286

spots. Not minding the stench from the open drains or the rot drifting in from the Chamar basti.

The door of Parijat's hut was open, giving it a gap-toothed smile. The kutcha path throbbed with evening activity. End of day's play for the Bhangis till the upper-caste bowels churned and emptied again, till their drains got clogged with the sludge of homemade soaps. It was the hour of mud chulhas. Smoke from the cook fires twirled out of the thatched roofs in a listlessness only smoke can attain. *Cluck-cluck-cluck-cluck...* Someone's chicken ran past Parijat's feet followed by a girl in hot pursuit.

Parijat stepped on the mud porch. The drum beats of her pumping blood reached a crescendo in her ears, muffling all sounds of the evening. She drew a long breath and entered the freezing hut. The miasma of sweat and mauda (or was it the other liquor, the name of which she could never get right?) had made the hut lose its dim self-regard. It was dark within; her retinas expanded and familiar forms begin to take shape. A weary trunk on one side, mud pots lined on a shelf made of a wooden plank, a darkened fireplace, a torn saree hanging from a hook on the wall, two eyes gleaming back from the cot.

'There you are, finally. I've been waiting for you,' her husband said, the words coming out weak.

Parijat took a couple of nervous steps and stopped.

'Come, sit, my pari, we need to talk.' Bhola patted the torn mattress sagging on the cot. His other hand, sticking to the chest, held a greasy bottle, half-empty.

The old cot groaned as she perched herself at the other end.

'We have to live in a nation, which was cut to pieces at birth ... If only Bapu and Bhagat Singh had joined forces ... History will hold the British Raj accountable to what it did to the subcontinent. And the sawarna upper castes will be held accountable for what they did to the Dalit untouchables. To *us*...' His words had the drag of a handcart. 'Does this sound familiar?'

Oh yes, it did. More of it coursed through her head. *Don't despair. The world order as we know it is languishing an era is coming to a close. If not us, our next generation will live in an Al-Hind that doesn't treat them as polluted.* She had always hung on to her brother Valmiki's words, whether there was any truth in it or not.

'You know what is worse than living the life that we live? It is living in false hope. While your brother is busy giving speeches to khadi-clad students, plotting a future for the Harijan, the untouchables, who have no future, and romancing with the daughter of an aristocrat, here I am, taking police beatings on his behalf.' His face shone with liquor-induced perspiration. He tapped on the cot again. She moved closer to him, his sour breath washing over her face.

'We were born in drains, my pari, we will die in drains. There are no seven upper worlds for us. Only the seven under worlds—the seven hells. Can we disrupt this balance?' He lifted his good hand and stroked her cheek. 'Can we?'

Parijat failed to nod on time and the back of his hand struck her jaw, throwing her back on the cot.

He took a swig off the bottle, staring at the torn saree suspended on the wall. Parijat propped herself up, eyes and cheek stinging. A low buzz in her ear.

'We can't,' Bhola picked up the conversation from where he'd left it, caressing her thigh as he did, still coherent with his talk. He became eloquent when he was drunk. A louse trooped down his sideburn and sensing the sudden lack of cover, scrambled back into his hair. 'I tolerated it all this while, you going to deliver your brothers' love letters. The bastard, putting you and me at risk for his shenanigans. And that Dada Bhai's daughter, Sanaz ... giving you a rupee for your services, huh? Would she throw the coin in your basket or put it in your hand?'

He inserted two fingers into her mouth and pressed her slashed tongue. Parijat gagged and tasted salt. Tears streamed down her cheeks.

'Did she touch you or not? Or would she only touch your dear brother?'

Parijat could see his crooked teeth grinding in rage.

'Did she pity you the same way you pity me? A rupee, thoo!' He spat on the side. 'Why didn't she give you those tiny studs in her earlobes instead?' He pulled his fingers out of her mouth chafing the insides with his nails, and wiped her saliva on her ghaghra in harsh smacks.

Parijat rubbed away tears from her eyes and the back of her hand came splotched with kohl.

'Were you dreaming of having her as your bhabhi ... your sister-in-law? Gracing our hut with her royal half-smile? Her mother, Mena Bai, welcoming us in her fortress and serving you quails and malai barfi? Dada Bhai dropping the boy's family back home in his car after we have cleared his shit?' His Adam's apple jumped as he gurgled out a laugh. Spittle made bubbles around the corners of his lips.

His eyelids drooped. Parijat tried to get up from the cot, her mouth tasting of unwashed laundry. Bhola gathered the flesh of her arm in a pinch and pressed hard, making her collapse on the cot again.

'What's the hurry, huh?' He took in a long swig.

Parijat rubbed her arm, pain warming up the flesh.

'My ardhangini … my half of the en-entire…' Bhola's tongue lolled to a side. He pulled it in with effort. 'Get this straight in here.' He tapped her forehead with his cracked nails. 'There are upper castes and there are upper-caste aristocrats. There are un-untouchables and there are untouchable aristocrats. Your brother is the latter. And you, my dear ardhangini, will always remain an ass-wiper. Don't you for-forget that.'

The dusk had deepened into night. The sounds from the streets had diminished with people retiring to their personal nightmares in their shanties.

'So now the whole of Mewar knows about you and G-gokul, your rakhi *brother*.' Bhola smirked. 'I am a *loola*, na, a grovelling handicap? He is a sturdy young man … huh?' He began to knead her thigh with his knuckle, pressing up to the bones. Parijat, having no tongue to bite, winced with each thrust. 'That's what you want no, my pari, my ardhangini? See how I address you so respectfully. Your brother Valmiki demands men should n-n-never abuse women.'

He let out a chortle, grabbed a handful of Parijat's curls and threw her on the cot, a few strands plucked from the roots hanging between his fingers. Her head stung and throbbed. She tried to scramble out from the other side. The thick glass bottle of liquor hit her chest and pain ruptured in a red light. Her breaths came out in short bursts as Bhola pulled up her ghaghra with his shrunken hand and undid his dhoti with the other.

'I am your pati parmeshwar, your husband g-god.' The stench of a wet mongrel hung above her in a cloud. The cot was a slab of ice. The dark hut a scream that had died in silence. *Squick-squick* … a cry of a pig from the Chamar basti crawled over Parijat's body along with Bhola's twisted limbs. He held her neck with his good hand before thrusting his way in.

'What-if-I-killed-Sanaz … I-killed-that-bitch … I-killed-that-bitch…' he panted in an inebriated, metrical soliloquy.

Her tranquil forest stream gurgled below her eyelids. She forced her aching eyes shut, her hands bunching up the bedding in her fists, and willed herself away from the here and now. The teardrops trickling into her ears were not tears, they were the morning dew on bajra fields. The cot poking her was her brother Valmiki's reckless embrace. The slaver-filled mouth was her mother's pot of Raab, hot and savoury. The din in her ears was Dada Bhai handing her the toffees and saying—*here, child, take this*—over and over and over.

Till it was over. For now. Bhola sank on to her before rolling to the side. She opened her eyes to the present. The stink returned. So did the cold and dark.

She gingerly touched the spot where the bottle had hit her ribs. It felt sore. Like the rest of her. Pain radiated from between her thighs and ended on her tongue where words came to die. Bit by bit, she rolled the ghaghra down her legs, feeling the new and old memories that had left their marks on her waist, her stomach, her thighs, her calves. Ladle marks, brass vase marks, broken handi marks, bottle marks. Bestowed on her by her aunt, her father, Rao Sahib's men, Bhola. Beatings didn't matter. She had learnt early on that life was a sum of your scars.

Bhola lay by her side. Spent. Exposed. Unloved. She pulled the rough blanket from the side of the cot and tucked him in. He had done her an immeasurable favour by marrying her, bringing her away from the accursed village, close to her beloved Valmiki, close to Dada Bhai, close to having a semblance of life. She could not bear Bhola any grudge.

Her husband had not killed Sanaz, as he claimed. He couldn't possibly. He was just a drunken braggart, seeking solace in his imagination. She would make sure he never says that in front of Valmiki. The petite smiling Sanaz, clandestinely handing Parijat her 'pocket money'. 'Get your rose water, Didi…' she would whisper pressing the coin into her palm. Valmiki's letters were to Sanaz what rose water was to Parijat. Panacea.

She walked up to the doused clay stove, sat on her haunches and wiped her eyes with the scullery rag. The delicate Sanaz. Dead. Was this the fate of all girls who transgressed? Was there always a living witch lying in wait to give them a kiss of death or … to cut their tongues? She drew out a folded envelope from her bosom, the one that she would never hand over to Sanaz, shredded it to pieces and sprinkled it over the ashes of the cook fire. Tomorrow, as the girl who loved her brother would be lowered in the ground, Valmiki's letter would go up in flames. A burial and a pyre, a fitting end to an unfitting story.

Valmiki would not be contained, she knew, whenever the news reached him. He would rage within. Waste away in the cavity of his chest. Become a haunted house no one could enter. She needed to bundle up all her nerve and pack it inside her. Convey to him soundlessly that he was fortunate to be loved for two years. Two years! An eternity for someone who had not got two whole hours of it in her life.

Parijat's stomach churned with hunger. Tonight, she would not sleep. The winter fog rolled in the lanes of the Bhangi shantytown, bringing along dreams brittle with misfortunes and exhaustion. She brought her wrist close to her nose, breathed deeply and snatched a gossamer-fine fragrance of rose from her racing pulse. The stench had not overpowered the roses. A thin smile lifted her damp, swollen cheeks. Till the time you were not made to eat the shit you collected, till the time your brother was alive and breathing, life had a rosy side.

32

Hariharan

Ghanta Ghar Mohalla

Udaipur

'I'LL GIVE YOU *ONE*, YOU!' HARIHARAN WAGGLED HIS LEATHER mojdi at an urchin who tee-heed kicking his football back to his gang. 'About time someone put these feral foxes back in their cages!' He shouted down the Ghanta Ghar lane, slipping his foot in the mojdi again and dusting his white pyjama where the football had hit him. He stood hammered by the day, his crispness gone with the starch of his clothes. The woollen shawl was thrown carelessly around his shoulders, his topi stuffed rudely in his pocket. He knew when it was time for appearances. And when it was time for action.

The bustle of the Ghanta Ghar market had died down long before he stepped into this quiet lane. Two-storey stone buildings stood in attention on both the sides of the dirt path. The merchants had counted their coins and slammed shut their shops. The vendors had pulled their carts or lugged their goods home. They had returned to the comfort of the familiar bickering of their wives, who would treat them as their very own Maharanas, serve them hot dal-roti before they touched the food themselves, and rub their toughened toes at night before lying down on the bedding at the base of their husband's cot. Scattered in the lane were kites, some with tails, some tailless, severed, in frays and tatters. The prized kites that the whole city had fought for were laid to unrest on knobbly branches and peeping jharokhas.

The January evenings were ghosts of their chirpy June sisters. They let out their foggy breaths fuzzing the few streetlamps and huddled in morose corners with knees drawn, their teeth biting the passersby.

A fragrant curd-kadi cooked in one kitchen. *Chunnn* ... a gatta curry garnished with asafoetida in the next. The aromas hung thick in the lane, unable to escape the lull of the sleepy winter twilight. Hariharan, thankfully, had eaten his meals. He had rushed home twice to eat between coercions, manipulations, a scandalous murder and the police interrogation. He was all but not a disobedient son. His father had advised him strictly— Have your meals on time! You don't eat to work. You work to eat.

One day he would own a cycle. Not an ordinary Phillips, but a Raleigh from London. And then he would go flying on the streets, nodding to envious glances, reaching home on time for meals between deals. Ha! He liked the idea.

There was a disquiet in his demeanour. It was not Sanaz's death. It was something more rudimentary. He had been obligated to have a cold drink, a glass of RoohAfza today at the Bohra-Muslim Kamruddin's place! It had left him much too polluted to finish the last and defining job of the day. There had been no time to purify himself after the act. His flapping body manoeuvred the next bend in the lane. A low guttural *Baaaaa* made his legs come to a jolting halt. Well, well! The promise of the offering he had made to his personal deity Laddoo Gopal at the start of the day had paid off! He noted it feverishly in his mental ledger. A black-and-white cow with ponderous udders stood right in the middle of the road, peeing a thick yellow stream that flooded around her hind legs and ran in a small rivulet to the side.

God sent! Hariharan ignored the crunch of his knees as he subjected them to a pounding sprint. Short-winded, he reached the cow's rear, spread his legs, bent his back, crushing his belly on his thighs, cupped his hands in the holy stream and gulped it down. The caustic taste revived his senses and sharpened his wits, till the flow reduced to a dribble. He collected the last of it lovingly in the cusp and splashed the warm urine on his face. There, now he was cleansed. Gau Mata, the holy cow, will help ferry his future to safe banks. He pulled out his kerchief, off-white now, dabbed his face, and walked in confident strides towards Lal Chand Mahajan's house, a one-man Dandi March, even without a dandi-stick. The inspiration behind his pertinacity was the great Mahatma Gandhi ji Sahib, after all.

The two stone steps to the wooden door with a brass knocker looked exactly as they had in the pre-dawn hours of that fateful Markar Sankranti. Indolent. In judgement of every visitor who came a-knocking. A door that would intuitively spurn away or accept its suitors. Rajput royals who had lost their ancestral wealth to liquor and women, Sunni Muslims seeking dowry loans to pack away their daughters, Shia Bohras whose cloth shops had been burnt to threads by refugees from Pakistan, Shudras trying to pay for their elders' kariyawar, Bhil tribals from the forest afflicted by draught or loss of cattle … the wooers were as varied and enticing as a door could hope for.

A pinkish-grey spinning top left by an urchin lay lopsided on a step. The dark umbilical cord of drain water from the hunkering houses met and ran in the middle of the path. A lone streetlamp down the lane woke up from the daylong slumber with a wheeze and blinking eye.

Thak-thak-thak … The brass knob clutched in Hariharan's fat fingers whacked the door. Once. Once again. Tenacious like hindsight.

A voice, colder than the evening air, asked from within, 'Whozz it?'

'I am here to see Lal Chand Mahajan ji.'

'At the hour of the evening meal? Who has died?'

'The egg-laying hen has died!' Hariharan met the jab with his own nettle sting. The quota for his day's niceties lay expended. He shook his head in self-deprecation and solicited again, 'Please, tell Mahajan ji Sahib that his humble servant Hariharan stands on his doorstep.'

Long moments of silence followed. Not awkward, but angry.

Hariharan fiddled his thumbs, cursing himself for losing his patience. He had never been angsty, self-absorbed and rude like today's youth. The virtue of patience had been instilled in him quite impatiently. By his father. Who was perpetually and forever in debt. Dependent on help from others to run his household. One such benefactor of their family was Abdul Chacha. He had chosen the plump Hariharan from his cache of siblings to be the lucky apprentice. Every morning, he had to reach his tiny clockmaker's shop and sweep it before Abdul Chacha arrived. There were dusty blueprints, brass pliers, riveting hammers, turns, die screw plates, spring winder, balance truing calliper … all the shiny tools that could create a clock to keep pace with the movement of the sun and stars. The market for his wares was small and well-paying—the nobles and aristocrats and every man who was not rich enough but wanted to flaunt his social status by owning a clock. For hours, Abdul Chacha would bend double over his scarred wooden desk. When he needed a break, he would get up and close the shop door. With Hariharan inside.

The first time it happened, he had cringed to the wall, hot with embarrassment, as Chacha had reached out not for his hammer but for Hariharan. Within moments, the shop that smelt of machine oil began reeking of a toilet. The eight-year-old Hariharan had fumbled with his dhoti, wiping his tears, once Chacha finished and returned to work. This went on for days and months, the break increasing to twice a day, depending on Chacha's workload. The day Hariharan gathered the courage to tell this to his father, he had come running from the clockmaker's shop, shivering and feverish. Baba had continued to roll and squeeze laddoos in his fist in the sweetmeat shop as he listened to his son. Then he had wiped his hands, walked to Hariharan and slapped him hard with the back of his hand, causing a nosebleed.

'You fat little whore! Here I am, trying to have you learn a precious life skill, and you…! Slouching in the corner with your lousy attitude. If you breathe this to your mother or anyone … you thankless wimp…' He had let his threat hang in the sultry shop, its walls greased with sweat and oil. And now a few drops of blood. That was the day Hariharan, covered in blood and

slobber and an old man's semen, had opened his mental ledger
and made the first note. To be patient and wait for his time. Till
his father became a snivelling, dribbling idiot his grandfather
had become. Till he could get back at all the old Abduls and
Alis who didn't have their hearts or foreskin in place. Laddoo
Gopal, the only one who listened to his woes, would help him
through. One day, he would have riches and power. He had on
his side that which his father and the clockmaker didn't have:
time. He had smiled at his father through pain and hurt, and
never stopped smiling.

A loud thunk, the scrape of metal on wood, and the door
flung open to the moneylender Mahajan's lair. Hariharan let
out the breath he was holding. The smell of chillies sizzling
in ghee managed to escape into the mohalla before Hariharan
stepped inside and the entrance was closed shut. Rumour had
it that Lal Chand Mahajan kept a jar of ghee in lock and key.
It was only to be taken out when *he* was home, and not for
cooking meals for his old hag or scrawny grandchildren.

The slightly bent figure of Mahajan was wrapped in his
prickly shawl. He hobbled on his elephant foot towards his
dingy office. The passage that led to the room where wealth
grew like fungus was less blurry now. The light from the first-
storey lamps fell tepidly on the ground floor. Mahajan was
known not to light one extra lamp than strictly necessary. He
preferred not to blow up his hard-embezzled money in smoke.

The rattle of a bunch of keys, the squeak of a reluctant lock
and the door cracked open. Without a word, Mahajan scuffled
to his kerosene lamp on the taak and lighted it, placing the
used match in the stack of its head-burnt brethren. Nothing
went to waste in Lal Chand Mahajan's household. Every little
twig was an extra second worth of fuel in cook fire. The lamp,

eager to prove its worth, puttered and cackled before the flame whooshed up. It faintly lit a room so dry that the air crunched as they moved.

'I heard you visited Kamruddin Hathiwala after you came to see me today.' Mahajan placed his diminished butt on the flat mattress amid the parchment rolls, sloping table with an ink pot and worn-out silk cloth with its exhibit of coins. He luxuriously extended his grand elephant foot to join the display. The presence of his mammoth leg filled the diminutive room.

Hariharan joined his hands in a namaste and lowered his gaze from the moneylender's bulbous nose, buying time. How did real-time news reach this place, which seemed to lie forever suspended in a spider's web? His bladder, full of holy cow piddle, began to press against the wall of his stomach.

'I did, Huzoor. You will not believe it…' Hariharan avoided his gaze as he unrolled a tattered mattress and sat on it, letting out loose clouds of dust and stirring the fleas to action. 'It was very rich of Kamruddin to pull four cashews from his pocket and chomp on them as he spoke to me. What a nawab, that!'

Mahajan scooped out a handful of cashews from the folds in his shawl and held it in his fist. He popped one in his mouth and Hariharan witnessed the nut being ground to a pulp between antiquated teeth. The small act confirmed what this merchant of desiccated dreams didn't have: lack of imagination.

'What I mean is, respected Mahajan ji, that myself is not used to such luxuries in life. Cashews are not meant for the underprivileged class to which yours truly belongs.' Hariharan folded his stiff legs. The day had left him with only one possible solution to his career advancement. To what he had noted in his ledger as an eight-year-old. He had every intention of making it work. 'I had gone there to ask that old Bohra merchant to give up any hope of marrying Dada Bhai's daughter Sanaz ... convince him that it was a bad, bad proposition. To marry into a family whose illustrious reputation was soon coming to an end would be the worst affliction he would bring upon his respected self. He could find other young and beautiful virgin brides without reducing his wealth substantially by sharing it with Dada Bhai. I told him that, in my humble opinion, the aristocrat would never be able to pay back the debt.' Hariharan concluded his hurried explanation.

'Oh, and I thought you had Dada Bhai's best interests at heart.' The edge of Mahajan's dhoti was coming undone at the seams. His voice as frayed as his well-worn garment.

'*Interest* is what the politicians call "a disputed territory".' Hariharan's jowls hurt with all the smiling he had done today. He cast a glance around the darkling chamber. The narrow room where dusk prevailed at all times. The dark-skinned natives who came into this room with folded hands were slaughtered without using a sword or a gun or a bludgeon. Slain by Mahajan, who was neither beast nor human. A Narasimha sent by gods to counter a boon of happiness granted by them. 'I am sure you too have the best interests of your clients at heart, respected Mahajan ji, but I understand the interests of your family come first.'

Mahajan smiled. The gold tooth glimmered in the lamplight. It was a shrewd, greasy smile. Slimy as the egg whites Hariharan had chanced upon in Abdul Chacha's shop.

'You know how these meat eaters are, Mahajan ji ... Sahib.' Hariharan was running out of deference. 'These people acquire the traits of the animals they consume. Kamruddin is hoof-headed, but Dada Bhai has the good qualities of a goat—mild and perseverant. If he lands the catechu tender—he has a strong possibility of getting it—he will make it work ... pay back your interest *and* the principal.'

Mahajan didn't eat dogs, but he was a belligerent bitch, crouching teeth-bared, biding her time. Silence stretched languorously. The odour of personal histories rolled up in parchments mixed with the pungent cow urine splashed on Hariharan's person. He was not unnerved.

'Lal Chand ji, Dada Bhai rents a garage in Hathipol for his car. He hasn't been able to pay the rental for the last eleven months. The Bohra man who owns that space is losing his patience. He might soon kick them out.' He shuffled in his place to press his penis with his ankle, willing it to restrain. To request the use of a bathroom now would break the flow of negotiation. It would be a naked show of weakness. 'There's this other Mahajan who gave him a loan ... Dada Bhai is paying his interest regularly, but has not paid back a paisa of the principal. If we decide, we can bring him the summons of seizure of all his properties, a kurki, amid drumbeats and public disgrace.'

'And why are you telling me this?' Lal Chand subjected another cashew to its final grinding.

'He is rammed from all sides. The only hope of his deliverance from this situation—his daughter's marriage to a wealthy merchant—is now gone. The polite British, who sipped tea with him over hunting tales, have left with their loot. His beloved Maharana ji Sahib is only a figurehead with good intentions. Unless he borrows money from you on a higher interest, he will not be able to bid for the government's catechu tender. He is a drowning man.'

'And?'

'And I demand a greater cut in your profits.'

A raucous laugh rang in the hibernation chamber of this snakelet. 'You do, do you now? It seems Laxmi ji has appointed me to write an obituary to your ambitions, respected Hariharan ji.'

The statue of Goddess Laxmi, anointed with oil and sitting content in the corner amid her garden of parijat flowers (fresh now), heard the scheming men placidly. She was the most looked-after being in the Mahajan household.

Hariharan's concerns about a bright future for his children competed hard with his concern about not urinating on the misused mattress.

'I do demand that!' His bladder threatened to wet the moneylender's sanctum sanctorum. He felt dizzy trying to hold on. 'I have enough reason to demand it, Lal Chand ji. Once I tell you that, there will be no taking it back. You and I will become partners in crime. The choice is yours.'

Mahajan confused the urgency of his bladder with his confidence. The sarcastic smile began to falter. He scratched his grey stubble with a grey fingernail.

'You want to know the reason?' Hariharan bent forward, placing his hand on the moneylender's table, his ankle on his stalk.

Mahajan's curiosity, as full as Hariharan's sac, could not stop a nod.

'What if I tell you that Kamruddin was not convinced by me? That he still wanted to marry Sanaz and lend Dada Bhai all the money interest-free?' He pushed on despite the great urge emanating from his abdomen.

Mahajan's eyes shone with anticipation in his sepulchral chamber.

'What if I say I got rid of the possibility of Kamruddin lending money to Dada Bhai? What if ... what if I had Sanaz taken *out of the way?*'

Hariharan's revelation had the quality of unreality that dreams and promises are made of. But one is inclined to believe in both.

He got up, holding on to his dignity with vehemence, and walked to the door, where he stopped and turned to look at the old man disfigured with years of elephantiasis and greed. The man's lips were parted, as if a corpse were trying to be seductive.

'Do we have a deal?' Hariharan asked, unable to breathe.

The vile old man looked at him in thrall, the first true sign of respect Hariharan was to receive in his lionized life and times that would span decades and grow taller in their telling; even Rao Sahib, who squirmed his nose as if Hariharan was someone's smelly underpants, would one day need his respectable services. Mahajan nodded, once, twice, so slowly Hariharan feared his treacherous pouch would empty then and there.

'Tomorrow,' concluded Hariharan, before he slammed the door open, and without another glance at the astonished corpse, shuffled across the corridor, which the faintest yellow lamp light had made translucent.

He unbolted the heavy latch of the main door with a sweep, stepped out into the lane in the frosty night air, closed the door unceremoniously behind him and went panting to the side. Before he could lift his dhoti and hunker down on the empty lane, the holy cow urine, now mixed with his own, poured in a copious warm line down his legs and made a shallow pool around his camel-leather mojdi. He abandoned himself to the intense relief spreading from the melody of an emptying vesicle. And from a future secured tightly in a knot.

Woof-woof-woof... A pie-dog claiming its nightly domain barked non-stop somewhere down the row of middle-class houses.

A lavish smile spread across Hariharan's person, a lump rose up his throat, he entwined the ringed fingers of both hands and bowed his head reverentially to Laddoo Gopal—the baby Krishna, shut his mental ledger for the day and on legs quaking with pain, traipsed down the road to success.

33

Nathu

Near Jogion ka Guda

Aravalli Hills

HIS HEART AND THE SUN, BOTH HAD SUNK. THE BROW OF THE
horizon had turned scarlet. The dusk had spread itself
around the hills with fastidious care. The birds, whose calls
Nathu could identify accurately, cried in disparate unison. He
was not a nobody here. He was Nathu, son of Jaitya of the
village Jogoin ka Guda. Here he knew his neighbouring trees
and hills and pockets of water. Here, he could read the mood
of winds and foresee a crying monsoon or a dry-eyed draught.

Nathu's legs had carried him out of the Udaipur city walls,
back to his much-loved hills and brown-green valleys, in a fever
pitch. A thick line of fecund black ants lay amputated by Nathu's
misplaced step. He took their tiny bites with equanimity as he

went up the hilly trail—the goat track that had expanded into a path by prolonged human use. He was halfway away from home. Halfway away from a dying (or dead?) father. From a pregnant wife. From a dead bull. From the three-hundred per cent interest that the village moneylending Bohra would charge for his father's kariyawar—the gifts to be given to gods to ensure his smooth passage.

The bad-tempered crump of a red jungle fowl with two hens alarmed the patch of forest about Nathu's presence. The cock's tail was a flaming inferno matching the dusk sky. Nathu trod on. Thorns of ber bushes scratched his flaying hands, urging him to slow down. Crickets had begun to drone, vibrating their scraper wings. A spotted owlet looked down at him from his hollow with faultless, moon eyes.

Nathu's lips moved, but no words escaped.

Why, Ba, why...

Dry leaves crunched beneath his hard mojdi. Shoe bites bit him harder than the cold. He lunged forward in wrath. The wilderness with multiple ears, eyes, skins, claws, teeth, fur, souls and memories sensed the anger in him and withdrew into itself.

A tracker of trackers—Ba! Attacked by a leopard, which was so easily traceable. You had not chanced upon her. You had walked up to her, Ba ... with complete knowledge!

Last evening, something lay mutilated in Nathu's chest as he had sat by his father's death bed listening to him speak during a short spell of consciousness.

'Nathu ji ...you have a remarkable, practical wife ... and a life of your own. What am I left with? With your Bai gone ... even Bhoora gone ... I am just an extra mouth to feed.'

'D-did you d-d-do it?' Words chafed Nathu's tongue.

'Yes, I ventured near the leopard intentionally. You know Dada Bhai, Nathu ji, don't you? The villagers have lost cattle, but Dada Bhai would not have killed the leopard. She is with two cubs. And he is too disciplined a hunter to shoot a mother.' His father, who addressed him with the additional courtesy of 'ji' that no one else thought he deserved, stared at him with eyes burning with fever.

'But if the leopard attacked a ha-ha-human, Da-dada Bhai would k-come and shoot her, right?' Blood rushed to Nathu's temples, thumping like the fists of the kids who would force him to speak without a stutter.

Jaitya's reply was a grunt of pain. In the quiet that stretched, Nathu smelt his rotting father and felt a strong guilt-laden desire to step out of the hut and draw in a lungful of winter air.

'The hope of the entire village is pinned on you, my son. Get Dada Bhai here to cull the cattle lifter; don't inform him that she is with cubs. And ... and don't inform that I am dying. Spare him the pain for as long as you can. Promise me, you'll spare him the pain...' He beseeched, giving him a pitiful smile. 'I am only going to the scented forests of Rana ji ... the "happy hunting grounds" Dada Bhai calls them.' Here, his father gripped his hand. 'The villagers will respect you, Nathu ji, when you bring Dada Bhai to help them out. You will step in my shoes then ... *Hangaar karwa chalo!* With the war cry of a beat, he had slipped back into the delusory state.

A shudder ran across Nathu's shoulders remembering the last evening with his father. Birds had hushed. The dubious opaqueness of twilight had ceded way to stoic dark. Solid and unbreakable in its wake. The night belched out the cry of a nightjar. Nathu's eyes burnt with rage. The thorny bush forest was a rogue: hiding forked-tongued snakes and slit-eyed cats, unleashing blood-sucking mosquitoes, carrying sibilant whispers, feeding vultures with the flesh of her own denizens and hyenas with their bones. A conjurer. With spoors of aromas. With sacs of poison.

Nathu quickened his pace. His father, his own Ba, a human sacrifice for the village that never accepted Nathu for what he was.

I am not strong, Ba ... I am not strong. I cannot bear this burden of you trying to make a strong man out of me.

There was no running away from the jungle, however fast he ran. Jaitya had left him to deal with the brutal world alone.

'You d-d-d-didn't toughen me up, Ba ... it's not fair!' Twigs snapped around his ankles.

Jaitya was not a leopard kill. He was killed by his goodness. To what end? Nathu had failed him. Failed to bring Dada Bhai. Failed to put himself in his father's shoes. Jaitya's life worth nothing. Lost in vain.

The hill on his side had a rain-fed stream. Dry and fissured as his lips now. Jaitya often brought him here in the monsoons to catch fish that magically appeared with the first showers. Nathu was close to his village. Then why didn't he feel at home? His pace slackened. The road meandering below his feet stilled. Nathu gripped his fingers around the throat of the fleeing truth.

The truth, the real reason why he went to Dada Bhai in Udaipur, leaving his dying father. The hairy whisper of his wife Thawari in his ear this morning—*Go, Nathu, go. If you can bring back Dada Bhai, he sure will pay for Ba's kariyawar. We can't afford a loan. I am pregnant.* The revelation had made his world spin. He had gone running to Udaipur, away from a mangled, dying man, not out of love for his Ba's last wish, the wish of a man who had sacrificed his life selflessly, but for Dada

Bhai to pay for his funeral rites. So that he and his wife and the unborn child could avoid getting sucked into the ledgers of the village moneylender.

Anger transmigrated into despondency. It grew inside him, became larger, pushing his organs to the sides. It hurt his skin like pus-filled boils. He was not the ideal son that the village … that *his Ba* … thought him to be. He was a mean-spirited coward the world could do without. His wife Thawari, his unborn child could do without. A blotch on the legacy of his great father—a man who could talk to animals in their own ancient language, a man silenced for nought.

Lethargy had settled on the range, hill after hill after hill. The path on his right that went down the hillock led to the huts of his village, bunched up in the valley of Dholi Ghati. He gave it one appraising look. Goat herds had returned home. Thin lines of smoke from cook fires were the threads held loosely by an illusionist in the night sky. Somewhere out there, in the dewy ground, a once-spirited bull Bhoora lay alone and disintegrating. And a man who spoke to animals would soon go up in smoke.

The path on Nathu's left led to his Ba's fields. Where Bhoora was killed. Where Jaitya was attacked. Where the leopard lurked with her two cubs.

Jaitya had often cooed in little Nathu's ears, so that he learnt his lessons by heart, 'Forest is our mother, Nathu ji. Our real Annadata. She sustains and regulates life, shares milk from her bosom and sheds her fingers to give us firewood and healing herbs.' Today, Nathu saw this sorceress of a forest for what she was. She sat masticating on the dead, ejecting snarling cats to tear unsuspecting victims, drooling silver baits of streams, oozing worms to feed on their planted crops, and hiding her cunning in the prickly bushes of a whore's labia.

Fear coiled around Nathu's stomach. He could not return to the diseased city with living witches hanging in its hair. He could not return to his hut, to a father whose death wish he didn't fulfil. He could not become a man bowed with the weight of feeding a child and paying monstrous interests that would endure through his sorry lifetime. A lifetime of going every morning to defecate in a watchful forest and returning from the low-yielding fields to an underfed wife, her rounded form wearing away like the dried stalks of their corn. He could not go back to being what he always was. Inadequate.

Nathu reached out for support. Too afraid to touch anything in the deceitful night, he slunk his hand in his pocket and felt the two rounded tidi-ke-patthar tied on a thick string. He always carried the flint stones to light a fire or a friendly bidi. He drew out the stones and absently struck them. A rasp. A spark. As if in response, a dozen fireflies winked on the path that went to the fields. If ever there was a cue by their forest deity Rana ji, this was one.

The cold froze his flesh. The jungle's cloudy breath formed a crust on his skin. A gust of breeze, as if the forest had broken wind, cleared the fog for a moment. A deciding moment. Nathu's feet turned away from his home. Pebbles crunched. Frogs called to him. A jackal howled her disapproval. A lapwing warned. He dropped the tidi-ke-patthar in the bushes as he strode, one step after the other, on the path towards the field cultivated dotingly by his father; strode, one step after the other, to the mouth of the snarking she-forest.

The rays from the Makar Sankranti moon of 1950, a waning crescent, fell impotently on the clumps of grasses shifting with snakes. Their small cultivated patch came into view, smelling of cherished memories.

'Where do fish go in ss-summers, Ba?' He heard his own words spoken long ago by the dried forest stream as their handsome bull Bhoora stood cramming grass between his block-teeth, and Jaitya sat on his haunches digging roots of the dholi-musli herb.

'Why, Nathu ji, didn't you know?' Jaitya had tilted his head in surprise. 'They come to my head to hide. Where do you think I got all this silver hair from?'

The winter night rang with Nathu's disconsolate giggles as he walked towards the leopard hiding in the tall stalks with her two cubs, shrinking with her babies till the time she could evade detection, till the very last moment she could avoid a disagreeable attack. Nathu walked closer and closer and closer. Shackles uncoiling around his ankles. Laughing aloud. Inhaling the intoxicating winter night. Perceiving a blaze: the flash of a leaping leopard followed by the sigh of parting corn stalks. Carrying, till his very end, a dead father in his laughter.

12.15 AM

The Night Before
Makar Sankranti, 1950

34

Ahad

Dada Bhai's House

Bohrawadi

An IMMENSE SILENCE HUNG OVER THE TALLEST HOUSE IN Bohrawadi. From where the jeevti dakkan spawned out of the night. Crawled in the imagination of a world surrendered to dreams. It was the time she was in her element, when shadows split and gave her form, when she attained a fluidity that would make her seep through the phlegmatic will of the staunchest naysayers.

Ahad, who had sneaked out of the room that he shared with his brothers Sa'ad and Zain, scaled the steps from the second to the third floor, expecting a sunken-eyed, hurricane-haired houri to reveal herself any moment.

There was only one lamp on every floor, placed in a taak. A single burning eye. The lamp placed in the taak on the second floor was a pocket-sized avatar of the sun god in a halo of yellow light, whispering in a mystifying, godly tongue. Sa'ad Bhaiya had once sworn that there was an unseen mechanism at work in the house at night. It had made Ahad remember the first time he had seen the entrails of their B-Model Ford—the crisscrossing veins and a dark chugging heart that was hidden inside the green exterior. Who could have thought that? *Ya Ali, Ya Ali* ... he chanted, just like the women who beat their chest in perfect rhythm during the Muharram majlis organized by Ammi, his mother. Badi Bi had categorically told him that Ali kept bad spirits at bay. Who knew it better than the ancient widow, privy to the secrets of Hatim Tai and Aladdin's genie?

The winter ran a knife beneath his skin, pin-pricked his ears, numbed his lips. His butthole itched with fear.

'I need to give you my homemade kaada for de-worming, Rajkumar,' Badi Bi had said last evening, seeing him scratch his bottom. 'All these English medicines your parents give you will not even rid a potato of worms! Here, have another bowl of kheer...'

He hated potatoes. Same as coriander. And jelly! They called him Jelly Belly at his school, Vidya Bhawan. Cockeyed Kailash had christened him that. He had caught Ahad running after his father's tonga that brought them to school. Ahad loved running alongside the horse for the last stretch, his stomach prancing like a happy ball.

One day, he would become the greatest kite-fighter of the walled city and then he would show ... no, Dada Bhai insisted they treat their adversaries with dignity ... he would just wink at Kailash. But there was *no way* he was taking him along to the Hariyali Amavas carnival again! Last year, they both had seen on display a jet-black man with kinky hair—a Habshi! Let Cockeyed Kailash miss that treat.

Ahad had painstakingly, with Badi Bi's help, made the best possible manjha—the abrasive string for kite-flying—coating it in atta mixed with powdered glass. It was a surprise for his elder brothers. Maybe, they would let him fly a kite when they got tired. Actually, Ismail had done most of the work, but Ahad had hid the manjha in the guest room, right below the sloping table. And what did Dada Bhai tell him before going to bed? That his friend Rao Sahib is visiting tomorrow! He needed to retrieve the manjha and keep it safely in his trunk. What if Rao sahib arrived and occupied the guest room before Ahad got up? Life can be tricky, Badi Bi often said. Truth be told, Ahad had a tiny bit of a problem getting up before the sun. He could try to wake up early, but what could he do about life being tricky?

The guest room on the third floor was the cave of the forty thieves. He was Ali Baba, who had to say 'Open Sesame!' to reclaim his treasure. Nah … the room was a sleeping tiger. Striped. Savage. Just three more steps to the third floor, a spring across the veranda, yank open the mouth of the tiger, snatch the manjha and run out before the beast snaps his jaws shut … a death-defying mission. The future kite-flying champion of Udaipur must put his life on the line and brave these odds.

The familiar scent of jasmine wafted in a small ringlet around Ahad's nose and dispersed. A one-thousand-year-old smell. What was it doing three steps away from the third floor at midnight? It was followed by a distant laugh that died as abruptly. Ahad's legs wobbled. His cheeks tingled. Cold held him in a clutch on the perilous, railing-less stone steps. His legs wanted to slump on the stairs. But what a place to slump on!

In the middle of nowhere. Hanging in the ether. He flashed a glance around the corner. A jharokha, providing relief to the stretched-out wall, let in the moonlight, tepid and infirm. He felt a finger trail on the back of his neck. Ahad rushed up the last three steps, driven to action by the image of something long dead.

He could hear his own belly flaps and breaths. The witch had expectorated him out of the steps. Ahad had invaded her domain with impunity.

Leaning on the wall at the landing on the third floor, he stared down the dark steps, expecting the witch to be crawling on all fours after him, teeth embedded on her gaunt neck, two long hair coming out of a chin wart, lumpy veins on a bald head, ribs moving like snakes ... when he heard the evil titter again. He dribbled in his chequered knicker. Mucus ran down his nostrils. Muffled words reached him, making them sound outside time. He turned quickly to see if the witch stood leaning her back on his. Thankfully, the stone wall had his back. He peeped into the veranda.

'Do you think the travelling Prithvi Theatres will play *Death of a Salesman*? The Pulitzer went to its author last year.'

Why, that was his sister Sanaz! Ahad inched towards her room. A pencil-thin line of light seeped out of the door, which was split open an inch.

'Don't expect your father to take you all the way to watch it, Sanaz. You know about his state of affairs.'

Ahad felt warmth spread inside him hearing his mother speak.

'But I don't, Ammi! What do you think I am? A leech?'

The speech had a ground-glass quality to it. Manjha sharp. Why was Sanaz Apa always combative with Ammi?

'He has ordered a copy of Orwell's *1984* for you from London. You have been harping about it since its release last year.'

Ammi sounded like a lullaby; Ahad could just go in, fold up and sleep placing his head on her lap. He stood his ground like a man.

'I was not harping about it!'

'Oh yes, you were just having a conversation around it with him, for the twentieth time.'

The mean snicker again. Sanaz Apa was always, always pitting herself against Ammi.

'Really, Ammi, why are you in my room at this hour? Not to discuss President Truman's policies or the coining of the term Big Bang, I guess.'

The soft thud of a glass being kept on a table. 'Do *you* want to be the Big Bang of your father's ruin?'

'What is that supposed to mean, Ammi?'

'You know very well.'

'And here you talk about empowering women, huh? What about empowering your own daughter?'

'If she wasn't empowered, she wouldn't be talking to me in this tone.'

Ahad could smell jasmine all around. It was his mother Mena Bai's attar, not an aroma sent out by the jeevti dakkan to tease and freeze him. A gecko near the lamp caught an insect and sat with a mouth that had sprouted wings. Ahad's wet knicker felt cold on his thighs.

'I beg you, think about your father, Sanaz. He doesn't know anything about this. Think of his reputation ... what he has done for the society ... the tribals ... how many lives depend on Mahila Sabha that we run to educate women, to teach them life skills.'

'Will I not make an example, Ammi, the fruit of yours and Dada Bhai's labours to create an egalitarian society?'

An indistinct scraping of a chair's legs on carpet. Ammi must be getting up.

'You are already an example. An intelligent, educated girl, the very image of modernity mixed with tradition. And well, as far as societies are concerned, they have to be weaned into change. Last year, in South Africa, they imposed a ban on mixed marriages. Ours, like theirs, is a long-drawn fight, child. It calls for sacrifices.'

'Am I to be that sacrifice?'

'You are to be a beacon, Sanaz, not a sacrifice.' A dry rustle of cotton. 'I don't care if I am Mewar's very own Suparnakha ... many well-meaning Laxmans who want to uphold the sanctity of women are hoping to chop off my nose.' Ammi's sad laugh. 'But I dearly, desperately care about your father. You know it is not just the royals who have been disenfranchised. Your father has lost his livelihood. Don't ruin him socially too, child. You very well know about his heart condition. He will die an untimely death.'

'All this emotional blackmailing ... Valmiki was right. No one cares about us. *No one!*' Sanaz Apa sounded nasal. She had restored to the cowardice of tears.

'You are a very perceptive girl, Sanaz, aren't you? I beg you not to be so stubborn, please...'

Ammi's helplessness was clear like the sharp flavour of fresh coriander on dal. Ahad wanted to give her a hug.

'Where do you think I inherited my stubbornness from?' Sanaz Apa's voice was melted chocolate now, too sweet and hot for the tongue.

'You are barely seventeen and such a bright student. You'll soon be attending Aligarh Muslim University. Finish your studies, find your footing ... and then, Sanaz, then you marry whom you please. I swear upon Allah ... I swear upon *your father* ... I will stand by you.' Ammi's words were the soft swish of mud slipping down a dug-out grave. 'It will be done quickly. We can go there tomorrow morning ... it's safe ... it is a very early stage.'

A confused Ahad managed a peek through the crack in the door, but could only see the lit-up wall cramped with shadows.

'Stop it, Ammi! I am not doing it, you understand? I am keeping it.' An angry sob and a sniff. 'Mothers forget what it feels to be in love. Didn't Dada Bhai marry you against the wishes of his mother? What was your age? Nine?'

Ahad could smell his knicker and urine-soaked pouches. He quivered. No wonder frogs hibernated in winters. Above ground, and that too three floors above it, was no place to be in the cold. *Allah, Sanaz Apa, just agree with Ammi and let her go!*

'I have not forgotten what it is to be in love. I am still in love with your father. And *I* am expecting *too*.'

Expecting what ... Ahad wondered. Another package from Ammi's Mamu in Mombasa who had two wives? He always sent whacky gifts, which Ahad totally loved!

To his surprise, Sanaz Apa didn't bite. She just sucked in a breath. Maybe she was expecting too? Good, his sister and mother were conciliating.

'Will you think about it, Sanaz ... Please give it a thought at least. Too much is at stake, including your whole life.'

The quiet stretched, making room for the jeevti dakkan to sneak in again. The paranormal closed in on Ahad from the open-sky roof, the walls, the stairs. Goading him into a flight.

'I have decided, Ammi. It is mine, it is *ours* ... Mine and Valmiki's. I will not get rid of it. My answer is a categorical no.' Sanaz's reply came just in time. Ahad was ready to flee back to his quarters, where Zain Bhaiya lay talking to people in his dreams. One of them, Ahad deeply suspected, was a girl.

'Have your milk,' Ammi gave the familiar command. There was no getting past her and milk.

The light falling through the crack in the door began to move frantically. Ahad skipped back to the landing and stuck himself to the wall, hands pinned to the sides. He hoped Ammi had not heard his swinging jelly-belly.

Sanaz Apa's door screeched open. Ammi must have stepped out before Sanaz Apa latched it from inside, ill-manneredly. A long moment passed. Ahad tiptoed to the corner of the landing and stuck his head out to spy. Ammi stood filling the night with jasmines. One hand on the brass door handle, the other holding an empty glass of milk. She seemed ill. Tortured like tea bleeding slowly in boiling water. Her hand shook worse than Ahad's legs. She kept looking at the emptiness of the glass, as if it was the saddest thing that could happen to anyone before Makar Sankranti. Her silhouette was the cardboard cut-out of Mahatma Gandhi that Vidya Bhawan had erected in their annual function. She walked, shoulders hunched, towards the wrinkle of lamplight.

Tchak tchak tchak ... the gecko called nine times.

'Don't judge me,' Ammi stopped near the slowly burning lamp in the taak and told the worldly-wise gecko. The gecko looked at her with a dignified expression and made no comments. 'Just two drops. It is just two drops to make her bleed. She will be okay in two or three days.' Ammi's waterlogged words fell

heavy in the stillness of the night. '*Parvardigar* ... forgive me.'
Her eyes found the roof searching for god.

Even with a nose stuck out in defiance, hair spiking out of
her bun, hand gripping the glass like a beggar's bowl, Ammi was
the most beautiful person in the world.

Ahad watched his crumpled mother in a cotton saree with
grinding adoration as she straightened and floated up the flight
of steps, as silent as dew drops that didn't really drop. They
appeared. Just as Ammi disappeared.

Phew ... finally. All clear! Ahad smacked his lips and
tasted metallic excitement, as if he had bit a solid char-anna
coin. From the attic of his head, he drew out all his mothball-
smelling courage and walked towards the guest room, which
hid his shining riches—a killer manjha! He would be able to
invoke favours from his brothers with an offering so significant.

Jeevti dakkan flew away with fears. Feet slapped the veranda.
Night sang with crickets. Hands undid a door. And through the
warm breath forming mist around his face, Ahad could picture
the most sensational Makar Sankranti of his life.

Acknowledgements

Dada bhai is loosely inspired from the life and times of my grandfather T.H. Tehsin, the monopoly holder of arms and ammunition business in the erstwhile Mewar, and later the acting Mayor of Udaipur. He loved his forests, tribals and *watan* too much to leave them in the face of the imminent fall of his fortunes with Independence. He rejected Jinnah's two-nation theory. Going to Pakistan, despite being offered a generous share in a fleet of merchant ships and mining by his friend, was unthinkable for him. He would live his days with his people—his Rajput brothers and Bhil *khoju-shikaris*—and be buried in his motherland, even if he died penniless.

My grandmother, Khurshid Banu, was disabled but never believed she was. She was one of the initiators of the women's literacy movement in Rajasthan and continued her efforts despite people throwing stones at their house. She was the Vice President of All India Women's Conference, state chapter, of which Maharani Gayatri Devi was the president. In 1942, she formed Bazm-e-Niswan, a women's study group with a library, to spread Gandhi's message and increase awareness about the country's socio-political situation.

Bohot bohot shukriya, Dadaji and Dadijaan ... and Badi Bi, on whose ample waist the keys of their house dangled, lifelong.

While a few of the characters (and the house) may be inspired from real life, the story is entirely fictitious, dug out from my compost heap during the first Covid lockdown. The inputs of the era and devil in the details came from the Tehsins—Riaz, Rafiq, Raza, Habiba and Himalay. I picked their brains till they were raw. I got inputs from Naveen Singh ji on the Rajput ways of life, from Rtd. IG Nisar Farooqui on the police force and from Dr Satish Sharma on the local vegetation. Errors, if any, are my own. Riaz chacha and Raffu chacha (Rafiq Tehsin) will never see the book. I'll tell them all about it in my dream-world, where I meet them often.

A fat thanks to Kan (Kanishka Gupta), my agent par excellence, who gave invaluable feedback.

Thank you, my editor Prerna Gill and the entire team of my publisher HarperCollins for believing in the witch, and artist— for the beautiful cover.

Aditya, can I ever thank you enough for reading each line with the diligence of a tailorbird and for making me pink cocktails to end my writing days? For holding my hand in cities and leaving me on my own in forests? Clearly, I can't.

About the Author

Arefa Tehsin is the author of many fiction and non-fiction books and contributes pieces to *The Indian Express*, *The Hindu*, *Deccan Herald*, TERI's *Terra Green*, Scroll.in, *Outlook Money* and others.

Her books have been shortlisted for awards like NEEV Book Award, FICCI Best Book of the Year Award and *The Hindu* Young World Best Author Award. *The Elephant Bird* was read at 3,200+ locations in India from the slums to the Presidential Library on the International Literacy Day, 2016, and translated into more than forty languages. Arefa spent her childhood treading jungles with her naturalist father, exploring caves and chasing snakes. She was appointed the Honorary Wildlife Warden of Udaipur.

30 Years *of*

![HarperCollins logo] HarperCollins *Publishers* India

At HarperCollins, we believe in telling the best stories and finding the widest possible readership for our books in every format possible. We started publishing 30 years ago; a great deal has changed since then, but what has remained constant is the passion with which our authors write their books, the love with which readers receive them, and the sheer joy and excitement that we as publishers feel in being a part of the publishing process.

Over the years, we've had the pleasure of publishing some of the finest writing from the subcontinent and around the world, and some of the biggest bestsellers in India's publishing history. Our books and authors have won a phenomenal range of awards, and we ourselves have been named Publisher of the Year the greatest number of times. But nothing has meant more to us than the fact that millions of people have read the books we published, and somewhere, a book of ours might have made a difference.

As we step into our fourth decade, we go back to that one word – a word which has been a driving force for us all these years.

Read.